More Annotated H. P. Lovecraft

Previous books in this series:

The Annotated H. P. Lovecraft

More Annotated H. P. Lovecraft

annotations by Peter Cannon and S. T. Joshi

A Dell Trade Paperback

A DELL TRADE PAPERBACK

Published by
Dell Publishing
a division of
Random House, Inc.
1540 Broadway
New York, New York 10036

Edited by John Gregory Betancourt and Leigh Grossman

Special thanks to Amy West, Katherine Macdonald, and Kathleen Jayes

Library of Congress Cataloging in Publication Data

Lovecraft, H. P. (Howard Phillips), 1890–1937.
    More annotated H.P. Lovecraft / annotations by S.T. Joshi.
        p.   cm.
    Includes bibliographical references.
    ISBN 0-440-50875-4
    1. Horror tales, American. I. Joshi, S. T., 1958–   .
II. Title.
PS3523.0833A6   1999b
813'.52—dc21   99-23457
                                                                CIP

Printed in the United States of America

Published simultaneously in Canada

August 1999

10 9 8 7 6 5 4 3 2 1
FFG

Typeset by Jackson Typesetting, Jackson, Michigan

To the memory of Andrew Heyl

Acknowledgments

The texts of these stories are derived from the Arkham House corrected edition of Lovecraft's collected fiction (1984–86) produced under the editorship of S. T. Joshi. This edition was founded upon consultation of autograph manuscripts, typescripts, and early publications, and eliminated many errors from previous editions. The texts as presented here correct a few further errors. The editors and publisher are grateful to Arkham House Publishers, Inc., for permission to reprint the stories and to David E. Schultz for providing the stories on disk.

For assistance in the annotations, I am grateful to Rusty Burke, Joann Hand, James Hand, Sarah Mason, Bob Mason, Ann Brooke Mason, and Lawrence Tucker.

For permission to use photographs in this book, I am grateful to Mollie L. Burleson, Jason C. Eckhardt, and Steven J. Mariconda.

—Peter Cannon

Introduction

In 1917, prompted by W. Paul Cook and other amateur journalists who had been impressed by two youthful excursions into the weird, "The Beast in the Cave" (1905) and "The Alchemist" (1908), H. P. Lovecraft wrote "The Tomb" and "Dagon," the tales that mark the start of his career as an author of horror fiction. Over the next few years he would circulate in the amateur press some three dozen stories, none of them longer than a few thousand words. Ranging from Poe-esque narratives of madness and obsession to dreamlike fantasies in the manner of Lord Dunsany, they show Lovecraft, like any apprentice writer, imitating certain favorite authors on his way to finding his own voice.

Perhaps because of his great fondness for New England, its natural landscape and colonial architecture in particular, Lovecraft did not immediately recognize its suitability as a setting for supernatural horror. Eventually, though, he was able to rise above his literary influences and find inspiration, as Nathaniel Hawthorne had nearly a century earlier, in the history and folklore of New England.

Sad to say, Lovecraft's prejudices mar his initial efforts in this direction. His first tale with a distinct New England setting, "The Terrible Old Man" (1920), amounts to little more than a polemic against the intrusion of people he regarded as "foreigners," that is, the non-English immigrants who came in the nineteenth century as cheap labor to fill the factories of an increasingly industrialized America. His disavowed sketch, "The Street" (1920), is even more tainted by bigotry.

It would take these two false starts before he produced "The Picture in the House" (1920), his first story to effectively employ local New England color. Its opening paragraph amounts to a kind of aesthetic manifesto, with its declaration that "the true epicure in the terrible . . . esteems most of all the ancient, lonely farmhouses of backwoods New England." Here Lovecraft serves notice that he will rely less on stock Gothic trappings and more on his native region as a source for horror.

In a letter dating to 1930, Lovecraft explained to Robert E. Howard, his fellow *Weird Tales* writer, the psychological underpinnings of the tale:

> *It is the night-black Massachusetts legendry which packs the really macabre "kick". Here is material for a really profound study in group-neuroticism; for certainly, no one can deny the existence of a profoundly morbid streak in the Puritan imagination. What you say of the dark Saxon-Scandinavian heritage as a possible source of the atavistic impulses brought out by emotional repression, isolation, climactic rigour, and the nearness of the vast unknown forest with its coppery savages, is of vast interest to me, insomuch as I have often both said and written exactly the same thing! Have you seen*

my old story "The Picture in the House"? If not, I
must send you a copy. The introductory paragraph
virtually sums up the idea you advance. (Selected
Letters III, 174–75)

"The Picture in the House" is also significant for the introduction of what would evolve into Lovecraft's quintessential fictional town, Arkham, Massachusetts. The origin of this name has been a matter of some debate among Lovecraft scholars, but it is all but certain that he had no specific New England town or location in mind at the time he composed "The Picture in the House."

Lovecraft's next Arkham tale happens also to be his first professional work of fiction, the six-part serial "Herbert West—Reanimator" (1921–22). Commissioned by his amateur friend George Julian Houtain for a humor magazine Houtain was starting called *Home Brew*, it appeared serially under the generic title "Grewsome Tales" in the first six issues of that magazine (February-June 1922). While the local color is perfunctory at best, it is the story in which Miskatonic University makes its debut.

Lovecraft always considered "Herbert West—Reanimator" the worst of his tales because it was written to order and, in its following Houtain's requirement for a startling climax at the end of each segment, violated his emphasis (derived from Poe) for "singleness of impression" (*Selected Letters* I, 158) in a short story. "In this enforced, laboured, and artificial sort of composition there is nothing of art or natural gracefulness; for of necessity there must be a superfluity of strainings and repetitions in order to make each history compleat. My sole inducement is the monetary reward, which is a guinea [i.e., $5.00] per tale" (*Selected Letters* I, 157).

At the time Lovecraft began to write "Herbert West," in the fall of 1921, he was unemployed (except for sporadic work as a literary revisionist), with no prospects for work, and with his family inheritance slowly but inexorably dwindling. Five dollars (or about a quarter of a cent per word) was, even then, a very low rate for original fiction, but Lovecraft could ill afford to turn down any means of bringing in a few dollars. Although *Home Brew* therefore became the first venue for Lovecraft's professionally published fiction, he was no doubt relieved when that "vile rag" (*Selected Letters* IV, 170), folded sometime in 1924.

Despite such self-criticism Lovecraft did take considerable care in the tale's construction. The plot builds in neat, logical increments from one section to the next. It may in fact be a virtue that Herbert West's grotesque antics are more likely to raise a smile than a shudder. Readers of those first six issues of Houtain's humor magazine should not have been disappointed by this blackly comic farce of a horror story.

The wild exuberance of "Herbert West" continues in "The Hound" (1922), which Lovecraft would years later dismiss as "a piece of junk" (*Selected Letters* III, 192). Again, in a mood of severe self-assessment, he seems to have forgotten that he could only have written this extravagant narrative with tongue at least partly in cheek. Like the earlier tale, "The Hound" has a kind of naive charm, not least because the anonymous narrator and his pal St. John, for all their "decadent" pursuits, never indulge in any sexual escapades. It would remain for Poppy Z. Brite in her story "Thy Tongue Shall Taste of Wormwood," an obvious homage to "The Hound," to lay on the eroticism so conspicuously lacking in Lovecraft's tale.

In early October, 1924, the prospect of viewing some colonial-era buildings drew Lovecraft from New York, where he had been living since his marriage to Sonia Greene the previous March, to Elizabeth, New Jersey. There he was captivated by an old house (alas, no longer standing), because it reminded him of a house on Benefit Street in Providence where his aunt Lillian Clark once resided. Later that month he wrote "The Shunned House," his first tale to make use of an actual New England locale, undisguised. It is a heartfelt exercise, but after a lyrical and leisurely opening this lengthy story bogs down in a welter of data concerning births, marriages, and deaths. The horror ultimately unearthed is inert and despatched with relative ease.

As in "The Hound," the most important relationship in "The Shunned House" is between two men, the unnamed narrator and his beloved "antiquarian uncle," Elihu Whipple. Whipple is probably a composite portrait of Lovecraft's two learned uncles-in-law and maternal grandfather, all of whom were long gone by the 1920s. The tale's dominant mood is wistful and nostalgic—fear scarcely enters the equation—hinting at the homesickness that Lovecraft was beginning to express in letters to his aunts as the emotional strain between him and Sonia worsened. They would separate at year's end.

His next two stories, "The Horror at Red Hook" and "He," both composed in August 1925, reflect Lovecraft's disillusionment with New York. Two months later he wrote his friend and fellow fantasist Clark Ashton Smith: "The idea that black magic exists in secret today, or that hellish antique rites still survive in obscurity, is one that I have used & shall use again. When you see my new tale 'The Horror at Red Hook', you will see what use I make of the idea in connexion with the gangs of young loafers & herds of evil-looking foreigners that one sees everywhere in New York." (*Selected Letters* II, 27) Once again racism makes a poor premise for a horror tale.

"The Horror at Red Hook" may well represent a stab at writing a commercial occult detective yarn. It seems unlikely that Lovecraft would have bothered to give so much irrelevant information about his improbable protagonist, the Irish dreamer turned Brooklyn policeman, unless he had conceived of him as a series character. Mercifully we have only a single adventure featuring detective Thomas Malone. For once Lovecraft was not being overly modest when he said of "The Horror of Red Hook," "The tale is long and rambling, and I don't think it is very good." (*Se-lected Letters* II, 20)

That said, it should be noted that "The Horror at Red Hook" was one of the few Lovecraft stories anthologized in his lifetime, in Christine Campbell Thomson's *You'll Need a Night Light* (1927). In addition, the tale is dignified by a mention in the *Encyclopedia of New York City* (1995), edited by Kenneth T. Jackson, under the entry for Red Hook: "The ambience of the neighborhood in the 1930s and 1940s is conveyed in Arthur Miller's play *The View from the Bridge*, Elia Kazan's film *On the Water-front*, and H. P. Lovecraft's short story 'The Horror at Red Hook.' "

Lovecraft would produce his best story with a New York setting only when he knew he was on the verge of leaving what he had come to call the "pest zone." Written in March 1926, "Cool Air" repeats the peculiar lodger theme first used in "The Music of Erich Zann" (1921). But where the narrator of the earlier tale fit the romantic type of the poor student, alone in some imaginary neighborhood of what appears to be Paris, the narrator of "Cool Air" be-longs to the gritty, recognizable world of Manhattan, where he struggles to make a living by writing for cheap magazines. His speech is plain and to the point, free of the sort of lofty rhetoric that, for example, opens "The Picture in the House." "Cool Air" shows Lovecraft capa-ble of using an understated, naturalistic style to power-ful effect.

With his return to Providence from New York exile in the spring of 1926, Lovecraft entered the most intensely productive period of his writing career. The first tale to flow from his pen was "The Call of Cthulhu," which he had plotted a full year earlier, as recorded in his diary entry for August 12–13, 1925: "Write out story plot—'The Call of Cthulhu.' " The result was Lovecraft's most ambi-tious and complex tale to date, a dense and subtle narra-tive in which the horror gradually builds to cosmic proportions. Appropriately enough it is the source for August Derleth's popular if problematic label, the "Cthulhu Mythos."

As in "The Shunned House," the narrator (identified as Francis Wayland Thurston only in a sort of footnote to the title) investigates evidence of weirdness in Providence. He even has an elderly "grand-uncle," but unlike Elihu Whipple, Professor George Gammell Angell is dead and off-stage, the apparent victim of foul play. Thurston evinces no sentiment over his relative's loss, in contrast to the feelings of the earlier tale's narrator for his late uncle. Thurston may betray his sensitivity to colonial architecture in passing, but his focus is firmly on the outré artifacts that point to disturbing doings in New Orleans, the South Pacific, and elsewhere around the globe. By the end he is too overwhelmed by cosmic angst over the entire human race to waste tears over the merely personal.

When it appeared in *Weird Tales*, "The Call of Cthulhu" impressed many of that magazine's readers, including Robert E. Howard, the creator of Conan, who was moved to write to "The Eyrie," the *Weird Tales* letters column: "Mr. Lovecraft's latest story, 'The Call of Cthulhu,' is indeed a masterpiece, which I am sure will live as one of the highest achievements of literature. Mr. Lovecraft holds a unique position in the literary world; he has grasped, to all intents, the worlds outside our paltry ken. His scope is unlimited, and his range is cosmic."

The tale also attracted the attention of an anthologist, T. Everett Harré, who reprinted it in a volume entitled *Beware After Dark!* (1929). A few months before his death, Lovecraft described "The Call of Cthulhu" as "rather middling—not as bad as the worst, but full of cheap and cumbrous touches." (*Selected Letters* V, 348) This modest assessment does nothing to undermine the story's standing as one of his bleakest fictional expressions of man's insignificant place in the universe.

A couple of months after writing "The Call of

Cthulhu," Lovecraft returned to more down to earth, or "beneath the earth," horror in "Pickman's Model." Set in Boston, which he knew well from amateur journalist conventions there earlier in the decade, it presents a vision of colonial (and modern) New England threatened by monsters—ghouls who haunt graveyards, cellars, and subways—that make the aged cannibal of "The Picture in the House" seem a harmless crank by comparison. Lovecraft described "Pickman's Model" to one correspondent as "one of my very tamest and mildest effusions" (*Selected Letters* II, 170). Indeed, the tale is filled with touches of sardonic humor the equal of anything in Ambrose Bierce.

Lovecraft uses a colloquial, conversational style as in "Cool Air," though here there are two voices, that of the respectable clubman Thurber and that of the morbid painter Richard Upton Pickman. Both the framing narrative and the sub-narrative are rich with references to New England lore. The tale is a well-nigh perfect example of Poe's unity of effect principle. The one weakness is the contrived ending, though it is hard to imagine how else Thurber might have emerged alive from Pickman's hellish studio with some final piece of confirming evidence. In "Pickman's Model" Lovecraft succeeded in painting in prose a story as meticulous in its realism and as shocking in its implications as any portrait from the fiendish brush of Richard Upton Pickman.

Lovecraft's liberating surge of creativity in the wake of his escape from New York lasted into the following year. Other works of this period include two of his three short novels, *The Dream-Quest of Unknown Kadath* (1926–27) and *The Case of Charles Dexter Ward* (1927), as well as the tale Lovecraft himself would rate as his best, "The Colour Out of Space" (1927). Thereafter his pace slowed considerably, and in the remaining decade of his life he was to write on average only one original story a year. With the exception of *At the Mountains of Madness* (1931), they all employ New England settings, and even the narrator of that novel cannot help invoking the Boston subway to describe the horror he discovers in the cold wastes of Antarctica.

Lovecraft's last story to set Arkham at center stage is "The Thing on the Doorstep" (1933). While the early parts of "The Shadow Out of Time" (1934–35) take place in Arkham, the narrator, Nathaniel Wingate Peaslee, is at pains to explain at the outset that despite "the traditions of horror, madness, and witchcraft which lurked behind the ancient Massachusetts town," the shadow that fell so suddenly upon him was from "*outside* sources"; these later carry him in his dreams far beyond Arkham. By contrast, in "The Thing on the Doorstep" the action is limited to Arkham, with an occasional foray to Innsmouth and the remote Maine forest.

Most critics agree that "The Thing on the Doorstep," together with "The Dreams in the Witch House" (1932), rank as the poorest of Lovecraft's later tales. In the context of an obvious and melodramatic plot, punctuated by patches of histrionic monologue in the mouth of the protagonist, the poet Edward Derby, the Arkham background comes across as rather formulaic. Fortunately, the tale has some redeeming features. "The Thing on the Doorstep" is the only Lovecraft story with a strong or important female character—though of course the malign Ephraim Waite has usurped his daughter Asenath's consciousness. If Lovecraft avoids exploring the possibilities inherent in this gender-swapping situation, his narrator, the staid Daniel Upton, has plenty to say about Edward Derby's psychological development or lack of it. Where cosmic forces usually overtake the typical Lovecraft hero such as Peaslee by chance, here Derby has only his own weak personality to blame for his falling victim to his wife's nefarious designs.

"The Haunter of the Dark," Lovecraft's last original tale, represents a return to form at shorter length. He wrote it in November 1935, prompted by the acceptance of both *At the Mountains of Madness* and "The Shadow

Out of Time" by *Astounding*, a major science fiction magazine. The protagonist, Robert Blake, owes his origin to Lovecraft's young protégé, Robert Bloch (author of *Psycho*), but Blake's chief interest is as a self-portrait of the author, a contented bachelor living in a near-colonial-vintage house in the College Hill area of Providence, Rhode Island, with friendly cats lying just outside his window. Never mind that Blake will meet his doom after inadvertently stirring up a horror lurking in the steeple of a distant church visible from that window. At the end of the day "The Haunter of the Dark" amounts to a vision of H. P. Lovecraft in paradise.

—PETER CANNON

The Picture in the House

Searchers after horror haunt strange, far places. For them are the catacombs of Ptolemais,[1] and the carven mausolea of the nightmare countries. They climb to the moonlit towers of ruined Rhine castles,[2] and falter down black cob-

---

"The Picture in the House" was written on December 12, 1920, and was first published in the "July 1919" issue of the *National Amateur*, which actually came out in the summer of 1921. It is one of Lovecraft's most frequently reprinted stories.

[1] *catacombs of Ptolemais*: Cemeteries of the early Christians, located in any of several Middle Eastern or North African cities named in honor of the line of ancient Egyptian kings, from Ptolemy I (d. 284 B.C.) to Ptolemy XIV (47–30 B.C.).

[2] *Rhine castles*: The Rhine river with its spectacular scenery and background of legendary lore was a common setting for early Gothic novels.

webbed steps beneath the scattered stones of forgotten cities in Asia. The haunted wood and the desolate mountain are their shrines, and they linger around the sinister monoliths on uninhabited islands.[3] But the true epicure in the terrible,[4] to whom a new thrill of unutterable ghastliness is the chief end and justification of existence, esteems most of all the ancient, lonely farmhouses of backwoods New England; for there the dark elements of strength, solitude, grotesqueness, and ignorance combine to form the perfection of the hideous.

Most horrible of all sights are the little unpainted wooden houses remote from travelled ways, usually squatted upon some damp, grassy slope or leaning against some gigantic outcropping of rock. Two hundred years and more they have leaned or squatted there, while vines have crawled and the trees have swelled and spread. They are almost hidden now in lawless luxuriances of green and guardian shrouds of shadow; but the small-paned windows[5] still stare shockingly, as if blinking through a lethal stupor which wards off madness by dulling the memory of unutterable things.

In such houses have dwelt generations of strange people, whose like the world has ever seen. Seized with a gloomy and fanatical belief which exiled them from their kind, their ancestors sought the wilderness for freedom. There the scions of a conquering race indeed flourished free from

---

[3] *sinister monoliths on uninhabited islands*: Possibly an oblique reference to the mysterious stone heads carved out of volcanic rock on Easter Island, a small island in the South Pacific that belongs to Chile.

[4] *epicure in the terrible*: An epicure is a person who appreciates the finer things of life; derived from Epicurus (341–270 B.C.), a Greek philosopher who believed that pleasure is the end of all morality and that real pleasure is achieved through a life of prudence, honor, and justice. A major collection of Lovecraft criticism takes its title from this phrase: *An Epicure in the Terrible: A Centennial Anthology of Essays in Honor of H. P. Lovecraft*, edited by David E. Schultz and S. T. Joshi (1991).

[5] *small-paned windows*: Houses in colonial America were typically built with windows divided into multiple sections because glass was expensive. It was cheaper and easier to replace smaller panes when they broke.

the restrictions of their fellows, but cowered in an appalling slavery to the dismal phantasms of their own minds. Divorced from the enlightenment of civilisation, the strength of these Puritans[6] turned into singular channels; and in their isolation, morbid self-repression, and struggle for life with relentless Nature, there came to them dark furtive traits from the prehistoric depths of their cold Northern heritage. By necessity practical and by philosophy stern, these folk were not beautiful in their sins. Erring as all mortals must, they were forced by their rigid code to seek concealment above all else; so that they came to use less and less taste in what they concealed. Only the silent, sleepy, staring houses in the backwoods can tell all that has lain hidden since the early days; and they are not communicative, being loath to shake off the drowsiness which helps them forget. Sometimes one feels that it would be merciful to tear down these houses, for they must often dream.

It was to a time-battered edifice of this description that I was driven one afternoon in November, 1896, by a rain of such chilling copiousness that any shelter was preferable to exposure. I had been travelling for some time amongst the people of the Miskatonic Valley[7] in quest of certain genealogical data; and from the remote, devious, and problematical nature of my course, had deemed it convenient to employ a bicycle despite the lateness of the season. Now I found myself upon an apparently abandoned road which I had chosen as the shortest cut to Arkham;[8] overtaken by the storm at a point far from any town, and

---

[6] *Puritans*: The earliest European settlers of Massachusetts, who first arrived at Plymouth in 1620. They were religious dissenters who believed man was sinful by nature and could attain virtue through hard work. In the popular imagination they have been stereotyped as stern, grim folk. Perhaps the most distinguished American author to give the Puritans fictional treatment is Nathaniel Hawthorne (1804–1864), who was an influence on Lovecraft.

[7] *Miskatonic Valley*: The first mention of the "Miskatonic" region in the Lovecraft canon, here referring to a river valley. See note 3 to "Herbert West—Reanimator" for the derivation of the word *Miskatonic*.

confronted with no refuge save the antique and repellent wooden building which blinked with bleared windows from between two huge leafless elms near the foot of a rocky hill. Distant though it was from the remnant of a road, the house none the less impressed me unfavourably the very moment I espied it. Honest, wholesome structures do not stare at travellers so slyly and hauntingly, and in my genealogical researches I had encountered legends of a century before which biassed me against places of this kind. Yet the force of the elements was such as to overcome my scruples, and I did not hesitate to wheel my machine up the weedy rise to the closed door which seemed at once so suggestive and secretive.

I had somehow taken it for granted that the house was abandoned, yet as I approached it I was not so sure; for though the walks were indeed overgrown with weeds, they seemed to retain their nature a little too well to argue complete desertion. Therefore instead of trying the door I knocked, feeling as I did so a trepidation I could scarcely explain. As I waited on the rough, mossy rock which served as a doorstep, I glanced at the neighbouring windows and the panes of the transom above me, and noticed that although old, rattling, and almost opaque with dirt, they were not broken. The building, then, must still be

---

[8] *Arkham*: The first mention of Lovecraft's preeminent fictional town, which he would identify in later years as loosely corresponding to Salem, Massachusetts. At this point there is no evidence Lovecraft envisioned a series of tales set in or near this or any other fictional New England towns. In his article "Arkham Country: In Rescue of the Lost Searchers" (*Lovecraft Studies* 39, [summer 1998]: 1–20), Robert D. Marten makes a persuasive case that Lovecraft derived the uncommon prefix *Ark-* from the town of Arkwright, Rhode Island, now assimilated into Fiskville, Rhode Island. Sir Richard Arkwright invented the "spinning frame" which revolutionized the manufacture of cloth. In the 1780s, a mill-worker named Samuel Slater brought the process from England to the United States, where he established, with the financial backing of Moses Brown, the first successful textile factory at Pawtucket, Rhode Island. Thus Lovecraft came up with *Arkham* as a typical name for a New England factory town. Given Salem's development into an industrial center in the nineteenth century, the link with Arkham is all the more appropriate. For Arkham's connection to the neighborhing town of Bolton, see note 27 to "Herbert West—Reanimator."

inhabited, despite its isolation and general neglect. How- ever, my rapping evoked no response, so after repeating the summons I tried the rusty latch and found the door unfastened. Inside was a little vestibule with walls from which the plaster was falling, and through the doorway came a faint but peculiarly hateful odour. I entered, car- rying my bicycle, and closed the door behind me. Ahead rose a narrow staircase, flanked by a small door probably leading to the cellar, while to the left and right were closed doors leading to rooms on the ground floor.

Leaning my cycle against the wall I opened the door at the left, and crossed into a small low-ceiled chamber but dimly lighted by its two dusty windows and furnished in the barest and most primitive possible way. It appeared to be a kind of sitting-room, for it had a table and several chairs, and an immense fireplace above which ticked an antique clock on a mantel. Books and papers were very few, and in the prevailing gloom I could not readily dis- cern the titles. What interested me was the uniform air of archaism as displayed in every visible detail. Most of the houses in this region I had found rich in relics of the past, but here the antiquity was curiously complete; for in all the room I could not discover a single article of definitely post-revolutionary date. Had the furnishings been less humble, the place would have been a collector's paradise.

As I surveyed this quaint apartment, I felt an increase in that aversion first excited by the bleak exterior of the house. Just what it was that I feared or loathed, I could by no means define; but something in the whole atmosphere seemed redolent of unhallowed age, of unpleasant crude- ness, and of secrets which should be forgotten. I felt disin- clined to sit down, and wandered about examining the various articles which I had noticed. The first object of my curiosity was a book of medium size lying upon the table and presenting such an antediluvian aspect that I marvelled at beholding it outside a museum or library. It was bound in leather with metal fittings, and was in an

Drawing of butcher shop of the cannibal
Anziques. Taken from W. H. Wesley's
drawing (copied from Pigafetta's *Regnum
Congo*) included in Thomas Henry Hux-
ley's essay, "On the Natural History of
Man-Like Apes," from *Man's Place in Na-
ture and Other Anthropological Essays*
(New York: D. Appleton & Co., 1894).

excellent state of preservation; being altogether
an unusual sort of vol-
ume to encounter in an
abode so lowly. When I
opened it to the title page
my wonder grew even
greater, for it proved to be
nothing less rare than Pigafetta's account of the
Congo region,[9] written in
Latin from the notes of
the sailor Lopez and
printed at Frankfort in
1598. I had often heard of
this work, with its curi-
ous illustrations by the
brothers De Bry,[10] hence
for a moment forgot my
uneasiness in my desire
to turn the pages before
me. The engravings were
indeed interesting, drawn
wholly from imagination
and careless descriptions,
and represented negroes
with white skins and
Caucasian features; nor
would I soon have closed
the book had not an ex-
ceedingly trivial circum-

[9] *Pigafetta's account of the Congo region*: An actual book, by Filippo Pigafetta
(1533–1604). As S. T. Joshi points out in *H. P. Lovecraft: A Life* (1996), since
Lovecraft derived his information for the *Regnum Congo* (to use its Latin title)
from Thomas Henry Huxley's essay "On the History of the Man-like Apes," he
erred in a number of respects. The book was first published in Italian in 1591
and subsequently in English (1597) and German (1597) prior to its Latin translation in 1598. Lovecraft never consulted the De Bry plates themselves, only a
partial and rather inaccurate reproduction in the appendix to Huxley's essay.

stance upset my tired nerves and revived my sensation of disquiet. What annoyed me was merely the persistent way in which the volume tended to fall open of itself at Plate XII, which represented in gruesome detail a butcher's shop of the cannibal Anziques.[11] I experienced some shame at my susceptibility to so slight a thing, but the drawing nevertheless disturbed me, especially in connexion with some adjacent passages descriptive of Anzique gastronomy.

I had turned to a neighbouring shelf and was examining its meagre literary contents—an eighteenth-century Bible, a *Pilgrim's Progress*[12] of like period, illustrated with grotesque woodcuts and printed by the almanack-maker Isaiah Thomas,[13] the rotting bulk of Cotton Mather's *Magnalia Christi Americana*,[14] and a few other books of evidently equal age—when my attention was aroused by the unmistakable sound of walking in the room overhead. At first astonished and startled, considering the lack of response to my recent knocking at the door, I immediately afterward concluded that the walker had just awakened from a sound sleep; and listened with less surprise as the footsteps sounded on the creaking stairs. The tread was heavy, yet seemed to contain a curious quality of cau-

---

[10] *the brothers De Bry*: Johann Theodor De Bry (1561–1623) and Johann Israel De Bry (1570–1611) illustrated a number of books in the late sixteenth and early seventeenth centuries.

[11] *Anziques*: Natives of the Kingdom of Anziku, an historic African state in the vicinity of the Congo River.

[12] *Pilgrim's Progress*: Christian allegory by the Englishman John Bunyan (1628–88). In its day the most common book to be found in people's homes after the Bible.

[13] *Isaiah Thomas*: Isaiah Thomas (1749–1831) was a radical anti-British printer and journalist, founder of the *Massachusetts Spy*, which carried the first reports of the battles of Lexington and Concord in 1775.

[14] *Cotton Mather's Magnalia Christi Americana*: Cotton Mather (1663–1728), clergyman and author, was a leading figure in colonial Massachusetts. His *Magnalia Christi Americana* (1702) is an ecclesiastical history of New England, showing the working of God's will in the history of Massachusetts.

tiousness; a quality which I disliked the more because the tread was heavy. When I had entered the room I had shut the door behind me. Now, after a moment of silence during which the walker may have been inspecting my bicycle in the hall, I heard a fumbling at the latch and saw the panelled portal swing open again.

In the doorway stood a person of such singular appearance that I should have exclaimed aloud but for the restraints of good breeding. Old, white-bearded, and ragged, my host possessed a countenance and physique which inspired equal wonder and respect. His height could not have been less than six feet, and despite a general air of age and poverty he was stout and powerful in proportion. His face, almost hidden by a long beard which grew high on the cheeks, seemed abnormally ruddy and less wrinkled than one might expect; while over a high forehead fell a shock of white hair little thinned by the years. His blue eyes, though a trifle bloodshot, seemed inexplicably keen and burning. But for his horrible unkemptness the man would have been as distinguished-looking as he was impressive. This unkemptness, however, made him offensive despite his face and figure. Of what his clothing consisted I could hardly tell, for it seemed to me no more than a mass of tatters surmounting a pair of high, heavy boots; and his lack of cleanliness surpassed description.

The appearance of this man, and the instinctive fear he inspired, prepared me for something like enmity; so that I almost shuddered through surprise and a sense of uncanny incongruity when he motioned me to a chair and addressed me in a thin, weak voice full of fawning respect and ingratiating hospitality. His speech was very curious, an extreme form of Yankee dialect I had thought long extinct; and I studied it closely as he sat down opposite me for conversation.

"Ketched in the rain, be ye?"[15] he greeted. "Glad ye was nigh the haouse en' hed the sense ta come right in. I calc-'late I was asleep, else I'd a heerd ye—I ain't as young as

I uster be, an' I need a paowerful sight o' naps naowadays. Trav'lin' fur? I hain't seed many folks 'long this rud sence they tuk off the Arkham stage."

I replied that I was going to Arkham, and apologised for my rude entry into his domicile, whereupon he continued.

"Glad ta see ye, young Sir—new faces is scurce arount here, an' I hain't got much ta cheer me up these days. Guess yew hail from Bosting,[16] don't ye? I never ben thar, but I kin tell a taown man when I see 'im—we hed one fer deestrick schoolmaster in 'eighty-four, but he quit suddent an' no one never heerd on 'im sence—" Here the old man lapsed into a kind of chuckle, and made no explanation when I questioned him. He seemed to be in an aboundingly good humour, yet to possess those eccentricities which one might guess from his grooming. For some time he rambled on with an almost feverish geniality, when it struck me to ask him how he came by so rare a book as Pigafetta's *Regnum Congo*. The effect of this volume had not left me, and I felt a certain hesitancy in speaking of it; but curiosity overmastered all the vague fears which had steadily accumulated since my first glimpse of the house. To my relief, the question did not

---

[15] "*Ketched in the rain, be ye!*": The first use of (archaic) New England dialect in Lovecraft's fiction—and the start of the first notable monologue in Lovecraft, who avoided dialogue as such because he felt he had no aptitude for it. Jason Eckhardt in his article "The Cosmic Yankee," included in *An Epicure in the Terrible*, has suggested that Lovecraft derived it largely from James Russell Lowell's *Biglow Papers* (1848–62). Lovecraft owned Lowell's poems and was clearly familiar with much of his work. It should also be noted that, at the period Lovecraft was writing, representing dialect phonetically to the point of unintelligibility was common. Modern writers tend to be more sparing in their use of dialect.

This old-fashioned speech fits a character who is a survival of the eighteenth century. Old men—both beyond and within a normal life span—often appear in Lovecraft's fiction, the first example being the title character of "The Terrible Old Man" (1920). For more on this topic, see Peter Cannon's "Lovecraft's Old Men" in his *"Sunset Terrace Imagery in Lovecraft" and Other Essays* (1990).

[16] *Bosting*: Boston. The largest town in colonial Massachusetts. This reference suggests that Arkham is in the vicinity of Boston, and hence unlikely to be very far inland. See note 8 on Arkham above.

seem an awkward one; for the old man answered freely and volubly.

"Oh, thet Afriky book? Cap'n Ebenezer Holt traded me thet in 'sixty-eight—him as was kilt in the war." Something about the name of Ebenezer Holt caused me to look up sharply. I had encountered it in my genealogical work, but not in any record since the Revolution. I wondered if my host could help me in the task at which I was labouring, and resolved to ask him about it later on. He continued.

"Ebenezer was on a Salem merchantman for years, an' picked up a sight o' queer stuff in every port. He got this in London, I guess—he uster like ter buy things at the shops. I was up ta his haouse onct, on the hill, tradin' hosses, when I see this book. I relished the picters, so he give it in on a swap. 'Tis a queer book—here, leave me git on my spectacles—" The old man fumbled among his rags, producing a pair of dirty and amazingly antique glasses with small octagonal lenses and steel bows. Donning these, he reached for the volume on the table and turned the pages lovingly.

"Ebenezer cud read a leetle o' this—'tis Latin—but I can't. I hed two er three schoolmasters read me a bit, and Passon Clark,[17] him they say got draownded in the pond—kin yew make anything outen it?" I told him that I could, and translated for his benefit a paragraph near the beginning. If I erred, he was not scholar enough to correct me; for he seemed childishly pleased at my English version. His proximity was becoming obnoxious, yet I saw no way to escape without offending him. I was amused at the childish fondness of this ignorant old man for the pictures in a book he could not read, and wondered how much better he could read the few books in English which adorned his room. This revelation of simplicity removed much of the ill-defined apprehension I had felt, and I smiled as my host rambled on:

[17] *Passon Clark*: Dialect for Parson Clark. A parson is a Protestant clergyman.

"Queer haow picters kin set a body thinkin'. Take this un here near the front. Hev yew ever seed trees like thet, with big leaves a-floppin' over an' daown? And them men—them can't be niggers—they dew beat all. Kinder like Injuns, I guess, even ef they be in Afriky. Some o' these here critters looks like monkeys, or half monkeys an' half men, but I never heerd o' nothing like this un." Here he pointed to a fabulous creature of the artist, which one might describe as a sort of dragon with the head of an alligator.

"But naow I'll shew ye the best un—over here nigh the middle—" The old man's speech grew a trifle thicker and his eyes assumed a brighter glow; but his fumbling hands, though seemingly clumsier than before, were entirely adequate to their mission. The book fell open, almost of its own accord and as if from frequent consultation at this place, to the repellent twelfth plate shewing a butcher's shop amongst the Anzique cannibals. My sense of restlessness returned, though I did not exhibit it. The especially bizarre thing was that the artist had made his Africans look like white men—the limbs and quarters hanging about the walls of the shop were ghastly, while the butcher with his axe was hideously incongruous. But my host seemed to relish the view as much as I disliked it.

"What d'ye think o' this—ain't never see the like hereabouts, eh? When I see this I telled Eb Holt, 'Thar's suthin' ta stir ye up an' make yer blood tickle!' When I read the Scripter about slayin'—like them Midianites[18] was slew—I kinder think things, but I ain't got no picter of it. Here a body kin see all they is to it—I s'pose 'tis sinful, but ain't we all born an' livin' in sin?—Thet feller

---

[18] *Midianites*: A nomadic people who were enemies of the Israelites. The specific passage of Scripture here referred to may be Judges 7:25: "And they took the two princes of Midian, Oreb and Zeeb; they killed Oreb at the rock of Oreb, and Zeeb they killed at the wine press of Zeeb, as they pursued Midian; and they brought the heads of Oreb and Zeeb to Gideon beyond the Jordan."

bein' chopped up gives me a tickle every time I look at 'im—I hev ta keep lookin' at 'im—see whar the butcher cut off his feet? Thar's his head on thet bench, with one arm side of it, an' t'other arm's on the graound side o' the meat block.''

As the man mumbled on in his shocking ecstasy the expression on his hairy, spectacled face became indescribable, but his voice sank rather than mounted. My own sensations can scarcely be recorded. All the terror I had dimly felt before rushed upon me actively and vividly, and I knew that I loathed the ancient and abhorrent creature so near me with an infinite intensity. His madness, or at least his partial perversion, seemed beyond dispute. He was almost whispering now, with a huskiness more terrible than a scream, and I trembled as I listened.

"As I says, 'tis queer haow picters sets ye thinkin'. D'ye know, young Sir, I'm right sot on this un here. Arter I got the book off Eb I uster look at it a lot, especial when I'd heerd Passon Clark rant o' Sundays in his big wig.[19] Onct I tried suthin' funny—here, young Sir, don't git skeert—all I done was ter look at the picter afore I kilt the sheep for market—killin' sheep was kinder more fun arter lookin' at it—'' The tone of the old man now sank very low, sometimes becoming so faint that his words were hardly audible. I listened to the rain, and to the rattling of the bleared, small-paned windows, and marked a rumbling of approaching thunder quite unusual for the season. Once a terrific flash and peal shook the frail house to its foundations, but the whisperer seemed not to notice.

"Killin' sheep was kinder more fun—but d'ye know,

---

[19] *big wig*: Wigs were fashionable among the upper classes in the eighteenth century. They went out of fashion at the time of the French Revolution (1789), when many aristocrats lost their heads (and their wigs) to the guillotine. In *The Case of Charles Dexter Ward*, Dr. Willett is disturbed because Ward knows "so much about the way the fat sherriff's wig fell off" at a play put on at a Providence theatre in 1762. Lovecraft was delighted by the pen-and-ink sketch his artist friend Virgil Finlay (1914–71) did showing him dressed as an eighteenth-century gentleman, complete with periwig.

AMATEUR
CORRESPONDENT

MAY-JUNE
1937

Dedication

This issue is respectfully dedicated to the memory of Howard Phillips Lovecraft, who died March 15, 1937, at the age of forty-six. Called by many the dean of modern writers of weird fiction, he will be mourned by every reader of fantasy, not only for the excellence of his writings but also for the fine calibre of mind typified therein.

Portrait of H. P. Lovecraft as an eighteenth-century gentleman by Virgil Finlay, first published on the cover of *Amateur Correspondent* (May-June 1937).

'twan't quite *satisfyin'*. Queer haow a *cravin'* gits a holt on ye— As ye love the Almighty, young man, don't tell nobody, but I swar ter Gawd thet picter begun ta make me *hungry fer victuals I couldn't raise nor buy*—here, set still, what's ailin' ye?—I didn't do nothin', only I wondered haow 'twud be ef I *did*— They say meat makes blood an' flesh, an' gives ye new life, so I wondered if 'twudn't make a man live longer an' longer ef 'twas *more the same*—" But the whisperer never continued. The interruption was not produced by my fright, nor by the rapidly increasing storm amidst whose fury I was presently to open my eyes on a smoky solitude of blackened ruins. It was produced by a very simple through somewhat unusual happening.

The open book lay flat between us, with the picture staring repulsively upward. As the old man whispered the words *"more the same"* a tiny spattering impact was heard, and something shewed on the yellowed paper of the upturned volume. I thought of the rain and of a leaky roof, but rain is not red. On the butcher's shop of the Anzique cannibals a small red spattering glistened picturesquely, lending vividness to the horror of the engraving. The old man saw it, and stopped whispering even before my expression of horror made it necessary; saw it and glanced quickly toward the floor of the room he had left an hour before. I followed his glance, and beheld just above us on the loose plaster of the ancient ceiling a large irregular spot of wet crimson which seemed to spread even as I viewed it. I did not shriek or move, but merely shut my eyes. A moment later came the titanic thunderbolt of thunderbolts; blasting that accursed house of unutterable secrets and bringing the oblivion which alone saved my mind.[20]

---

[20] *alone saved my mind*: This deus ex machina ending may well have been inspired by the conclusion to Poe's story "The Fall of the House of Usher," in which the narrator survives to tell his tale only because the House of Usher literally collapses.

Herbert West— Reanimator

I. *From the Dark*[1]

Of Herbert West,[2] who was my friend in college and in after life, I can speak only with extreme terror. This terror is not due altogether to the sinister manner of his recent

---

"Herbert West—Reanimator" was written between the autumn of 1921 and the summer of 1922. It was commissioned by George Julian Houtain for his short-lived humor magazine, *Home Brew*, and appeared serially (under the generic title "Grewsome Tales") in the first six issues of that magazine (February–June 1922); after Lovecraft's death it was reprinted in *Weird Tales*.

[1] First published in *Home Brew*, February 1922; reprinted in *Weird Tales*, March 1942.

disappearance, but was engendered by the whole nature of
his life-work, and first gained its acute form more than
seventeen years ago, when we were in the third year of
our course at the Miskatonic University[3] Medical School
in Arkham.[4] While he was with me, the wonder and diabolism of his experiments fascinated me utterly, and I was
his closest companion. Now that he is gone and the spell
is broken, the actual fear is greater. Memories and possibilities are ever more hideous than realities.

The first horrible incident of our acquaintance was the
greatest shock I ever experienced, and it is only with reluc-
tance that I repeat it. As I have said, it happened when
we were in the medical school, where West had already
made himself notorious through his wild theories on the
nature of death and the possibility of overcoming it artificially. His views, which were widely ridiculed by the faculty and his fellow-students, hinged on the essentially
mechanistic nature of life;[5] and concerned means for op-

---

[2] It is difficult to know where Lovecraft came up with the name Herbert West.
West is by no means a specifically New England name, even though most of
the story takes place in New England.

[3] This is Lovecraft's first mention of this celebrated imaginary institution of
higher learning, although the Miskatonic Valley had been cited in an earlier
tale, "The Picture in the House" (1920). It is very likely modeled upon Brown
University; its medical school had been established in 1811. The name *Miska-
tonic* is probably an adaptation of several Indian place-names in New England,
most notably Housatonic, a river in western Massachusetts and Connecticut.
Of the name Lovecraft remarks that it "is simply a jumble of Algonquin roots"
(*Selected Letters*, III, 432). Will Murray ("Roots of the Miskatonic," *Crypt of
Cthulhu* No. 45 [Candlemas 1987]:6–9) presents a hypothetical translation as
"Red mountain place."

[4] This is the second mention of this imaginary Massachusetts city; its first cita-
tion occurred in "The Picture in the House" (1920). See note 8 to that story and
also note 27 below.

[5] When Lovecraft stated that "my philosophical position [is] that of a mechanistic materialist" (*Selected Letters*, II, 60), he was making two separate but related
assertions. Mechanism refers to the uniformity of the laws of cause and effect
and the absence of free will; materialism is (as defined by Hugh Elliot in *Modern
Science and Materialism* [London: Longmans, Green, 1919], 138—a book Lovecraft read) "the denial of any form of existence other than those envisaged by
physics and chemistry, that is to say, other existences that have some kind of
palpable material characteristics and qualities."

erating the organic machinery of mankind by calculated chemical action after the failure of natural processes. In his experiments with various animating solutions he had killed and treated immense numbers of rabbits, guinea-pigs, cats, dogs, and monkeys, till he had become the prime nuisance of the college. Several times he had actually obtained signs of life in animals supposedly dead; in many cases violent signs; but he soon saw that the perfection of this process, if indeed possible, would necessarily involve a lifetime of research. It likewise become clear that, since the same solution never worked alike on different organic species, he would require human subjects for further and more specialised progress. It was here that he first came into conflict with the college authorities, and was debarred from future experiments by no less a dignitary than the dean of the medical school himself—the learned and benevolent Dr. Allan Halsey,[6] whose work in behalf of the stricken is recalled by every old resident of Arkham.

I had always been exceptionally tolerant of West's pursuits, and we frequently discussed his theories, whose ramifications and corollaries were almost infinite. Holding with Haeckel[7] that all life is a chemical and physical pro-

---

[6] *Dr. Allan Halsey*: Halsey is the name of one of the older families in Providence; the so-called "Halsey mansion" at 140 Prospect Street in Providence was well known to Lovecraft, as he later based his novel *The Case of Charles Dexter Ward* (1927) upon it. The name Allan is perhaps derived from Edgar Allan Poe.

[7] *Haeckel*: Ernst Haeckel (1834–1919), German scientist and philosopher. Lovecraft was much influenced by his volumes, *Die Welträthsel* (1899; tr. as *The Riddle of the Universe*, 1900) and *Anthropogenie* (1874; tr. as *The Evolution of Man*, 1903), which propounded the Darwinian theory of evolution and ridiculed the idea of an immaterial and immortal soul. Cf. Lovecraft's essay "Final Words" (1921): "One might ask, to the confounding of those who aver that men have 'souls' whilst beasts have not, . . . just how the evolving organism began to acquire 'spirit' after it crossed the boundary betwixt advanced ape and primitive human? It is rather hard to believe in 'soul' when one has not a jot of evidence for its existence; when all the psychic life of man is demonstrated to be precisely analogous to that of other animals—presumably 'soulless'. . . . Haeckel's *Evolution of Man*, in its final edition, leaves very little to be said" (*In Defence of Dagon* [West Warwick, RI: Necronomicon Press, 1985], 37).

cess, and that the so-called "soul" is a myth, my friend
believed that artificial reanimation of the dead can depend
only on the condition of the tissues; and that unless actual
decomposition has set in, a corpse fully equipped with
organs may with suitable measures be set going again in
the peculiar fashion known as life. That the psychic or
intellectual life might be impaired by the slight deterioration of sensitive brain-cells which even a short period of
death would be apt to cause, West fully realised. It had at
first been his hope to find a reagent which would restore
vitality before the actual advent of death, and only repeated failures on animals had shewn him that the natural
and artificial life-motions were incompatible. He then
sought extreme freshness in his specimens, injecting his
solutions into the blood immediately after the extinction
of life. It was this circumstance which made the professors
so carelessly sceptical, for they felt that true death had
not occurred in any case. They did not stop to view the
matter closely and reasoningly.

It was not long after the faculty had interdicted his work
that West confided to me his resolution to get fresh
human bodies in some manner, and continue in secret the
experiments he could no longer perform openly. To hear
him discussing ways and means was rather ghastly, for at
the college we had never procured anatomical specimens
ourselves. Whenever the morgue proved inadequate, two
local negroes attended to this matter, and they were seldom questioned. West was then a small, slender, spectacled youth with delicate features, yellow hair, pale blue
eyes, and a soft voice, and it was uncanny to hear him
dwelling on the relative merits of Christchurch Cemetery
and the potter's field.[8] We finally decided on the potter's
field, because practically every body in Christchurch was
embalmed; a thing of course ruinous to West's researches.

---

[8] *potter's field*: A burial place for the poor and for strangers; derived from Mat-
thew 27:7: "And they took counsel, and brought with them the potter's field,
to bury strangers in."

A New England cemetery (photo by Will Murray).

I was by this time his active and enthralled assistant, and helped him make all his decisions, not only concerning the source of bodies but concerning a suitable place for our loathsome work. It was I who thought of the deserted Chapman farmhouse beyond Meadow Hill,[9] where we fitted up on the ground floor an operating room and a laboratory, each with dark curtains to conceal our midnight doings. The place was far from any road, and in sight of no other house, yet precautions were none the less necessary; since rumours of strange lights, started by chance nocturnal roamers, would soon bring disaster on our enter-

---

[9] *Meadow Hill*: An imaginary place cited in several other stories by Lovecraft, including "The Unnamable" (1923), "The Colour Out of Space" (1927), and "The Dreams in the Witch House" (1932). For the Chapman farmhouse, see note 12 below.

prise. It was agreed to call the whole thing a chemical laboratory if discovery should occur. Gradually we equipped our sinister haunt of science with materials either purchased in Boston or quietly borrowed from the college—materials carefully made unrecognisable save to expert eyes—and provided spades and picks for the many burials we should have to make in the cellar. At the college we used an incinerator, but the apparatus was too costly for our unauthorised laboratory. Bodies were always a nuisance—even the small guinea-pig bodies from the slight clandestine experiments in West's room at the boarding-house.

We followed the local death-notices like ghouls, for our specimens demanded particular qualities. What we wanted were corpses interred soon after death and without artificial preservation; preferably free from malforming disease, and certainly with all organs present. Accident victims were our best hope. Not for many weeks did we hear of anything suitable; though we talked with morgue and hospital authorities, ostensibly in the college's interest, as often as we could without exciting suspicion. We found that the college had first choice in every case, so that it might be necessary to remain in Arkham during the summer, when only the limited summer-school classes were held. In the end, though, luck favoured us; for one day we heard of an almost ideal case in the potter's field; a brawny young workman drowned only the morning before in Sumner's Pond, and buried at the town's expense without delay or embalming. That afternoon we found the new grave, and determined to begin work soon after midnight.

It was a repulsive task that we undertook in the black small hours, even though we lacked at that time the special horror of graveyards which later experiences brought to us. We carried spades and oil dark lanterns, for although electric torches were then manufactured, they were not as satisfactory as the tungsten contrivances of today. The process of unearthing was slow and sordid—it might have

Graves in St. John's Churchyard (Benefit Street), Providence (photo by Steven J. Mariconda).

been gruesomely poetical if we had been artists instead of scientists[10]—and we were glad when our spades struck wood. When the pine box was fully uncovered West scrambled down and removed the lid, dragging out and propping up the contents. I reached down and hauled the contents out of the grave, and then both toiled hard to restore the spot to its former appearance. The affair made us rather nervous, especially the stiff form and vacant face of our first trophy, but we managed to remove all traces of our visit. When we had patted down the last shovelful of earth we put the specimen in a canvas sack and set out for the old Chapman place beyond Meadow Hill.

On an improvised dissecting-table in the old farmhouse, by the light of a powerful acetylene lamp, the specimen

---

[10] Cf. Lovecraft's "The Hound" (1922): "We were no vulgar ghouls, but worked only under certain conditions of mood, landscape, environment, weather, season, and moonlight. These pastimes [graverobbing] were to us the most exquisite form of aesthetic expression, and we gave their details a fastidious technical care" (*Dagon and Other Macabre Tales*, 173).

was not very spectral looking. It had been a sturdy and apparently unimaginative youth of wholesome plebeian type—large-framed, grey-eyed, and brown-haired—a sound animal without psychological subtleties, and probably having vital processes of the simplest and healthiest sort.[11] Now, with the eyes closed, it looked more asleep than dead; though the expert test of my friend soon left no doubt on that score. We had at last what West had always longed for—a real dead man of the ideal kind, ready for the solution as prepared according to the most careful calculations and theories for human use. The tension on our part became very great. We knew that there was scarcely a chance for anything like complete success, and could not avoid hideous fears at possible grotesque results of partial animation. Especially were we apprehensive concerning the mind and impulses of the creature, since in the space following death some of the more delicate cerebral ceils might well have suffered deterioration. I, myself, still held some curious notions about the traditional "soul" of man, and felt an awe at the secrets that might be told by one returning from the dead. I wondered what sights this placid youth might have seen in inaccessible spheres, and what he could relate if fully restored to life. But my wonder was not overwhelming, since for the most part I shared the materialism of my friend. He was calmer than I as he forced a large quantity of his fluid into a vein

---

[11] This description seems typical of Lovecraft's evaluation of the mental and psychological attributes of common people. Cf. the speech of the extraterrestrial entity who inhabits the body of a denizen of the Catskill Mountains, Joe Slater, in "Beyond the Wall of Sleep" (1919): " 'His gross body could not undergo the needed adjustments between ethereal life and planet life. He was too much of an animal, too little a man . . .' " (*Dagon and Other Macabre Tales*, 34). See also Lovecraft's evaluation of the work of Theodore Dreiser: "He does understand the undercurrents of certain heavy, mediocre characters . . . At the same time, I cannot summon up any real interest in his painful photographs. . . . The amount of real interest in the draggled flounderings of a muddled lower-middle-class mind in the toils of social inhibition would seem to me definitely limited. For a while it may symbolise the writhings of man in the clutch of the infinite, but after the novelty of the analogy has worn off one loses patience with the spectacle of sheer, stupid, ox-like misery." (*Selected Letters*, II, 80)

of the body's arm, immediately binding the incision securely.

The waiting was gruesome, but West never faltered. Every now and then he applied his stethoscope to the specimen, and bore the negative results philosophically. After about three-quarters of an hour without the least sign of life he disappointedly pronounced the solution inadequate, but determined to make the most of his opportunity and try one change in the formula before disposing of his ghastly prize. We had that afternoon dug a grave in the cellar, and would have to fill it by dawn—for although we had fixed a lock on the house we wished to shun even the remotest risk of a ghoulish discovery. Beside, the body would not be even approximately fresh the next night. So taking the solitary acetylene lamp into the adjacent laboratory, we left our silent guest on the slab in the dark, and bent every energy to the mixing of a new solution; the weighing and measuring supervised by West with an almost fanatical care.

The awful event was very sudden, and wholly unexpected. I was pouring something from one test-tube to another, and West was busy over the alcohol blast-lamp which had to answer for a Bunsen burner in this gasless edifice, when from the pitch-black room we had left there burst the most appalling and daemoniac succession of cries that either of us had ever heard. Not more unutterable could have been the chaos of hellish sound if the pit itself had opened to release the agony of the damned, for in one inconceivable cacophony was centred all the supernal terror and unnatural despair of animate nature. Human it could not have been—it is not in man to make such sounds—and without a thought of our late employment or its possible discovery both West and I leaped to the nearest window like stricken animals; overturning tubes, lamp, and retorts, and vaulting madly into the starred abyss of the rural night. I think we screamed ourselves as we stumbled frantically toward the town, though as we

reached the outskirts we put on a semblance of restraint—
just enough to seem like belated revellers staggering home
from a debauch.

We did not separate, but managed to get to West's room,
where we whispered with the gas up until dawn. By then
we had calmed ourselves a little with rational theories and
plans for investigation, so that we could sleep through the
day—classes being disregarded. But that evening two items
in the paper, wholly unrelated, made it again impossible
for us to sleep. The old deserted Chapman house had inexplicably burned to an amorphous heap of ashes;[12] that we
could understand because of the upset lamp. Also, an attempt had been made to disturb a new grave in the potter's
field, as if by futile and spadeless clawing at the earth.
That we could not understand, for we had patted down
the mould very carefully.

And for seventeen years after that West would look frequently over his shoulder, and complain of fancied footsteps behind him. Now he has disappeared.

II. *The Plague-Daemon*[13]

I shall never forget that hideous summer sixteen years
ago, when like a noxious afrite[14] from the halls of Eblis[15]

---

[12] This scene seems to reflect an actual incident Lovecraft witnessed in early
1920 while living at 598 Angell Street in Providence: "But *the* event of the
season was the burning of the large Chapman house last Wednesday night—the
yellow house across two lawns to the north of #598 Angell. . . . Where that
evening had stood the unoccupied Chapman house, recently sold and undergoing
repairs, was now a titanic pillar of roaring, living flame amidst the deserted
night—reaching into the illimitable heavens and lighting the country for miles
around." (*Selected Letters*, I, 108)

Lovecraft may also have been thinking of the scene in Mary Shelley's *Frankenstein* in which the monster, rebuffed by the cottagers to whom he had made
overtures of friendship, sets fire to their abode: "I lighted the dry branch of a
tree, and danced with fury around the devoted cottage, my eyes still fixed on
the western horizon, the edge of which the moon nearly touched. A part of its
orb was at length hid, and I waved my brand; it sunk, and, with a loud scream,
I fired the straw, and heath, and bushes, which I had collected. The wind fanned
the fire, and the cottage was quickly enveloped by the flames, which clung
to it, and licked it with their forked and destroying tongues." (*The Essential*

typhoid stalked leeringly through Arkham. It is by that satanic scourge that most recall the year, for truly terror brooded with bat-wings over the piles of coffins in the tombs of Christchurch Cemetery; yet for me there is a greater horror in that time—a horror known to me alone now that Herbert West has disappeared.

West and I were doing post-graduate work in summer classes at the medical school of Miskatonic University, and my friend had attained a wide notoriety because of his experiments leading toward the revivication of the dead. After the scientific slaughter of uncounted small animals the freakish work had ostensibly stopped by order of our sceptical dean, Dr. Allan Halsey; though West had continued to perform certain secret tests in his dingy boarding-house room, and had on one terrible and unforgettable occasion taken a human body from its grave in the potter's field to a deserted farmhouse beyond Meadow Hill.

I was with him on that odious occasion, and saw him inject into the still veins the elixir which he thought would to some extent restore life's chemical and physical processes. It had ended horribly—in a delirium of fear

---

Frankenstein, ed. Leonard Wolf [New York: Penguin/Plume, 1993], 188–89)

[13] First published in *Home Brew,* March 1922; reprinted in *Weird Tales,* July 1942. "Daemon" is Lovecraft's habitual archaic spelling of *demon.*

[14] *afrite:* An evil demon or monster in the Islamic religion; also spelled *afreet* and *afrit.* Cf. William Beckford's *History of the Caliph Vathek* (1786): "Those inviolable asylums were defended against the Divas and the Afrits by waving streamers, on which were inscribed, in characters of gold that flashed like lightning, the names of Alla and the Prophet." Samuel Henley, in his notes to *Vathek,* defines afrits as follows: "They were a kind of Medusa, or Lamia, supposed to be the most terrible and cruel of all the orders of the dives" (i.e., devils).

[15] *halls of Eblis:* Eblis is the Devil of the Islamic religion. Lovecraft probably learned of it from Beckford's *Vathek* (see note 14 above), which he read in 1921 and which he describes as follows in "Supernatural Horror in Literature": "*Vathek* is a tale of the grandson of the Caliph Haroun, who, tormented by that ambition for super-terrestrial power, pleasure, and learning which animates the average Gothic villain or Byronic hero . . . is lured by an evil genius to seek the subterranean throne of the mighty and fabulous pre-Adamite sultans in the fiery halls of Eblis, the Mohametan Devil." (*Dagon and Other Macabre Tales,* 383)

which we gradually came to attribute to our own over-wrought nerves—and West had never afterward been able to shake off a maddening sensation of being haunted and hunted.[16] The body had not been quite fresh enough; it is obvious that to restore normal mental attributes a body must be very fresh indeed; and a burning of the old house had prevented us from burying the thing. It would have been better if we could have known it was underground.

After that experience West had dropped his researches for some time; but as the zeal of the born scientist slowly returned, he again became importunate with the college faculty, pleading for the use of the dissecting-room and of fresh human specimens for the work he regarded as so overwhelmingly important. His pleas, however, were wholly in vain; for the decision of Dr. Halsey was inflexible, and the other professors all endorsed the verdict of their leader. In the radical theory of reanimation they saw nothing but the immature vagaries of a youthful enthusiast whose slight form, yellow hair, spectacled blue eyes, and soft voice gave no hint of the supernormal—almost diabolical—power of the cold brain within. I can see him now as he was then—and I shiver. He grew sterner of face, but never elderly.[17] And now Sefton Asylum[18] has had the mishap and West has vanished.

West clashed disagreeably with Dr. Halsey near the end

---

[16] Perhaps another echo of *Frankenstein*, especially the scene in which Victor Frankenstein, after reanimating the monster, flees in horror from it: "I traversed the streets, without any clear conception of where I was, or what I was doing. My heart palpitated in the sickness of fear; and I hurried on with irregular steps, not daring to look about me . . ." Frankenstein then quotes a stanza from Coleridge's *Rime of the Ancient Mariner*, one of Lovecraft's favorite poems from earliest childhood:

Like one who, on a lonely road,
Doth walk in fear and dread,
And, having once turn'd round, walks on,
And turns no more his head;
Because he knows a frightful fiend
Doth close behind him tread.

(*The Essential Frankenstein*, 89)

of our last undergraduate term in a wordy dispute that did less credit to him than to the kindly dean in point of courtesy. He felt that he was needlessly and irrationally retarded in a supremely great work; a work which he could of course conduct to suit himself in later years, but which he wished to begin while still possessed of the exceptional facilities of the university. That the tradition-bound elders should ignore his singular results on animals, and persist in their denial of the possibility of reanimation, was inexpressibly disgusting and almost incomprehensible to a youth of West's logical temperament. Only greater maturity could help him understand the chronic mental limitations of the "professor-doctor" type—the product of generations of pathetic Puritanism;[19] kindly, conscientious, and sometimes gentle and amiable, yet always narrow, intolerant, custom-ridden, and lacking in perspective. Age has more charity for these incomplete yet high-souled characters, whose worst real vice is timidity, and who are ultimately punished by general ridicule for their intellec-

---

[17] Cf. Joseph Curwen in *The Case of Charles Dexter Ward*, who uses alchemy to preserve the appearance of youth even in advanced old age: "Now the first odd thing about Joseph Curwen was that he did not seem to grow much older than he had been on his arrival. . . . [A]lways did he retain the nondescript aspect of a man not greatly over thirty or thirty-five." (*At the Mountains of Madness and Other Novels*, 117–18)

[18] *Sefton Asylum*: Imaginary, although there are many towns in central Massachusetts with -*ton* endings (e.g., Grafton).

[19] Lovecraft's attitude to New England Puritanism was mixed. In reference to seventeenth-century Puritans he writes harshly in "The Picture in the House": "There [in New England] the scions of a conquering race indeed flourished free from the restrictions of their fellows, but cowered in an appalling slavery to the dismal phantasms of their own minds. Divorced from the enlightenment of civilisation, the strength of these Puritans turned into singular channels; and in their isolation, morbid self-repression, and struggle for life with relentless Nature, there came to them dark furtive traits from the prehistoric depths of their cold Northern heritage." But Lovecraft's use of the term here really denotes the Puritan-Victorian social codes of nineteenth- and early twentieth-century New England, to which he was occasionally much more sympathetic. ". . . as for Puritan inhibitions—I admire them more every day. They are attempts to make of life a work of art—to fashion a pattern of beauty in the hog-wallow that is animal existence . . . a Puritan in the conduct of life is the only kind of man one may honestly respect" (*Selected Letters*, I, 315).

tual sins—sins like Ptolemaism, Calvinism, anti-Darwinisn,
anti-Nietzscheism, and every sort of Sabbatarianism and
sumptuary legislation.[20] West, young despite his marvellous scientific acquirements, had scant patience with good
Dr. Halsey and his erudite colleagues; and nursed an increasing resentment, coupled with a desire to prove his
theories to these obtuse worthies in some striking and
dramatic fashion. Like most youths, he indulged in elabo-

---

[20] *Ptolemaism*: A denial of the Copernican theory that the earth revolves around
the sun and a return to the geocentric theory of Ptolemy.

   Calvinism: The rigid Protestant theology evolved by John Calvin (1509–1564),
who asserted that the souls of certain human beings (the "elect") are predestined
for salvation without regard to any actions performed in life, while all others—
regardless of their actions in life—are doomed to eternal punishment in Hell.

   anti-Darwinism: A denial of the theory of evolution of Charles Darwin
(1809–1882). Cf. Lovecraft's remarks on G. K. Chesterton in "The Defence Re-
opens!" (1921): ". . . when a man soberly tries to dismiss the results of Darwin
we need not give him too much of our valuable time. The exact details of
organic progress as described in *The Origin of Species* and *The Descent of Man*
may admit of correction or amplification; but to attack the essential principle,
which alone is of universal importance, is pathetic." (*In Defence of Dagon*, 17)

   anti-Nietzscheism: Lovecraft had fallen under the influence of the German
philosopher Friedrich Nietzsche (1844–1900) beginning around 1919. "Lest you
fancy that I am making an idol of Nietzsche . . . let me state clearly that I do
not swallow him whole. His ethical system is a joke—or a poet's dream, which
amounts to the same thing. It is in his method, and his account of the basic
origin and actual relation of existing ideas and standards, which make him the
master figure of the modern age and founder of unvarnished sincerity in philosophical thought." (*Selected Letters*, I, 134) Cf. also the essay "Nietzscheism
and Realism" (1921; actually a collection of excerpts of letters written to his
future wife Sonia H. Greene), which embodies Lovecraft's political theories as
influenced by Nietzsche.

   Sabbatarianism: Strict observance of the Sabbath. Cf. Lovecraft's "A Confession of Unfaith" (1922): "Hitherto [at the age of twelve] my philosophy had been
distinctly juvenile and empirical. . . . In ethical questions I had no analytical
interest because I did not realise that they were questions. I accepted Victori-
anism, with consciousness of many prevailing hypocrisies aside from Sabbat-
arian and supernatural matters, without dispute . . ." (*Autobiographical Writings*
[West Warwick, RI: Necronomicon Press, 1992], 15) It does not appear that Lovecraft ever regularly attended a church, although on various occasions in his
youth his mother would compel him to enroll in Sunday school, from which
he would be withdrawn because of his clear-cut atheism.

   sumptuary legislation: Legislation "regulating expenditure, esp. with a view
to restraining excess in food, dress, equipage, etc." (*Oxford English Dictionary*).
Both Sabbatarianism and sumptuary legislation are direct references to New
England's "blue laws," which prohibited many activities (especially shopping or
the purchase of liquor) on Sundays.

rate day-dreams of revenge, triumph, and final magnanimous forgiveness.

And then had come the scourge, grinning and lethal, from the nightmare caverns of Tartarus.[21] West and I had graduated about the time of its beginning, but had remained for additional work at the summer school, so that we were in Arkham when it broke with full daemoniac fury upon the town. Though not as yet licenced physicians, we now had our degrees, and were pressed frantically into public service as the numbers of the stricken grew. The situation was almost past management, and deaths ensued too frequently for the local undertakers fully to handle. Burials without embalming were made in rapid succession, and even the Christchurch Cemetery receiving tomb was crammed with coffins of the unembalmed dead. This circumstance was not without effect on West, who thought often of the irony of the situation— so many fresh specimens, yet none for his persecuted researches! We were frightfully overworked, and the terrific mental and nervous strain made my friend brood morbidly.

But West's gentle enemies were no less harassed with prostrating duties. College had all but closed, and every doctor of the medical faculty was helping to fight the typhoid plague. Dr. Halsey in particular had distinguished himself in sacrificing service, applying his extreme skill with whole-hearted energy to cases which many others shunned because of danger or apparent hopelessness. Before a month was over the fearless dean had become a popular hero, though he seemed unconscious of his fame as he struggled to keep from collapsing with physical fatigue and nervous exhaustion. West could not withhold admiration for the fortitude of his foe, but because of this was even more determined to prove to him the truth of his amazing doctrines. Taking advantage of the disorgani-

----

[21] *Tartarus*: A region in the Greek underworld.

sation of both college work and municipal health regulations, he managed to get a recently deceased body smuggled into the university dissecting-room one night, and in my presence injected a new modification of his solution. The thing actually opened its eyes, but only stared at the ceiling with a look of soul-petrifying horror before collapsing into an inertness from which nothing could rouse it. West said it was not fresh enough—the hot summer air does not favour corpses. That time we were almost caught before we incinerated the thing, and West doubted the advisability of repeating his daring misuse of the college laboratory.

The peak of the epidemic was reached in August. West and I were almost dead, and Dr. Halsey did die on the 14th. The students all attended the hasty funeral on the 15th, and bought an impressive wreath, though the latter was quite overshadowed by the tributes sent by wealthy Arkham citizens and by the municipality itself. It was almost a public affair, for the dean had surely been a public benefactor. After the entombment we were all somewhat depressed, and spent the afternoon at the bar of the Commercial House; where West, though shaken by the death of his chief opponent, chilled the rest of us with references to his notorious theories. Most of the students went home, or to various duties, as the evening advanced; but West persuaded me to aid him in "making a night of it". West's landlady saw us arrive at his room about two in the morning, with a third man between us; and told her husband that we had all evidently dined and wined rather well.[22]

Apparently this acidulous[23] matron was right; for about 3 a.m. the whole house was aroused by cries coming from West's room, where when they broke down the door they

---

[22] In other words, the landlady believes that West and the narrator are merely carrying a friend who has lapsed into a drunken stupor.

[23] *acidulous*: "Slightly sour, sourish, sub-acid"; hence, "sour-tempered" (*Oxford English Dictionary*).

found the two of us unconscious on the blood-stained car-
pet, beaten, scratched, and mauled, and with the remnants
of West's bottles and instruments around us. Only an open
window told us what had become of our assailant, and
many wondered how he himself had fared after the terrific
leap from the second story to the lawn which he must
have made. There were some strange garments in the
room, but West upon regaining consciousness said they
did not belong to the stranger, but were specimens collected for bacteriological analysis in the course of investigations on the transmission of germ diseases. He ordered
them burnt as soon as possible in the capacious fireplace.
To the police we both declared ignorance of our late companion's identity. He was, West nervously said, a conge-
nial stranger whom we had met at some downtown bar of
uncertain location. We had all been rather jovial, and West
and I did not wish to have our pugnacious companion
hunted down.

That same night saw the beginning of the second Arkham horror—the horror that to me eclipsed the plague
itself. Christchurch Cemetery was the scene of a terrible
killing; a watchman having been clawed to death in a
manner not only too hideous for description, but raising
a doubt as to the human agency of the deed. The victim
had been seen alive considerably after midnight—the
dawn revealed the unutterable thing. The manager of a
circus at the neighbouring town of Bolton[24] was questioned, but he swore that no beast had at any time escaped
from its cage. Those who found the body noted a trail of
blood leading to the receiving tomb, here a small pool of
red lay on the concrete just outside the gate. A fainter
trail led away toward the woods, but it soon gave out.

The next night devils danced on the roofs of Arkham,
and unnatural madness howled in the wind. Through the
fevered town had crept a curse which some said was

---

[24] *Bolton*: See note 27 below.

greater than the plague, and which some whispered was the embodied daemon-soul of the plague itself. Eight houses were entered by a nameless thing which strewed red death in its wake—in all, seventeen maimed and shapeless remnants of bodies were left behind by the voiceless, sadistic monster that crept abroad. A few persons had half seen it in the dark, and said it was white and like a malformed ape or anthropomorphic fiend. It had not left behind quite all that it had attacked, for sometimes it had been hungry. The number it had killed was fourteen; three of the bodies had been in stricken homes and had not been alive.

On the third night frantic bands of searchers, led by the police, captured it in a house on Crane Street[25] near the Miskatonic campus. They had organised the quest with care, keeping in touch by means of volunteer telephone stations, and when someone in the college district had reported hearing a scratching at a shuttered window, the net was quickly spread. On account of the general alarm and precautions, there were only two more victims, and the capture was effected without major casualties. The thing was finally stopped by a bullet, though not a fatal one, and was rushed to the local hospital amidst universal excitement and loathing.

For it had been a man. This much was clear despite the nauseous eyes, the voiceless simianism, and the daemoniac savagery. They dressed its wound and carted it to the asylum at Sefton, where it beat its head against the wall of a padded cell for sixteen years—until the recent mishap, when it escaped under circumstances that few like to mention. What had most disgusted the researchers of Arkham was the thing they noticed with the monster's face was cleaned—the mocking, unbelievable resemblance to a

---

[25] *Crane Street*: The central character of "The Shadow Out of Time" (1934–35), Nathaniel Wingate Peaslee, resides at 27 Crane Street in Arkham. The Cranes were a prominent and wealthy family in New England, especially in Ipswich, Massachusetts.

learned and self-sacrificing martyr who had been entombed but three days before —the late Dr. Allan Halsey,
public benefactor and dean of the medical school of Miskatonic University.

To the vanished Herbert West and to me the disgust
and horror were supreme. I shudder tonight as I think of
it; shudder even more than I did that morning when West
muttered through his bandages,

"Damn it, it wasn't *quite* fresh enough!"

III. *Six Shots by Midnight*[26]

It is uncommon to fire all six shots of a revolver with
great suddenness when one would probably be sufficient,
but many things in the life of Herbert West were uncommon. It is, for instance, not often that a young physician
leaving college is obliged to conceal the principles which
guide his selection of a home and office, yet that was the
case with Herbert West. When he and I obtained our degrees at the medical school of Miskatonic University, and
sought to relieve our poverty by setting up as general prac-
titioners, we took great care not to say that we chose our
house because it was fairly well isolated, and as near as
possible to the potter's field.

Reticence such as this is seldom without a cause, nor
indeed was ours; for our requirements were those resulting
from a life-work distinctly unpopular. Outwardly we were
doctors only, but beneath the surface were aims of far
greater and more terrible moment—for the essence of Herbert West's existence was a quest amid black and forbidden realms of the unknown, in which he hoped to uncover
the secret of life and restore to perpetual animation the
graveyard's cold clay. Such a quest demands strange mate-

[26] First published in *Home Brew*, April 1922; reprinted in *Weird Tales*, September 1942.

rials, among them fresh human bodies; and in order to keep supplied with these indispensable things one must live quietly and not far from a place of informal interment. West and I had met in college, and I had been the only one to sympathise with his hideous experiments. Gradually I had come to be his inseparable assistant, and now that we were out of college we had to keep together. It was not easy to find a good opening for two doctors in company, but finally the influence of the university secured us a practice in Bolton[27]—a factory town near Arkham, the seat of the college. The Bolton Worsted Mills are the largest in the Miskatonic Valley, and their polyglot employees[28] are never popular as patients with the local physicians. We chose our house with the greatest care, seizing at last on a rather run-down cottage near the end of Pond Street; five numbers from the closest neighbour, and separated from the local potter's field by only a stretch

---

[27] *Bolton*: While there is a small town in east central Massachusetts called Bolton, Lovecraft may well have been unaware of it when he created his town of the same name. As Robert D. Marten observes in his article "Arkham Country: In Rescue of the Lost Searchers" (*Lovecraft Studies* 39 [Summer 1998]: 1–20): "The actual Bolton is among the smallest and quietest of the state's many towns. It would surprise me not at all to learn that Lovecraft never noticed that Massachusetts already had a 'Bolton' when he concocted his own. If he ever came to know there was an actual Bolton, I suspect he would feel obligated at least to modify the name of the invented town." (p. 15)

In fact, Lovecraft had a more obvious source for "industrial" Bolton—the town by that name in Lancashire, England, now part of Greater Manchester. In the late eighteenth century it developed into a major center of cotton-textile manufacturing and later had factories that packed poultry and produced textile and other machinery, as well as chemicals, leather goods, furniture, carpets, and paper. In addition, Sir Richard Arkwright invented the "spinning frame" there in 1769. For the relation of Arkwright to Arkham, see note 8 to "The Picture in the House."

[28] *polyglot employees*: A dim reference to Lovecraft's disapproval of the number of immigrants, particularly from eastern Europe, who had come to New England in the early decades of the century and secured work in mills, factories, and the like. Cf. "Vermont—A First Impression" (1927): "All through the nearer countryside [of southern New England] the stigmata of change are spreading. Reservoirs, billboards, and concrete roads, power lines, garages, and flamboyant inns, squalid immigrant nests and grimy mill villages; these things and things like them have brought ugliness, tawdriness, and commonplaceness to the urban penumbra." (*Miscellaneous Writings*, 293)

of meadow land, bisected by a narrow neck of the rather dense forest which lies to the north. The distance was greater than we wished, but we could get no nearer house without going on the other side of the field, wholly out of the factory district. We were not much displeased, however, since there were no people between us and our sinister source of supplies. The walk was a trifle long, but we could haul our silent specimens undisturbed.

Our practice was surprisingly large from the very first—large enough to please most young doctors, and large enough to prove a bore and a burden to students whose real interest lay elsewhere. The mill-hands were of somewhat turbulent inclinations; and besides their many natural needs, their frequent clashes and stabbing affrays gave us plenty to do. But what actually absorbed our minds was the secret laboratory we had fitted up in the cellar—the laboratory with the long table under the electric lights, where in the small hours of the morning we often injected West's various solutions into the veins of the things we dragged from the potter's field. West was experimenting madly to find something which would start man's vital motions anew after they had been stopped by the thing we call death, but had encountered the most ghastly obstacles. The solution had to be differently compounded for different types—what would serve for guinea-pigs would not serve for human beings, and different human specimens required large modifications.

The bodies had to be exceedingly fresh, or the slight decomposition of brain tissue would render perfect reanimation impossible. Indeed, the greatest problem was to get them fresh enough—West had had horrible experiences during his secret college researches with corpses of doubtful vintage. The results of partial or imperfect animation were much more hideous than were the total failures, and we both held fearsome recollections of such things. Ever since our first daemoniac session in the deserted farmhouse on Meadow Hill in Arkham, we had felt a brooding menace; and West, though a calm, blond, blue-eyed scientific automaton in most respects, often confessed to a shuddering sensation of stealthy pursuit. He half felt that he was followed—a psychological delusion of shaken nerves, enhanced by the undeniably disturbing fact that at least one of our reanimated specimens was still alive—a frightful carnivorous thing in a padded cell at Sefton. Then there was another—our first—whose exact fate we had never learned.

We had fair luck with specimens in Bolton—much better than in Arkham. We had not been settled a week before we got an accident victim on the very night of burial, and made it open its eyes with an amazingly rational expression before the solution failed. It had lost an arm—if it had been a perfect body we might have succeeded better. Between then and the next January we secured three more; one total failure, one case of marked muscular motion, and one rather shivery thing—it rose of itself and uttered a sound. Then came a period when luck was poor; interments fell off, and those that did occur were of specimens either too diseased or too maimed for use. We kept track of all the deaths and their circumstances with systematic care.

One March night, however, we unexectedly obtained a specimen which did not come from the potter's field. In Bolton the prevailing spirit of Puritanism had outlawed the sport of boxing—with the usual result. Surreptitious and ill-conducted bouts among the mill-workers were common, and occasionally professional talent of low grade was imported. This late winter night there had been such a match; evidently with disastrous results, since two timorous Poles had come to us with incoherently whispered entreaties to attend to a very secret and desperate case. We followed them to an abandoned barn, where the remnants of a crowd of frightened foreigners were watching a silent black form on the floor.

The match had been between Kid O'Brien—a lubberly[29] and now quaking youth with a most un-Hibernian hooked nose—and Buck Robinson, "The Harlem Smoke".[30] The negro had been knocked out, and a moment's examination shewed us that he would permanently remain so. He was a loathsome, gorilla-like thing, with abnormally long arms which I could not help calling fore legs, and a face that conjured up thoughts of unspeakable Congo secrets and tom-tom poundings under an eerie moon.[31] The body must have looked even worse in life—but the world holds many ugly things. Fear was upon the whole pitiful crowd, for they did not know what the law would exact of them if the affair were not hushed up; and they were grateful when West, in spite of my involuntary shudders, offered to get rid of the thing quietly—for a purpose I knew too well.

There was bright moonlight over the snowless landscape, but we dressed the thing and carried it home between us through the deserted streets and meadows, as we had carried a similar thing one horrible night in Arkham. We approached the house from the field in the rear, took the specimen in the back door and down the cellar stairs, and prepared it for the usual experiment. Our fear of the police was absurdly great, though we had timed our trip to avoid the solitary patrolman of that section.

The result was wearily anticlimactic. Ghastly as our prize appeared, it was wholly unresponsive to every solution we injected in its black arm; solutions prepared from experience with white specimens only. So as the hour

---

[29] *lubberly*: "Coarse of figure and dull of intellect, loutish" (*Oxford English Dictionary*).

[30] Prize-fighting (presumably of the bare-knuckled variety) was common among working-class people in the United States at this time. The mention of Kid O'Brien's "un-Hibernian hooked nose" suggests that he was not in reality Irish, but probably Jewish; perhaps he was wishing to capitalize on the fame of John L. Sullivan, the great Irish-American boxer of the 1880s.

[31] Lovecraft had set an earlier tale, "Facts Concerning the Late Arthur Jermyn and His Family" (1920), in the Belgian Congo.

grew dangerously near to dawn, we did as we had done with the others—dragged the thing across the meadows to the neck of the woods near the potter's field, and buried it there in the best sort of grave the frozen ground would furnish. The grave was not very deep, but fully as good as that of the previous specimen—the thing which had risen of itself and uttered a sound. In the light of our dark lanterns we carefully covered it with leaves and dead vines, fairly certain that the police would never find it in a forest so dim and dense.

The next day I was increasingly apprehensive about the police, for a patient brought rumours of a suspected fight and death. West had still another source of worry, for he had been called in the afternoon to a case which ended very threateningly. An Italian woman had become hysterical over her missing child—a lad of five who had strayed off early in the morning and failed to appear for dinner—and had developed symptoms highly alarming in view of an always weak heart. It was a very foolish hysteria, for the boy had often run away before; but Italian peasants are exceedingly superstitious, and this woman seemed as much harassed by omens as by facts. About seven o'clock in the evening she had died, and her frantic husband had made a frightful scene in his efforts to kill West, whom he wildly blamed for not saving her life. Friends had held him when he drew a stiletto, but West departed amidst his inhuman shrieks, curses, and oaths of vengeance. In his latest affliction the fellow seemed to have forgotten his child, who was still missing as the night advanced. There was some talk of searching the woods, but most of the family's friends were busy with the dead woman and the screaming man. Altogether, the nervous strain upon West must have been tremendous. Thoughts of the police and of the mad Italian both weighed heavily.

We retired about eleven, but I did not sleep well. Bolton had a surprisingly good police force for so small a town, and I could not help fearing the mess which would ensue if the affair of the night before were ever tracked down. It might mean the end of all our local work—and perhaps prison for both West and me. I did not like those rumours of a fight which were floating about. After the clock had struck three the moon shone in my eyes, but I turned over without rising to pull down the shade. Then came the steady rattling at the back door.

I lay still and somewhat dazed, but before long heard West's rap on my door. He was clad in dressing-gown and slippers, and had in his hands a revolver and an electric flashlight. From the revolver I knew that he was thinking more of the crazed Italian than of the police.

"We'd better both go," he whispered. "It wouldn't do not to answer it anyway, and it may be a patient—it would be like one of those fools to try the back door."

So we both went down the stairs on tiptoe, with a fear partly justified and partly that which comes only from the soul of the weird small hours. The rattling continued, growing somewhat louder. When we reached the door I cautiously unbolted it and threw it open, and as the moon streamed revealingly down on the form silhouetted there, West did a peculiar thing. Despite the obvious danger of attracting notice and bringing down on our heads the dreaded police investigation—a thing which after all was mercifully averted by the relative isolation of our cottage—my friend suddenly, excitedly, and unnecessarily emptied all six chambers of his revolver into the nocturnal visitor.

For that visitor was neither Italian nor policeman. Looming hideously against the spectral moon was a gigantic misshapen thing not to be imagined save in nightmares—a glassy-eyed, ink-black apparition nearly on all fours, covered with bits of mould, leaves, and vines, foul with caked blood, and having between its glistening teeth a snow-white, terrible, cylindrical object terminating in a tiny hand.

IV. *The Scream of the Dead*[32]

The scream of a dead man gave to me that acute and added horror of Dr. Herbert West which harassed the latter years of our companionship. It is natural that such a thing as a dead man's scream should give horror, for it is obviously not a pleasing or ordinary occurrence; but I was used to similar experiences, hence suffered on this occasion only because of a particular circumstance. And, as I have implied, it was not of the dead man himself that I became afraid.

Herbert West, whose associate and assistant I was, possessed scientific interests far beyond the usual routine of a village physician. That was why, when establishing his practice in Bolton, he had chosen an isolated house near the potter's field. Briefly and brutally stated, West's sole absorbing interest was a secret study of the phenomena of life and its cessation, leading toward the reanimation of the dead through injections of an excitant solution. For this ghastly experimenting it was necessary to have a constant supply of very fresh human bodies; very fresh because even the least decay hopelessly damaged the brain structure, and human because we found that the solution had to be compounded differently for different types of organisms. Scores of rabbits and guinea-pigs had been killed and treated, but their trail was a blind one. West head never fully succeeded because he had never been able to secure a corpse sufficiently fresh. What he wanted were bodies from which vitality had only just departed; bodies with every cell intact and capable of receiving again the

[32] First published in *Home Brew*, May 1922; reprinted in *Weird Tales*, November 1942.

impulse toward that mode of motion called life.[33] There was hope that this second and artificial life might be made perpetual by repetitions of the injection, but we had learned that an ordinary natural life would not respond to the action. To establish the artificial motion, natural life must be extinct—the specimens must be very fresh, but genuinely dead.

The awesome quest had begun when West and I were students at the Miskatonic University Medical School in Arkham, vividly conscious for the first time of the thoroughly mechanical nature of life. That was seven years before, but West looked scarcely a day older now—he was small, blond, clean-shaven, soft-voiced, and spectacled, with only an occasional flash of a cold blue eye to tell of the hardening and growing fanaticism of his character under the pressure of his terrible investigations. Our experiences had often been hideous in the extreme; the results of defective reanimation, when lumps of graveyard clay had been galvanised into morbid, unnatural, and brainless motion by various modifications of the vital solution.

One thing had uttered a nerve-shattering scream; another had risen violently, beaten us both to unconsciousness, and run amuck in a shocking way before it could be placed behind asylum bars; still another, a loathsome African monstrosity, had clawed out of its shallow grave and done a deed[34]—West had had to shoot that object. We could not get bodies fresh enough to shew any trace of reason when reanimated, so had perforce created nameless horrors. It was disturbing to think that one, perhaps two, of our monsters still lived—that thought haunted us shad-

---

[33] Cf. Lovecraft's essay "The Materialist Today" (1926): "To the materialist, *mind* seems very clearly not a *thing*, but a *mode of motion* or *form of energy*." (*Miscellaneous Writings*, 177)

[34] Cf. "The Lurking Fear" (1922): "In a hamlet twenty miles away an orgy of fear had followed the bolt which brought me above ground, and a nameless thing had dropped from an overhanging tree into a weak-roofed cabin. It had done a deed . . ." (*Dagon and Other Macabre Tales*, 194)

owingly, till finally West disappeared under frightful circumstances. But at the time of the scream in the cellar
laboratory of the isolated Bolton cottage, our fears were
subordinate to our anxiety for extremely fresh specimens.
West was more avid than I, so that it almost seemed to
me that he looked half-covetously at any very healthy living physique.

It was in July, 1910, that the bad luck regarding specimens began to turn. I had been on a long visit to my
parents in Illinois,[35] and upon my return found West in a
state of singular elation. He had, he told me excitedly, in
all likelihood solved the problem of freshness through an
approach from an entirely new angle—that of artificial
preservation. I had known that he was working on a new
and highly unusual embalming compound, and was not
surprised that it had turned out well; but until he explained the details I was rather puzzled as to how such a
compound could help in our work, since the objectionable
staleness of the specimens was largely due to delay occurring before we secured them. This, I now saw, West
had clearly recognised; creating his embalming compound
for future rather than immediate use, and trusting to fate
to supply again some very recent and unburied corpse, as
it had years before when we obtained the negro killed in
the Bolton prize-fight. At last fate had been kind, so that
on this occasion there lay in the secret cellar laboratory a
corpse whose decay could not by any possibility have
begun. What would happen on reanimation, and whether
we could hope for a revival of mind and reason, West did
not venture to predict. The experiment would be a landmark in our studies, and he had saved the new body for

---

[35] Lovecraft's father was from New York State and his mother from Rhode Island,
but members of his more distant maternal line did come from Illinois. James
Phillips (1794–1878), uncle of Lovecraft's grandfather Whipple Phillips, was born
in Rhode Island, but in 1843 became one of the original settlers of the temper-
ance town of Delavan, Illinois (about twenty miles south of Peoria).

my return, so that both might share the spectacle in accustomed fashion.

West told me how he had obtained the specimen. It had been a vigorous man; a well-dressed stranger just off the train on his way to transact some business with the Bolton Worsted Mills.[36] The walk through the town had been long, and by the time the traveller paused at our cottage to ask the way to the factories his heart had become greatly overtaxed. He had refused a stimulant, and had suddenly dropped dead only a moment later. The body, as might be expected, seemed to West a heaven-sent gift. In his brief conversation the stranger had made it clear that he was unknown in Bolton, and a search of his pockets subsequently revealed him to be one Robert Leavitt of St. Louis, apparently without a family to make instant inquiries about his disappearance. If this man could not be restored to life, no one would know of our experiment. We buried our materials in a dense strip of woods between the house and the potter's field. If, on the other hand, he could be restored, our fame would be brilliantly and perpetually established. So without delay West had injected into the body's wrist the compound which would hold it fresh for use after my arrival. The matter of the presumably weak heart, which to my mind imperiled the success of our experiment, did not appear to trouble West extensively. He hoped at last to obtain what the had never obtained before—a rekindled spark of reason and perhaps a normal, living creature.

So on the night of July 18, 1910,[37] Herbert West and I stood in the cellar laboratory and gazed at a white, silent

---

[36] Lovecraft's father, Winfield Scott Lovecraft (1853–1898), was listed on his medical records as a "Commercial Traveller" (probably for Gorham & Co., Silversmiths of Providence); i.e., a traveling salesman who sold to the trade (not door-to-door). His territory appears generally to have been the Boston area, but on at least one occasion he traveled as far as Chicago.

[37] Lovecraft's father had died on July 19, 1898. The critical events of "The Shadow out of Time" (1934–35) occur July 17–18, 1935.

figure beneath the dazzling arc-light. The embalming compound had worked uncannily well, for as I stared fascinat-
edly at the sturdy frame which had lain two weeks
without stiffening I was moved to seek West's assurance
that the thing was really dead. This assurance he gave
readily enough; reminding me that the reanimating solution was never used without careful tests as to life; since
it could have no effect if any of the original vitality were
present. As West proceeded to take preliminary steps, I
was impressed by the vast intricacy of the new experiment; an intricacy so vast that he could trust no hand less
delicate than his own. Forbidding me to touch the body,
he first injected a drug in the wrist just beside the place
his needle had punctured when injecting the embalming
compound. This, he said, was to neutralise the compound
and release the system to a normal relaxation so that the
reanimating solution might freely work when injected.
Slightly later, when a change and a gentle tremor seemed
to affect the dead limbs, West stuffed a pillow-like object
violently over the twitching face, not withdrawing it until
the corpse appeared quiet and ready for our attempt at
reanimation. The pale enthusiast now applied some last
perfunctory tests for absolute lifelessness, withdrew satisfied, and finally injected into the left arm an accurately
measured amount of the vital elixir, prepared during the
afternoon with a greater care than we had used since college days, when our feats were new and groping. I cannot
express the wild, breathless suspense with which we
waited for results on this first really fresh specimen—the
first we could reasonably expect to open its lips in rational
speech, perhaps to tell of what it had seen beyond the
unfathomable abyss.

West was a materialist, believing in no soul and attributing all the working of consciousness to bodily phenomena; consequently he looked for no revelation of hideous
secrets from gulfs and caverns beyond death's barrier. I did
not wholly disagree with him theoretically, yet held vague

instinctive remnants of the primitive faith of my forefathers; so that I could not help eyeing the corpse with a certain amount of awe and terrible expectation. Besides—I could not extract from my memory that hideous, inhuman shriek we heard on the night we tried our first experiment in the deserted farmhouse at Arkham.

Very little time had elapsed before I saw the attempt was not to be a total failure. A touch of colour came to cheeks hitherto chalk-white, and spread out under the curiously ample stubble of sandy beard. West, who had his hand on the pulse of the left wrist, suddenly nodded significantly; and almost simultaneously a mist appeared on the mirror inclined above the body's mouth. There followed a few spasmodic muscular motions, and then an audible breathing and visible motion of the chest. I looked at the closed eyelids, and thought I detected a quivering. Then the lids opened, shewing eyes which were grey, calm, and alive, but still unintelligent and not even curious.

In a moment of fantastic whim I whispered questions to the reddening ears; questions of other worlds of which the memory might still be present. Subsequent terror drove them from my mind, but I think the last one, which I repeated, was: "Where have you been?" I do not yet know whether I was answered or not, for no sound came from the well-shaped mouth; but I do know that at that moment I firmly thought the thin lips moved silently, forming syllables I would have vocalised as "only now"[38] if that phrase had possessed any sense or relevancy. At that moment, as I say, I was elated with the conviction that the one great goal had been attained; and that for the first time a reanimated corpse had uttered distinct words impelled by actual reason. In the next moment there was

---

[38] It is not clear what the significance of the words "only now" is. Perhaps the man is recalling his final conversation with West before his death, and is saying, "I have only now come into town," or something of the sort.

no doubt about the triumph; no doubt that the solution
had truly accomplished, at least temporarily, its full mission of restoring rational and articulate life to the dead.
But in that triumph there came to me the greatest of all
horrors—not horror of the thing that spoke, but of the
deed that I had witnessed and of the man with whom my
professional fortunes were joined.

For that very fresh body, at last writhing into full and
terrifying consciousness with eyes dilated at the memory
of its last scene on earth, threw out its frantic hands in a
life and death struggle with the air; and suddenly collapsing into a second and final dissolution from which there
could be no return, screamed out the cry that will ring
eternally in my aching brain:

"Help! Keep off, you cursed little tow-head fiend—keep
that damned needle away from me!"

V. *The Horror from the Shadows*[39]

Many men have related hideous things, not mentioned
in print, which happened on the battlefields of the Great
War.[40] Some of these things have made me faint, others
have convulsed me with devastating nausea, while still
others have made me tremble and look behind me in the
dark; yet despite the worst of them I believe I can myself
relate the most hideous thing of all—the shocking, the
unnatural, the unbelievable horror from the shadows.

In 1915 I was a physician with the rank of First Lieutenant in a Canadian regiment in Flanders, one of many
Americans to precede the government itself into the gigantic struggle.[41] I had not entered the army on my own ini-

---

[39] First published in *Home Brew*, June 1922; reprinted in *Weird Tales*, September 1943.

[40] *Great War*: World War I.

[41] See note 12 to "The Rats in the Walls." (*Annotated Lovecraft*, 28)

tiative, but rather as a natural result of the enlistment of the man whose indispensable assistant I was—the celebrated Boston surgical specialist, Dr. Herbert West. Dr. West had been avid for a chance to serve as surgeon in a great war, and when the chance had come he carried me with him almost against my will. There were reasons why I would have been glad to let the war separate us; reasons why I found the practice of medicine and the companionship of West more and more irritating; but when he had gone to Ottawa and through a colleague's influence secured a medical commission as Major, I could not resist the imperious persuasion of one determined that I should accompany him in my usual capacity.

When I say that Dr. West was avid to serve in battle, I do not mean to imply that he was either naturally warlike or anxious for the safety of civilisation. Always an ice-cold intellectual machine; slight, blond, blue-eyed, and spectacled; I think he secretly sneered at my occasional martial enthusiasms and censures of supine neutrality.[42] There was, however, something he wanted in embattled Flanders;[43] and in order to secure it he had to assume a military exterior. What he wanted was not a thing which many persons want, but something connected with the peculiar branch of medical science which he had chosen quite clandestinely to follow, and in which he had

---

[42] Lovecraft, as a lifelong Anglophile, was infuriated at American neutrality in World War I prior to April 1917, and wrote many polemics in verse and prose excoriating President Woodrow Wilson and America's failure to come to the aid of "Mother England." Cf. "The Renaissance of Manhood" (*Conservative* 1, No. 3 [October 1915]:8): "After the degrading debauch of craven pacifism through which our sodden and feminised public has lately floundered, a slight sense of shame seems to be appearing, and the outcries of peace-at-any-price maniacs are less violent than they were a few months ago. Military training for business and professional men has been provided at Plattsburg, N.Y., and the high schools of Providence, R.I. have established, despite the wails of the unwarlike, efficient courses in martial instruction and drilling."

[43] *Flanders*: A region in the Low Countries now comprising portions of Belgium and the Netherlands, and a major theatre of war during World War I. This was where Lovecraft's idol Lord Dunsany had been sent in 1916 with the Royal Inniskilling Fusiliers.

achieved amazing and occasionally hideous results. It was, in fact, nothing more or less than an abundant supply of freshly killed men in every stage of dismemberment.

Herbert West needed fresh bodies because his life-work was the reanimation of the dead. This work was not known to the fashionable clientele who had so swiftly built up his fame after his arrival in Boston; but was only too well known to me, who had been his closest friend and sole assistant since the old days in Miskatonic University Medical School at Arkham. It was in those college days that he had begun his terrible experiments, first on small animals and then on human bodies shockingly obtained. There was a solution which he injected into the veins of dead things, and if they were fresh enough they responded in strange ways. He had had much trouble in discovering the proper formula, for each type of organism was found to need a stimulus especially adapted to it. Terror stalked him when he reflected on his partial failures; nameless things resulting from imperfect solutions or from bodies insufficiently fresh. A certain number of these failures had remained alive—one was in an asylum while others had vanished—and as he thought of conceivable yet virtually impossible eventualities he often shivered beneath his usual stolidity.

West had soon learned that absolute freshness was the prime requisite for useful specimens, and had accordingly resorted to frightful and unnatural expedients in body-snatching. In college, and during our early practice together in the factory town of Bolton, my attitude toward him had been largely one of fascinated admiration; but as his boldness in methods grew, I began to develop a gnawing fear. I did not like the way he looked at healthy living bodies; and then there came a nightmarish session in the cellar laboratory when I learned that a certain specimen had been a living body when he secured it. That was the first time he had ever been able to revive the quality of rational thought in a corpse; and his success, obtained at such a loathsome cost, had completely hardened him.

Of his methods in the intervening five years I dare not speak. I was held to him by sheer force of fear, and witnessed sights that no human tongue could repeat. Gradually I came to find Herbert West himself more horrible than anything he did—that was when it dawned on me that his once normal scientific zeal for prolonging life had subtly degenerated into a mere morbid and ghoulish curiosity and secret sense of charnel picturesqueness. His interest became a hellish and perverse addiction to the repellently and fiendishly abnormal; he gloated calmly over artificial monstrosities which would make most healthy men drop dead from fright and disgust; he became, behind his pallid intellectuality, a fastidious Baudelaire of physical experiment—a languid Elagabalus of the tombs.[44]

Dangers he met unflinchingly; crimes he committed unmoved. I think the climax came when he had proved his point that rational life can be restored, and had sought new worlds to conquer by experimenting on the reanimation of detached parts of bodies. He had wild and original ideas on the independent vital properties of organic cells and nerve-tissue separated from natural physiological systems; and achieved some hideous preliminary results in the form of never-dying, artificially nourished tissue obtained from the nearly hatched eggs of an indescribable

---

[44] *Baudelaire*: Charles Pierre Baudelaire (1821–1867), whose poetry collection *Les Fleurs du mal* (1857; usually translated as *The Flowers of Evil*) was much admired by Lovecraft. In a letter to Wilfred B. Talman, Lovecraft wrote: "'. . . I am reminded of what Baudelaire once asked an aspiring decadent poet who copied—and even exceeded—his colourful Satanism without reflecting to any dangerous extent his genius. A trifle exasperated by the ostentatious 'shockingness' of the young man, Baudelaire 'went him one better' by asking very gravely—'Have you ever tasted young children's brains? They're quite delightful, and taste exactly like walnuts!' " (*Selected Letters*, II, 105–6)

Elagabalus: M. Aurelius Antoninus, sometimes referred to as Heliogabalus, Emperor of Rome (218–222). The name derives from the sun-god of Emesa (in modern-day Syria), Elah-Gabal, whom the emperor worshiped, introduced to Rome, and adopted as his own name. He became notorious as a decadent voluptuary and was murdered by his own troops.

tropical reptile. Two biological points he was exceedingly anxious to settle—first, whether any amount of consciousness and rational action may be possible without the brain, proceeding from the spinal cord and various nerve-centres; and second, whether any kind of ethereal, intangible relation distinct from the material cells may exist to link the surgically separated parts of what has previously been a single living organism. All this research work required a prodigious supply of freshly slaughtered human flesh—and that was why Herbert West had entered the Great War.

The phantasmal, unmentionable thing occurred one midnight late in March, 1915, in a field hospital behind the lines at St. Eloi.[45] I wonder even now if it could have been other than a daemoniac dream of delirium. West had a private laboratory in an east room of the barn-like temporary edifice, assigned him on his plea that he was devising new and radical methods for the treatment of hitherto hopeless cases of maiming. There he worked like a butcher in the midst of his gory wares—I could never get used to the levity with which he handled and classified certain things. At times he actually did perform marvels of surgery for the soldiers; but his chief delights were of a less public and philanthropic kind, requiring many explanations of sounds which seemed peculiar even amidst that babel of the damned. Among these sounds were frequent revolver-shots—surely not uncommon on a battlefield, but distinctly uncommon in an hospital. Dr. West's reanimated specimens were not meant for long existence or a large audience. Besides human tissue, West employed much of the reptile embryo tissue which he had cultivated with such singular results. It was better than human material for maintaining life in organless fragments, and that was now my friend's chief activity. In a dark corner of the laboratory, over a queerly incubating burner, he kept a

---

[45] *St. Eloi*: A hamlet about three miles southeast of Ypres in Belgium, where a battle between the Germans and the British was fought on March 14, 1915.

large covered vat full of this reptilian cell-matter; which multiplied and grew puffily and hideously.

On the night of which I speak we had a splendid new specimen—a man at once physically powerful and of such high mentality that a sensitive nervous system was assured. It was rather ironic, for he was the officer who had helped West to his commission, and who was now to have been our associate. Moreover, he had in the past secretly studied the theory of reanimation to some extent under West. Major Sir Eric Moreland Clapham-Lee, D.S.O.,[46] was the greatest surgeon in our division, and had been hastily assigned to the St. Eloi sector when news of the heavy fighting reached headquarters. He had come in an aëroplane piloted by the intrepid Lieut. Ronald Hill, only to be shot down when directly over his destination. The fall had been spectacular and awful; Hill was unrecognisable afterward, but the wreck yielded up the great surgeon in a nearly decapitated but otherwise intact condition. West had greedily seized the lifeless thing which had once been his friend and fellow-scholar; and I shuddered when he finished severing the head, placed it in his hellish vat of pulpy reptile-tissue to preserve it for future experiments, and proceeded to treat the decapitated body on the operating table. He injected new blood, jointed certain veins, arteries, and nerves at the headless neck, and closed the ghastly aperture with engrafted skin from an unidentified specimen which had borne an officer's uniform. I knew what he wanted—to see if this highly organised body could exhibit, without its head, any of the signs of mental life which had distinguished Sir Eric Moreland Clapham-Lee. Once a student of reanimation, this silent trunk was now gruesomely called upon to exemplify it.

---

[46] *D.S.O.*: Distinguished Service Order, an order of military merit established in 1886 by Queen Victoria. It was awarded only to officers, but not necessarily for service in action (as is the Victoria Cross). The royal warrant instituting the order declares that it is awarded "for individual instances of meritorious or distinguished service in war."

I can still see Herbert West under the sinister electric light as he injected his reanimating solution into the arm of the headless body. The scene I cannot describe—I should faint if I tried it, for there is madness in a room full of classified charnel things, with blood and lesser human debris almost ankle-deep on the slimy floor, and with hideous reptilian abnormalities sprouting, bubbling, and baking over a winking bluish-green spectre of dim flame in a far corner of black shadows.

The specimen, as West repeatedly observed, had a splendid nervous system. Much was expected of it; and as a few twitching motions began to appear, I could see the feverish interest on West's face. He was ready, I think, to see proof of his increasingly strong opinion that consciousness, reason, and personality can exist independently of the brain—that man has no central connective spirit, but is merely a machine of nervous matter, each section more or less complete in itself. In one triumphant demonstration West was about to relegate the mystery of life to the category of myth. The body now twitched more vigorously, and beneath our avid eyes commenced to heave in a frightful way. The arms stirred disquietingly, the legs drew up, and various muscles contracted in a repulsive kind of writhing. Then the headless thing threw out its arms in a gesture which was unmistakably one of desperation—an intelligent desperation apparently sufficient to prove every theory of Herbert West. Certainly, the nerves were recalling the man's last act in life; the struggle to get free of the falling aëroplane.

What followed, I shall never positively know. It may have been wholly an hallucination from the shock caused at the instant by the sudden and complete destruction of the building in a cataclysm of German shell-fire—who can gainsay it, since West and I were the only proved survivors? West liked to think that before his recent disappearance, but there were times when he could not; for it was queer that we both had the same hallucination. The hideous occurrence itself was very simple, notable only for what it implied.

The body on the table had risen with a blind and terrible groping, and we had heard a sound. I should not call that sound a voice, for it was too awful. And yet its timbre was not the most awful thing about it. Neither was its message—it had merely screamed, "Jump, Ronald, for God's sake, jump!" The awful thing was its source.

For it had come from the large covered vat in that ghoulish corner of crawling black shadows.

VI. *The Tomb-Legions*[47]

When Dr. Herbert West disappeared a year ago, the Boston police questioned me closely. They suspected that I was holding something back, and perhaps suspected graver things; but I could not tell them the truth because they would not have believed it.[48] They knew, indeed, that West had been connected with activities beyond the credence of ordinary men; for his hideous experiments in the reanimation of dead bodies had long been too extensive to admit of perfect secrecy; but the final soul-shattering catastrophe held elements of daemoniac phantasy which make even me doubt the reality of what I saw.

I was West's closest friend and only confidential assistant. We had met years before, in medical school, and from the first I had shared his terrible researches. He had slowly tried to perfect a solution which, injected into the veins

---

[47] First published in *Home Brew*, July 1922; reprinted in *Weird Tales*, November 1943.

[48] Cf. Lovecraft's "The Statement of Randolph Carter" (1919), which similarly concerns two explorers into the bizarre, one of whom (Harley Warren) disappears. Randolph Carter states at the beginning of the tale: "I repeat to you, gentlemen, that your inquisition is fruitless. Detain me here forever if you will; confine or execute me if you must have a victim to propitiate the illusion you call justice; but I can say no more than I have said already." (*At the Mountains of Madness and Other Novels*, 299)

of the newly deceased, would restore life; a labour demanding an abundance of fresh corpses and therefore involving the most unnatural actions. Still more shocking were the products of some of the experiments—grisly masses of flesh that had been dead, but that West waked to a blind, brainless, nauseous animation. These were the usual results, for in order to reawaken the mind it was necessary to have specimens so absolutely fresh that no decay could possibly affect the delicate brain-cells.

This need for very fresh corpses had been West's moral undoing. They were hard to get, and one awful day he had secured his specimen while it was still alive and vigorous. A struggle, a needle, and a powerful alkaloid had transformed it to a very fresh corpse, and the experiment had succeeded for a brief and memorable moment; but West had emerged with a soul calloused and seared, and a hardened eye which sometimes glanced with a kind of hideous and calculating appraisal at men of especially sensitive brain and especially vigorous physique. Toward the last I became acutely afraid of West, for he began to look at me that way. People did not seem to notice his glances, but they noticed my fear; and after his disappearance used that as a basis for some absurd suspicions.

West, in reality, was more afraid than I; for his abominable pursuits entailed a life of furtiveness and dread of every shadow. Partly it was the police he feared; but sometimes his nervousness was deeper and more nebulous, touching on certain indescribable things into which he had injected a morbid life, and from which he had not seen that life depart. He usually finished his experiments with a revolver, but a few times he had not been quick enough. There was that first specimen on whose rifled grave marks of clawing were later seen. There was also that Arkham professor's body which had done cannibal things before it had been captured and thrust unidentified into a madhouse cell at Sefton, where it beat the walls for sixteen years. Most of the other possibly surviving results were things less easy to speak of—for in later years West's scientific zeal had degenerated to an unhealthy and fantastic mania, and he had spent his chief skill in vitalising not entire human bodies but isolated parts of bodies, or parts joined to organic matter other than human. It had become fiendishly disgusting by the time he disappeared; many of the experiments could not even be hinted at in print. The Great War, through which both of us served as surgeons, had intensified this side of West.

In saying that West's fear of his specimens was nebulous, I have in mind particularly its complex nature. Part of it came merely from knowing of the existence of such nameless monsters, while another part arose from apprehension of the bodily harm they might under certain circumstances do him. Their disappearance added horror to the situation—of them all West knew the whereabouts of only one, the pitiful asylum thing. Then there was a more subtle fear—a very fantastic sensation resulting from a curious experiment in the Canadian army in 1915. West, in the midst of a severe battle, had reanimated Major Sir Eric Moreland Clapham-Lee, D.S.O., a fellow-physician who knew about his experiments and could have duplicated them. The head had been removed, so that the possibilities of quasi-intelligent life in the trunk might be investigated. Just as the building was wiped out by a German shell, there had been a success. The trunk had moved intelligently; and, unbelievable to relate, we were both sickeningly sure that articulate sounds had come from the detached head as it lay in a shadowy corner of the laboratory. The shell had been merciful, in a way—but West could never feel as certain as he wished, that we two were the only survivors. He used to make shuddering conjectures about the possible actions of a headless physician with the power of reanimating the dead.

West's last quarters were in a venerable house of much elegance, overlooking one of the oldest burying-grounds in

A New England burying ground (photo by Will Murray).

Boston.[49] He had chosen the place for purely symbolic and
fantastically aesthetic reasons, since most of the interments were of the colonial period and therefore of little
use to a scientist seeking very fresh bodies. The laboratory
was in a sub-cellar secretly constructed by imported workmen, and contained a huge incinerator for the quiet and
complete disposal of such bodies, or fragments and syn-
thetic mockeries of bodies, as might remain from the morbid experiments and unhallowed amusements of the
owner. During the excavation of this cellar the workmen
had struck some exceedingly ancient masonry; undoubtedly connected with the old burying-ground, yet far too

---

[49] Among the oldest burying grounds in Boston are King's Chapel Burying
Ground (1630), the churchyard of the Old North Church (1650), the Granary
Burying Ground on Tremont Street (1660), Copp's Hill Burying Ground in the
North End (1660), and the churchyard of the Old South Meeting House (1669).
Lovecraft set a later story, "Pickman's Model" (1926), in part in Copp's Hill
Burying Ground.

deep to correspond with any known sepulchre therein. After a number of calculations West decided that it represented some secret chamber beneath the tomb of the Averills, where the last interment had been made in 1768. I was with him when he studied the nitrous, dripping walls laid bare by the spades and mattocks[50] of the men, and was prepared for the gruesome thrill which would attend the uncovering of centuried grave-secrets; but for the first time West's new timidity conquered his natural curiosity, and he betrayed his degenerating fibre by ordering the masonry left intact and plastered over. Thus it remained till that final hellish night; part of the walls of the secret laboratory. I speak of West's decadence, but must add that it was a purely mental and intangible thing. Outwardly he was the same to the last—calm, cold, slight, and yellow-haired, with spectacled blue eyes and a general aspect of youth which years and fears seemed never to change. He seemed calm even when he thought of that clawed grave and looked over his shoulder; even when he thought of the carnivorous thing that gnawed and pawed at Sefton bars.

The end of Herbert West began one evening in our joint study when he was dividing his curious glance between the newspaper and me. A strange headline item had struck at him from the crumpled pages, and a nameless titan claw had seemed to reach down through sixteen years. Something fearsome and incredible had happened to Sefton Asylum fifty miles away, stunning the neighbourhood and baffling the police. In the small hours of the morning a body of silent men had entered the grounds and their leader had aroused the attendants. He was a menacing military figure who talked without moving his lips and whose voice seemed almost ventriloquially connected with an immense black case he carried. His expressionless face was handsome to the point of radiant beauty, but had

---

[50] *mattock*: "An agricultural tool . . . used for loosening hard ground, grubbing up trees, etc." (*Oxford English Dictionary*)

shocked the superintendent when the hall light fell on
it—for it was a wax face with eyes of painted glass.[51] Some
nameless accident had befallen this man. A larger man
guided his steps; a repellent hulk whose bluish face
seemed half eaten away by some unknown malady. The
speaker had asked for the custody of the cannibal monster
committed from Arkham sixteen years before; and upon
being refused, gave a signal which precipitated a shocking
riot. The fiends had beaten, trampled, and bitten every
attendant who did not flee; killing four and finally suc-
ceeding in the liberation of the monster. Those victims
who could recall the event without hysteria swore that the
creatures had acted less like men than like unthinkable
automata guided by the wax-faced leader. By the time help
could be summoned, every trace of the men and of their
mad charge had vanished.

From the hour of reading this item until midnight, West
sat almost paralysed. At midnight the doorbell rang, startling him fearfully. All the servants were asleep in the
attic, so I answered the bell. As I have told the police,
there was no wagon in the street; but only a group of
strange-looking figures bearing a large square box which
they deposited in the hallway after one of them had
grunted in a highly unnatural voice, "Express—prepaid."
They filed out of the house with a jerky tread, and as I
watched them go I had an odd idea that they were turning
toward the ancient cemetery on which the back of the
house abutted. When I slammed the door after them West
came downstairs and looked at the box. It was about two
feet square, and bore West's correct name and present address. It also bore the inscription, "From Eric Moreland
Clapham-Lee, St. Eloi, Flanders". Six years before, in Flanders, a shelled hospital had fallen upon the headless reani-

<hr>

[51] Cf. "The Festival" (1923): ". . . the more I looked at the old man's bland face
the more its very blandness terrified me. The eyes never moved, and the skin
was too much like wax. Finally I was sure it was not a face at all, but a fiendishly
cunning mask." (*Dagon and Other Macabre Tales*, 211)

mated trunk of Dr. Clapham-Lee, and upon the detached head which—perhaps—had uttered articulate sounds.

West was not even excited now. His condition was more ghastly. Quickly he said, "It's the finish—but let's incinerate—this." We carried the thing down to the laboratory—listening. I do not remember many particulars—you can imagine my state of mind—but it is a vicious lie to say it was Herbert West's body which I put into the incinerator. We both inserted the whole unopened wooden box, closed the door, and started the electricity. Nor did any sound come from the box, after all.

It was West who first noticed the falling plaster on that part of the wall where the ancient tomb masonry had been covered up. I was going to run, but he stopped me. Then I saw a small black aperture, felt a ghoulish wind of ice, and smelled the charnel bowels of a putrescent earth. There was no sound, but just then the electric lights went out and I saw outlined against some phosphorescence of the nether world a horde of silent toiling things which only insanity—or worse—could create. Their outlines were human, semi-human, fractionally human, and not human at all—the horde was grotesquely heterogeneous. They were removing the stones quietly, one by one, from the centuried wall. And then, as the breach became large enough, they came out into the laboratory in single file; led by a stalking thing with a beautiful head made of wax. A sort of mad-eyed monstrosity behind the leader seized on Herbert West. West did not resist or utter a sound. Then they all sprang at him and tore him to pieces before my eyes, bearing the fragments away into that subterranean vault of fabulous abominations. West's head was carried off by the wax-headed leader, who wore a Canadian officer's uniform. As it disappeared I saw that the blue eyes behind the spectacles were hideously blazing with their first touch of frantic, visible emotion.

Servants found me unconscious in the morning. West was gone. The incinerator contained only unidentifiable

ashes. Detectives have questioned me, but what can I say?
The Sefton tragedy they will not connect with West; not
that, nor the men with the box, whose existence they
deny. I told them of the vault, and they pointed to the
unbroken plaster wall and laughed. So I told them no
more. They imply that I am a madman or a murderer—
probably I am mad. But I might not be mad if those accursed tomb-legions had not been so silent.

The Hound

In my tortured ears there sounds unceasingly a nightmare whirring and flapping, and a faint, distant baying as of some gigantic hound.[1] It is not dream—it is not, I fear, even madness—for too much has already happened to give me these merciful doubts. St. John is a mangled corpse; I alone know why, and such is my knowledge that I am about to blow out my brains for fear I shall be mangled

"The Hound" was written in September 1922. It was one of the five tales that Lovecraft originally submitted to *Weird Tales* in 1923, all of which the editor Edwin Baird accepted. "The Hound" was published in the February 1924 issue.

[1] *gigantic hound*: An echo of Conan Doyle's Hound of the Baskervilles. In a letter dating to 1918, Lovecraft wrote: "As to 'Sherlock Holmes'—I used to be infatuated with him! I read every Sherlock Holmes story published. . . ." As a twelve-year-old boy he would have taken especial note of *The Hound of the Baskervilles*, serialized in 1902–03, as the first new Sherlock Holmes adventure to appear since the detective's apparent death in "The Final Problem" (1893).

in the same way. Down unlit and illimitable corridors of
eldritch phantasy sweeps the black, shapeless Nemesis[2]
that drives me to self-annihilation.

May heaven forgive the folly and morbidity which led
us both to so monstrous a fate! Wearied with the com-
monplaces of a prosaic world, where even the joys of romance and adventure soon grow stale, St. John and I had
followed enthusiastically every aesthetic and intellectual
movement which promised respite from our devastating
ennui. The enigmas of the Symbolists[3] and the ecstasies
of the pre-Raphaelites[4] all were ours in their time, but
each new mood was drained too soon of its diverting novelty and appeal. Only the sombre philosophy of the Decadents[5] could hold us, and this we found potent only by
increasing gradually the depth and diabolism of our pene-
trations. Baudelaire[6] and Huysmans[7] were soon exhausted

---

[2] *Nemesis*: In Greek mythology, Nemesis was the agent of the gods' retribution
against those who violated sacred law. Also the title of a Lovecraft poem, a
stanza of which serves as the epigraph for "The Haunter of the Dark."

[3] *Symbolists*: A literary school that originated in France at the end of the nineteenth century, in reaction to the naturalism and realism of the period. The
movement sought to convey impressions by suggestion rather than by direct
statement. The first Symbolists were poets, who experimented with form, notably free verse. Their critics accused them of being morbid.

[4] *pre-Raphaelites*: A brotherhood of English poets and painters founded in 1848
by Dante Gabriel Rossetti (1828–82), W. Holman Hunt (1827–1910), and John
Millais (1829–96). A later convert was the painter Edward Burne-Jones (1833–98).
Dismayed by the poor quality of the British art of their day, they turned to what
they perceived as the comparative simplicity of the medieval world for their
inspiration. Their work was meticulous in detail and highly mannered in style.

[5] *Decadents*: At the end of the nineteenth century those authors who found
inspiration, in both their lives and their writings, in aestheticism and in the
morbid and the macabre. They admired the French Symbolists and Charles
Baudelaire. One of the leading Decadents in England was the playwright Oscar
Wilde (1854–1900).

[6] *Baudelaire*: Charles Baudelaire (1821–67), French poet and critic, author of *Les
Fleurs du mal*. An erratic and moody personality, he felt a great affinity with
Edgar Allan Poe (1809–1849), whose works he translated and brought to the
attention of the French public. He was a forerunner of the Symbolists. In a 1922
letter to his friend Frank Belknap Long, Lovecraft writes: "The Freudism of such
decadents as Baudelaire mildly amuses me." (*Selected Letters* I, 172) See note
45 to "Herbert West—Reanimator."

of thrills, till finally there remained for us only the more
direct stimuli of unnatural personal experiences and ad-
ventures. It was this frightful emotional need which led
us eventually to that detestable course which even in my
present fear I mention with shame and timidity—that hideous extremity of human outrage, the abhorred practice of
grave-robbing.

I cannot reveal the details of our shocking expeditions,
or catalogue even partly the worst of the trophies adorning
the nameless museum we prepared in the great stone
house where we jointly dwelt, alone and servantless. Our
museum was a blasphemous, unthinkable place, where
with the satanic taste of neurotic virtuosi we had assembled an universe of terror and decay to excite our jaded
sensibilities. It was a secret room, far, far underground;
where huge winged daemons carven of basalt and onyx
vomited from wide grinning mouths weird green and or-
ange light, and hidden pneumatic pipes ruffled into kaleidoscopic dances of death the lines of red charnel things
hand in hand woven in voluminous black hangings.
Through these pipes came at will the odours our moods
most craved; sometimes the scent of pale funeral lilies,
sometimes the narcotic incense of imagined Eastern
shrines of the kingly dead, and sometimes—how I shudder
to recall it!—the frightful, soul-upheaving stenches of the
uncovered grave.

Around the walls of this repellent chamber were cases
of antique mummies alternating with comely, life-like
bodies perfectly stuffed and cured by the taxidermist's art,
and with headstones snatched from the oldest churchyards
of the world. Niches here and there contained skulls of

---

[7] *Huysmans*: Joris-Karl Huysmans (1848–1907), French novelist and occultist.
His novel *A rebours* (1884, translated as *Against the Grain*) describes a spiritual
quest for mystical meaning that captures the mood of the Decadents. He later
became absorbed in Roman Catholicism. "The Hound" has many echoes of
Huysmans and of *A Rebours* in particular, as Steven J. Mariconda has demonstrated in " 'The Hound'—A Dead Dog?," an essay collected in Mariconda's *On
the Emergence of "Cthulhu" and Other Observations* (1995).

all shapes, and heads preserved in various stages of dissolution. There one might find the rotting, bald pates of
famous noblemen, and the fresh and radiantly golden
heads of new-buried children. Statues and paintings there
were, all of fiendish subjects and some executed by St.
John and myself. A locked portfolio, bound in tanned
human skin, held certain unknown and unnamable drawings which it was rumoured Goya[8] had perpetrated but
dared not acknowledge. There were nauseous musical instruments, stringed, brass, and wood-wind, on which St.
John and I sometimes produced dissonances of exquisite
morbidity and cacodaemoniacal ghastliness; whilst in a
multitude of inlaid ebony cabinets reposed the most incredible and unimaginable variety of tomb-loot ever assembled by human madness and perversity. It is of this
loot in particular that I must not speak—thank God I had
the courage to destroy it long before I thought of destroying myself.

The predatory excursions on which we collected our unmentionable treasures were always artistically memorable
events. We were no vulgar ghouls, but worked only under
certain conditions of mood, landscape, environment,
weather, season, and moonlight. These pastimes were to
us the most exquisite form of aesthetic expression, and
we gave their details a fastidious technical care. An inappropriate hour, a jarring lighting effect, or a clumsy manip-
ulation of the damp sod, would almost totally destroy for
us that ecstatic titillation which followed the exhumation
of some ominous, grinning secret of the earth. Our quest
for novel scenes and piquant conditions was feverish and
insatiate—St. John was always the leader, and he it was

---

[8] *Goya*: Francisco Goya y Lucientes (1746–1828), Spanish painter and graphic
artist. In his old age he painted a number of macabre murals, including "Saturn
Devouring His Children," "Witches' Sabbath," and "The Three Fates." A com-
ment in a 1923 letter to Frank Belknap Long suggests that Lovecraft knew Goya
only by reputation: "Goya? Yes, child, I must learn of him. Undoubtedly he is
akin to the horror I relish, though as yet pictorial art is remoter than literary
art from my centres of consciousness." (*Selected Letters* I, 228)

who led the way at last to that mocking, that accursed spot which brought us our hideous and inevitable doom.

By what malign fatality were we lured to that terrible Holland churchyard?[9] I think it was the dark rumour and legendry, the tales of one buried for five centuries, who had himself been a ghoul in his time and had stolen a potent thing from a mighty sepulchre. I can recall the scene in these final moments—the pale autumnal moon over the graves, casting long horrible shadows; the grotesque trees, drooping sullenly to meet the neglected grass and the crumbling slabs; the vast legions of strangely colossal bats that flew against the moon; the antique ivied church pointing a huge spectral finger at the livid sky; the phosphorescent insects that danced like death-fires under the yews in a distant corner; the odours of mould, vegetation, and less explicable things that mingled feebly with the night-wind from over the far swamps and seas; and worst of all, the faint deep-toned baying of some gigantic hound which we could neither see nor definitely place. As we heard this suggestion of baying we shuddered, remembering the tales of the peasantry; for he whom we sought had centuries before been found in this selfsame spot, torn and mangled by the claws and teeth of some unspeakable beast.

I remembered how we delved in this ghoul's grave with our spades, and how we thrilled at the picture of ourselves, the grave, the pale watching moon, the horrible shadows, the grotesque trees, the titanic bats, the antique church, the dancing death-fires, the sickening odours, the gently moaning night-wind, and the strange, half-heard, directionless baying, of whose objective existence we could scarcely be sure. Then we struck a substance harder than the damp mould, and beheld a rotting oblong box crusted

---

[9] *Holland churchyard*: Lovecraft appears to have used Holland as a setting because the graveyard that inspired him to write "The Hound," that of the Dutch Reformed Church (1796) in Brooklyn, was full of crumbling gravestones inscribed in Dutch.

with mineral deposits from the long-undisturbed ground. It was incredibly tough and thick, but so old that we finally pried it open and feasted our eyes on what it held.

Much—amazingly much—was left of the object despite the lapse of five hundred years. The skeleton, though crushed in places by the jaws of the thing that had killed it, held together with surprising firmness, and we gloated over the clean white skull and its long, firm teeth and its eyeless sockets that once had glowed with a charnel fever like our own. In the coffin lay an amulet[10] of curious and exotic design, which had apparently been worn around the sleeper's neck. It was the oddly conventionalised figure of a crouching winged hound, or sphinx with a semi-canine face, and was exquisitely carved in antique Oriental fashion from a small piece of green jade. The expression on its features was repellent in the extreme, savouring at once of death, bestiality, and malevolence. Around the base was an inscription in characters which neither St. John nor I could identify; and on the bottom, like a maker's seal, was graven a grotesque and formidable skull.

Immediately upon beholding this amulet we knew that we must possess it; that this treasure alone was our logical pelf[11] from the centuried grave. Even had its outlines been unfamiliar we would have desired it, but as we looked more closely we saw that it was not wholly unfamiliar. Alien it indeed was to all art and literature which sane and balanced readers know, but we recognised it as the thing hinted of in the forbidden *Necronomicon*[12] of the

[10] *amulet*: Something worn as a charm against evil.

[11] *pelf*: Riches or in this context booty.

[12] *Necronomicon of the mad Arab Abdul Alhazred*: The first mention of Lovecraft's archetypal forbidden tome, which he would elaborate on in later tales, most notably "The Dunwich Horror," where he quotes an extensive passage. Abdul Alhazred is first mentioned in "The Nameless City" (1921). Lovecraft claimed that he invented the name after reading Lang's *Arabian Nights* as a child, though elsewhere he says that he may have asked an adult, possibly the family lawyer, to make up an Arab name for him. For a discussion of the grammar and etymology of these names, see note 60 to "The Dunwich Horror" in *The Annotated H. P. Lovecraft* (1997), edited by S. T. Joshi.

mad Arab Abdul Alhazred; the ghastly soul-symbol of the corpse-eating cult of inaccessible Leng,[13] in Central Asia. All too well did we trace the sinister lineaments described by the old Arab daemonologist; lineaments, he wrote, drawn from some obscure supernatural manifestation of the souls of those who vexed and gnawed at the dead.

Seizing the green jade object, we gave a last glance at the bleached and cavern-eyed face of its owner and closed up the grave as we found it. As we hastened from that abhorrent spot, the stolen amulet in St. John's pocket, we thought we saw the bats descend in a body to the earth we had so lately rifled, as if seeking for some cursed and unholy nourishment. But the autumn moon shone weak and pale, and we could not be sure. So, too, as we sailed the next day away from Holland to our home, we thought we heard the faint distant baying of some gigantic hound in the background. But the autumn wind moaned sad and wan, and we could not be sure.

II.

Less than a week after our return to England, strange things began to happen. We lived as recluses; devoid of friends, alone, and without servants in a few rooms of an ancient manor-house on a bleak and unfrequented moor;[14] so that our doors were seldom disturbed by the knock of the visitor. Now, however, we were troubled by what seemed to be frequent fumblings in the night, not only around the doors but around the windows also, upper as

---

[13] *inaccessible Leng*: Lovecraft first mentions Leng in his dream-world fantasy, "Celephaïs" (1920). Here, as part of his demythologizing process, he has located it in Central Asia. Leng will reappear as "the plateau of Leng" in *The Dream-Quest of Unknown Kadath* and *At the Mountains of Madness*. See also note 96 to *At the Mountains of Madness*. (*Annotated Lovecraft*, 226)

[14] *unfrequented moor*: Another echo of *The Hound of the Baskervilles*, which is mainly set on Dartmoor in Devon.

well as lower. Once we fancied that a large, opaque body
darkened the library window when the moon was shining
against it, and another time we thought we heard a whirring or flapping sound not far off. On each occasion investigation revealed nothing, and we began to ascribe the
occurrences to imagination alone—that same curiously
disturbed imagination which still prolonged in our ears
the faint far baying we thought we had heard in the Holland churchyard. The jade amulet now reposed in a niche
in our museum, and sometimes we burned strangely
scented candles before it. We read much in Alhazred's *Necronomicon* about its properties, and about the relation of
ghouls' souls to the objects it symbolised; and were disturbed by what we read. Then terror came.

On the night of September 24, 19—,[15] I heard a knock
at my chamber door. Fancying it St. John's, I bade the
knocker enter, but was answered only by a shrill laugh.
There was no one in the corridor. When I aroused St. John
from his sleep, he professed entire ignorance of the event,
and became as worried as I. It was that night that the
faint, distant baying over the moor became to us a certain
and dreaded reality. Four days later, whilst we were both
in the hidden museum, there came a low, cautious
scratching at the single door which led to the secret library
staircase. Our alarm was now divided, for besides our fear
of the unknown, we had always entertained a dread that
our grisly collection might be discovered. Extinguishing
all lights, we proceeded to the door and threw it suddenly
open; whereupon we felt an unaccountable rush of air, and
heard as if receding far away a queer combination of rus-
tling, tittering, and articulate chatter. Whether we were
mad, dreaming, or in our senses, we did not try to determine. We only realised, with the blackest of apprehen-

---

[15] *19—*: A device common in gothic fiction to disguise dates. Poe gave dates in
his tales typically as 18—.

sions, that the apparently disembodied chatter was beyond a doubt *in the Dutch language.*

After that we lived in growing horror and fascination. Mostly we held to the theory that we were jointly going mad from our life of unnatural excitements, but sometimes it pleased us more to dramatise ourselves as the victims of some creeping and appalling doom. Bizarre manifestations were now too frequent to count. Our lonely house was seemingly alive with the presence of some malign being whose nature we could not guess, and every night that daemoniac baying rolled over the windswept moor, always louder and louder. On October 29 we found in the soft earth underneath the library window a series of footprints utterly impossible to describe. They were as baffling as the hordes of great bats which haunted the old manor-house in unprecedented and increasing numbers.

The horror reached a culmination on November 18, when St. John, walking home after dark from the distant railway station, was seized by some frightful carnivorous thing and torn to ribbons. His screams had reached the house, and I had hastened to the terrible scene in time to hear a whir of wings and see a vague black cloudy thing silhouetted against the rising moon. My friend was dying when I spoke to him, and he could not answer coherently. All he could do was to whisper, "The amulet—that damned thing—."[16] Then he collapsed, an inert mass of mangled flesh.

I buried him the next midnight in one of our neglected gardens, and mumbled over his body one of the devilish rituals he had loved in life. And as I pronounced the last daemoniac sentence I heard afar on the moor the faint baying of some gigantic hound. The moon was up, but I

---

[16] *that damned thing:* "The Damned Thing" is the title of a horror story by Ambrose Bierce (1842–1914?), an American journalist and satirist, best known today for *The Devil's Dictionary* and his Civil War tales.

dared not look at it. And when I saw on the dim-litten moor a wide nebulous shadow sweeping from mound to mound, I shut my eyes and threw myself face down upon the ground. When I arose trembling, I know not how much later, I staggered into the house and made shocking obeisances before the enshrined amulet of green jade.

Being now afraid to live alone in the ancient house on the moor, I departed on the following day for London, taking with me the amulet after destroying by fire and burial the rest of the impious collection in the museum. But after three nights I heard the baying again, and before a week was over felt strange eyes upon me whenever it was dark. One evening as I strolled on Victoria Embankment[17] for some needed air, I saw a black shape obscure one of the reflections of the lamps in the water. A wind stronger than the night-wind rushed by, and I knew that what had befallen St. John must soon befall me.

The next day I carefully wrapped the green jade amulet and sailed for Holland. What mercy I might gain by returning the thing to its silent, sleeping owner I knew not; but I felt that I must at least try any step conceivably logical. What the hound was, and why it pursued me, were questions still vague; but I had first heard the baying in that ancient churchyard, and every subsequent event including St. John's dying whisper had served to connect the curse with the stealing of the amulet. Accordingly I sank into the nethermost abysses of despair when, at an inn in Rotterdam, I discovered that thieves had despoiled me of this sole means of salvation.

The baying was loud that evening, and in the morning I read of a nameless deed in the vilest quarter of the city. The rabble were in terror, for upon an evil tenement had

---

[17] *Victoria Embankment*: Fashionable London walkway running along the north side of the Thames between Westminster and Blackfriars. Lovecraft longed to visit England, but he was never able to afford to travel beyond North America.

fallen a red death[18] beyond the foulest previous crime of
the neighbourhood. In a squalid thieves' den an entire family had been torn to shreds by an unknown thing which
left no trace, and those around had heard all night above
the usual clamour of drunken voices a faint, deep, insistent note as of a gigantic hound.

So at last I stood again in that unwholesome churchyard
where a pale winter moon cast hideous shadows, and
leafless trees drooped sullenly to meet the withered, frosty
grass and cracking slabs, and the ivied church pointing a
jeering finger at the unfriendly sky, and the night-wind
howled maniacally from over frozen swamps and frigid
seas. The baying was very faint now, and it ceased altogether as I approached the ancient grave I had once violated, and frightened away an abnormally large horde of
bats which had been hovering curiously around it.

I know not why I went thither unless to pray, or gibber
out insane pleas and apologies to the calm white thing
that lay within; but, whatever my reason, I attacked the
half-frozen sod with a desperation partly mine and partly
that of a dominating will outside myself. Excavation was
much easier than I expected, though at one point I encountered a queer interruption; when a lean vulture darted
down out of the cold sky and pecked frantically at the
grave-earth until I killed him with a blow of my spade.
Finally I reached the rotting oblong box and removed the
damp nitrous cover. This is the last rational act I ever
performed.

For crouched within that centuried coffin, embraced by
a close-packed nightmare retinue of huge, sinewy, sleeping
bats, was the bony thing my friend and I had robbed; not
clean and placid as we had seen it then, but covered with
caked blood and shreds of alien flesh and hair, and leering

---

[18] *red death*: A tip of the hat to Poe's story "The Masque of the Red Death."
The fictional red death is analogous to the black death (or the bubonic plague)
that afflicted medieval Europe.

sentiently at me with phosphorescent sockets and sharp ensanguined fangs yawning twistedly in mockery of my inevitable doom. And when it gave from those grinning jaws a deep, sardonic bay as of some gigantic hound, and I saw that it held in its gory, filthy claw the lost and fateful amulet of green jade, I merely screamed and ran away idiotically, my screams soon dissolving into peals of hysterical laughter.

Madness rides the star-wind . . . claws and teeth sharpened on centuries of corpses . . . dripping death astride a Bacchanale[19] of bats from night-black ruins of buried temples of Belial.[20] . . . Now, as the baying of that dead, fleshless monstrosity grows louder and louder, and the stealthy whirring and flapping of those accursed web-wings circles closer and closer, I shall seek with my revolver the oblivion which is my only refuge from the unnamed and unnamable.

---

[19] *Bacchanale*: A Roman religious festival in honor of Bacchus, the god of wine. It later degenerated into an occasion for drunken and licentious behavior and was banned by law.

[20] *Belial*: A Biblical name for Satan. "What accord has Christ with Belial?" 2 Corinthians 6:15. This name also crops up in the passage from the Reverend Abijah Hoadley's sermon cited in "The Dunwich Horror." See note 22 to "The Dunwich Horror" (*Annotated Lovecraft*, 111).

The Shunned House

I.

From even the greatest of horrors irony is seldom absent. Sometimes it enters directly into the composition of the events, while sometimes it relates only to their fortuitous position among persons and places. The latter sort

---

"The Shunned House" was written October 16–19, 1924. The tale having been rejected by *Weird Tales*, Lovecraft agreed to let his amateur friend W. Paul Cook bring it out as a chapbook. Cook printed but did not bind about 300 copies in the summer of 1928. Because of ill health he never finished the job. In the mid-1930s Cook sent Robert Barlow most of the unbound sheets, but Barlow ended up binding only about eight copies, including one in natural leather for Lovecraft. Exasperated by his friend's dilatoriness, Lovecraft resigned himself to the prospect that his first "book" was a total loss. It remained for Arkham House to bind the bulk of the loose sheets and issue a proper edition of *The Shunned House* after Lovecraft's death.

is splendidly exemplified by a case in the ancient city of
Providence, where in the late forties Edgar Allan Poe used
to sojourn often during his unsuccessful wooing of the
gifted poetess, Mrs. Whitman.[1] Poe generally stopped at
the Mansion House in Benefit Street—the renamed
Golden Ball Inn whose roof has sheltered Washington, Jef-
ferson, and Lafayette[2]—and his favourite walk led north-
ward along the same street to Mrs. Whitman's home and
the neighbouring hillside churchyard of St. John's,[3] whose
hidden expanse of eighteenth-century gravestones had for
him a peculiar fascination.

Now the irony is this. In this walk, so many times repeated, the world's greatest master of the terrible and the
bizarre was obliged to pass a particular house on the eastern side of the street; a dingy, antiquated structure perched
on the abruptly rising side-hill, with a great unkempt yard
dating from a time when the region was partly open country. It does not appear that he ever wrote or spoke of it,
nor is there any evidence that he even noticed it. And yet
that house, to the two persons in possession of certain

---

[1] *Mrs. Whitman*: Poe became engaged to Sarah Helen Power Whitman (1803–78),
a widow, in 1848 and wrote the second of his two "To Helen" poems about
her. Lovecraft explains why they never married in a 1934 letter: "The engagement was finally broken off through the influence of Mrs. Whitman's mother—
old Mrs. Power—who objected to Poe's drinking habits. Many of the older Providence people remembered Poe, and refused to appreciate his work because of
his frequent drunken appearances on our streets. The mother of my elder aunt's
husband knew Mrs. Whitman, and so prejudiced her son against Poe that he
always argued with me when I defended him." Lovecraft also noted that "Mrs.
Whitman was a very passable poetess—smooth and pleasing, though in no way
original or distinguished." (*Selected Letters* IV, 399–400)

[2] *Lafayette*: In a 1924 letter Lovecraft says that Washington and Lafayette
stopped at this Providence landmark in 1790. (*Selected Letters* I, 286)

[3] *St. John's*: In the letter cited in note 1 above, Lovecraft says of the house where
Mrs. Whitman lived: "The rear of this house overlooks the hidden churchyard
of St. John's, where Poe used to wander on moonlight nights." Lovecraft liked
to take visitors to St. John's churchyard at night, one of whom, an attractive
young woman named Helen Sully, became so frightened when Lovecraft started
to tell her ghostly stories that she fled from the place. See Helen Sully's brief
memoir, "Memories of Lovecraft: II," in *Lovecraft Remembered* (1998), edited
by Peter Cannon.

information, equals or outranks in horror the wildest phantasy of the genius who so often passed it unknowingly, and stands starkly leering as a symbol of all that is unutterably hideous.

The house was—and for that matter still is—of a kind to attract the attention of the curious. Originally a farm or semi-farm building, it followed the average New England colonial lines of the middle eighteenth century—the prosperous peaked-roof sort, with two stories and dormerless attic, and with the Georgian doorway and interior panelling dictated by the progress of taste at that time. It faced south, with one gable end buried to the lower windows in the eastward rising hill, and the other exposed to the foundations toward the street. Its construction, over a century and a half ago, had followed the grading and straightening of the road in that especial vicinity; for Benefit Street—at first called Back Street—was laid out as a lane winding amongst the graveyards of the first settlers, and straightened only when the removal of the bodies to the North Burial Ground[4] made it decently possible to cut through the old family plots.

At the start, the western wall had lain some twenty feet up a precipitous lawn from the roadway; but a widening of the street at about the time of the Revolution sheared off most of the intervening space, exposing the foundations so that a brick basement wall had to be made, giving the deep cellar a street frontage with door and two windows above ground, close to the new line of public travel. When the sidewalk was laid out a century ago the last of the intervening space was removed; and Poe in his walks must have seen only sheer ascent of dull grey brick flush with the sidewalk and surmounted at a height of ten feet by the antique shingled bulk of the house proper.

The farm-like grounds extended back very deeply up the

---

[4] *North Burial Ground*: Sarah Helen Whitman is buried in the North Burial Ground.

THE HOUSE

'Tis a grove-circled dwelling
     Set close to a hill,
Where the branches are telling
     Strange legends of ill;
Over timbers so old
     That they breathe of the dead,
Crawl the vines, green and cold,
     By strange nourishment fed;
And no man knows the juices they suck
from the depths of their dank slimy bed.

In the gardens are growing
     Tall blossoms and fair,
Each pallid bloom throwing
     Perfume on the air;
But the afternoon sun
     With its red slanting rays
Makes the picture loom dun
     On the curious gaze,
And above the sweet scent of the blos-
soms rise odours of numberless days.

The rank grasses are waving
     On terrace and lawn,
Dim memories saving
     Of things that have gone;
The stones of the walks
     Are encrusted and wet,
And a strange spirit stalks
     When the red sun has set.
And the soul of the watcher is fill'd with
faint pictures he fain would forget.

It was in the hot Junetime
     I stood by that scene,
When the gold rays of noontime
     Beat bright on the green.
But I shiver'd with cold,
     Groping feebly for light,
As a picture unroll'd—
     And my age-spanning sight
Saw the time I had been there before
flash like fulgury out of the night.

                                    WARD PHILLIPS.

H. P. Lovecraft's poem "The House": first appearance, in *The Philosopher* 1,
No. 1 (December 1920). The poem is also about the "shunned house" on Benefit Street.

hill, almost to Wheaton Street. The space south of the
house, abutting on Benefit Street, was of course greatly
above the existing sidewalk level, forming a terrace
bounded by a high bank wall of damp, mossy stone pierced
by a steep flight of narrow steps which led inward between
canyon-like surfaces to the upper region of mangy lawn,
rheumy brick walls, and neglected gardens whose disman-
tled cement urns, rusted kettles fallen from tripods of
knotty sticks, and similar paraphernalia set off the
weather-beaten front door with its broken fanlight, rotting
Ionic pilasters, and wormy triangular pediment.[5]

What I heard in my youth about the shunned house was
merely that people died there in alarmingly great numbers.
That, I was told, was why the original owners had moved

---

[5] *wormy triangular pediment*: This house, built in 1763, has been considerably
restored since Lovecraft's day. It had inspired him to write a poem in 1920,
"The House."

out some twenty years after building the place. It was plainly unhealthy, perhaps because of the dampness and fungous growth in the cellar, the general sickish smell, the draughts of the hallways, or the quality of the well and pump water. These things were bad enough, and these were all that gained belief among the persons whom I knew. Only the notebooks of my antiquarian uncle, Dr. Elihu Whipple,[6] revealed to me at length the darker, vaguer surmises which formed an undercurrent of folklore among old-time servants and humble folk; surmises which never travelled far, and which were largely forgotten when Providence grew to be a metropolis with a shifting modern population.

The fact is, that the house was never regarded by the solid part of the community as in any real sense "haunted". There were no widespread tales of rattling chains, cold currents of air, extinguished lights, or faces at the window. Extremists sometimes said the house was "unlucky", but that is as far as even they went. What was really beyond dispute is that a frightful proportion of persons died there; or more accurately, *had* died there, since after some peculiar happenings over sixty years ago the building had become deserted through the sheer impossibility of renting it. These persons were not all cut off suddenly by any one cause; rather did it seem that their vitality was insidiously sapped, so that each one died the sooner from whatever tendency to weakness he may have naturally had. And those who did not die displayed in varying degree a type of anaemia or consumption, and sometimes a decline of the mental faculties, which spoke ill for the salubriousness of the building. Neighbouring

---

[6] *Elihu Whipple*: The character of Elihu Whipple may owe something to Lovecraft's beloved grandfather, Whipple Phillips (1833–1904), as well as to his two learned uncles-in-law, Dr. Franklin Chase Clark (1847–1915) and Edward Francis Gamwell (1869–1936). Whipple is the most benevolent of Lovecraft's elderly male characters, in contrast to such evil old men as the cannibalistic rustic in "The Picture in the House."

houses, it must be added, seemed entirely free form the noxious quality.

This much I knew before my insistent questioning led my uncle to shew me the notes which finally embarked us both on our hideous investigation. In my childhood the shunned house was vacant, with barren, gnarled, and terrible old trees, long, queerly pale grass, and nightmarishly misshapen weeds in the high terraced yard where birds never lingered. We boys used to overrun the place, and I can still recall my youthful terror not only at the morbid strangeness of this sinister vegetation, but at the eldritch atmosphere and odour of the dilapidated house, whose unlocked front door was often entered in quest of shudders. The small-paned windows were largely broken, and a nameless air of desolation hung round the precarious panelling, shaky interior shutters, peeling wall-paper, falling plaster, rickety staircases, and such fragments of battered furniture as still remained. The dust and cobwebs added their touch of the fearful; and brave indeed was the boy who would voluntarily ascend the ladder to the attic, a vast raftered length lighted only by small blinking windows in the gable ends, and filled with a massed wreckage of chests, chairs, and spinning-wheels which infinite years of deposit had shrouded and festooned into monstrous and hellish shapes.

But after all, the attic was not the most terrible part of the house. It was the dank, humid cellar which somehow exerted the strongest repulsion on us, even though it was wholly above ground on the street side, with only a thin door and window-pierced brick wall to separate it from the busy sidewalk. We scarcely knew whether to haunt it in spectral fascination, or to shun it for the sake of our souls and our sanity. For one thing, the bad odour of the house was strongest there; and for another thing, we did not like the white fungous growths which occasionally sprang up in rainy summer weather from the hard earth floor. Those fungi, grotesquely like the vegetation in the yard outside, were truly horrible in their outlines; detestable parodies of toadstools and Indian pipes,[7] whose like we had never seen in any other situation. They rotted quickly, and at one stage became slightly phosphorescent; so that nocturnal passers-by sometimes spoke of witch-fires glowing behind the broken panes of the foetor-spreading windows.

We never—even in our wildest Hallowe'en moods—visited this cellar by night, but in some of our daytime visits could detect the phosphorescence, especially when the day was dark and wet. There was also a subtler thing we often thought we detected—a very strange thing which was, however, merely suggestive at most. I refer to a sort of cloudy whitish pattern on the dirt floor—a vague, shifting deposit of mould or nitre[8] which we sometimes thought we could trace amidst the sparse fungous growths near the huge fireplace of the basement kitchen. Once in a while it struck us that this patch bore an uncanny resemblance to a doubled-up human figure, though generally no such kinship existed, and often there was no whitish deposit whatever. On a certain rainy afternoon when this illusion seemed phenomenally strong, and when, in addition, I had fancied I glimpsed a kind of thin, yellowish, shimmering exhalation rising from the nitrous pattern toward the yawning fireplace, I spoke to my uncle about the matter. He smiled at this odd conceit, but it seemed that his smile was tinged with reminiscence. Later I heard that a similar notion entered into some of the wild ancient tales of the common folk—a notion likewise alluding to ghoulish, wolfish shapes taken by smoke from the great chimney, and queer contours assumed by certain of the sinuous tree-roots that thrust their way into the cellar through the loose foundation-stones.

---

[7] *Indian pipes*: An Indian pipe is a waxy white leafless herb that typically feeds on the products of organic breakdown and decay.

[8] *nitre*: Potassium or sodium nitrate. Potassium nitrate is also known as saltpeter, a white, crystalline salt used in preserving meat and in medicine.

II.

Not till my adult years did my uncle set before me the notes and data which he had collected concerning the shunned house. Dr. Whipple was a sane, conservative physician of the old school, and for all his interest in the place was not eager to encourage young thoughts toward the abnormal. His own view, postulating simply a building and location of markedly unsanitary qualities, had nothing to do with abnormality; but he realised that the very picturesqueness which aroused his own interest would in a boy's fanciful mind take on all manner of gruesome imaginative associations.

The doctor was a bachelor; a white-haired, clean-shaven, old-fashioned gentleman, and a local historian of note, who had often broken a lance with such controversial guardians of tradition as Sidney S. Rider and Thomas W. Bicknell.[9] He lived with one manservant in a Georgian homestead with knocker and iron-railed steps, balanced eerily on a steep ascent of North Court Street beside the ancient brick court and colony house where his grandfather—a cousin of that celebrated privateersman, Capt. Whipple, who burnt His Majesty's armed schooner *Gaspee* in 1772—had voted in the legislature on May 4, 1776, for the independence of the Rhode-Island Colony.[10] Around him in the damp, low-ceiled library with the musty white

[9] *Sidney S. Rider and Thomas W. Bicknell*: Sidney Smith Ryder (1833–1917) was a prolific editor and publisher as well as the author of numerous historical tracts on Rhode Island. Thomas W. Bicknell (1834–1925) is most noted for his five-volume *History of the State of Rhode Island and Providence Plantations* (1920), one of many historical works he wrote over a long career.

[10] *Rhode-Island Colony*: Lovecraft also records this act of defiance against British rule, which occurred in May 1772, in *The Case of Charles Dexter Ward*: "Capt. Whipple led the mob who burnt the revenue ship *Gaspee*. . . ." Abraham Whipple (1733–1819) became a captain in the Continental Navy in 1775. During the war he captured eight East Indiamen with cargoes worth more than $1,000,000.

panelling, heavy carved overmantel, and small-paned, vine-shaded windows, were the relics and records of his ancient family, among which were many dubious allusions to the shunned house in Benefit Street. That pest spot lies not far distant—for Benefit runs ledgewise just above the court-house along the precipitous hill up which the first settlement climbed.

When, in the end, my insistent pestering and maturing years evoked from my uncle the hoarded lore I sought, there lay before me a strange enough chronicle. Long-winded, statistical, and drearily genealogical as some of the matter was, there ran through it a continuous thread of brooding, tenacious horror and preternatural malevolence which impressed me even more than it had impressed the good doctor. Separate events fitted together uncannily, and seemingly irrelevant details held mines of hideous possibilities. A new and burning curiosity grew in me, compared to which my boyish curiosity was feeble and inchoate. The first revelation led to an exhaustive research, and finally to that shuddering quest which proved so disastrous to myself and mine. For at last my uncle insisted on joining the search I had commenced, and after a certain night in that house he did not come away with me. I am lonely without that gentle soul whose long years were filled only with honour, virtue, good taste, benevolence, and learning. I have reared a marble urn to his memory in St. John's churchyard—the place that Poe loved— the hidden grove of giant willows on the hill, where tombs and headstones huddle quietly between the hoary bulk of the church and the houses and bank walls of Benefit Street.

The history of the house, opening amidst a maze of dates, revealed no trace of the sinister either about its construction or about the prosperous and honourable family who built it. Yet from the first a taint of calamity, soon increased to boding significance, was apparent. My uncle's carefully compiled record began with the building of the structure in 1763, and followed the theme with an unusual amount of detail. The shunned house, it seems, was first inhabited by William Harris[11] and his wife Rhoby Dexter, with their children, Elkanah, born in 1755, Abigail, born in 1757, William, Jr., born in 1759, and Ruth, born in 1761. Harris was a substantial merchant and seaman in the West India trade, connected with the firm of Obadiah Brown and his nephews. After Brown's death in 1761, the new firm of Nicholas Brown[12] & Co. made him master of the brig *Prudence,* Providence-built, of 120 tons, thus enabling him to erect the new homestead he had desired ever since his marriage.

The site he had chosen—a recently straightened part of the new and fashionable Back Street, which ran along the side of the hill above crowded Cheapside—was all that could be wished, and the building did justice to the location. It was the best that moderate means could afford, and Harris hastened to move in before the birth of a fifth child which the family expected. That child, a boy, came in December; but was still-born. Nor was any child to be born alive in that house for a century and a half.

The next April sickness occurred among the children, and Abigail and Ruth died before the month was over. Dr. Job Ives[13] diagnosed the trouble as some infantile fever, though others declared it was more of a mere wasting-

---

[11] *William Harris*: A William Harris was one of the leaders of the first twelve settlers of Rhode Island who in 1638 argued with Roger Williams that they deserved more land on account of their seniority. Harris was later engaged in property disputes in Pawtuxet, Rhode Island. In 1679 he was captured by Barbary pirates and in 1681 was ransomed, but he died before he could reach home.

[12] *Nicholas Brown*: Nicholas Brown (1729–91) was a merchant and partner in the firm of Obadiah Brown & Co. with his uncle and his three brothers. He dealt in secret imports during the Revolution for the Continental Congress, and was a supporter of Rhode Island College, later Brown University.

In *The Case of Charles Dexter Ward* Ezra Weeden consults "all four of the Brown brothers, John, Joseph, Nicholas, and Moses, Nicholas, who formed the recognised local magnates," in his effort to extirpate Joseph Curwen.

[13] *Dr. Job Ives*: A fictional character, though perhaps meant to be related to the Ives family distinguished in Connecticut annals.

away or decline. It seemed, in any event, to be contagious; for Hannah Bowen, one of the two servants, died of it in the following June. Eli Liddeason, the other servant, constantly complained of weakness; and would have returned to his father's farm in Rehoboth but for a sudden attachment for Mehitabel Pierce, who was hired to succeed Hannah. He died the next year—a sad year indeed, since it marked the death of William Harris himself, enfeebled as he was by the climate of Martinique, where his occupation had kept him for considerable periods during the preceding decade.

The widowed Rhoby Harris never recovered from the shock of her husband's death, and the passing of her first-born Elkanah two years later was the final blow to her reason. In 1768 she fell victim to a mild form of insanity, and was thereafter confined to the upper part of the house; her elder maiden sister, Mercy Dexter, having moved in to take charge of the family. Mercy was a plain, raw-boned woman of great strength; but her health visibly declined from the time of her advent. She was greatly devoted to her unfortunate sister, and had an especial affection for her only surviving nephew William, who from a sturdy infant had become a sickly, spindling lad. In this year the servant Mehitabel died, and the other servant, Preserved Smith, left without coherent explanation—or at least, with only some wild tales and a complaint that he disliked the smell of the place. For a time Mercy could secure no more help, since the seven deaths and case of madness, all occurring within five years' space, had begun to set in motion the body of fireside rumour which later became so bizarre. Ultimately, however, she obtained new servants from out of town; Ann White, a morose woman from the part of North Kingstown now set off as the township of Exeter, and a capable Boston man named Zenas Low.

It was Ann White who first gave definite shape to the sinister idle talk. Mercy should have known better than

to hire anyone from the Nooseneck Hill country, for that
remote bit of backwoods was then, as now, a seat of the
most uncomfortable superstitions. As lately as 1892 an
Exeter community[14] exhumed a dead body and ceremoni-
ously burnt its heart in order to prevent certain alleged
visitations injurious to the public health and peace, and
one may imagine the point of view of the same section in
1768. Ann's tongue was perniciously active, and within a
few months Mercy discharged her, filling her place with
a faithful and amiable Amazon from Newport, Maria
Robbins.

Meanwhile poor Rhoby Harris, in her madness, gave
voice to dreams and imaginings of the most hideous sort.
At times her screams became insupportable, and for long
periods she would utter shrieking horrors which necessi-
tated her son's temporary residence with his cousin, Peleg
Harris, in Presbyterian-Lane near the new college building.
The boy would seem to improve after these visits, and had
Mercy been as wise as she was well-meaning, she would
have let him live permanently with Peleg. Just what Mrs.
Harris cried out in her fits of violence, tradition hesitates
to say; or rather, presents such extravagant accounts that
they nullify themselves through sheer absurdity. Certainly
it sounds absurd to hear that a woman educated only in
the rudiments of French often shouted for hours in a
coarse and idiomatic form of that language, or that the
same person, alone and guarded, complained wildly of a
staring thing which bit and chewed at her. In 1772 the
servant Zenas died, and when Mrs. Harris heard of it she
laughed with a shocking delight utterly foreign to her. The
next year she herself died, and was laid to rest in the
North Burial Ground beside her husband.

---

[14] *Exeter community*: In her essay "Some Strange New England Mortuary Prac-
tices: Lovecraft Was Right" (*Lovecraft Studies* 29, Fall 1993: 13–18), Faye Ringel
points out that several articles on this incident appeared in the *Providence Journal* in 1892. She goes on to examine the vampire legendry in Exeter, Rhode
Island, and vicinity.

Upon the outbreak of trouble with Great Britain in 1775, William Harris, despite his scant sixteen years and feeble constitution, managed to enlist in the Army of Observation under General Greene;[15] and from that time on enjoyed a steady rise in health and prestige. In 1780, as a Captain in Rhode Island forces in New Jersey under Colonel Angell,[16] he met and married Phebe Hetfield of Elizabethtown,[17] whom he brought to Providence upon his honourable discharge in the following year.

The young soldier's return was not a thing of unmitigated happiness. The house, it is true, was still in good condition; and the street had been widened and changed in name from Back Street to Benefit Street. But Mercy Dexter's once robust frame had undergone a sad and curious decay, so that she was now a stooped and pathetic figure with hollow voice and disconcerting pallor—qualities shared to a singular degree by the one remaining servant Maria. In the autumn of 1782 Phebe Harris gave birth to a still-born daughter, and on the fifteenth of the next May Mercy Dexter took leave of a useful, austere, and virtuous life.

William Harris, at last thoroughly convinced of the radically unhealthful nature of his abode, now took steps toward quitting and closing it forever. Securing temporary quarters for himself and his wife at the newly opened Golden Ball Inn, he arranged for the building of a new and finer house in Westminster Street, in the growing part of

---

[15] *General Greene*: Nathanael Greene (1742–86) was a Rhode Islander who served as a high-ranking officer in the Continental Army. In 1780 he took command of the Army of the South. His strategy in the Carolinas helped force the British general Cornwalis to Yorktown.

[16] *Colonel Angell*: Israel Angell (1740–1832) was born in Providence and sired seventeen children. At the start of the Revolutionary War he commanded the Rhode Island Volunteers. He participated in the siege of Boston and the battles of Brandywine, Red Bank, and Monmouth.

[17] *Elizabethtown*: The former name of Elizabeth, New Jersey, where in October 1924 Lovecraft saw an old house that reminded him of the Babbit house on Benefit St. in Providence. A few days after visiting Elizabeth, Lovecraft wrote "The Shunned House."

the town across the Great Bridge. There, in 1785, his son
Dutee was born; and there the family dwelt till the en-
croachments of commerce drove them back across the
river and over the hill to Angell Street, in the newer East
Side residence district, where the late Archer Harris built
his sumptuous but hideous French-roofed mansion in
1876. William and Phebe both succumbed to the yellow
fever epidemic of 1797, but Dutee was brought up by his
cousin Rathbone Harris, Peleg's son.

Rathbone was a practical man, and rented the Benefit
Street house despite William's wish to keep it vacant. He
considered it an obligation to his ward to make the most
of all the boy's property, nor did he concern himself with
the deaths and illnesses which caused so many changes of
tenants, or the steadily growing aversion with which the
house was generally regarded. It is likely that he felt only
vexation when, in 1804, the town council ordered him to
fumigate the place with sulphur, tar, and gum camphor
on account of the much-discussed deaths of four persons,
presumably caused by the then diminishing fever epidemic. They said the place had a febrile smell.

Dutee himself thought little of the house, for he grew
up to be a privateersman, and served with distinction on
the *Vigilant* under Capt. Cahoone[18] in the War of 1812.
He returned unharmed, married in 1814, and became a
father on that memorable night of September 23, 1815,
when a great gale[19] drove the waters of the bay over half
the town, and floated a tall sloop well up Westminster
Street so that its masts almost tapped the Harris windows
in symbolic affirmation that the new boy, Welcome, was
a seaman's son.

Welcome did not survive his father, but lived to perish
gloriously at Fredericksburg[20] in 1862. Neither he nor his

---

[18] *Capt. Cahoone*: Lieutenant John C. Cahoone of Rhode Island had command
of the ship *Tartar* in an attack on Louisburg in 1744 during the French-Canadian
Wars. It is thus fitting that a fictional Rhode Island naval captain should bear
this name.

son Archer knew of the shunned house as other than a nuisance almost impossible to rent—perhaps on account of the mustiness and sickly odour of unkept old age. Indeed, it never was rented after a series of deaths culminating in 1861, which the excitement of the war tended to throw into obscurity. Carrington Harris, last of the male line, knew it only as a deserted and somewhat picturesque centre of legend until I told him my experience. He had meant to tear it down and build an apartment house on the site, but after my account decided to let it stand, install plumbing, and rent it. Nor has he yet had any difficulty in obtaining tenants. The horror has gone.

III.

It may well be imagined how powerfully I was affected by the annals of the Harrises. In this continuous record there

---

[19] *great gale*: This was an actual storm. Lovecraft could have learned about it from any of several Rhode Island histories he had in his library, including William R. Staples' *Annals of the Town of Providence, from Its First Settlement, to the Organization of the City Government, in June, 1832* (Providence: Knowles & Vose, 1843). This volume includes extracts from the report that Moses Brown made on the storm in 1818: "The storm of rain commenced on the 22d, from the N. E.; moderate through the day, but at night the wind increased. On the morning of the 23d, the wind blew with increased severity from the east, and about 9 A. M. veered to E. S. E., at 10 or before, to S. E., and from this time to half past 11, the storm was tremendous, and beyond, far beyond, any in the memory of any man living. Before 12, the wind veered to S. W. and greatly abated." . . . "The damage by the extreme violence of the wind, extended to driving from their anchors and fastenings all the vessels, save two or three, that lay in the harbor and at the wharves; some against the bridge with such force as to open a free passage for others to follow to the northern extremity of the cove above the bridge, to the number of between thirty and forty, of various descriptions from five hundred tons, downwards." . . . "A sloop of about sixty tons floated across Weybosset-street and lodged in Pleasant-street, her mast standing above and she by the side of a three story brick house." (pp. 379–80)

[20] *Fredericksburg*: A Confederate victory in the Civil War, fought on December 13, 1862, between Ambrose Burnside's Army of the Potomac and Robert E. Lee's Army of Northern Virginia. The Southerners had the advantage of being positioned on the heights above the town of Fredericksburg, Virginia, from which the Federals made several doomed assaults. Lovecraft sympathized with the South, and once wrote a poem, "On Genl. Robert Edward Lee."

seemed to me to brood a persistent evil beyond anything in Nature as I had known it; an evil clearly connected with the house and not with the family. This impression was confirmed by my uncle's less systematic array of miscellaneous data—legends transcribed from servant gossip, cuttings from the papers, copies of death-certificates by fellow-physicians, and the like. All of this material I cannot hope to give, for my uncle was a tireless antiquarian and very deeply interested in the shunned house; but I may refer to several dominant points which earn notice by their recurrence through many reports from diverse sources. For example, the servant gossip was practically unanimous in attributing to the fungous and malodorous *cellar* of the house a vast supremacy in evil influence. There had been servants—Ann White especially—who would not use the cellar kitchen, and at least three well-defined legends bore upon the queer quasi-human or diabolic outlines assumed by tree-roots and patches of mould in that region. These latter narratives interested me profoundly, on account of what I had seen in my boyhood, but I felt that most of the significance had in each case been largely obscured by additions from the common stock of local ghost lore.

Ann White, with her Exeter superstition, had promulgated the most extravagant and at the same time most consistent tale; alleging that there must lie buried beneath the house one of those vampires—the dead who retain their bodily form and live on the blood or breath of the living—whose hideous legions send their preying shapes or spirits abroad by night. To destroy a vampire one must, the grandmothers say, exhume it and burn its heart, or at least drive a stake through that organ; and Ann's dogged insistence on a search under the cellar had been prominent in bringing about her discharge.

Her tales, however, commanded a wide audience, and were the more readily accepted because the house indeed stood on land once used for burial purposes. To me their interest depended less on this circumstance than on the peculiarly appropriate way in which they dovetailed with certain other things—the complaint of the departing servant Preserved Smith, who had preceded Ann and never heard of her, that something "sucked his breath" at night; the death-certificates of fever victims of 1804, issued by Dr. Chad Hopkins,[21] and shewing the four deceased persons all unaccountably lacking in blood; and the obscure passages of poor Rhoby Harris's ravings, where she complained of the sharp teeth of a glassy-eyed, half-visible presence.

Free from unwarranted superstition though I am, these things produced in me an odd sensation, which was intensified by a pair of widely separated newspaper cuttings relating to deaths in the shunned house—one from the *Providence Gazette and Country-Journal* of April 12, 1815, and the other from the *Daily Transcript and Chronicle* of October 27, 1845—each of which detailed an appallingly grisly circumstance whose duplication was remarkable. It seems that in both instances the dying person, in 1815 a gentle old lady named Stafford and in 1845 a school-teacher of middle age named Eleazar Durfee, became transfigured in a horrible way; glaring glassily and attempting to bite the throat of the attending physician. Even more puzzling, though, was the final case which put an end to the renting of the house—a series of anaemia deaths preceded by progressive madnesses wherein the patient would craftily attempt the lives of his relatives by incisions in the neck or wrist.

This was in 1860 and 1861, when my uncle had just begun his medical practice; and before leaving for the front he heard much of it from his elder professional colleagues. The really inexplicable thing was the way in which the

---

[21] *Dr. Chad Hopkins*: A Thomas Hopkins settled in Providence about 1638. One of his descendants was Stephen Hopkins (1707–85), colonial governor of Rhode Island and signer of the Declaration of Independence.

victims—ignorant people, for the ill-smelling and widely shunned house could now be rented to no others—would babble maledictions in French, a language they could not possibly have studied to any extent. It made one think of poor Rhoby Harris nearly a century before, and so moved my uncle that he commenced collecting historical data on the house after listening, some time subsequent to his return from the war, to the first-hand account of Drs. Chase and Whitmarsh. Indeed, I could see that my uncle had thought deeply on the subject, and that he was glad of my own interest—an open-minded and sympathetic interest which enabled him to discuss with me matters at which others would merely have laughed. His fancy had not gone so far as mine, but he felt that the place was rare in its imaginative potentialities, and worthy of note as an inspiration in the field of the grotesque and macabre.

For my part, I was disposed to take the whole subject with profound seriousness, and began at once not only to review the evidence, but to accumulate as much more as I could. I talked with the elderly Archer Harris, then owner of the house, many times before his death in 1916; and obtained from him and his still surviving maiden sister Alice an authentic corroboration of all the family data my uncle had collected. When, however, I asked them what connexion with France or its language the house could have, the confessed themselves as frankly baffled and ignorant as I. Archer knew nothing, and all that Miss Harris could say was that an old allusion her grandfather, Dutee Harris, had heard of might have shed a little light. The old seaman, who had survived his son Welcome's death in battle by two years, had not himself known the legend; but recalled that his earliest nurse, the ancient Maria Robbins, seemed darkly aware of something that might have lent a weird significance to the French ravings of Rhoby Harris, which she had so often heard during the last days of that hapless woman. Maria had been at the shunned house from 1769 till the removal of the family in 1783, and had seen Mercy Dexter die. Once she hinted to the child Dutee of a somewhat peculiar circumstance in Mercy's last moments, but he had soon forgotten all about it save that it was something peculiar. The granddaughter, moreover, recalled even this much with difficulty. She and her brother were not so much interested in the house as was Archer's son Carrington, the present owner, with whom I talked after my experience.

Having exhausted the Harris family of all the information it could furnish, I turned my attention to early town records and deeds with a zeal more penetrating than that which my uncle had occasionally shewn in the same work. What I wished was a comprehensive history of the site from its very settlement in 1636—or even before, if any Narragansett Indian legend could be unearthed to supply the data. I found, at the start, that the land had been part of the long strip of home lot granted originally to John Throckmorton; one of many similar strips beginning at the Town Street beside the river and extending up over the hill to a line roughly corresponding with the modern Hope Street. The Throckmorton lot had later, of course, been much subdivided; and I became very assiduous in tracing that section through which Back or Benefit Street was later run. It had, a rumour indeed said, been the Throckmorton graveyard; but as I examined the records more carefully, I found that the graves had all been transferred at an early date to the North Burial Ground on the Pawtucket West Road.

Then suddenly I came—by a rare piece of chance, since it was not in the main body of records and might easily have been missed—upon something which aroused my keenest eagerness, fitting in as it did with several of the queerest phases of the affair. It was the record of a lease, in 1697, of a small tract of ground to an Etienne Roulet and wife. At last the French element had appeared—that, and another deeper element of horror which the name conjured up from the darkest recesses of my weird and hetero-

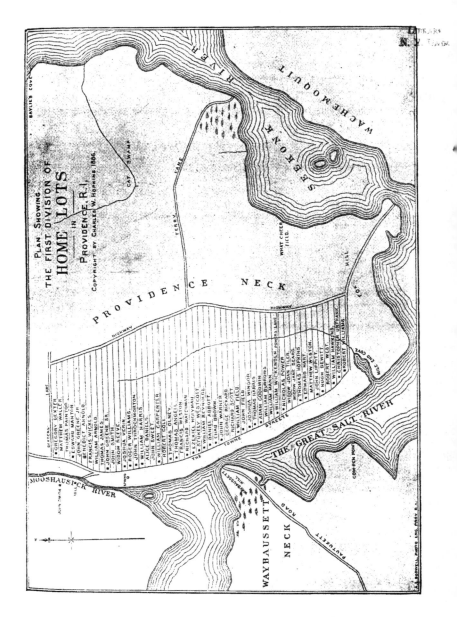

Map of the first settlement of Providence. Taken from Edward Field, ed., *State of Rhode Island and Providence Plantations at the End of the Century: A History* (Boston: Mason Publishing Co., 1902), Vol. 3.

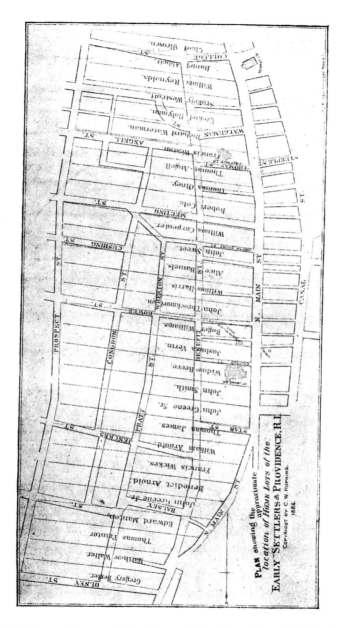

Map of the first settlement of Providence. Taken from Edward Field, ed., *State of Rhode Island and Providence Plantations at the End of the Century: A History* (Boston: Mason Publishing Co., 1902), Vol. 3.

geneous reading—and I feverishly studied the platting of the locality as it had been before the cutting through and partial straightening of Back Street between 1747 and 1758. I found what I had half expected, that where the shunned house now stood the Roulets had laid out their graveyard behind a one-story and attic cottage, and that no record of any transfer of graves existed. The document, indeed, ended in much confusion; and I was forced to ransack both the Rhode Island Historical Society and Shepley Library[22] before I could find a local door which the name Etienne Roulet would unlock. In the end I did find something; something of such vague but monstrous import that I set about at once to examine the cellar of the shunned house itself with a new and excited minuteness.

The Roulets, it seemed, had come in 1696 from East Greenwich, down the west shore of Narragansett Bay. They were Huguenots[23] from Caude, and had encountered much opposition before the Providence selectmen allowed them to settle in the town. Unpopularity had dogged them in East Greenwich, whither they had come in 1686, after the revocation of the Edict of Nantes,[24] and rumour said that the cause of dislike extended beyond mere racial and national prejudice, or the land disputes which involved

---

[22] *Rhode Island Historical Society and Shepley Library*: The Rhode Island Historical Society, founded in 1822, has its headquarters at the John Brown House on Power Street. In the 1930s Lovecraft did genealogical research into his family there. Col. George L. Metcalf organized the Shepley Library in 1921, establishing it in what had previously been a Mormon church. In the fall of 1923, in the company of his aunt Lillian Clark, Lovecraft visited the Shepley Library, which housed a museum "where may be found the greatest of all collections of Rhode-Island relicks and antiquities" (*Selected Letters* I, 268). In 1938 the Shepley Library closed and the collection was sold to the Rhode Island Historical Society.

[23] *Huguenots*: French Protestants, typically skilled artisans and members of the bourgeoisie, who gained certain property and religious rights under the Edict of Nantes in 1598. After the revocation of the Edict of Nantes, they fled France in large numbers, many to America.

[24] *Edict of Nantes*: A decree promulgated by King Henry IV to restore internal peace in France that defined the rights of the Huguenots. As part of a policy to ensure Catholic supremacy, Louis XIV revoked the Edict of Nantes in 1685.

other French settlers with the English in rivalries which
not even Governor Andros[25] could quell. But their ardent
Protestantism—too ardent, some whispered—and their evident distress when virtually driven from the village down
the bay, had moved the sympathy of the town fathers.
Here the strangers had been granted a haven; and the swarthy Etienne Roulet, less apt at agriculture than at reading
queer books and drawing queer diagrams, was given a cler-
ical post in the warehouse at Pardon Tillinghast's wharf,
far south in Town Street. There had, however, been a riot
of some sort later on—perhaps forty years later, after old
Roulet's death—and no one seemed to hear of the family
after that.

For a century and more, it appeared, the Roulets had
been well remembered and frequently discussed as vivid
incidents in the quiet life of a New England seaport.
Etienne's son Paul, a surly fellow whose erratic conduct
had probably provoked the riot which wiped out the family, was particularly a source of speculation; and though
Providence never shared the witchcraft panics of her Puritan neighbours, it was freely intimated by old wives that
his prayers were neither uttered at the proper time nor
directed toward the proper object. All this had undoubtedly formed the basis of the legend known by old Maria
Robbins. What relation it had to the French ravings of
Rhoby Harris and other inhabitants of the shunned house,
imagination or future discovery alone could determine. I
wondered how many of those who had known the legends
realised that additional link with the terrible which my
wide reading had given me; that ominous item in the annals of morbid horror which tells of the creature *Jacques*

---

[25] *Governor Andros*: Sir Edmund Andros (1637–1714) was the colonial governor
of New England at this time. His suppression of charters and colonial assemblies, his interference with local customs and rights, and his overbearing ways
led to his seizure in 1689 by Boston colonials, who sent him and other officials
back to England as prisoners. He was soon released and returned to serve as
governor of Virginia.

Roulet, of Caude,[26] who in 1598 was condemned to death as a daemoniac but afterward saved from the stake by the Paris parliament and shut in a madhouse. He had been found covered with blood and shreds of flesh in a wood, shortly after the killing and rending of a boy by a pair of wolves. One wolf was seen to lope away unhurt. Surely a pretty hearthside tale, with a queer significance as to name and place; but I decided that the Providence gossips could not have generally known of it. Had they known, the coincidence of names would have brought some drastic and frightened action—indeed, might not its limited whispering have precipitated the final riot which erased the Roulets from the town?

I now visited the accursed place with increased frequency; studying the unwholesome vegetation of the garden, examining all the walls of the building, and poring over every inch of the earthen cellar floor. Finally, with Carrington Harris's permission, I fitted a key to the disused door opening from the cellar directly upon Benefit Street, preferring to have a more immediate access to the outside world than the dark stairs, ground floor hall, and front door could give. There, where morbidity lurked most thickly, I searched and poked during long afternoons when the sunlight filtered in through the cobwebbed aboveground windows, and a sense of security glowed from the unlocked door which placed me only a few feet from the placid sidewalk outside. Nothing new rewarded my efforts—only the same depressing mustiness and faint suggestions of noxious odours and nitrous outlines on the floor—and I fancy that many pedestrians must have watched me curiously through the broken panes.

At length, upon a suggestion of my uncle's, I decided to try the spot nocturnally; and one stormy midnight ran the

---

[26] *Jacques Roulet, of Caude*: A real person whom Lovecraft read about in John Fiske's *Myths and Myth-Makers* (1872), a source for his early views on the anthropology of religion.

beams of an electric torch over the mouldy floor with its
uncanny shapes and distorted, half-phosphorescent fungi.
The place had dispirited me curiously that evening, and I
was almost prepared when I saw—or thought I saw—
amidst the whitish deposits a particularly sharp definition
of the "huddled form" I had suspected from boyhood. Its
clearness was astonishing and unprecedented—and as I
watched I seemed to see again the thin, yellowish, shimmering exhalation which had startled me on that rainy
afternoon so many years before.

Above the anthropomorphic patch of mould by the fireplace it rose; a subtle, sickish, almost luminous vapour
which as it hung trembling in the dampness seemed to
develop vague and shocking suggestions of form, gradually
trailing off into nebulous decay and passing up into the
blackness of the great chimney with a foetor in its wake.
It was truly horrible, and the more so to me because of
what I knew of the spot. Refusing to flee, I watched it
fade—and as I watched I felt that it was in turn watching
me greedily with eyes more imaginable than visible. When
I told my uncle about it he was greatly aroused; and after
a tense hour of reflection, arrived at a definite and drastic
decision. Weighing in his mind the importance of the matter, and the significance of our relation to it, he insisted
that we both test—and if possible destroy—the horror of
the house by a joint night or nights of aggressive vigil in
that musty and fungus-cursed cellar.

IV.

On Wednesday, June 25, 1919,[27] after a proper notifica-
tion of Carrington Harris which did not include surmises

---

[27] *June 25, 1919*: Lovecraft's aunt, Mrs. Lillian Clark, was living at 135 Benefit
Street in 1919–20 as a companion to Mrs. H. C. Babbit (so spelled in the 1920
U.S. census).

as to what we expected to find, my uncle and I conveyed to the shunned house two camp chairs and a folding camp cot, together with some scientific mechanism of greater weight and intricacy. These we placed in the cellar during the day, screening the windows with paper and planning to return in the evening for our first vigil. We had locked the door from the cellar to the ground floor; and having a key to the outside cellar door, we were prepared to leave our expensive and delicate apparatus—which we had obtained secretly and at great cost—as many days as our vigils might need to be protracted. It was our design to sit up together till very late, and then watch singly till dawn in two-hour stretches, myself first and then my companion; the inactive member resting on the cot.

The natural leadership with which my uncle procured the instruments from the laboratories of Brown University and the Cranston Street Armoury, and instinctively assumed direction of our venture, was a marvellous commentary on the potential vitality and resilience of a man of eighty-one. Elihu Whipple had lived according to the hygienic laws he had preached as a physician, and but for what happened later would be here in full vigour today. Only two persons suspect what did happen—Carrington Harris and myself. I had to tell Harris because he owned the house and deserved to know what had gone out of it. Then too, we had spoken to him in advance of our quest; and I felt after my uncle's going that he would understand and assist me in some vitally necessary public explanations. He turned very pale, but agreed to help me, and decided that it would now be safe to rent the house.

To declare that we were not nervous on that rainy night of watching would be an exaggeration both gross and ridiculous. We were not, as I have said, in any sense childishly superstitions, but scientific study and reflection had taught us that the known universe of three dimensions embraces the merest fraction of the whole cosmos of substance and energy. In this case an overwhelming prepon-

derance of evidence from numerous authentic sources
pointed to the tenacious existence of certain forces of great
power and, so far as the human point of view is concerned,
exceptional malignancy. To say that we actually believed
in vampires or werewolves would be a carelessly inclusive
statement. Rather must it be said that we were not prepared to deny the possibility of certain unfamiliar and unclassified modifications of vital force and attenuated
matter; existing very infrequently in three-dimensional
space because of its more intimate connexion with other
spatial units, yet close enough to the boundary of our own
to furnish us occasional manifestations which we, for lack
of a proper vantage-point, may never hope to understand.

In short, it seemed to my uncle and me that an incontro-
vertible array of facts pointed to some lingering influence
in the shunned house; traceable to one or another of the
ill-favoured French settlers of two centuries before, and
still operative through rare and unknown laws of atomic
and electronic motion. That the family of Roulet had possessed an abnormal affinity for outer circles of entity—
dark spheres which for normal folk hold only repulsion
and terror—their recorded history seemed to prove. Had
not, then, the riots of those bygone seventeen-thirties set
moving certain kinetic patterns in the morbid brain of one
or more of them—notably the sinister Paul Roulet—which
obscurely survived the bodies murdered and buried by
the mob, and continued to function in some multiple-
dimensioned space along the original lines of force determined by a frantic hatred of the encroaching community?

Such a thing was surely not a physical or biochemical
impossibility in the light of a newer science which includes the theories of relativity and intra-atomic action.[28]
One might easily imagine an alien nucleus of substance

---

[28] *relativity and intra-atomic action*: A reference to Einstein's theories of relativity and possibly quantum physics. See note 77 to *At the Mountains of Madness*
(*Annotated Lovecraft*, 77).

or energy, formless or otherwise, kept alive by impercepti-
ble or immaterial subtractions from the life-force or bodily
tissues and fluids of other and more palpably living things
into which it penetrates and with whose fabric it sometimes completely merges itself. It might be actively hos-
tile, or it might be dictated merely by blind motives of
self-preservation. In any case such a monster must of necessity be in our scheme of things an anomaly and an
intruder, whose extirpation forms a primary duty with
every man not an enemy to the world's life, health, and
sanity.

What baffled us was our utter ignorance of the aspect
in which we might encounter the thing. No sane person
had even seen it, and few had ever felt it definitely. It
might be pure energy—a form ethereal and outside the
realm of substance—or it might be partly material; some
unknown and equivocal mass of plasticity, capable of
changing at will to nebulous approximations of the solid,
liquid, gaseous, or tenuously unparticled states. The anthropomorphic patch of mould on the floor, the form of
the yellowish vapour, and the curvature of the tree-roots[29]
in some of the old tales, all argued at least a remote and
reminiscent connexion with the human shape; but how
representative or permanent that similarity might be,
none could say with any kind of certainty.

We had devised two weapons to fight it; a large and
specially fitted Crookes tube[30] operated by powerful storage batteries and provided with peculiar screens and re-
flectors, in case it proved intangible and opposable only
by vigorously destructive ether radiations, and a pair of

---

[29] *curvature of the tree-roots*: Lovecraft probably had in mind "the apple-tree
root which enter'd Roger Williams' coffin and is said to have follow'd the lines
of the skeleton," on display at the Rhode Island Historical Society (*Selected
Letters* V, 126). Roger Williams was the founder of Rhode Island.

[30] *Crookes tube*: A vacuum tube invented circa 1875 by Sir William Crookes
(1832–1919), an English chemist and physicist, for demonstrating the properties
of cathode rays.

military flame-throwers of the sort used in the world-war,
in case it proved partly material and susceptible of mechanical destruction—for like the superstitious Exeter rustics, we were prepared to burn the thing's heart out if
heart existed to burn. All this aggressive mechanism we
set in the cellar in positions carefully arranged with reference to the cot and chairs, and to the spot before the fireplace where the mould had taken strange shapes. That
suggestive patch, by the way, was only faintly visible
when we placed our furniture and instruments, and when
we returned that evening for the actual vigil. For a moment I half doubted that I had ever seen it in the more
definitely limned form—but then I thought of the legends.

Our cellar vigil began at 10 p.m., daylight saving time,
and as it continued we found no promise of pertinent de-
velopments. A weak, filtered glow from the rain-harassed
street-lamps outside, and a feeble phosphorescence from
the detestable fungi within, shewed the dripping stone of
the walls, from which all traces of whitewash had vanished; the dank, foetid, and mildew-tainted hard earth
floor with its obscene fungi; the rotting remains of what
had been stools, chairs, and tables, and other more shapeless furniture; the heavy planks and massive beams of the
ground floor overhead; the decrepit plank door leading to
bins and chambers beneath other parts of the house; the
crumbling stone staircase with ruined wooden hand-rail;
and the crude and cavernous fireplace of blackened brick
where rusted iron fragments revealed the past presence of
hooks, andirons, spit, crane, and a door to the Dutch
oven—these things, and our austere cot and camp chairs,
and the heavy and intricate destructive machinery we
had brought.

We had, as in my own former explorations, left the door
to the street unlocked; so that a direct and practical path
of escape might lie open in case of manifestations beyond
our power to deal with. It was our idea that our continued
nocturnal presence would call forth whatever malign en-

tity lurked there; and that being prepared, we could dispose of the thing with one or the other of our provided means as soon as we had recognised and observed it sufficiently. How long it might require to evoke and extinguish the thing, we had no notion. It occurred to us, too, that our venture was far from safe; for in what strength the thing might appear no one could tell. But we deemed the game worth the hazard, and embarked on it alone and unhesitatingly; conscious that the seeking of outside aid would only expose us to ridicule and perhaps defeat our entire purpose. Such was our frame of mind as we talked— far into the night, till my uncle's growing drowsiness made me remind him to lie down for his two-hour sleep.

Something like fear chilled me as I sat there in the small hours alone—I say alone, for one who sits by a sleeper is indeed alone; perhaps more alone than he can realise. My uncle breathed heavily, his deep inhalations and exhalations accompanied by the rain outside, and punctuated by another nerve-racking sound of distant dripping water within—for the house was repulsively damp even in dry weather, and in this storm positively swamp-like. I studied the loose, antique masonry of the walls in the fungus-light and the feeble rays which stole in from the street through the screened windows; and once, when the noisome atmosphere of the place seemed about to sicken me, I opened the door and looked up and down the street, feasting my eyes on familiar sights and my nostrils on the wholesome air. Still nothing occurred to reward my watching; and I yawned repeatedly, fatigue getting the better of apprehension.

Then the stirring of my uncle in his sleep attracted my notice. He had turned restlessly on the cot several times during the latter half of the first hour, but now he was breathing with unusual irregularity, occasionally heaving a sigh which held more than a few of the qualities of a choking moan. I turned my electric flashlight on him and found his face averted, so rising and crossing to the other

side of the cot, I again flashed the light to see if he seemed
in any pain. What I saw unnerved me most surprisingly,
considering its relative triviality. It must have been
merely the association of any odd circumstance with the
sinister nature of our location and mission, for surely the
circumstance was not in itself frightful or unnatural. It
was merely that my uncle's facial expression, disturbed
no doubt by the strange dreams which our situation
prompted, betrayed considerable agitation, and seemed not
at all characteristic of him. His habitual expression was
one of kindly and well-bred calm, whereas now a variety
of emotions seemed struggling within him. I think, on the
whole, that it was the *variety* which chiefly disturbed me.
My uncle, as he gasped and tossed in increasing perturba-
tion and with eyes that had now started open, seemed not
one but many men, and suggested a curious quality of
alienage from himself.

All at once he commenced to mutter, and I did not like
the look of his mouth and teeth as he spoke. The words
were at first indistinguishable, and then—with a tremendous start—I recognised something about them which
filled me with icy fear till I recalled the breadth of my
uncle's education and the interminable translations he had
made from anthropological and antiquarian articles in the
Revue des Deux Mondes.[31] For the venerable Elihu Whipple was muttering *in French*, and the few phrases I could
distinguish seemed connected with the darkest myths he
had ever adapted from the famous Paris magazine.

Suddenly a perspiration broke out on the sleeper's forehead, and he leaped abruptly up, half awake. The jumble
of French changed to a cry in English, and the hoarse voice
shouted excitedly, "My breath, my breath!" Then the
awakening became complete, and with a subsidence of facial expression to the normal state my uncle seized my

---

[31] *Revue des Deux Mondes*: A journal founded in 1829 that is today one of the
best-known French literary reviews.

hand and began to relate a dream whose nucleus of significance I could only surmise with a kind of awe.

He had, he said, floated off from a very ordinary series of dream-pictures into a scene whose strangeness was related to nothing he had ever read. It was of this world, and yet not of it—a shadowy geometrical confusion in which could be seen elements of familiar things in most unfamiliar and perturbing combinations. There was a suggestion of queerly disordered pictures superimposed one upon another; an arrangement in which the essentials of time as well as of space seemed dissolved and mixed in the most illogical fashion. In this kaleidoscopic vortex of phantasmal images were occasional snapshots, if one might use the term, of singular clearness but unaccountable heterogeneity.

Once my uncle thought he lay in a carelessly dug open pit, with a crowd of angry faces framed by straggling locks and three-cornered hats[32] frowning down on him. Again he seemed to be in the interior of a house—an old house, apparently—but the details and inhabitants were constantly changing, and he could never be certain of the faces or the furniture, or even of the room itself, since doors and windows seemed in just as great a state of flux as the more presumably mobile objects. It was queer— damnably queer—and my uncle spoke almost sheepishly, as if half expecting not to be believed, when he declared that of the strange faces many had unmistakably borne the features of the Harris family. And all the while there was a personal sensation of choking, as if some pervasive presence had spread itself through his body and sought to possess itself of his vital processes. I shuddered at the

---

[32] *three-cornered hats*: A type of hat, also known as a tricorne hat, fashionable in the late eighteenth century. In his article "Young Man Lovecraft," L. Sprague de Camp says that "Lovecraft once dressed up in colonial costume—or at least a three-cornered hat—and, so clad, had a photograph of himself published in a Providence newspaper." (*Lovecraft Remembered*, 175) As de Camp notes, no one has yet run down and reproduced this photograph.

thought of those vital processes, worn as they were by eighty-one years of continuous functioning, in conflict with unknown forces of which the youngest and strongest system might well be afraid; but in another moment reflected that dreams are only dreams, and that these uncomfortable visions could be, at most, no more than my uncle's reaction to the investigations and expectations which had lately filled our minds to the exclusion of all else.

Conversation, also, soon tended to dispel my sense of strangeness; and in time I yielded to my yawns and took my turn at slumber. My uncle seemed now very wakeful, and welcomed his period of watching even though the nightmare had aroused him far ahead of his allotted two hours. Sleep seized me quickly, and I was at once haunted with drams of the most disturbing kind. I felt, in my visions, a cosmic and abysmal loneness; with hostility surging from all sides upon some prison where I lay confined. I seemed bound and gagged, and taunted by the echoing yells of distant multitudes who thirsted for my blood. My uncle's face came to me with less pleasant associations than in waking hours, and I recall many futile struggles and attempts to scream. It was not a pleasant sleep, and for a second I was not sorry for the echoing shriek which clove through the barriers of dream and flung me to a sharp and startled awakeness in which every actual object before my eyes stood out with more than natural clearness and reality.

V.

I had been lying with my face away from my uncle's chair, so that in this sudden flash of awakening I saw only the door to the street, the more northerly window, and the wall and floor and ceiling toward the north of the room, all photographed with morbid vividness on my brain in a light brighter than the glow of the fungi or the rays from the street outside. It was not a strong or even a fairly strong light; certainly not nearly strong enough to read an average book by. But it cast a shadow of myself and the cot on the floor, and had a yellowish, penetrating force that hinted at things more potent than luminosity. This I perceived with unhealthy sharpness despite the fact that two of my other senses wee violently assailed. For on my ears rang the reverberations of that shocking scream, while my nostrils revolted at the stench which filled the place. My mind, as alert as my senses, recognised the gravely unusual; and almost automatically I leaped up and turned about to grasp the destructive instruments which we had left trained on the mouldy spot before the fire-place. As I turned, I dreaded what I was to see; for the scream had been in my uncle's voice, and I knew not against what menace I should have to defend him and myself.

Yet after all, the sight was worse than I had dreaded. There are horrors beyond horrors, and this was one of those nuclei of all dreamable hideousness which the cosmos saves to blast an accursed and unhappy few. Out of the fungus-ridden earth steamed up a vaporous corpse-light, yellow and diseased, which bubbled and lapped to a gigantic height in vague outlines half-human and half-monstrous, through which I could see the chimney and fireplace beyond. It was all eyes—wolfish and mocking—and the rugose[33] insect-like head dissolved at the top to a thin stream of mist which curled putridly about and finally vanished up the chimney. I say that I saw this thing, but it is only in conscious retrospection that I ever definitely traced its damnable approach to form. At the time it was to me only a seething, dimly phosphorescent cloud of fungous loathsomeness, enveloping and dissolving to an

---

[33] *rugose*: Wrinkled. Lovecraft later described the cone-shaped members of the Great Race as "rugose" in "The Shadow Out of Time."

abhorrent plasticity the one object to which all my attention was focussed. That object was my uncle—the venerable Elihu Whipple—who with blackening and decaying features leered and gibbered at me, and reached out dripping claws to rend me in the fury which this horror had brought.

It was a sense of routine which kept me from going mad. I had drilled myself in preparation for the crucial moment, and blind training saved me. Recognising the bubbling evil as no substance reachable by matter or material chemistry, and therefore ignoring the flame-thrower which loomed on my left, I threw on the current of the Crookes tube apparatus, and focussed toward that scene of immortal blasphemousness the strongest ether radiations which man's art can arouse from the spaces and fluids of Nature. There was a bluish haze and a frenzied sputtering, and the yellowish phosphorescence grew dimmer to my eyes. But I saw the dimness was only that of contrast, and that the waves from the machine had no effect whatever.

Then, in the midst of that daemoniac spectacle, I saw a fresh horror which brought cries to my lips and sent me fumbling and staggering toward that unlocked door to the quiet street, careless of what abnormal terrors I loosed upon the world, or what thoughts or judgments of men I brought down upon my head. In that dim blend of blue and yellow the form of my uncle had commenced a nauseous liquefaction whose essence eludes all description, and in which there played across his vanishing face such changes of identity as only madness can conceive. He was at once a devil and a multitude, a charnel-house and a pageant. Lit by the mixed and uncertain beams, that gelatinous face assumed a dozen—a score—a hundred—aspects; grinning, as it sank to the ground on a body that melted like tallow,[34] in the caricatured likeness of legions strange and yet not strange.

I saw the features of the Harris line, masculine and feminine, adult and infantile, and other features old and young, coarse and refined, familiar and unfamiliar. For a second there flashed a degraded counterfeit of a miniature of poor mad Rhoby Harris that I had seen in the School of Design Museum, and another time I thought I caught the raw-boned image of Mercy Dexter as I recalled her from a painting in Carrington Harris's house. It was frightful beyond conception; toward the last, when a curious blend of servant and baby visages flickered close to the fungous floor where a pool of greenish grease was spreading, it seemed as though the shifting features fought against themselves, and strove to form contours like those of my uncle's kindly face. I like to think that he existed at that moment, and that he tried to bid me farewell. It seems to me I hiccoughed a farewell from my own parched throat as I lurched out into the street; a thin stream of grease following me through the door to the rain-drenched sidewalk.

The rest is shadowy and monstrous. There was no one in the soaking street, and in all the world there was no one I dared tell. I walked aimlessly south past College Hill and the Athenaeum,[35] down Hopkins Street, and over the bridge to the business section where tall buildings seemed to guard me as the modern material things guard the world from ancient and unwholesome wonder. Then grey dawn unfolded wetly from the east, silhouetting the archaic hill and its venerable steeples, and beckoning me to the place where my terrible work was still unfinished. And in the

[34] *melted like tallow*: The image of a body dissolving in corruption is a recurring one in Lovecraft. His most likely sources are Poe's "Facts in the Case of M. Valdemar" and Arthur Machen's "The Novel of the White Powder" from *The Three Impostors*. See note 52 to "The Colour Out of Space." (*Annotated Lovecraft*, 85)

[35] *Athenaeum*: On his Providence visits Poe often stopped at the Athenaeum, "where he us'd to dream and ramble thro' the corridors," according to Lovecraft. (*Selected Letters* I, 292). The Doric-style building is located at 251 Benefit Street, south of the Babbit house. An athenaeum is a club devoted to the pursuit of literary and scientific knowledge. In classical Greek the name means temple of Athena. Athena was the goddess of wisdom.

end I went, wet, hatless, and dazed in the morning light, and entered that awful door in Benefit Street which I had left ajar, and which still swung cryptically in full sight of the early householders to whom I dared not speak.

The grease was gone, for the mouldy floor was porous. And in front of the fireplace was no vestige of the giant doubled-up form in nitre. I looked at the cot, the chairs, the instruments, my neglected hat, and the yellowed straw hat of my uncle. Dazedness was uppermost, and I could scarcely recall what was dream and what was reality. Then thought trickled back, and I knew that I had witnessed things more horrible than I had dreamed. Sitting down, I tried to conjecture as nearly as sanity would let me just what had happened, and how I might end the horror, if indeed it had been real. Matter it seemed not to be, nor ether, nor anything else conceivable by mortal mind. What, then, but some exotic *emanation*; some vampirish vapour such as Exeter rustics tell of as lurking over certain churchyards? This I felt was the clue, and again I looked at the floor before the fireplace where the mould and nitre had taken strange forms. In ten minutes my mind was made up, and taking my hat I set out for home, where I bathed, ate, and gave by telephone an order for a pickaxe, a spade, a military gas-mask, and six carboys[36] of sulphuric acid, all to be delivered the next morning at the cellar door of the shunned house in Benefit Street. After that I tried to sleep; and failing, passed the hours in reading and in the composition of inane verses to counteract my mood.

At 11 a.m. the next day I commenced digging. It was sunny weather, and I was glad of that. I was still alone, for as much as I feared the unknown horror I sought, there was more fear in the thought of telling anybody. Later I told Harris only through sheer necessity, and because he

---

[36] *six carboys*: A carboy is a large cylindrical container for liquids, typically made of glass or metal.

had heard odd tales from old people which disposed him ever so little toward belief. As I turned up the stinking black earth in front of the fireplace, my spade causing a viscous yellow ichor to ooze from the white fungi which it severed, I trembled at the dubious thoughts of what I might uncover. Some secrets of inner earth are not good for mankind, and this seemed to me one of them.

My hand shook perceptibly, but still I delved; after a while standing in the large hole I had made. With the deepening of the hole, which was about six feet square, the evil smell increased; and I lost all doubt of my imminent contact with the hellish thing whose emanations had cursed the house for over a century and a half. I wondered what it would look like—what its form and substance would be, and how big it might have waxed through long ages of life-sucking. At length I climbed out of the hole and dispersed the heaped-up dirt, then arranging the great carboys of acid around and near two sides, so that when necessary I might empty them all down the aperture in quick succession. After that I dumped earth only along the other two sides; working more slowly and donning my gas-mask as the smell grew. I was nearly unnerved at my proximity to a nameless thing at the bottom of a pit.

Suddenly my spade struck something softer than earth. I shuddered, and made a motion as if to climb out of the hole, which was now as deep as my neck. Then courage returned, and I scraped away more dirt in the light of the electric torch I had provided. The surface I uncovered was fishy and glassy—a kind of semi-putrid congealed jelly with suggestions of translucency. I scraped further, and saw that it had form. There was a rift where a part of the substance was folded over. The exposed area was huge and roughly cylindrical; like a mammoth soft blue-white stovepipe doubled in two, its largest part some two feet in diameter. Still more I scraped, and then abruptly I leaped out of the hole and away from the filthy thing; frantically unstopping and tilting the heavy carboys, and precipitating their corrosive contents one after another down that charnel gulf and upon the unthinkable abnormality whose titan *elbow*[37] I had seen.

The blinding maelstrom of greenish-yellow vapour which surged tempestuously up from that hole as the floods of acid descended, will never leave my memory. All along the hill people tell of the yellow day, when virulent and horrible fumes arose from the factory waste dumped in the Providence River, but I know how mistaken they are as to the source. They tell, too, of the hideous roar which at the same time came from some disordered water-pipe or gas main underground—but again I could correct them if I dared. It was unspeakably shocking, and I do not see how I lived through it. I did faint after emptying the fourth carboy, which I had to handle after the fumes had begun to penetrate my mask; but when I recovered I saw that the hold was emitting no fresh vapours.

The two remaining carboys I emptied down without particular result, and after a time I felt it safe to shovel the earth back into the pit. It was twilight before I was done, but fear had gone out of the place. The dampness was less foetid, and all the strange fungi had withered to a kind of harmless greyish powder which blew ash-like along the floor. One of earth's nethermost terrors had perished forever; and if there be a hell, it had received at last the daemon soul of an unhallowed thing. And as I patted down the last spadeful of mould, I shed the first of the many tears with which I have paid unaffected tribute to my beloved uncle's memory.[38]

The next spring no more pale grass and strange weeds came up in the shunned house's terraced garden, and shortly afterward Carrington Harris rented the place. It is still spectral, but its strangeness fascinates me, and I shall

---

[37] *titan elbow*: This "titan *elbow*" is foreshadowed by the "five-headed monster" which turns out to be a giant paw in "Under the Pyramids," the story that Lovecraft ghostwrote for Harry Houdini, the magician and escape artist, a few months before he composed "The Shunned House."

find mixed with my relief a queer regret when it is torn down to make way for a tawdry shop or vulgar apartment building. The barren old trees in the yard have begun to bear small, sweet apples, and last year the birds nested in their gnarled boughs.

---

[38] *my beloved uncle's memory.* The narrator's grief at his granduncle's death may well reflect Lovecraft's feelings at his grandfather's death. At any rate, it is extremely rare for a Lovecraft character to show emotion in the face of ordinary human tragedy. The most notable example appears in "The Rats in the Walls," where Delapore laments the loss of his son: "I bought Exham Priory in 1918, but was almost immediately distracted from my plans of restoration by the return of my son as a maimed invalid. During the two years that he lived I thought of nothing but his care, having even placed my business under the direction of partners." (*Annotated Lovecraft,* 29)

The Horror at Red Hook

"There are sacraments of evil as well as of good about us, and we live and move to my belief in an unknown world, a place where there are caves and shadows and dwellers in twilight. It is possible that man may sometimes return on the track of evolution, and it is my belief that an awful lore is not yet dead."

—Arthur Machen.[1]

"The Horror at Red Hook" was written August 1–2, 1925. It was first published in the January 1927 issue of *Weird Tales*.

[1] *Arthur Machen*: Lovecraft discovered the work of the Welsh writer Arthur Machen (1863–1947) in 1923. A number of references to Machen occur in Lovecraft's fiction from 1925 on, notably in "The Dunwich Horror" (see note 69 in the *Annotated Lovecraft*, 136). Lovecraft considered Machen's "The White People" the second greatest weird tale ever written after Algernon Blackwood's "The Willows." This epigraph comes from Machen's story "The Red Hand."

I.

Not many weeks ago, on a street corner in the village of Pascoag, Rhode Island, a tall, heavily built, and wholesome-looking pedestrian furnished much speculation by a singular lapse of behaviour. He had, it appears, been descending the hill by the road from Chepachet;[2] and encountering the compact section, had turned to his left into the main thoroughfare where several modest business blocks convey a touch of the urban. At this point, without visible provocation, he committed his astonishing lapse; staring queerly for a second at the tallest of the buildings before him, and then, with a series of terrified, hysterical shrieks, breaking into a frantic run which ended in a stumble and fall at the next crossing. Picked up and dusted off by ready hands, he was found to be conscious, organically unhurt, and evidently cured of his sudden nervous attack. He muttered some shamefaced explanations involving a strain he had undergone, and with downcast glance turned back up the Chepachet road, trudging out of sight without once looking behind him. It was a strange incident to befall so large, robust, normal-featured, and capable-looking a man, and the strangeness was not lessened by the remarks of a bystander who had recognised him as the boarder of a well-known dairyman on the outskirts of Chepachet.

He was, it developed, a New York police detective named Thomas F. Malone, now on a long leave of absence under medical treatment after some disproportionately ar-

---

[2] *Pascoag, Rhode Island . . . Chepachet*: Lovecraft visited Chepachet and Pascoag in the northwestern corner of Rhode Island in September 1923. He described Chepachet as "a veritable bucolic poem—a study in ancient New-England village atmosphere, with its deep, grass-bordered gorge, its venerable bridge, and its picturesque, centuried houses." (*Selected Letters* I, 251) He found Pascoag equally charming.

The Horror at Red Hook 125

duous work on a gruesome local case which accident had
made dramatic. There had been a collapse of several old
brick buildings during a raid in which he had shared, and
something about the wholesale loss of life, both of prisoners and of his companions, had peculiarly appalled him. As
a result, he had acquired an acute and anomalous horror of
any buildings[3] even remotely suggesting the ones which
had fallen in, so that in the end mental specialists forbade
him the sight of such things for an indefinite period. A
police surgeon with relatives in Chepachet had put forward that quaint hamlet of wooden colonial houses as an
ideal spot for the psychological convalescence; and thither
the sufferer had gone, promising never to venture among
the brick-lined streets of larger villages till duly advised
by the Woonsocket specialist with whom he was put in
touch. This walk to Pascoag for magazines had been a
mistake, and the patient had paid in fright, bruises, and
humiliation for his disobedience.

So much the gossips of Chepachet and Pascoag knew;
and so much, also, the most learned specialists believed.
But Malone had at first told the specialists much more,
ceasing only when he saw that utter incredulity was his
portion. Thereafter he held his peace, protesting not at all
when it was generally agreed that the collapse of certain
squalid brick houses in the Red Hook section of Brooklyn,[4]
and the consequent death of many brave officers, had un-
seated his nervous equilibrium. He had worked too hard,
all said, in trying to clean up those nests of disorder and
violence; certain features were shocking enough, in all

---

[3] *acute and anomalous horror of any buildings*: In "Pickman's Model" the narrator suffers from an analogous subway phobia. Likewise the narrator of "Cool
Air" fears a cool draught of air.

[4] *Red Hook section of Brooklyn*: Settled in 1636, Red Hook became one of the
busiest shipping centers in the United States in the nineteenth century. Al Ca-
pone made his start as a petty criminal in Red Hook before moving to Chicago.
At the time Lovecraft was living in Brooklyn, Italian dockworkers dominated
the neighborhood, but there were also many Middle Easterners. Today Red Hook
is largely inhabited by blacks and Latinos.

169 Clinton Street, Lovecraft's address in Brooklyn (photo by Steven J. Mariconda).

conscience, and the unexpected tragedy was the last straw. This was a simple explanation which everyone could understand, and because Malone was not a simple person he perceived that he had better let it suffice. To hint to unimaginative people of a horror beyond all human conception—a horror of houses and blocks and cities leprous and cancerous with evil dragged from elder worlds—would be merely to invite a padded cell instead of restful rustication, and Malone was a man of sense despite his mysticism. He had the Celt's far vision of weird and hidden things, but the logician's quick eye for the outwardly unconvincing; an amalgam which had led him far afield in the forty-two years of his life, and set him in strange places for a Dublin University[5] man born in a Georgian villa near Phoenix Park.

And now, as he reviewed the things he had seen and felt and apprehended, Malone was content to keep unshared the secret of what could reduce a dauntless fighter to a quivering neurotic; what could make old brick slums and seas of dark, subtle faces a thing of nightmare and eldritch portent. It would not be the first time his sensations had been forced to bide uninterpreted—for was not his very act of plunging into the polyglot abyss of New York's underworld a freak beyond sensible explanation? What could he tell the prosaic of the antique witcheries and grotesque marvels discernible to sensitive eyes amidst the poison cauldron where all the varied dregs of unwholesome ages mix the venom and perpetuate their obscene terrors? He had seen the hellish green flame of secret wonder in this blatant, evasive welter of outward greed and inward blasphemy, and had smiled gently when all the New-Yorkers he knew scoffed at his experiment in police work. They had been very witty and cynical, deriding his fantastic pursuit of unknowable mysteries and assuring him that in these days New York held nothing but cheapness and vulgarity. One of them had wagered him a heavy sum that he could not—despite many poignant

---

[5] *Dublin University*: Also known as Trinity College, Dublin. It was founded in 1591 by Queen Elizabeth I. By making Thomas Malone an educated gentleman, Lovecraft appears to be deliberately avoiding the stereotypical Irish policeman.

things to his credit in the *Dublin Review*[6]—even write a truly interesting story of New York low life; and now, looking back, he perceived that cosmic irony had justified the prophet's words while secretly confuting their flippant meaning. The horror, as glimpsed at last, could not make a story—for like the book cited by Poe's German authority,[7] *"es lässt sich nicht lesen*—it does not permit itself to be read."

II.

To Malone the sense of latent mystery in existence was always present. In youth he had felt the hidden beauty and ecstasy of things, and had been a poet; but poverty and sorrow and exile had turned his gaze in darker directions, and he had thrilled at the imputations of evil in the world around. Daily life had for him come to be a phantasmagoria of macabre shadow-studies; now glittering and leering with concealed rottenness as in Beardsley's best manner,[8] now hinting terrors behind the commonest shapes and objects as in the subtler and less obvious work of Gustave Doré.[9] He would often regard it as merciful that most persons of high intelligence jeer at the inmost

---

[6] *Dublin Review*: A fictional periodical. Lovecraft may have had in mind *The Dublin Magazine* (1923–58), the major Irish literary journal of its day.

[7] *Poe's German authority*: A quotation that appears in Poe's story "The Man of the Crowd." This reinforces the idea that the horror is incomprehensible.

[8] *Beardsley's best manner*: Aubrey Beardsley (1872–98), the foremost English illustrator of the 1890s, exemplified the aesthetic movement in Englist art. He did the frontispiece for Arthur Machen's *The Great God Pan and the Inmost Light* (1894).

[9] *Gustave Doré*: Gustave Doré (1832–83), the French illustrator and painter, excelled in weird or fantastic scenes. As a child Lovecraft dreamed of creatures he called "night-gaunts," which later surfaced in his short novel *The Dream-Quest of Unknown Kadath*. In a 1916 letter he said: "perhaps the idea for these figures came from an edition de luxe of *Paradise Lost* with illustrations by Doré" (*Selected Letters* I, 35).

mysteries; for, he argued, if superior minds were ever placed in fullest contact with the secrets preserved by ancient and lowly cults, the resultant abnormalities would soon not only wreck the world, but threaten the very integrity of the universe. All this reflection was no doubt morbid, but keen logic and a deep sense of humour ably offset it. Malone was satisfied to let his notions remain as half-spied and forbidden visions to be lightly played with; and hysteria came only when duty flung him into a hell of revelation too sudden and insidious to escape.

He had for some time been detailed to the Butler Street station in Brooklyn when the Red Hook matter came to his notice. Red Hook is a maze of hybrid squalor near the ancient waterfront opposite Governors Island,[10] with dirty highways climbing the hill from wharves to that higher ground where the decayed lengths of Clinton and Court Streets lead off toward the Borough Hall.[11] Its houses are mostly of brick, dating from the first quarter to the middle of the nineteenth century, and some of the obscurer alleys and byways have that alluring antique flavour which conventional reading leads us to call "Dickensian."[12] The population is a hopeless tangle and enigma; Syrian, Spanish, Italian, and negro elements impinging upon one another, and fragments of Scandinavian and American belts lying not far distant. It is a babel of sound and filth, and sends out strange cries to answer the lapping of oily waves at its grimy piers and the monstrous organ litanies of the harbour whistles. Here long ago a brighter picture dwelt, with clear-eyed mariners on the lower streets and homes

---

[10] *Governors Island*: An island off the southern tip of Manhattan, bought by the Dutch from the Indians in 1637. It received its present name when the British set it aside as the colonial governors' residence in 1698.

[11] *Borough Hall*: Brooklyn's equivalent of city hall, which would have been a familiar landmark to Lovecraft when he was living at 169 Clinton Street.

[12] *"Dickensian"*: Characteristic of Charles Dickens (1812–70), the great Victorian author whose sentimentality was anathema to Lovecraft. "Chas. Dickens I cannot bear," he wrote in 1918 (*Selected Letters* I, 73).

of taste and substance where the larger houses line the
hill. One can trace the relics of this former happiness in
the trim shapes of the buildings, the occasional graceful
churches, and the evidences of original art and background
in bits of detail here and there—a worn flight of steps, a
battered doorway, a wormy pair of decorative columns or
pilasters, or a fragment of once green space with bent and
rusted iron railing. The houses are generally in solid
blocks, and now and then a many-windowed cupola[13]
arises to tell of days when the households of captains and
ship-owners watched the sea.

From this tangle of material and spiritual putrescence
the blasphemies of an hundred dialects assail the sky.
Hordes of prowlers reel shouting and singing along the
lanes and thoroughfares, occasional furtive hands suddenly
extinguish lights and pull down curtains, and swarthy, sin-
pitted faces disappear from windows when visitors pick
their way through. Policemen despair of order or reform,
and seek rather to erect barriers protecting the outside
world from the contagion. The clang of the patrol is answered by a kind of spectral silence, and such prisoners
as are taken are never communicative. Visible offences are
as varied as the local dialects, and run the gamut from the
smuggling of rum and prohibited aliens through diverse
stages of lawlessness and obscure vice to murder and mu-
tilation in their most abhorrent guises. That these visible
affairs are not more frequent is not to the neighbourhood's
credit, unless the power of concealment be an art demanding credit. More people enter Red Hook than leave
it—or at least, than leave it by the landward side—and
those who are not loquacious are the likeliest to leave.

Malone found in this state of things a faint stench of
secrets more terrible than any of the sins denounced by
citizens and bemoaned by priests and philanthropists. He
was conscious, as one who united imagination with scien-

---

[13] *cupola*: A small architectural feature built on top of a roof.

tific knowledge, that modern people under lawless conditions tend uncannily to repeat the darkest instinctive patterns of primitive half-ape savagery in their daily life and ritual observances; and he had often viewed with an anthropologist's shudder the chanting, cursing processions of blear-eyed and pockmarked young men which wound their way along in the dark small hours of morning. One saw groups of these youths incessantly; sometimes in leering vigils on street corners, sometimes in doorways playing eerily on cheap instruments of music, sometimes in stupefied dozes or indecent dialogues around cafeteria tables near Borough Hall, and sometimes in whispering converse around dingy taxicabs drawn up at the high stoops of crumbling and closely shuttered old houses. They chilled and fascinated him more than he dared confess to his associates on the force, for he seemed to see in them some monstrous thread of secret continuity; some fiendish, cryptical, and ancient pattern utterly beyond and below the sordid mass of facts and habits and haunts listed with such conscientious technical care by the police. They must be, he felt inwardly, the heirs of some shocking and primordial tradition; the sharers of debased and broken scraps from cults and ceremonies older than mankind. Their coherence and definiteness suggested it, and it shewed in the singular suspicion of order which lurked beneath their squalid disorder. He had not read in vain such treatises as Miss Murray's *Witch-Cult in Western Europe*;[14] and knew that up to recent years there had certainly survived among peasants and furtive folk a frightful and clandestine system of assemblies and orgies descended from dark religions antedating the Aryan world, and ap-

---

[14] *Miss Murray's Witch-Cult in Western Europe*: This landmark work of anthropology by Margaret A. Murray, published in 1921, made the claim that the witch-cult in both Europe and America had its origin in a pre-Aryan race that was driven underground but continued to lurk in the hidden corners of the earth. Now regarded by modern scholars as highly unlikely, this bizarre theory appealed to Lovecraft, who thought Arthur Machen had put a similar idea of a primitive race's survival to effective use in his fiction.

pearing in popular legends as Black Masses and Witches'
Sabbaths. That these hellish vestiges of old Turanian-
Asiatic magic[15] and fertility-cults were even now wholly
dead he could not for a moment suppose, and he frequently wondered how much older and how much blacker
than the very worst of the muttered tales some of them
might really be.

III.

It was the case of Robert Suydam[16] which took Malone
to the heart of things in Red Hook. Suydam was a lettered
recluse of ancient Dutch family, possessed originally of
barely independent means, and inhabiting the spacious but
ill-preserved mansion which his grandfather had built in
Flatbush[17] when the village was little more than a pleasant
group of colonial cottages surrounding the steepled and
ivy-clad Reformed Church with its iron-railed yard of
Netherlandish gravestones.[18] In his lonely house, set back
from Martense Street[19] amidst a yard of venerable trees,
Suydam had read and brooded for some six decades except
for a period a generation before, when he had sailed for
the old world and remained there out of sight for eight
years. He could afford no servants, and would admit but

[15] *Turanian-Asiatic magic*: Turan is a sparsely populated desert region in west
Turkistan in Central Asia. One of Arthur Machen's sketches in *Ornaments in
Jade* (1924) is called "The Turanians."

[16] *Robert Suydam*: Suydam is an old Dutch New York name. There is a Suydam
Street in Brooklyn.

[17] *Flatbush*: Settled in 1652, Flatbush was one of the six original towns that
made up Brooklyn. Before they separated at the end of 1924, Lovecraft and his
wife Sonia lived in Flatbush, at 259 Parkside Avenue.

[18] *Netherlandish gravestones*: This is the same church that was an inspiration
for "The Hound."

[19] *Martense Street*: Martense is another old Dutch New York name. The villain
in Lovecraft's tale "The Lurking Fear" is named Jan Martense.

259 Parkside, Sonia's address in Brooklyn (photo by Steven J. Mariconda).

few visitors to his absolute solitude; eschewing close friendships and receiving his rare acquaintances in one of the three ground-floor rooms which he kept in order—a vast, high-ceiled library whose walls were solidly packed with tattered books of ponderous, archaic, and vaguely repellent aspect. The growth of the town and its final ab-

sorption in the Brooklyn district had meant nothing to
Suydam, and he had come to mean less and less to the
town. Elderly people still pointed him out on the streets,
but to most of the recent population he was merely a
queer, corpulent old fellow whose unkempt white hair,
stubbly beard, shiny black clothes, and gold-headed cane
earned him an amused glance and nothing more. Malone
did not know him by sight till duty called him to the
case, but had heard of him indirectly as a really profound
authority on mediaeval superstition, and had once idly
meant to look up an out-of-print pamphlet of his on the
Kabbalah[20] and the Faustus legend,[21] which a friend had
quoted from memory.

Suydam became a "case" when his distant and only relatives sought court pronouncements on his sanity. Their
action seemed sudden to the outside world, but was really
undertaken only after prolonged observation and sorrowful
debate. It was based on certain odd changes in his speech
and habits; wild references to impending wonders, and unaccountable hauntings of disreputable Brooklyn neigh-
bourhoods. He had been growing shabbier and shabbier
with the years, and now prowled about like a veritable
mendicant; seen occasionally by humiliated friends in subway stations, or loitering on the benches around Borough
Hall in conversation with groups of swarthy, evil-looking
strangers. When he spoke it was to babble of unlimited
powers almost within his grasp, and to repeat with knowing leers such mystical words or names as "Sephiroth",
"Ashmodai", and "Samael".[22] The court action revealed
that he was using up his income and wasting his principal

---

[20] *Kabbalah*: A medieval and modern system of Jewish theosophy and mysticism, marked by belief in creation through emanation and a cipher method of
interpreting Scripture.

[21] *Faustus legend*: In this legend a sixteenth-century German doctor, Johann
Faust, sells his soul to the devil in exchange for youth, knowledge, and magical
power. The villainous Joseph Curwen exemplifies this theme in *The Case of
Charles Dexter Ward*.

in the purchase of curious tomes imported from London and Paris, and in the maintenance of a squalid basement flat in the Red Hook district where he spent nearly every night, receiving odd delegations of mixed rowdies and foreigners, and apparently conducting some kind of ceremonial service behind the green blinds of secretive windows. Detectives assigned to follow him reported strange cries and chants and prancing of feet filtering out from these nocturnal rites, and shuddered at their peculiar ecstasy and abandon despite the commonness of weird orgies in that sodden section. When, however, the matter came to a hearing, Suydam managed to preserve his liberty. Before the judge his manner grew urbane and reasonable, and he freely admitted the queerness of demeanour and extravagant cast of language into which he had fallen through excessive devotion to study and research. He was, he said, engaged in the investigation of certain details of European tradition which required the closest contact with foreign groups and their songs and folk dances. The notion that any low secret society was preying upon him, as hinted by his relatives, was obviously absurd; and shewed how sadly limited was their understanding of him and his work. Triumphing with his calm explanations, he was suffered to depart unhindered; and the paid detectives of the Suydams, Corlears, and Van Brunts[23] were withdrawn in resigned disgust.

It was here that an alliance of Federal inspectors and police, Malone with them, entered the case. The law had

---

[22] *"Sephiroth", "Ashmodai", and "Samael"*: In the philosophy of the Kabbalah, Sephiroth is the ten hypostatized attributes by means of which the Infinite enters into relation with the finite. Ashmodai, a form of Ashmodeus, is an evil spirit in Jewish demonology, while the Persian form of the word means a demon of lust. In rabbinical tradition, Samael is the incarnation of Leviathan, the demon seducer of Eve.

[23] *Suydams, Corlears, and Van Brunts*: More old Dutch names associated with the founding of New Amsterdam. Corlear's Hook was a former neighborhood on Manhattan's Lower East Side. Rutgert Joesten Van Brunt (d. before 1713) was an important landowner and political leader.

watched the Suydam action with interest, and had in
many instances been called upon to aid the private detectives. In this work it developed that Suydam's new associates were among the blackest and most vicious criminals
of Red Hook's devious lanes, and that at least a third of
them were known and repeated offenders in the matter of
thievery, disorder, and the importation of illegal immigrants. Indeed, it would not have been too much to say
that the old scholar's particular circle coincided almost
perfectly with the worst of the organised cliques which
smuggled ashore certain nameless and unclassified Asian
dregs wisely turned back by Ellis Island.[24] In the teeming
rookeries of Parker Place—since renamed—where Suydam
had his basement flat, there had grown up a very unusual
colony of unclassified slant-eyed folk who used the Arabic
alphabet but were eloquently repudiated by the great mass
of Syrians in and around Atlantic Avenue. They could all
have been deported for lack of credentials, but legalism is
slow-moving, and one does not disturb Red Hook unless
publicity forces one to.

These creatures attended a tumbledown stone church,[25]
used Wednesdays as a dance-hall, which reared its Gothic
buttresses near the vilest part of the waterfront. It was
nominally Catholic; but priests throughout Brooklyn denied the place all standing and authenticity, and policemen agreed with them when they listened to the noises
it emitted at night. Malone used to fancy he heard terrible
cracked bass notes from a hidden organ far underground
when the church stood empty and unlighted, whilst all
observers dreaded the shrieking and drumming which accompanied the visible services. Suydam, when questioned,

---

[24] *Ellis Island*: Between 1892 and 1943 this island in New York harbor served
as the chief immigration port for the United States. Its buildings now house an
immigration museum.

[25] *tumbledown stone church*: This church, now demolished, was actually used
as a dance-hall.

The "dance-hall" church in Red Hook (now destroyed) (photo by Steven J. Mariconda).

said he thought the ritual was some remnant of Nestorian Christianity[26] tinctured with the Shamanism of Thibet.[27] Most of the people, he conjectured, were of Mongoloid stock, originating somewhere in or near Kurdistan—and Malone could not help recalling that Kurdistan is the land

of Yezidis,[28] last survivors of the Persian devil-worshippers.
However this may have been, the stir of the Suydam investigation made it certain that these unauthorised newcomers were flooding Red Hook in increasing numbers;
entering through some marine conspiracy unreached by
revenue officers and harbour police, overrunning Parker
Place and rapidly spreading up the hill, and welcomed
with curious fraternalism by the other assorted denizens
of the region. Their squat figures and characteristic squinting physiognomies, grotesquely combined with flashy
American clothing, appeared more and more numerously
among the loafers and nomad gangsters of the Borough
Hall section; till at length it was deemed necessary to
compute their numbers, ascertain their sources and occupations, and find if possible a way to round them up and
deliver them to the proper immigration authorities. To
this task Malone was assigned by agreement of Federal
and city forces, and as he commenced his canvass of Red
Hook he felt poised upon the brink of nameless terrors,
with the shabby, unkempt figure of Robert Suydam as
arch-fiend and adversary.

IV.

Police methods are varied and ingenious. Malone, through
unostentatious rambles, carefully casual conversations,
well-timed offers of hip-pocket liquor, and judicious dialogues with frightened prisoners, learned many isolated

---

[26] *Nestorian Christianity*: A branch of Christianity based on the teachings of an
abbot of Antioch, Nestorius (d. 451?), who opposed the title of Mother of God
for the Virgin on the grounds that Mary bore Jesus as a man, among other
heresies. Nestorian communities exist today in Iran, Iraq, and India.

[27] *Shamanism of Thibet*: Among tribal peoples, a shaman is a magician, medium,
or healer, with a mystic connection to the spirit world.

[28] *Yezidis*: Natives of the old city of Yazd or Yezd in central Iran. It was an
important Zoroastrian center in Sassanid times.

facts about the movement whose aspect had become so menacing. The newcomers were indeed Kurds, but of a dialect obscure and puzzling to exact philology. Such of them as worked lived mostly as dock-hands and unlicenced pedlars, though frequently serving in Greek restaurants and tending corner news stands. Most of them, however, had no visible means of support; and were obviously connected with underworld pursuits, of which smuggling and "bootlegging"[29] were the least indescribable. They had come in steamships, apparently tramp freighters, and had been unloaded by stealth on moonless nights in rowboats which stole under a certain wharf and followed a hidden canal to a secret subterranean pool beneath a house. This wharf, canal, and house Malone could not locate, for the memories of his informants were exceedingly confused, while their speech was to a great extent beyond even the ablest interpreters; nor could he gain any real data on the reasons for their systematic importation. They were reticent about the exact spot from which they had come, and were never sufficiently off guard to reveal the agencies which had sought them out and directed their course. Indeed, they developed something like acute fright when asked the reasons for their presence. Gangsters of other breeds were equally taciturn, and the most that could be gathered was that some god or great priesthood had promised them unheard-of powers and supernatural glories and rulerships in a strange land.

The attendance of both newcomers and old gangsters at Suydam's closely guarded nocturnal meetings was very regular, and the police soon learned that the erstwhile recluse had leased additional flats to accommodate such guests as knew his password; at last occupying three entire houses and permanently harbouring many of his queer

---

[29] "bootlegging": New York was a major port for rumrunning during Prohibition. During this lawless period Police Commissioner Grover Whalen estimated there were 32,000 speakeasies in New York City. For Lovecraft's attitude toward Prohibition, see note 119 to "The Dunwich Horror" (Annotated Lovecraft, 159).

companions. He spent but little time now at his Flatbush home, apparently going and coming only to obtain and return books; and his face and manner had attained an appalling pitch of wildness. Malone twice interviewed him, but was each time brusquely repulsed. He knew nothing, he said, of any mysterious plots or movements; and had no idea how the Kurds could have entered or what they wanted. His business was to study undisturbed the folklore of all the immigrants of the district; a business with which policemen had no legitimate concern. Malone mentioned his admiration for Suydam's old brochure on the Kabbalah and other myths, but the old man's softening was only momentary. He sensed an intrusion, and rebuffed his visitor in no uncertain way; till Malone withdrew disgusted, and turned to other channels of information.

What Malone would have unearthed could he have worked continuously on the case, we shall never know. As it was, a stupid conflict between city and Federal authority suspended the investigations for several months, during which the detective was busy with other assignments. But at no time did he lose interest, or fail to stand amazed at what began to happen to Robert Suydam. Just at the time when a wave of kidnappings and disappearances spread its excitement over New York, the unkempt scholar embarked upon a metamorphosis as startling as it was absurd. One day he was seen near Borough Hall with clean-shaved face, well-trimmed hair, and tastefully immaculate attire, and on every day thereafter some obscure improvement was noticed in him. He maintained his new fastidiousness without interruption, added to it an unwonted sparkle of eye and crispness of speech, and began little by little to shed the corpulence which had so long deformed him. Now frequently taken for less than his age, he acquired an elasticity of step and buoyancy of demeanour to match the new tradition, and shewed a curious darkening of the hair which somehow did not suggest dye. As the months passed, he commenced to dress less and less conservatively, and finally astonished his new friends by renovating and redecorating his Flatbush mansion, which he threw open in a series of receptions, summoning all the acquaintances he could remember, and extending a special welcome to the fully forgiven relatives who had so lately sought his restraint. Some attended through curiosity, others through duty; but all were suddenly charmed by the dawning grace and urbanity of the former hermit. He had, he asserted, accomplished most of his allotted work; and having just inherited some property from a half-forgotten European friend, was about to spend his remaining years in a brighter second youth which ease, care, and diet had made possible to him. Less and less was he seen at Red Hook, and more and more did he move in the society to which he was born. Policemen noted a tendency of the gangsters to congregate at the old stone church and dance-hall instead of at the basement flat in Parker Place, though the latter and its recent annexes still overflowed with noxious life.

Then two incidents occurred—wide enough apart, but both of intense interest in the case as Malone envisaged it. One was a quiet announcement in the *Eagle*[30] of Robert Suydam's engagement to Miss Cornelia Gerritsen[31] of Bayside, a young woman of excellent position, and distantly related to the elderly bridegroom-elect; whilst the other was a raid on the dance-hall church by city police, after a report that the face of a kidnapped child had been seen for a second at one of the basement windows. Malone had participated in this raid, and studied the place with much care when inside. Nothing was found—in fact, the building was entirely deserted when visited—but the sensitive

---

[30] *Eagle*: Founded in 1841 as an organ for the Democratic Party, the *Brooklyn Eagle* evolved into the largest daily and Sunday newspaper in Brooklyn. It ceased publication in 1955.

[31] *Gerritsen*: Wolfert Gerritsen, an early seventeenth-century settler of Brooklyn, built a house and mill on Gerritsen Creek, now part of Marine Park.

Celt was vaguely disturbed by many things about the interior. There were crudely painted panels he did not like—panels which depicted sacred faces with peculiarly worldly and sardonic expressions, and which occasionally took liberties that even a layman's sense of decorum could scarcely countenance. Then, too, he did not relish the Greek inscription on the wall above the pulpit; an ancient incantation which he had once stumbled upon in Dublin college days, and which read, literally translated,

> "O friend and companion of night, thou who rejoicest in the baying of dogs and spilt blood, who wanderest in the midst of shades among the tombs, who longest for blood and bringest terror to mortals, Gorgo, Mormo,[32] thousand-faced moon, look favourably on our sacrifices!"

When he read this he shuddered, and thought vaguely of the cracked bass organ notes he fancied he had heard beneath the church on certain nights. He shuddered again at the rust around the rim of a metal basin which stood on the altar, and paused nervously when his nostrils seemed to detect a curious and ghastly stench from somewhere in the neighbourhood. That organ memory haunted him, and he explored the basement with particular assiduity before he left. The place was very hateful to him; yet after all, were the blasphemous panels and inscriptions more than mere crudities perpetrated by the ignorant?

By the time of Suydam's wedding the kidnapping epidemic had become a popular newspaper scandal. Most of the victims were young children of the lowest classes, but the increasing number of disappearances had worked up a sentiment of the strongest fury. Journals clamoured for

---

[32] *Gorgo, Mormo*: Gorgo may be a variation on Gorgon, the snake-haired female monster that could turn men to stone. Mormo is a ghastly ghoul who served as an emissary of Hecate.

action from the police, and once more the Butler Street station sent its men over Red Hook for clues, discoveries, and criminals. Malone was glad to be on the trail again, and took pride in a raid on one of Suydam's Parker Place houses. There, indeed, no stolen child was found, despite the tales of screams and the red sash picked up in the areaway; but the paintings and rough inscriptions on the peeling walls of most of the rooms, and the primitive chemical laboratory in the attic, all helped to convince the detective that he was on the track of something tremendous. The paintings were appalling—hideous monsters of every shape and size, and parodies on human outlines which cannot be described. The writing was in red, and varied from Arabic to Greek, Roman, and Hebrew letters. Malone could not read much of it, but what he did decipher was portentous and cabbalistic enough. One frequently repeated motto was in a sort of Hebraised Hellenistic Greek, and suggested the most terrible daemon-evocations of the Alexandrian decadence:

"HEL * HELOYM * SOTHER * EMMANVEL * SA-
BAOTH   *   AGLA   *   TETRAGRAMMATON   *
AGYROS   *   OTHEOS   *   ISCHYROS   *   ATHA-
NATOS * IEHOVA * VA * ADONAI * SADAY *
HOMOVSION * MESSIAS * ESCHEREHEYE."[33]

Circles and pentagrams loomed on every hand, and told indubitably of the strange beliefs and aspirations of those who dwelt so squalidly here. In the cellar, however, the strangest thing was found—a pile of genuine gold ingots covered carelessly with a piece of burlap, and bearing upon their shining surfaces the same weird hieroglyphics which also adorned the walls. During the raid the police encountered only a passive resistance from the squinting Orientals that swarmed from every door. Finding nothing relevant, they had to leave all as it was; but the precinct captain wrote Suydam a note advising him to look closely to the character of his tenants and protégés in view of the growing public clamour.

V.

Then came the June wedding and the great sensation. Flatbush was gay for the hour about high noon, and pennanted motors thronged the streets near the old Dutch church where an awning stretched from door to highway. No local event ever surpassed the Suydam-Gerritsen nuptials in tone and scale, and the party which escorted bride and groom to the Cunard Pier[34] was, if not exactly the smart-

---

[33] *ESCHEREHEYE*: Lovecraft may have copied this incantation from the article on "Magic" in the 9th edition of the *Encyclopaedia Britannica*, which he owned. In an undated letter, reproduced as an article with the title "The Incantation from Red Hook" in *The Occult Lovecraft* (Saddle River, N.J.: Gerry de la Ree, 1975), he explains the background: "About that incantation from 'Red Hook'— it is actually a relic of ancient rituals, and is mentioned in more than one history of magic, so that I can hardly sign it in such a way as to indicate authorship. I don't wonder that a Latin teacher was stumped by that Herbraised-Hellenistic incantation . . . , for it is a piece of late-ancient or medieval illiteracy which probably has no straightforward or syntactical sense anyway! E. B. Tylor, the well-known anthropologist, calls it 'an illustration of magical scholarship in its lowest stage.' When I wrote 'Red Hook' in 1925 I thought this formula was Alexandrian in origin, but later reading makes me inclined to place it in the Middle Ages. It was first used, no doubt, by Jewish Cabalists, and later adopted by European magicians generally. I am no scholar—knowing sadly little Greek and no Hebrew at all—hence can't pretend to give a real translation. I merely took it as I found it in a history of magic (where there was no attempt to translate this or any other formula) and tried to get as good a notion as I could of the principle words—recalling my meagre and long-ago Greek course and relying on Dr. William Smith's Bible dictionary for Hebraic lore. The result was something like:

'O Lord God Deliverer; Lord-Messenger of Hosts: Thou-art-a-mighty god-forever; Magically fourfold assemblage; And anointed one, together and in succession!'

But I don't fancy this is accurate; for as I said, I am no savant and the incantation is a decadent ungrammatical and misspelled piece of crudeness which would baffle even the wisest." (pp. 23–24) Lovecraft goes on to translate the individual words in the incantation, not always accurately.

[34] *Cunard Pier*: Sir Samuel Cunard (1787–1865), a Canadian, established the first regular trans-Atlantic steamship service. This was the start of the noted Cunard Line.

est, at least a solid page from the Social Register.[35] At five o'clock adieux were waved, and the ponderous liner edged away from the long pier, slowly turned its nose seaward, discarded its tug, and headed for the widening water spaces that led to old world wonders. By night the outer harbour was cleared, and late passengers watched the stars twinkling above an unpolluted ocean.

Whether the tramp steamer or the scream was first to gain attention, no one can say. Probably they were simultaneous, but it is of no use to calculate. The scream came from the Suydam stateroom, and the sailor who broke down the door could perhaps have told frightful things if he had not forthwith gone completely mad—as it is, he shrieked more loudly than the first victims, and thereafter ran simpering about the vessel till caught and put in irons. The ship's doctor who entered the stateroom and turned on the lights a moment later did not go mad, but told nobody what he saw till afterward, when he corresponded with Malone in Chepachet. It was murder—strangulation—but one need not say that the claw-mark on Mrs. Suydam's throat could not have come from her husband's or any other human hand, or that upon the white wall there flickered for an instant in hateful red a legend which, later copied from memory, seems to have been nothing less than the fearsome Chaldee letters of the word "LILITH".[36] One need not mention these things because they vanished so quickly—as for Suydam, one could at least bar others from the room until one knew what to think oneself. The doctor has distinctly assured Malone that he did not see *IT*. The open porthole, just before he turned on the lights, was clouded for a second with a certain

---

[35] *Social Register*: A book listing socially prominent people in the United States.

[36] *Chaldee letters of the word "LILITH"*: The Chaldeans were an ancient Semitic people that became dominant in Babylonia. They were reputed to be versed in the occult arts. Lilith is an evil female spirit in Semitic mythology that roams desolate places and attacks children.

phosphorescence, and for a moment there seemed to echo in the night outside the suggestion of a faint and hellish tittering; but no real outline met the eye. As proof the doctor points to his continued sanity.

Then the tramp steamer claimed all attention. A boat put off, and a horde of swart, insolent ruffians in officers' dress swarmed aboard the temporarily halted Cunarder. They wanted Suydam or his body—they had known of his trip, and for certain reasons were sure he would die. The captain's deck was almost a pandemonium;[37] for at the instant, between the doctor's report from the stateroom and the demands of the men from the tramp, not even the wisest and gravest seaman could think what to do. Suddenly the leader of the visiting mariners, an Arab with a hatefully negroid mouth, pulled forth a dirty, crumpled paper and handed it to the captain. It was signed by Robert Suydam, and bore the following odd message:

"In case of sudden or unexplained accident or death on my part, please deliver me or my body unquestioningly into the hands of the bearer and his associates. Everything, for me, and perhaps for you, depends on absolute compliance. Explanations can come later—do not fail me now.
ROBERT SUYDAM."

Captain and doctor looked at each other, and the latter whispered something to the former. Finally they nodded rather helplessly and led the way to the Suydam stateroom. The doctor directed the captain's glance away as he unlocked the door and admitted the strange seamen, nor did he breathe easily till they filed out with their burden after an unaccountably long period of preparation. It was wrapped in bedding from the berths, and the doctor was

---

[37] *pandemonium*: A wild uproar. In Milton's *Paradise Lost* Pandemonium is the capital of Hell.

glad that the outlines were not very revealing. Somehow the men got the thing over the side and away to their tramp steamer without uncovering it. The Cunarder started again, and the doctor and a ship's undertaker sought out the Suydam stateroom to perform what last services they could. Once more the physician was forced to reticence and even to mendacity, for a hellish thing had happened. When the undertaker asked him why he had drained off all of Mrs. Suydam's blood, he neglected to affirm that he had not done so; nor did he point to the vacant bottle-spaces on the rack, or to the odour in the sink which shewed the hasty disposition of the bottles' original contents. The pockets of those men—if men they were—had bulged damnably when they left the ship. Two hours later, and the world knew by radio all that it ought to know of the horrible affair.

VI.

That same June evening, without having heard a word from the sea, Malone was desperately busy among the alleys of Red Hook. A sudden stir seemed to permeate the place, and as if apprised by "grapevine telegraph" of something singular, the denizens clustered expectantly around the dance-hall church and the houses in Parker Place. Three children had just disappeared—blue-eyed Norwegians from the streets toward Gowanus[38]—and there were rumours of a mob forming among the sturdy Vikings of that section. Malone had for weeks been urging his colleagues to attempt a general cleanup; and at last, moved by conditions more obvious to their common sense than the conjectures of a Dublin dreamer, they had agreed

[38] *Gowanus*: In the nineteenth century this Brooklyn neighborhood had a reputation for rowdiness, so much so that it was nicknamed the Gashouse District. Its many taverns and rooming-houses catered to transients, mostly seamen and laborers.

upon a final stroke. The unrest and menace of this evening had been the deciding factor, and just about midnight a raiding party recruited from three stations descended upon Parker Place and its environs. Doors were battered in, stragglers arrested, and candlelighted rooms forced to disgorge unbelievable throngs of mixed foreigners in figured robes, mitres, and other inexplicable devices. Much was lost in the melee, for objects were thrown hastily down unexpected shafts, and betraying odours deadened by the sudden kindling of pungent incense. But spattered blood was everywhere, and Malone shuddered whenever he saw a brazier or altar from which the smoke was still rising.

He wanted to be in several places at once, and decided on Suydam's basement flat only after a messenger had reported the complete emptiness of the dilapidated dance-hall church. The flat, he thought, must hold some clue to a cult of which the occult scholar had so obviously become the centre and leader; and it was with real expectancy that he ransacked the musty rooms, noted their vaguely charnel odour, and examined the curious books, instruments, gold ingots, and glass-stoppered bottles scattered carelessly here and there. Once a lean, black-and-white cat edged between his feet and tripped him, overturning at the same time a beaker half full of a red liquid. The shock was severe, and to this day Malone is not certain of what he saw; but in dreams he still pictures that cat as it scuttled away with certain monstrous alterations and peculiarities. Then came the locked cellar door, and the search for something to break it down. A heavy stool stood near, and its tough seat was more than enough for the antique panels. A crack formed and enlarged, and the whole door gave way—but from the *other* side; whence poured a howling tumult of ice-cold wind with all the stenches of the bottomless pit, and whence reached a sucking force not of earth or heaven, which, coiling sentiently about the paralysed detective, dragged him through the aperture and down unmeasured spaces filled with whispers and wails, and gusts of mocking laughter.

Of course it was a dream. All the specialists have told him so, and he has nothing to prove the contrary. Indeed, he would rather have it thus; for then the sight of old brick slums and dark foreign faces would not eat so deeply into his soul. But at the time it was all horribly real, and nothing can ever efface the memory of those nighted crypts, those titan arcades, and those half-formed shapes of hell that strode gigantically in silence holding half-eaten things whose still surviving portions screamed for mercy or laughed with madness. Odours of incense and corruption joined in sickening concert, and the black air was alive with the cloudy, semi-visible bulk of shapeless elemental things with eyes. Somewhere dark sticky water was lapping at onyx piers, and once the shivery tinkle of raucous little bells pealed out to greet the insane titter of a naked phosphorescent thing which swam into sight, scrambled ashore, and climbed up to squat leeringly on a carved golden pedestal in the background.

Avenues of limitless night seemed to radiate in every direction, till one might fancy that here lay the root of a contagion destined to sicken and swallow cities, and engulf nations in the foetor of hybrid pestilence. Here cosmic sin[39] had entered, and festered by unhallowed rites had commenced the grinning march of death that was to rot us all to fungous abnormalities too hideous for the grave's holding. Satan here held his Babylonish court, and in the blood of stainless childhood the leprous limbs of phospho-

---

[39] *cosmic sin*: The concept of "sin" was important to Machen, hence its use here if modified by the typically Lovecraftian adjective "cosmic." As a materialist Lovecraft took issue with Machen on this point: "People whose minds are—like Machen's—steeped in orthodox myths of religion, naturally find a poignant fascination in the conception of things which religion brands with outlawry and horror. Such people take the artificial and obsolete concept of 'sin' seriously, and find it full of dark allurement. . . . The whole idea of 'sin', with its overtones of unholy fascination, is in 1932 simply a curiosity of intellectual history." (*Selected Letters* IV, 4)

rescent Lilith were laved. Incubi and succubae[40] howled
praise to Hecate,[41] and headless moon-calves bleated to the
Magna Mater.[42] Goats leaped to the sound of thin accursed
flutes, and aegipans chased endlessly after misshapen
fauns over rocks twisted like swollen toads. Moloch and
Ashtaroth[43] were not absent; for in this quintessence of all
damnation the bounds of consciousness were let down,
and man's fancy lay open to vistas of every realm of horror
and every forbidden dimension that evil had power to
mould. The world and Nature were helpless against such
assaults from unsealed wells of night, nor could any sign
or prayer check the Walpurgis-riot[44] of horror which had
come when a sage with the hateful key had stumbled on a
horde with the locked and brimming coffer of transmitted
daemon-lore.

Suddenly a ray of physical light shot through these
phantasms, and Malone heard the sound of oars amidst
the blasphemies of things that should be dead. A boat with
a lantern in its prow darted into sight, made fast to an
iron ring in the slimy stone pier, and vomited forth several
dark men bearing a long burden swathed in bedding. They
took it to the naked phosphorescent thing on the carved
golden pedestal, and the thing tittered and pawed at the

---

[40] *incubi and succubae*: An incubus is an evil spirit that typically afflicts people
in their sleep, in particular a being that has sexual intercourse with women in
their sleep. A succubus or succuba is a demon that assumes female form to
have sexual intercouse with men in their sleep.

[41] *Hecate*: The goddess of the underworld in Greek mythology.

[42] *Magna Mater*: An aspect of the fertility goddess Cybele. See notes 15 and 16
to "The Rats in the Walls" (*Annotated Lovecraft*, 30–31).

[43] *Moloch and Ashtaroth*: Moloch is a Semitic deity worshipped through the
sacrifice of children. Ashtaroth is a variation on Astarte, the Phoenician goddess
of fertility and sexual love.

[44] *Walpurgis-riot*: Named for unknown reasons for Saint Walburga (d. c. 779),
Walpurgisnacht is the traditional German witches' sabbath held on the eve of
one of her feast days, May 1. Goethe's *Faust* includes a famous Walpurgisnacht
scene. See note 12 to "The Haunter of the Dark" for Lovecraft's account of how
the saint's name came to be associated with the witches' sabbath.

bedding. Then they unswathed it, and propped upright before the pedestal the gangrenous corpse of a corpulent old man with stubbly beard and unkept white air. The phosphorescent thing tittered again, and the men produced bottles from their pockets and anointed its feet with red, whilst they afterward gave the bottles to the thing to drink from.

All at once, from an arcaded avenue leading endlessly away, there came the daemoniac rattle and wheeze of a blasphemous organ, choking and rumbling out the mockeries of hell in a cracked, sardonic bass. In an instant every moving entity was electrified; and forming at once into a ceremonial procession, the nightmare horde slithered away in quest of the sound—goat, satyr,[45] and aegipan,[46] incubus, succuba, and lemur,[47] twisted toad and shapeless elemental, dog-faced howler and silent stutterer in darkness—all led by the abominable naked phosphorescent thing that had squatted on the carved golden throne, and that now strode insolently bearing in its arms the glassy-eyed corpse of the corpulent old man. The strange dark men danced in the rear, and the whole column skipped and leaped with Dionysiac[48] fury. Malone staggered after them a few steps, delirious and hazy, and doubtful of his place in this or any world. Then he turned, faltered, and sank down on the cold damp stone, gasping and shivering as the daemon organ croaked on, and the howling and

---

[45] *satyr*: A sylvan diety of Greek mythology who is fond of Dionysian revelry.

[46] *aegipan*: A term apparently derived from the Greek proper name Aigipan ("goat-Pan"), referring either to goat-footed Pan or to the son of Zeus and the nymph Aex ("she-goat"). In Greek art, Aigipan is represented as half-goat and half-fish.

[47] *lemur*: A tree-dwelling mammal, chiefly nocturnal, related to monkeys but forming a distinct family of its own. Once widespread, lemurs today are confined mainly to Madagascar.

[48] *Dionysiac*: Of a frenzied, sensuous, or orgiastic character. Dionysus was the Greek god of wine.

drumming and tinkling of the mad procession grew fainter and fainter.

Vaguely he was conscious of chanted horrors and shocking croakings afar off. Now and then a wail or whine of ceremonial devotion would float to him through the black arcade, whilst eventually there rose the dreadful Greek incantation whose text he had read above the pulpit of that dance-hall church.

"O friend and companion of night, though who rejoicest in the baying of dogs (*here a hideous howl burst forth*) and spilt blood (*here nameless sounds vied with morbid shriekings*), who wanderest in the midst of shades among the tombs (*here a whistling sigh occurred*), who longest for blood and bringest terror to mortals (*short, sharp cries from myriad throats*), Gorgo (*repeated as response*), Mormo (*repeated with ecstasy*), thousand-faced moon (*sighs and flute notes*), look favourably on our sacrifices!"

As the chant closed, a general shout went up, and hissing sounds nearly drowned the croaking of the cracked bass organ. Then a gasp as from many throats, and a babel of barked and bleated words—"Lilith, Great Lilith, behold the Bridegroom!" More cries, a clamour of rioting, and the sharp, clicking footfalls of a running figure. The footfalls approached, and Malone raised himself to his elbow to look.

The luminosity of the crypt, lately diminished, had now slightly increased; and in that devil-light there appeared the fleeing form of that which should not flee or feel or breathe—the glassy-eyed, gangrenous corpse of the corpulent old man, now needing no support, but animated by some infernal sorcery[49] of the rite just closed. After it raced the naked, tittering, phosphorescent thing that belonged on the carven pedestal, and still farther behind panted the

---

[49] *animated by some infernal sorcery*: Like one of Herbert West's experiments in "Herbert West—Reanimator," Suydam has become an animated corpse. Another exemplar of this Frankenstein theme is Doctor Muñoz in "Cool Air."

dark men, and all the dread crew of sentient loath-somenesses. The corpse was gaining on its pursuers, and seemed bent on a definite object, straining with every rotting muscle toward the carved golden pedestal, whose necromantic importance was evidently so great. Another moment and it had reached its goal, whilst the trailing throng laboured on with more frantic speed. But they were too late, for in one final spurt of strength which ripped tendon from tendon and sent its noisome bulk floundering to the floor in a state of jellyish dissolution, the staring corpse which had been Robert Suydam achieved its object and its triumph. The push had been tremendous, but the force had held out; and as the pusher collapsed to a muddy blotch of corruption[50] the pedestal he had pushed tottered, tipped, and finally careened from its onyx base into the thick waters below, sending up a parting gleam of carven gold as it sank heavily to undreamable gulfs of lower Tartarus.[51] In that instant, too, the whole scene of horror faded to nothingness before Malone's eyes; and he fainted amidst a thunderous crash which seemed to blot out all the evil universe.

VII.

Malone's dream, experienced in full before he knew of Suydam's death and transfer at sea, was curiously supplemented by some odd realities of the case; though that is no reason why anyone should believe it. The three old houses in Parker Place, doubtless long rotten with decay in its most insidious form, collapsed without visible

---

[50] *muddy blotch of corruption*: Another melted corpse. See note 33 to "The Shunned House."

[51] *Tartarus*: A region in the Greek underworld.

cause[52] while half the raiders and most of the prisoners were inside; and of both the greater number were instantly killed. Only in the basements and cellars was there much saving of life, and Malone was lucky to have been deep below the house of Robert Suydam. For he really was there, as no one is disposed to deny. They found him unconscious by the edge of a night-black pool, with a grotesquely horrible jumble of decay and bone, identifiable through dental work[53] as the body of Suydam, a few feet away. The case was plain, for it was hither that the smugglers' underground canal led; and the men who took Suydam from the ship had brought him home. They themselves were never found, or at least never identified; and the ship's doctor is not yet satisfied with the simple certitudes of the police.

Suydam was evidently a leader in extensive man-smuggling operations, for the canal to his house was but one of several subterranean channels and tunnels in the neighbourhood. There was a tunnel from this house to a crypt beneath the dance-hall church; a crypt accessible from the church only through a narrow secret passage in the north wall, and in whose chambers some singular and terrible things were discovered. The croaking organ was there, as well as a vast arched chapel with wooden benches and a strangely figured altar. The walls were lined with small cells, in seventeen of which—hideous to relate—solitary prisoners in a state of complete idiocy were found chained, including four mothers with infants of disturbingly strange appearance.[54] These infants died soon after expo-

[52] *collapsed without visible cause*: At the climax of Lovecraft's "The Street" (1920), perhaps his most overtly racist tale, a row of old houses collapses on the foreigners who inhabit them.

[53] *dental work*: In "The Thing on the Doorstep" the body of Asenath Waite is also identified through dental work.

[54] *infants of disturbingly strange appearance*: A minor example of the changeling or miscegenation theme found in such better tales as "Pickman's Model" and "The Dunwich Horror"

sure to the light; a circumstance which the doctors thought rather merciful. Nobody but Malone, among those who inspected them, remembered the sombre question of old Delrio:[55] *"An sint unquam daemones incubi et succubae, et an ex tali congressu proles nasci queat?"*

Before the canals were filled up they were thoroughly dredged, and yielded forth a sensational array of sawed and split bones of all sizes. The kidnapping epidemic, very clearly, had been traced home; though only two of the surviving prisoners could by any legal thread be connected with it. These men are now in prison, since they failed of conviction as accessories in the actual murders. The carved golden pedestal or throne so often mentioned by Malone as of primary occult importance was never brought to light, though at one place under the Suydam house the canal was observed to sink into a well too deep for dredging. It was choked up at the mouth and cemented over when the cellars of the new houses were made, but Malone often speculates on what lies beneath. The police, satisfied that they had shattered a dangerous gang of maniacs and man-smugglers, turned over the Federal authorities the unconvicted Kurds, who before their deportation were conclusively found to belong to the Yezidi clan of devil-worshippers. The tramp ship and its crew remain an elusive mystery, though cynical detectives are once more ready to combat its smuggling and rum-running ventures. Malone thinks these detectives shew a sadly limited perspective in their lack of wonder at the myriad unexplainable details, and the suggestive obscurity of the whole case; though he is just as critical of the newspapers, which saw only a morbid sensation and gloated over a minor

---

[55] *old Delrio*: Lovecraft found this quotation in the "Demonology" article in the 9th edition of the *Encyclopaedia Britannica*. The quotation itself comes from *Disquisitionum Magicarum Libri Sex* [*Six Books of Disquisitions on Magic*] (1603), by Martin Anton Del Rio (or Delrio) (1551–1608). The Latin translates as: "Have there ever been demons, incubi, and succubae, and from such a union can offspring be born?"

sadist cult which they might have proclaimed a horror from the universe's very heart. But he is content to rest silent in Chepachet, calming his nervous system and praying that time may gradually transfer his terrible experience from the realm of present reality to that of picturesque and semi-mythical remoteness.

Robert Suydam sleeps beside his bride in Greenwood Cemetery.[56] No funeral was held over the strangely released bones, and relatives are grateful for the swift oblivion which overtook the case as a whole. The scholar's connexion with the Red Hook horrors, indeed, was never emblazoned by legal proof; since his death forestalled the inquiry he would otherwise have faced. His own end is not much mentioned, and the Suydams hope that posterity may recall him only as a gentle recluse who dabbled in harmless magic and folklore.

As for Red Hook—it is always the same. Suydam came and went; a terror gathered and faded; but the evil spirit of darkness and squalor broods on amongst the mongrels in the old brick houses, and prowling bands still parade on unknown errands past windows where lights and twisted faces unaccountably appear and disappear. Age-old horror is a hydra with a thousand heads, and the cults of darkness are rooted in blasphemies deeper than the well of Democritus.[57] The soul of the beast is omnipresent and triumphant, and Red Hook's legions of blear-eyed, pock-marked youths still chant and curse and howl as they file from abyss to abyss, none knows whence or whither, pushed on by blind laws of biology which they may never understand. As of old, more people enter Red Hook than

---

[56] *Greenwood Cemetery*: A Brooklyn cemetery, commissioned in 1836, that is also a rural retreat. Prominent people buried there include the inventor Samuel F. B. Morse, the artist George Bellows, and the politician William M. "Boss" Tweed.

[57] *well of Democritus*: Democritus (c.460–c.370 B.C.), a Greek philosopher, first postulated that all things were made of atoms. Poe cites the well of Democritus in "A Descent into the Maelstrom." According to legend, the well is bottomless.

leave it on the landward side, and there are already rumours of new canals running underground to certain centres of traffic in liquor and less mentionable things.

The dance-hall church is now mostly a dance-hall, and queer faces have appeared at night at the windows. Lately a policeman expressed the belief that the filled-up crypt has been dug out again, and for no simply explainable purpose. Who are we to combat poisons older than history and mankind? Apes danced in Asia to those horrors, and the cancer lurks secure and spreading where furtiveness hides in rows of decaying brick.

Malone does not shudder without cause—for only the other day an officer overheard a swarthy squinting hag teaching a small child some whispered patois[58] in the shadow of an areaway. He listened, and thought it very strange when he heard her repeat over and over again,

> *"friend and companion of night, thou who rejoicest in the baying of dogs and spilt blood, who wanderest in the midst of shades among the tombs, who longest for blood and bringest terror to mortals, Gorgo, Mormo, thousand-faced moon, look favourably on our sacrifices!"*

---

[58] *patois*: A non-standard dialect; illiterate or provincial speech.

Cool Air

You ask me to explain why I am afraid of a draught of cool air;[1] why I shiver more than others upon entering a

"Cool Air" was written in March 1926. For inexplicable reasons, since it would appear to be just the sort of safe, macabre tale that he liked, Farnsworth Wright, editor of *Weird Tales*, rejected it. The story first appeared in the March 1928 issue of the short-lived *Tales of Magic and Mystery*.

[1] *draught of cool air*: Lovecraft himself was abnormally sensitive to cold. In his letters he frequently complains of its effects. In 1932 he wrote fellow *Weird Tales* author Robert E. Howard: "I can't write decently under 73° or 74°. From there down to freezing the effect of a falling temperature is simply increasing discomfort and sluggishness; but after that it begins to be painful to breathe. I can't go out at all under +20°, since the effects are varied and disastrous. First my lungs and throat get sore, and then I become sick at the stomach and lose anything I've eaten. My heart also pounds and palpitates. At about 17° or 16° my muscular and nervous coördination gets all shot to hell, and I have to flounder and stagger like a drunken man. When I try to walk ahead, I feel as if I were trying to swim through some viscous, hampering medium of resistance. Finally, at 15° or 14°, I begin to lose consciousness." (*Selected Letters* IV, 82–83)

cold room, and seem nauseated and repelled when the chill of evening creeps through the heat of a mild autumn day. There are those who say I respond to cold as others do to a bad odour, and I am the last to deny the impression. What I will do is to relate the most horrible circumstance I ever encountered, and leave it to you to judge whether or not this forms a suitable explanation of my peculiarity.

It is a mistake to fancy that horror is associated inextricably with darkness, silence, and solitude. I found it in the glare of mid-afternoon, in the clangour of a metropolis, and in the teeming midst of a shabby and commonplace rooming-house with a prosaic landlady and two stalwart men by my side. In the spring of 1923 I had secured some dreary and unprofitable magazine work in the city of New York; and being unable to pay any substantial rent, began drifting from one cheap boarding establishment to another in search of a room which might combine the qualities of decent cleanliness, endurable furnishings, and very reasonable price. It soon developed that I had only a choice between different evils, but after a time I came upon a house in West Fourteenth Street[2] which disgusted me much less than the others I had sampled.

The place was a four-story mansion of brownstone, dating apparently from the late forties, and fitted with woodwork and marble whose stained and sullied splendour argued a descent from high levels of tasteful opulence. In the rooms, large and lofty, and decorated with impossible paper and ridiculously ornate stucco cornices, there lingered a depressing mustiness and hint of obscure cookery; but the floors were clean, the linen tolerably regular, and

---

[2] *a house in West Fourteenth Street*: For his setting Lovecraft used the brownstone at 317 West Fourteenth Street that was briefly the home in 1925 of his bookseller friend George Kirk (1898–1962). Kirk was one of the original members of Lovecraft's New York literary gang, the Kalem Club. For information on Kirk and his relationship to Lovecraft, see Mara Kirk Hart's "Walkers in City: George Willard Kirk and Howard Phillips Lovecraft in New York City, 1924–1926," in *Lovecraft Remembered*.

317 West 14th Street (photo by Jason C. Eckhardt).

the hot water not too often cold or turned off, so that I came to regard it as at least a bearable place to hibernate till one might really live again. The landlady, a slatternly, almost bearded Spanish woman named Herrero, did not annoy me with gossip or with criticisms of the late-burning electric light in my third-floor front hall room; and my fellow-lodgers were as quiet and uncommunicative as one might desire, being mostly Spaniard a little above the coarsest and crudest grade.[3] Only the din of street cars in the thoroughfare below proved a serious annoyance.

I had been there about three weeks when the first odd incident occurred. One evening at about eight I heard a spattering on the floor and became suddenly aware that I had been smelling the pungent odour of ammonia for some time. Looking about, I saw that the ceiling was wet and dripping;[4] the soaking apparently proceeding from a corner on the side toward the street. Anxious to stop the matter at its source, I hastened to the basement to tell the landlady; and was assured by her that the trouble would quickly be set right.

"Doctair Muñoz," she cried as she rushed upstairs ahead of me, "he have speel hees chemicals. He ees too seek for doctair heemself—seecker and seecker all the time—but he weel not have no othair for help. He ees vairy queer in hees seeckness—all day he take funnee-smelling baths, and he cannot get excite or warm. All hees own house-work he do—hees leetle room are full of bottles and ma-chines, and he do not work as doctair. But he was great once—my fathair in Barcelona have hear of heem—and only joost now he feex a arm of the plumber that get hurt of sudden. He nevair go out, only on roof, and my boy Esteban, he breeng heem hees food and laundry and medi-ceens and chemicals. My Gawd, the sal-ammoniac[5] that man use for keep heem cool!"

Mrs. Herrero disappeared up the staircase to the fourth floor, and I returned to my room. The ammonia ceased to drip, and as I cleaned up what had spilled and opened the

---

[3] *Spaniards a little above the coarsest and crudest grade*: Poor Hispanics. Spanish-speaking West Indians and Cubans had been settling in increasing num-bers in New York since the Spanish-American War and the opening of trade with the Caribbean. Chelsea, the neighborhood north of West Fourteenth Street, had many tobacco factories run by Latin Americans at this period.

[4] *the ceiling was wet and dripping*: A motif that occurs in "The Picture in the House," though here it is merely the prelude to the horror not the climax as it is in the earlier story.

[5] *sal-ammoniac*: Ammonium chloride. Literally salt of Ammon, derived from the name of the Egyptian god, Amen, near one of whose temples this compound was prepared.

window for air, I heard the landlady's heavy footsteps
above me. Dr. Muñoz I had never heard, save for certain
sounds as of some gasoline-driven mechanism; since his
step was soft and gentle. I wondered for a moment what
the strange affliction of this man might be, and whether
his obstinate refusal of outside aid were not the result of
a rather baseless eccentricity. There is, I reflected tritely,
an infinite deal of pathos in the state of an eminent person
who has come down in the world.

I might never have known Dr. Muñoz had it not been
for the heart attack[6] that suddenly seized me one forenoon
as I sat writing in my room. Physicians had told me of
the danger of those spells, and I knew there was no time
to be lost; so remembering what the landlady had said
about the invalid's help of the injured workman, I dragged
myself upstairs and knocked feebly at the door above
mine. My knock was answered in good English by a curious voice some distance to the right, asking my name
and business; and these things being stated, there came an
opening of the door next to the one I had sought.

A rush of cool air greeted me; and though the day was
one of the hottest of late June, I shivered as I crossed the
threshold into a large apartment whose rich and tasteful
decoration surprised me in this nest of squalor and seedi-
ness. A folding couch now filled its diurnal role of sofa,
and the mahogany furniture, sumptuous hangings, old
paintings, and mellow bookshelves all bespoke a gentleman's study rather than a boarding-house bedroom. I now
saw that the hall room above mine—the "leetle room" of
bottles and machines which Mrs. Herrero had mentioned—was merely the laboratory of the doctor; and that
his main living quarters lay in the spacious adjoining room

---

[6] *heart attack*: Lovecraft may well have had his young New York friend Frank
Belknap Long (1901–1994) in mind when he selected this malady. Having had
his undergraduate career at New York University cut short by a heart attack,
Long had to be careful not to overexert himself during the period Lovecraft was
living in New York in the mid-1920s.

whose convenient alcoves and large contiguous bathroom permitted him to hide all dressers and obtrusive utilitarian devices. Dr. Muñoz, most certainly, was a man of birth, cultivation, and discrimination.

The figure before me was short but exquisitely proportioned, and clad in somewhat formal dress of perfect cut and fit. A high-bred face of masterful though not arrogant expression was adorned by a short iron-grey full beard, and an old-fashioned pince-nez[7] shielded the full, dark eyes and surmounted an aquiline nose which gave a Moorish touch to a physiognomy otherwise dominantly Celtiberian.[8] Thick, well-trimmed hair that argued the punctual calls of a barber was parted gracefully above a high forehead; and the whole picture was one of striking intelligence and superior blood and breeding.

Nevertheless, as I saw Dr. Muñoz in that blast of cool air, I felt a repugnance which nothing in his aspect could justify. Only his lividly inclined complexion and coldness of touch could have afforded a physical basis for this feeling, and even these things should have been excusable considering the man's known invalidism. It might, too, have been the singular cold that alienated me; for such chilliness was abnormal on so hot a day, and the abnormal always excites aversion, distrust, and fear.

But repugnance was soon forgotten in admiration, for the strange physician's extreme skill at once became manifest despite the ice-coldness and shakiness of his bloodless-looking hands. He clearly understood my needs at a glance, and ministered to them with a master's deftness;

---

[7] *old-fashioned pince-nez*: Eyeglasses clipped to the nose by a spring.

[8] *Celtiberian*: The Iberians were an ancient people who migrated from Africa to the Iberian Peninsula, the part of Europe south of the Pyrenees occupied today by Portugal and Spain. About the fourth century B.C. the Celts began to move into the region from the north and the two eventually merged into the Celtiberian nation. The Moors, a nomadic people of the northern shores of Africa, conquered Spain in the Dark Ages and established a civilization that excelled in art and architecture, as well as in medicine and science.

the while reassuring me in finely modulated though oddly hollow and timbreless voice that he was the bitterest of sworn enemies to death, and had sunk his fortune and lost all his friends in a lifetime of bizarre experiment devoted to its bafflement and extirpation. Something of the benevolent fanatic seemed to reside in him, and he rambled on almost garrulously as he sounded my chest and mixed a suitable draught of drugs fetched from the smaller laboratory room. Evidently he found the society of a well-born man a rare novelty in this dingy environment, and was moved to unaccustomed speech as memories of better days surged over him.

His voice, if queer, was at least soothing; and I could not even perceive that he breathed as the fluent sentences rolled urbanely out. He sought to distract my mind from my own seizure by speaking of his theories and experiments; and I remember his tactfully consoling me about my weak heart by insisting that will and consciousness are stronger than organic life itself, so that if a bodily frame be but originally healthy and carefully preserved, it may through a scientific enhancement of these qualities retain a kind of nervous animation[9] despite the most serious impairments, defects, or even absences in the battery of specific organs. He might, he half jestingly said, some day teach me to live—or at least to possess some kind of conscious existence—without any heart at all! For his part, he was afflicted with a complication of maladies requiring a very exact regimen which included constant cold. Any marked rise in temperature might, if prolonged, affect him fatally; and the frigidity of his habitation— some 55 or 56 degrees Fahrenheit—was maintained by an absorption system of ammonia cooling,[10] the gasoline engine of whose pumps I had often heard in my own room below.

---

[9] *nervous animation*: Lovecraft is here providing the same sort of pseudo-scientific basis as he had in "Herbert West—Reanimator" for his version of the Frankenstein theme.

Relieved of my seizure in a marvellously short while, I left the shivery place a disciple and devotee of the gifted recluse. After that I paid him frequent overcoated calls; listening while he told of secret researches and almost ghastly results, and trembling a bit when I examined the unconventional and astonishingly ancient volumes on his shelves. I was eventually, I may add, almost cured of my disease for all time by his skilful ministrations. It seems that he did not scorn the incantations of the mediaevalists, since he believed these cryptic formulae to contain rare psychological stimuli which might conceivably have singular effects on the substance of a nervous system from which organic pulsations had fled. I was touched by his account of the aged Dr. Torres of Valencia, who had shared his earlier experiments with him through the great illness of eighteen years before, whence his present disorders proceeded. No sooner had the venerable practitioner saved his colleague than he himself succumbed to the grim enemy he had fought. Perhaps the strain had been too great; for Dr. Muñoz made it whisperingly clear—though not in detail—that the methods of healing had been most extraordinary, involving scenes and processes not welcomed by elderly and conservative Galens.[11]

As the weeks passed, I observed with regret that my new friend was indeed slowly but unmistakably losing ground physically, as Mrs. Herrero had suggested. The livid aspect

[10] *an absorption system of ammonia cooling*: Here Lovecraft has his mechanical details right. Dr. Muñoz has in effect turned his apartment into a giant refrigerator. In the absorption system, common in commercial installations, ammonia is usually used as a refrigerant to cool brine that is then sent through pipes to cool the refrigerated space. A pump is necessary to operate the compressor that converts the gaseous refrigerant into a liquid.

Air conditioning at this period was unknown outside of factories. Portable or window-mounted air-conditioning units did not become widespread until after World War II.

[11] *Galens*: Galen (c. 130–c. 200) was a Greek who served as court physician to the Roman emperor Marcus Aurelius. He systematized the knowledge of medicine in his day and wrote numerous treatises on anatomy and physiology. Until the sixteenth century his authority was virtually undisputed.

of his countenance was intensified, his voice became more hollow and indistinct, his muscular motions were less perfectly coördinated, and his mind and will displayed less resilience and initiative. Of this sad change he seemed by no means unaware, and little by little his expression and conversation both took on a gruesome irony which restored in me something of the subtle repulsion I had originally felt.

He developed strange caprices, acquiring a fondness of exotic spices and Egyptian incense till his room smelled like the vault of a sepulchred Pharaoh in the Valley of Kings.[12] At the same time his demands for cold air increased, and with my aid he amplified the ammonia piping of his room and modified the pumps and feed of his refrigerating machine till he could keep the temperature as low as 34 or 40, and finally even 28; the bathroom and laboratory, of course, being less chilled, in order that water might not freeze, and that chemical processes might not be impeded. The tenant adjoining him complained of the icy air from around the connecting door, so I helped him fit heavy hangings to obviate the difficulty. A kind of growing horror, of outré and morbid cast, seemed to possess him. He talked of death incessantly, but laughed hollowly when such things as burial or funeral arrangements were gently suggested.

All in all, he became a disconcerting and even gruesome companion; yet in my gratitude for his healing I could not well abandon him to the strangers around him, and was careful to dust his room and attend to his needs each day, muffled in a heavy ulster[13] which I bought especially for the purpose. I likewise did much of his shopping, and

[12] *Valley of Kings*: The Valley of the Kings, Wadi Biban el-Muluk in Arabic, is the site of the tomb of Tutankhamen, the Egyptian pharaoh, unearthed by the Englishman Howard Carter in 1922. Things Egyptian were much in vogue at this period because of this sensational discovery.

[13] *heavy ulster*: A long loose overcoat of Irish (Ulster) origin made of coarse wool or other heavy material.

gasped in bafflement at some of the chemicals he ordered from druggists and laboratory supply houses.

An increasing and unexplained atmosphere of panic seemed to rise around his apartment. The whole house, as I have said, had a musty odour; but the smell in his room was worse—and in spite of all the spices and incense, and the pungent chemicals of the now incessant baths which he insisted on taking unaided. I perceived that it must be connected with his ailment, and shuddered when I reflected on what that ailment might be. Mrs. Herrero crossed herself when she looked at him, and gave him up unreservedly to me; not even letting her son Esteban continue to run errands for him. When I suggested other physicians, the sufferer would fly into as much of a rage as he seemed to dare to entertain. He evidently feared the physical effect of violent emotion, yet his will and driving force waxed rather than waned, and he refused to be confined to his bed. The lassitude of his earlier ill days gave place to a return of his fiery purpose, so that he seemed about to hurl defiance at the death-daemon even as that ancient enemy seized him. The pretence of eating, always curiously like a formality with him, he virtually abandoned; and mental power alone appeared to keep him from total collapse.

He acquired a habit of writing long documents of some sort, which he carefully sealed and filled with injunctions that I transmit after his death to certain persons whom he named—for the most part lettered East Indians, but including a once celebrated French physician now generally thought dead,[14] and about whom the most inconceivable things had been whispered. As it happened, I burned all these papers undelivered and unopened. His aspect and voice became utterly frightful, and his presence almost

[14] *a once celebrated French physician now generally thought dead*: Likewise Joseph Curwen, in *The Case of Charles Dexter Ward*, will correspond with fellow delvers into the unknown who should have been long dead.

unbearable. One September day an unexpected glimpse of him induced an epileptic fit in a man who had come to repair his electric desk lamp; a fit for which he prescribed effectively whilst keeping himself well out of sight. That man, oddly enough, had been through the terrors of the Great War[15] without having incurred any fright so thorough.

Then, in the middle of October, the horror of horrors came with stupefying suddenness. One night about eleven the pump of the refrigerating machine broke down, so that within three hours the process of ammonia cooling became impossible. Dr. Muñoz summoned me by thumping on the floor, and I worked desperately to repair the injury while my host cursed in a tone whose lifeless, rattling hollowness surpassed description. My amateur efforts, however, proved of no use; and when I had brought in a mechanic from a neighbouring all-night garage we learned that nothing could be done till morning, when a new piston would have to be obtained. The moribund hermit's rage and fear, swelling to grotesque proportions, seemed likely to shatter what remained of his failing physique; and once a spasm caused him to clap his hands to his eyes and rush into the bathroom. He groped his way out with face tightly bandaged, and I never saw his eyes again.

The frigidity of the apartment was now sensibly diminishing, and at about 5 a.m. the doctor retired to the bathroom, commanding me to keep him supplied with all the ice I could obtain at all-night drug stores and cafeterias. As I would return from my sometimes discouraging trips and lay my spoils before the closed bathroom door, I could hear a restless splashing within, and a thick voice croaking out the order for "More—more!" At length a warm day broke, and the shops opened one by one. I asked Esteban either to help with the ice-fetching whilst I obtained the pump piston, or to order the piston while I continued with

---

[15] *Great War*: World War I.

the ice; but instructed by his mother, he absolutely refused.

Finally I hired a seedy-looking loafer whom I encountered on the corner of Eighth Avenue to keep the patient supplied with ice from a little shop where I introduced him, and applied myself diligently to the task of finding a pump piston and engaging workmen competent to install it. The task seemed interminable, and I raged almost as violently as the hermit when I saw the hours slipping by in a breathless, foodless round of vain telephoning, and a hectic quest from place to place, hither and thither by subway and surface car.[16] About noon I encountered a suitable supply house far downtown, and at approximately 1:30 p.m. arrived at my boarding-place with the necessary paraphernalia and two sturdy and intelligent mechanics. I had done all I could, and hoped I was in time.

Black terror, however, had preceded me. The house was in utter turmoil, and above the chatter of awed voices I heard a man praying in a deep basso. Fiendish things were in the air, and lodgers told over the beads of their rosaries as they caught the odour from beneath the doctor's closed door. The lounger I had hired, it seems, had fled screaming and mad-eyed not long after his second delivery of ice; perhaps as a result of excessive curiosity. He could not, of course, have locked the door behind him; yet it was now fastened, presumably from the inside. There was no sound within save a nameless sort of slow, thick dripping.

Briefly consulting with Mrs. Herrero and the workmen despite a fear that gnawed my inmost soul, I advised the breaking down of the door; but the landlady found a way to turn the key from the outside with some wire device. We had previously opened the doors of all the other rooms on that hall, and flung all the windows to the very top.

---

[16] *surface car*: Streetcar. Electrified streetcars, running on tracks, handled more passengers than the elevated lines and subways at this time. Patronage fell throughout the 1920s with the advent of automobiles and the efforts of their manufacturers to have streetcars replaced with buses.

Now, noses protected by handkerchiefs, we tremblingly invaded the accursed south room which blazed with the warm sun of early afternoon.

A kind of dark, slimy trail led from the open bathroom door to the hall door, and thence to the desk, where a terrible little pool had accumulated. Something was scrawled there in pencil[17] in an awful, blind hand on a piece of paper hideously smeared as though by the very claws that traced the hurried last words. Then the trail led to the couch and ended unutterably.

What was, or had been, on the couch I cannot and dare not say here. But this is what I shiveringly puzzled out on the stickily smeared paper before I drew a match and burned it to a crisp; what I puzzled out in terror as the landlady and two mechanics rushed frantically from that hellish place to babble their incoherent stories at the nearest police station. The nauseous words seemed well-nigh incredible in that yellow sunlight, with the clatter of cars and motor trucks ascending clamorously from crowded Fourteenth Street, yet I confess that I believed them then. Whether I believe them now I honestly do not know. There are things about which it is better not to speculate, and all that I can say is that I hate the smell of ammonia, and grow faint at a draught of unusually cool air.

"The end," ran the noisome scrawl, "is here. No more ice—the man looked and ran away. Warmer every minute, and the tissues can't last. I fancy you know—what I said about the will and the nerves and the preserved body after the organs ceased to work. It was good theory, but couldn't keep up indefinitely. There was a gradual deterioration I had not foreseen. Dr. Torres knew, but the shock killed

---

[17] *scrawled there in pencil*: The decaying Dr. Muñoz anticipates the actions of Edward Derby, whose mind is trapped in the rotting corpse of his wife Asenath, at the climax of "The Thing on the Doorstep." Many of Lovecraft's protagonists have a tendency to write final messages in extremity. See Peter Cannon's essay "Letters, Diaries, and Manuscripts: The Handwritten Word in Lovecraft" in *An Epicure in the Terrible*.

him. He couldn't stand what he had to do—he had to get me in a strange, dark place when he minded my letter and nursed me back. And the organs never would work again. It had to be done my way—artificial preservation—*for you see I died that time eighteen years ago.*"

The Call of Cthulhu
(Found Among the
Papers of the Late
Francis Wayland
Thurston,[1] of Boston)

"Of such great powers or beings there may be conceivably a survival . . . a survival of a hugely remote
period when . . . consciousness was manifested, perhaps, in the shapes and forms long since withdrawn
before the tide of advancing humanity . . . forms of
which poetry and legend alone have caught a flying

*memory and called them gods, monsters, mythical
beings of all sorts and kinds. . . ."*

—Algernon Blackwood.[2]

I. *The Horror in Clay.*

The most merciful thing in the world, I think, is the
inability of the human mind to correlate all its contents.

"The Call of Cthulhu" was written during the summer of 1926. Farnsworth
Wright initially rejected it for *Weird Tales*, though he would later change his
mind, thanks to the intercession of Lovecraft's friend and fellow writer, Donald
Wandrei. In June 1927 Wandrei visited Farnsworth Wright at his office in Chicago, as described in his memoir "Lovecraft in Providence":

> I casually worked in a reference to a story, "The Call of Cthulhu," that
> Lovecraft was revising and finishing and which I thought was a wonderful
> tale. But I added that for some reason or other, Lovecraft had talked about
> submitting it to other magazines. I said I just couldn't understand why he
> was apparently planning to by-pass *Weird Tales* unless he was seeking to
> broaden his markets or widen his reading public. None of this was true, but
> I could see that my fanciful account took effect, in the way Wright began
> to fidget and show signs of agitation, for he rose and paced around his office.
> (*Lovecraft Remembered*, 315)

"The Call of Cthulhu" appeared in the February 1928 issue of *Weird Tales*.

[1] *Francis Wayland Thurston*: Lovecraft's narrator has an impeccable pedigree.
Francis Wayland (1796–1865) was the distinguished fourth president of Brown
University. Robert Lawton Thurston (1800–74) was a pioneer manufacturer of
steam engines, descended from Rhode Island founder Roger Williams and from
Edward Thurston, who was living in the Rhode Island colony as early as 1647.
   This tag line identifying the narrator was printed as a footnote in *Weird Tales*.
It was dropped in subsequent reprintings until restored as a footnote in the
corrected fifth printing of the Arkham House edition of *The Dunwich Horror*
(1981). Only in the corrected sixth printing, edited by S. T. Joshi, did it become
a sort of subtitle as Lovecraft orginally intended.

[2] *Algernon Blackwood*: Algernon Blackwood (1869–1951) was a prolific author
of supernatural stories, including "The Willows," which Lovecraft regarded as
the single greatest weird tale ever written, followed by Arthur Machen's "The
White People." When Lovecraft first read "The Willows," in 1924, he called it
"perhaps the most devastating piece of supernaturally hideous suggestion which
I have beheld in a decade" (letter to Lillian D. Clark, 29–30 September 1924,
John Hay Library). The epigraph is from chapter 10 of Blackwood's novel *The
Centaur* (1911). See also note 92 to "The Dunwich Horror" (*Annotated Love-
craft*, 144) concerning parallel passages in that story and Blackwood's "The
Wendigo."

We live on a placid island of ignorance in the midst of
black seas of infinity, and it was not meant that we should
voyage far. The sciences, each straining in its own direction, have hitherto harmed us little; but some day the
piecing together of dissociated knowledge will open up
such terrifying vistas of reality, and of our frightful position therein, that we shall either go mad from the revelation or flee from the deadly light into the peace and safety
of a new dark age.[3]

Theosophists[4] have guessed at the awesome grandeur of
the cosmic cycle wherein our world and human race form
transient incidents. They have hinted at strange survivals
in terms which would freeze the blood if not masked by
a bland optimism. But it is not from them that there came
the single glimpse of forbidden aeons which chills me
when I think of it and maddens me when I dream of it.
That glimpse, like all dread glimpses of truth, flashed out
from an accidental piecing together of separated things—
in this case an old newspaper item and the notes of a dead
professor. I hope that no one else will accomplish this
piecing out; certainly, if I live, I shall never knowingly
supply a link in so hideous a chain. I think that the professor, too, intended to keep silent regarding the part he
knew, and that he would have destroyed his notes had not
sudden death seized him.

My knowledge of the thing began in the winter of
1926–27 with the death of my grand-uncle George Gam-

[3] *The most merciful thing . . . new dark age*: Arguably the most famous passage
in Lovecraft's fiction, setting forth his view of man's precarious and insignificant
place in the cosmos. The opening sentence has been enshrined in the fifteenth
edition of *Bartlett's Familiar Quotations* (1980).

[4] *Theosophists*: Theosophy, meaning sacred science or divine truth or wisdom,
is a philosophical system with affinities with mysticism. Its first adherents were
supposedly the Philalethians, third-century Alexandrian philosophers. Madame
H. P. Blavatsky (1831–91), author of *Isis Unveiled* (1877) and *The Secret Doc-
trine* (1888–97), founded the Theosophical Society in 1875. Lovecraft had no
belief in theosophy, but its mix of religion and occultism did fire his imagination. See Robert M. Price's article, "HPL and HPB: Lovecraft's Use of Theosophy," in *Crypt of Cthulhu* no. 5 (Roodmas 1982): 3–9.

mell Angell,[5] Professor Emeritus of Semitic Languages in Brown University, Providence, Rhode Island. Professor Angell was widely known as an authority on ancient inscriptions, and had frequently been resorted to by the heads of prominent museums; so that his passing at the age of ninety-two may be recalled by many. Locally, interest was intensified by the obscurity of the cause of death. The professor had been stricken whilst returning from the Newport boat;[6] falling suddenly, as witnesses said, after having been jostled by a nautical-looking negro who had come from one of the queer dark courts on the precipitous hillside which formed a short cut from the waterfront to the deceased's home in Williams Street. Physicians were unable to find any visible disorder, but concluded after perplexed debate that some obscure lesion of the heart, induced by the brisk ascent of so steep a hill by so elderly a man, was responsible for the end. At the time I saw no reason to dissent from this dictum, but latterly I am inclined to wonder—and more than wonder.

As my grand-uncle's heir and executor, for he died a childless widower, I was expected to go over his papers with some thoroughness; and for that purpose moved his entire set of files and boxes to my quarters in Boston. Much of the material which I correlated will be later published by the American Archaeological Society,[7] but there

[5] *George Gammell Angell*: Another typical old Rhode Island name. *Gammell* appears to be a variant of *Gamwell* (indeed *Gamwell*, the name of one of Lovecraft's uncles-in-law, was evidently pronounced with a silent "w"), while *Angell* is the name of the street in the College Hill neighborhood on which Lovecraft lived as a boy. A Colonel Angell commanded Rhode Island troops in the Revolution. See note 15 to "The Shunned House."

[6] *Newport boat*: A regular boat service used to run along Narragansett Bay between Providence and Newport, Rhode Island. Lovecraft often took it in the summer. In August 1934 he wrote: "For the past three days I have been taking advantage of the incredibly low steamboat rates (15¢ round trip), and making diurnal voyages to ancient Newport. It is an admirable relaxation—a two-hour sail past green shores . . ." (*Selected Letters* IV, 52).

[7] *American Archaeological Society*: A fictitious organization. Its closest equivalent would be the Archaeological Institute of America, founded in 1879 and with its headquarters in Boston.

was one box which I found exceedingly puzzling, and which I felt much averse from shewing to other eyes. It had been locked, and I did not find the key till it occurred to me to examine the personal ring which the professor carried always in his pocket. Then indeed I succeeded in opening it, but when I did so seemed only to be confronted by a greater and more closely locked barrier. For what could be the meaning of the queer clay bas-relief and the disjointed jottings, ramblings, and cuttings[8] which I found? Had my uncle, in his latter years, become credulous of the most superficial impostures? I resolved to search out the eccentric sculptor responsible for this apparent disturbance of an old man's peace of mind.

The bas-relief was a rough rectangle less than an inch thick and about five by six inches in area; obviously of modern origin. Its designs, however, were far from modern in atmosphere and suggestion; for although the vagaries of cubism and futurism[9] are many and wild, they do not often reproduce that cryptic regularity which lurks in prehistoric writing. And writing of some kind the bulk of these designs seemed certainly to be; though my memory, despite much familiarity with the papers and collections of my uncle, failed in any way to identify this particular species, or even to hint at its remotest affiliations.

Above these apparent hieroglyphics was a figure of evidently pictorial intent, though its impressionistic execution forbade a very clear idea of its nature. It seemed to be a sort of monster, or symbol representing a monster, of

---

[8] *cuttings*: Lovecraft preferred the British *cutting* for an item removed from a newspaper as opposed to the American *clipping*.

[9] *cubism and futurism*: Cubism was a phase of Postimpressionism that stressed abstract form at the expense of other pictorial elements largely by use of intersecting, often transparent cubes and cones. Futurism began in Italy around 1910 and tried to give formal expression to the dynamics of mechanical processes. Lovecraft viewed most modern art as decadent, as reflected for example in his poem "Futurist Art" (1918). Futurism is also mentioned in *At the Mountains of Madness*. See note 150 to that novel (*Annotated Lovecraft*, 263).

a form which only a diseased fancy could conceive. If I say that my somewhat extravagant imagination yielded simultaneous pictures of an octopus, a dragon, and a human caricature, I shall not be unfaithful to the spirit of the thing. A pulpy, tentacled head surmounted a grotesque and scaly body with rudimentary wings; but it was the *general outline* of the whole which made it most shockingly frightful. Behind the figure was a vague suggestion of a Cyclopean[10] architectural background.

The writing accompanying this oddity was, aside from a stack of press cuttings, in Professor Angell's most recent hand; and made no pretence to literary style. What seemed to be the main document was headed "CTHULHU CULT"[11] in characters painstakingly printed to avoid the erroneous reading of a word so unheard-of. The manuscript was divided into two sections, the first of which was headed "1925—Dream and Dream Work of H. A. Wilcox, 7 Thomas St., Providence, R.I.", and the second, "Narrative of Inspector John R. Legrasse, 121 Bienville St., New Orleans, La., at 1908 A. A. S. Mtg.—Notes on Same, & Prof. Webb's Acct." The other manuscript papers were all brief notes, some of them accounts of the queer dreams of different persons, some of them citations from theosophical books and magazines (notably W. Scott-Elliot's *Atlantis*

---

[10] *Cyclopean*: A style of stone construction marked typically by the use of large irregular blocks without mortar. In another sense this word anticipates the Cyclops-like monster that emerges from the sea at story's end. See note 97 to "The Dunwich Horror" (*Annotated Lovecraft*, 148) and note 60 below.

[11] *CTHULHU CULT*: The first mention of Lovecraft's most famous monster. The pronunciation of *Cthulhu* not surprisingly has caused confusion. In a 1935 letter he made what may be considered the definitive statement on the matter: ". . . the word is supposed to represent a fumbling human attempt to catch the phonetics of an *absolutely non-human* word. The name of the hellish entity was invented by beings whose vocal organs were not like man's, hence it has no relation to the human speech equipment. . . . The actual sound—as nearly as human organs could imitate it or human letters record it—may be taken as something like *Khlûl'hloo*, with the first syllable pronounced gutturally and very thickly. The *u* is about like that in *full*; and the first syllable is not unlike *klul* in sound, since "the *h* represents the guttural thickness." (*Selected Letters* V, 10–11)

and the Lost Lemuria[12]), and the rest comments on long-surviving secret societies and hidden cults, with references to passages in such mythological and anthropological source-books as Frazer's *Golden Bough* and Miss Murray's *Witch-Cult in Western Europe*.[13] The cuttings largely alluded to outré mental illnesses and outbreaks of group folly or mania in the spring of 1925.

The first half of the principal manuscript told a very peculiar tale. It appears that on March 1st, 1925, a thin, dark young man of neurotic and excited aspect had called upon Professor Angell bearing the singular clay bas-relief, which was then exceedingly damp and fresh. His card bore the name of Henry Anthony Wilcox, and my uncle had recognised him as the youngest son of an excellent family slightly known to him, who had latterly been studying sculpture at the Rhode Island School of Design and living alone at the Fleur-de-Lys Building[14] near that institution. Wilcox was a precocious youth of known genius but great eccentricity, and had from childhood excited attention through the strange stories and odd dreams he was in the

---

[12] *Atlantis and the Lost Lemuria*: Actually a compendium published in 1925 of two books by W. Scott-Elliot, *The Story of Atlantis* (1896) and *The Lost Lemuria* (1904). Lovecraft read this volume in the spring of 1926, reporting in a letter: ". . . some of these hints about the lost 'City of the Golden Gates' & the shapeless monsters of archaic Lemuria are ineffably pregnant with fantastic suggestion; and I only wish I could get hold of more of the stuff." (*Selected Letters* II, 58) Lemuria was hypothesized to be a lost continent in the Indian Ocean. See note 130 to *At the Mountains of Madness* (*Annotated Lovecraft*, 250).

[13] *Frazer's Golden Bough and Miss Murray's Witch-Cult in Western Europe*: Lovecraft was probably familiar with the one-volume, abridged edition of Sir James George Frazer's monumental work on the anthropology of religion, *The Golden Bough*, published in several installments from 1890 onward. See note 14 to "The Horror at Red Hook" for the influence of Margaret A. Murray's *Witch-Cult in Western Europe* on Lovecraft.

[14] *Fleur-de-Lys Building*: An actual building at 7 Thomas Street, still standing. When Bertrand K. Hart, a columnist for the *Providence Journal*, read "The Call of Cthulhu" in 1929, he was startled to discover Lovecraft using a house he himself had once occupied. Hart wrote Lovecraft affecting to take umbrage and threatening to send a ghostly visitor to his residence on Barnes Street. Lovecraft responded with a sonnet, "The Messenger," describing the consequences of this nocturnal visit.

Fleur-de-Lys Building, 7 Thomas Street, Providence RI (photo by Steven J. Mariconda).

habit of relating. He called himself "psychically hypersensitive", but the staid folk of the ancient commercial city dismissed him as merely "queer". Never mingling much with his kind, he had dropped gradually from social visibility, and was now known only to a small group of aesthetes from other towns. Even the Providence Art Club,[15] anxious to preserve its conservatism, had found him quite hopeless.

On the occasion of the visit, ran the professor's manuscript, the sculptor abruptly asked for the benefit of his host's archaeological knowledge in identifying the hieroglyphics on the bas-relief. He spoke in a dreamy, stilted manner which suggested pose and alienated sympathy; and my uncle shewed some sharpness in replying, for the conspicuous freshness of the tablet implied kinship with anything but archaeology. Young Wilcox's rejoinder, which impressed my uncle enough to make him recall and record it verbatim, was of a fantastically poetic cast which must have typified his whole conversation, and which I have since found highly characteristic of him. He said, "It is new, indeed, for I made it last night in a dream of strange cities; and dreams are older then brooding Tyre, or the contemplative Sphinx, or garden-girdled Babylon."[16]

It was then that he began that rambling tale which suddenly played upon a sleeping memory and won the fevered interest of my uncle. There had been a slight earthquake tremor[17] the night before, the most considerable felt in New England for some years; and Wilcox's imagination

---

[15] *Providence Art Club*: The Providence Art Club, founded 1880, stands at 11 Thomas Street. The Fleur-de-Lys Building has belonged to the Providence Art Club since 1939.

[16] *garden-girdled Babylon*: In 1920 Lovecraft had a dream that later served as a plot germ for "The Call of Cthulhu": "I was in a museum somewhere in down town Providence . . . trying to sell the curator a bas-relief which *I* had just fashioned from clay. He asked me if I were crazy, attempting to sell him something *modern* when the museum was devoted to antiquities? . . . I replied to him in words which I remember *precisely*. 'This,' I said, 'was fashioned in my dreams; and the dreams of man are older than brooding Egypt or the contemplative Sphinx or garden-girdled Babylon.' " (*Selected Letters* I, 114) Lovecraft made a note of this in his commonplace book, hence the similarity of wording. Tyre, ancient city of Phoenicia, was flourishing by 1400 B.C.

[17] *slight earthquake tremor*: This was an actual earthquake, which Lovecraft felt on the night of February 28, 1925, while living in Brooklyn. In his diary he wrote: "house shakes 9:30 p m . . ."

had been keenly affected. Upon retiring, he had had an unprecedented dream of great Cyclopean cities of titan blocks and sky-flung monoliths, all dripping with green ooze and sinister with latent horror. Hieroglyphics had covered the walls and pillars, and from some undetermined point below had come a voice that was not a voice; a chaotic sensation which only fancy would transmute into sound, but which he attempted to render by the almost unpronounceable jumble of letters, *"Cthulhu fhtagn"*.

This verbal jumble was the key to the recollection which excited and disturbed Professor Angell. He questioned the sculptor with scientific minuteness; and studied with almost frantic intensity the bas-relief on which the youth had found himself working, chilled and clad only in his night-clothes, when waking had stolen bewilderingly over him. My uncle blamed his old age, Wilcox afterward said, for his slowness in recognising both hieroglyphics and pictorial design. Many of his questions seemed highly out-of-place to his visitor, especially those which tried to connect the latter with strange cults or societies; and Wilcox could not understand the repeated promises of silence which he was offered in exchange for an admission of membership in some widespread mystical or paganly religious body. When Professor Angell became convinced that the sculptor was indeed ignorant of any cult or system of cryptic lore, he besieged his visitor with demands for future reports of dreams. This bore regular fruit, for after the first interview the manuscript records daily calls of the young man, during which he related startling fragments of nocturnal imagery whose burden was always some terrible Cyclopean vista of dark and dripping stone, with a subterrene voice or intelligence shouting monotonously in enigmatical sense-impacts uninscribable save as gibberish. The two sounds most frequently repeated are those rendered by the letters *"Cthulhu"* and *"R'lyeh."*[18]

On March 23d, the manuscript continued, Wilcox failed to appear; and inquiries at his quarters revealed that he had been stricken with an obscure sort of fever and taken to the home of his family in Waterman Street. He had cried out in the night, arousing several other artists in the building, and had manifested since then only alternations of unconsciousness and delirium. My uncle at once telephoned the family, and from that time forward kept close watch of the case; calling often at the Thayer Street office of Dr. Tobey, whom he learned to be in charge. The youth's febrile mind, apparently, was dwelling on strange things; and the doctor shuddered now and then as he spoke of them. They included not only a repetition of what he had formerly dreamed, but touched wildly on a gigantic thing "miles high" which walked or lumbered about. He at no time fully described this object, but occasional frantic words, as repeated by Dr. Tobey, convinced the professor that it must be identical with the nameless monstrosity he had sought to depict in his dream-sculpture. Reference to this object, the doctor added, was invariably a prelude to the young man's subsidence into lethargy. His temperature, oddly enough, was not greatly above normal; but his whole condition was otherwise such as to suggest true fever rather than mental disorder.

On April 2nd at about 3 p.m. every trace of Wilcox's malady suddenly ceased. He sat upright in bed, astonished to find himself at home and completely ignorant of what had happened in dream or reality since the night of March 22nd. Pronounced well by his physician, he returned to his quarters in three days; but to Professor Angell he was of no further assistance. All traces of strange dreaming had vanished with his recovery, and my uncle kept no record of his night-thoughts after a week of pointless and irrelevant accounts of thoroughly usual visions.

[18] *R'lyeh*: The first mention of Lovecraft's version of Atlantis, which he originally considered calling *L'yeh*. Lovecraft first used the Atlantis theme in his tale of a German U-boat crew in the Great War, "The Temple" (1920).

Here the first part of the manuscript ended, but references to certain of the scattered notes gave me much material for thought—so much, in fact, that only the ingrained scepticism then forming my philosophy can account for my continued distrust of the artist. The notes in question were those descriptive of the dreams of various persons covering the same period as that in which young Wilcox had had his strange visitations. My uncle, it seems, had quickly instituted a prodigiously far-flung body of inquiries amongst nearly all the friends whom he could question without impertinence, asking for nightly reports of their dreams, and the dates of any notable visions for some time past. The reception of his request seems to have been varied; but he must, at the very least, have received more responses than any ordinary man could have handled without a secretary. This original correspondence was not preserved, but his notes formed a thorough and really significant digest. Average people in society and business—New England's traditional "salt of the earth"— gave an almost completely negative result, though scattered cases of uneasy but formless nocturnal impressions appear here and there, always between March 23d and April 2nd—the period of young Wilcox's delirium. Scientific men were little more affected, though four cases of vague description suggest fugitive glimpses of strange landscapes, and in one case there is mentioned a dread of something abnormal.

It was from the artists and poets that the pertinent answers came, and I know that panic would have broken loose had they been able to compare notes. As it was, lacking their original letters, I half suspected the compiler of having asked leading questions, or of having edited the correspondence in corroboration of what he had latently resolved to see. That is why I continued to feel that Wilcox, somehow cognisant of the old data which my uncle had possessed, had been imposing on the veteran scientist. These responses from aesthetes told a disturbing tale.

From February 28th to April 2nd a large proportion of
them had dreamed very bizarre things, the intensity of the
dreams being immeasurably the stronger during the period
of the sculptor's delirium. Over a fourth of those who reported anything, reported scenes and half-sounds not unlike those which Wilcox had described; and some of the
dreamers confessed acute fear of the gigantic nameless
thing visible toward the last. One case, which the note
describes with emphasis, was very sad. The subject, a
wisely known architect with leanings toward theosophy
and occultism, went violently insane on the date of young
Wilcox's seizure, and expired several months later after
incessant screamings to be saved from some escaped denizen of hell. Had my uncle referred to these cases by name
instead of merely by number, I should have attempted
some corroboration and personal investigation; but as it
was, I succeeded in tracing down only a few. All of these,
however, bore out the notes in full. I have often wondered
if all the objects of the professor's questioning felt as puzzled as did this fraction. It is well that no explanation
shall ever reach them.

The press cuttings, as I have intimated, touched on
cases of panic, mania, and eccentricity during the given
period. Professor Angell must have employed a cutting bureau, for the number of extracts was tremendous and the
sources scattered throughout the globe. Here was a nocturnal suicide in London, where a lone sleeper had leaped
from a window after a shocking cry. Here likewise a rambling letter to the editor of a paper in South America,
where a fanatic deduces a dire future from visions he has
seen. A despatch from California describes a theosophist
colony as donning white robes en masse for some "glorious fulfilment" which never arrives, whilst items from
India speak guardedly of serious native unrest toward the
end of March. Voodoo orgies multiply in Hayti,[19] and African outposts report ominous mutterings. American officers in the Philippines find certain tribes bothersome

about this time, and New York policemen are mobbed by hysterical Levantines[20] on the night of March 22–23. The west of Ireland, too, is full of wild rumour and legendry, and a fantastic painter named Ardois-Bonnot hangs a blasphemous "Dream Landscape" in the Paris spring salon of 1926. And so numerous are the recorded troubles in insane asylums, that only a miracle can have stopped the medical fraternity from noting strange parallelisms and drawing mystified conclusions. A weird bunch of cuttings, all told; and I can at this date scarcely envisage the callous rationalism with which I set them aside. But I was then convinced that young Wilcox had known of the older matters mentioned by the professor.

II. *The Tale of Inspector Legrasse.*

The older matters which had made the sculptor's dream and bas-relief so significant to my uncle formed the subject of the second half of his long manuscript. Once before, it appears, Professor Angell had seen the hellish outlines of the nameless monstrosity, puzzled over the unknown hieroglyphics, and heard the ominous syllables which can be rendered only as "*Cthulhu*"; and all this in so stirring and horrible a connexion that it is small wonder he pursued young Wilcox with queries and demands for data.

The earlier experience had come in 1908, seventeen years before, when the American Archaeological Society held its annual meeting in St. Louis. Professor Angell, as befitted one of his authority and attainments, had had a prominent part in all the deliberations; and was one of the

[19] *Voodoo orgies multiply in Hayti*: Voodoo is a religion, African in origin, practiced by certain Caribbean peoples, chiefly Haitians. *Hayti* is an obsolete variant spelling of *Haiti*.

[20] *hysterical Levantines*: The Levant was the collective name for the countries on the eastern shore of the Mediterranean from Egypt up to and including Turkey. Here the term refers to the many Jewish inhabitants of New York.

first to be approached by the several outsiders who took advantage of the convocation to offer questions for correct answering and problems for expert solution.

The chief of these outsiders, and in a short time the focus of interest for the entire meeting, was a commonplace-looking middle-aged man who had travelled all the way from New Orleans for certain special information unobtainable from any local source. His name was John Raymond Legrasse, and he was by profession an Inspector of Police. With him he bore the subject of his visit, a grotesque, repulsive, and apparently very ancient stone statuette whose origin he was at a loss to determine. It must not be fancied that Inspector Legrasse had the least interest in archaeology. On the contrary, his wish for enlightenment was prompted by purely professional considerations. The statuette, idol, fetish,[21] or whatever it was, had been captured some months before in the wooded swamps south of New Orleans during a raid on a supposed voodoo meeting; and so singular and hideous were the rites connected with it, that the police could not but realise that they had stumbled on a dark cult totally unknown to them, and infinitely more diabolic than even the blackest of the African voodoo circles. Of its origin, apart from the erratic and unbelievable tales extorted from the captured members, absolutely nothing was to be discovered; hence the anxiety of the police for any antiquarian lore which might help them to place the frightful symbol, and through it track down the cult to its fountain-head.

Inspector Legrasse was scarcely prepared for the sensation which his offering created. One sight of the thing had been enough to throw the assembled men of science into a state of tense excitement, and they lost no time in crowding around him to gaze at the diminutive figure whose utter strangeness and air of genuinely abysmal an-

---

[21] *fetish*: An object believed by primitive peoples to have magical power to protect or aid its owner.

tiquity hinted so potently at unopened and archaic vistas. No recognised school of sculpture had animated this terrible object, yet centuries and even thousands of years seemed recorded in its dim and greenish surface of unplaceable stone.

The figure, which was finally passed slowly from man to man for close and careful study, was between seven and eight inches in height, and of exquisitely artistic workmanship. It represented a monster of vaguely anthropoid outline,[22] but with an octopus-like head whose face was a mass of feelers, a scaly, rubbery-looking body, prodigious claws on hind and fore feet, and long, narrow wings behind. This thing, which seemed instinct with a fearsome and unnatural malignancy, was of a somewhat bloated corpulence, and squatted evilly on a rectangular block or pedestal covered with undecipherable characters. The tips of the wings touched the back edge of the block, the seat occupied the centre, whilst the long, curved claws of the doubled-up, crouching hind legs gripped the front edge and extended a quarter of the way down toward the bottom of the pedestal. The cephalopod[23] head was bent forward, so that the ends of the facial feelers brushed the backs of huge fore paws which clasped the croucher's elevated knees. The aspect of the whole was abnormally life-like, and the more subtly fearful because its source was so totally unknown. Its vast, awesome, and incalculable age was unmistakable; yet not one link did it shew with any known type of art belonging to civilisation's youth—or indeed to any other time. Totally separate and apart, its very material was a mystery; for the soapy, greenish-black stone with its golden or iridescent flecks and striations resembled nothing familiar to geology or mineralogy. The characters along the base were equally baffling; and no

---

[22] *anthropoid outline*: Resembling a man or an ape.

[23] *cephalopod*: A member of the most highly organized group of mollusks, including squids, octopuses, and cuttlefish.

H. P. Lovecraft's sketches of Pickman's Model and Cthulhu (taken from letters to F. Lee Baldwin, 27 July 1934 and 3 June 1934, respectively). (Courtesy of John Hay Library, Brown University)

member present, despite a representation of half the
world's expert learning in this field, could form the least
notion of even the remotest linguistic kinship. They, like
the subject and material, belonged to something horribly
remote and distinct from mankind as we know it; something frightfully suggestive of old and unhallowed cycles
of life in which our world and our conceptions have no
part.

And yet, as the members severally shook their heads
and confessed defeat at the Inspector's problem, there was
one man in that gathering who suspected a touch of bizarre familiarity in the monstrous shape and writing, and
who presently told with some diffidence of the odd trifle
he knew. This person was the late William Channing
Webb, Professor of Anthropology in Princeton University,
and an explorer of no slight note. Professor Webb had been
engaged, forty-eight years before, in a tour of Greenland
and Iceland in search of some Runic inscriptions[24] which
he failed to unearth; and whilst high up on the West
Greenland coast had encountered a singular tribe or cult
of degenerate Esquimaux[25] whose religion, a curious form
of devil-worship, chilled him with its deliberate blood-
thirstiness and repulsiveness. It was a faith of which other
Esquimaux knew little, and which they mentioned only
with shudders, saying that it had come down from horribly ancient aeons before ever the world was made. Besides
nameless rites and human sacrifices there were certain
queer hereditary rituals addressed to a supreme elder devil
or *tornasuk*; and of this Professor Webb had taken a care-

---

[24] *Runic inscriptions*: Runes are ancient characters used in Teutonic, Anglo-
Saxon, and Scandinavian inscriptions. With the coming of Christianity runes
were suppressed because of their pagan associations. The word *rune* comes from
an early Anglo-Saxon word meaning secret or mystery.

[25] *Esquimaux*: A now archaic spelling of Eskimos. The term *Eskimo* for the
people inhabiting the coastlines of the extreme north of Siberia, Canada, and
Greenland has gone out of fashion, replaced by *Inuit*. See note 64 to *At the
Mountains of Madness* (*Annotated Lovecraft*, 204).

ful phonetic copy from an aged *angekok* or wizard-priest, expressing the sounds in Roman letters as best he knew how. But just now of prime significance was the fetish which this cult had cherished, and around which they danced when the aurora[26] leaped high over the ice cliffs. It was, the professor stated, a very crude bas-relief of stone, comprising a hideous picture and some cryptic writing. And so far as he could tell, it was a rough parallel in all essential features of the bestial thing now lying before the meeting.

This data, received with suspense and astonishment by the assembled members, proved doubly exciting to Inspector Legrasse; and he began at once to ply his informant with questions. Having noted and copied an oral ritual among the swamp cult-worshippers his men had arrested, he besought the professor to remember as best he might the syllables taken down amongst the diabolist Esquimaux. There then followed an exhaustive comparison of details, and a moment of really awed silence when both detective and scientist agreed on the virtual identity of the phrase common to two hellish rituals so many worlds of distance apart. What, in substance, both the Esquimau wizards and the Louisiana swamp-priests had chanted to their kindred idols was something very like this—the word-divisions being guessed at from traditional breaks in the phrase as chanted aloud:

"*Ph'nglui mglw'nafh Cthulhu R'lyeh wgah'nagl fhtagn.*"

Legrasse had one point in advance of Professor Webb, for several among his mongrel prisoners had repeated to him what older celebrants had told them the words meant. This text, as given, ran something like this:

---

[26] *aurora*: The aurora borealis or northern lights. Arches or streaks of light visible in the night sky only in the higher latitudes.

"In his house at R'lyeh dead Cthulhu waits dreaming."

And now, in response to a general and urgent demand, Inspector Legrasse related as fully as possible his experience with the swamp worshippers; telling a story to which I could see my uncle attached profound significance. It savoured of the wildest dreams of myth-maker and theosophist, and disclosed an astonishing degree of cosmic imagination among such half-castes and pariahs as might be expected to possess it.

On November 1st, 1907, there had come to the New Orleans police a frantic summons from the swamp and lagoon country to the south. The squatters there, mostly primitive but good-natured descendants of Lafitte's men,[27] were in the grip of stark terror from an unknown thing which had stolen upon them in the night. It was voodoo, apparently, but voodoo of a more terrible sort than they had ever known; and some of their women and children had disappeared since the malevolent tom-tom had begun its incessant beating far within the black haunted woods where no dweller ventured. There were insane shouts and harrowing screams, soul-chilling chants and dancing devil-flames; and, the frightened messenger added, the people could stand it no more.

So a body of twenty police, filling two carriages and an automobile, had set out in the late afternoon with the shivering squatter as a guide. At the end of the passable road they alighted, and for miles splashed on in silence through the terrible cypress woods where day never came. Ugly roots and malignant hanging nooses of Spanish moss beset them, and now and then a pile of dank stones or fragment of a rotting wall intensified by its hint of morbid habitation a depression which every malformed tree and every fungous islet combined to create. At length the

---

[27] *Lafitte's men:* Jean Lafitte (c. 1780–1826?) led a band of pirates who operated off the Baratarian coast south of New Orleans. He and his men assisted the Americans in the battle of New Orleans against the British in 1814. A popular romantic figure in his day, Lafitte became a legend after his death.

squatter settlement, a miserable huddle of huts, hove in
sight; and hysterical dwellers ran out to cluster around the
group of bobbing lanterns. The muffled beat of tom-toms
was now faintly audible far, far ahead; and a curdling
shriek came at infrequent intervals when the wind shifted.
A reddish glare, too, seemed to filter through the pale un-
dergrowth beyond endless avenues of forest night. Reluc-
tant even to be left alone again, each one of the cowed
squatters refused point-blank to advance another inch
toward the scene of unholy worship, so Inspector Legrasse
and his nineteen colleagues plunged on unguided into
black arcades of horror that none of them had ever trod
before.

The region now entered by the police was one of traditionally evil repute, substantially unknown and untra-
versed by white men. There were legends of a hidden lake
unglimpsed by mortal sight, in which dwelt a huge, formless white polypous[28] thing with luminous eyes; and squatters whispered that bat-winged devils flew up out of
caverns in inner earth to worship it at midnight. They
said it had been there before D'Iberville, before La Salle,[29]
before the Indians, and before even the wholesome beasts
and birds of the woods. It was nightmare itself, and to see
it was to die. But it made men dream, and so they knew
enough to keep away. The present voodoo orgy was, indeed, on the merest fringe of this abhorred area, but that
location was bad enough; hence perhaps the very place
of the worship had terrified the squatters more than the
shocking sounds and incidents.

Only poetry or madness could do justice to the noises

---

[28] *polypous*: Characteristic of a polyp, an inverterbrate animal with a hollow
cylindrical body.

[29] *before D'Iberville, before La Salle*: Pierre le Moyne, sieur d'Iberville
(1661–1706), was the first European to ascertain the mouth of the Mississippi
River from the Gulf approach and explore its delta. Robert Cavelier, sieur de la
Salle (1643–87), another French explorer, descended the Mississippi from Canada
and claimed the region for France.

heard by Legrasse's men as they ploughed on through the black morass toward the red glare and the muffled tom-toms. There are vocal qualities peculiar to men, and vocal qualities peculiar to beasts; and it is terrible to hear the one when the source should yield the other. Animal fury and orgiastic licence here whipped themselves to daemoniac heights by howls and squawking ecstasies that tore and reverberated through those nighted woods like pestilential tempests from the gulfs of hell. Now and then the less organised ululation[30] would cease, and from what seemed a well-drilled chorus of hoarse voices would rise in singsong chant that hideous phrase or ritual:

> "Ph'nglui mglw'nafh Cthulhu R'lyeh wgah'nagl fhtagn."

Then the men, having reached a spot where the trees were thinner, came suddenly in sight of the spectacle itself. Four of them reeled, one fainted, and two were shaken into a frantic cry which the mad cacophony of the orgy fortunately deadened. Legrasse dashed swamp water on the face of the fainting man, and all stood trembling and nearly hypnotised with horror.

In a natural glade of the swamp stood a grassy island of perhaps an acre's extent, clear of trees and tolerably dry. On this now leaped and twisted a more indescribable horde of human abnormality than any but a Sime or an Angarola[31] could paint. Void of clothing, this hybrid spawn were braying, bellowing, and writhing about a monstrous

---

[30] *ululation*: A howl or wail.

[31] *Sime . . . Angarola*: Lovecraft may have discovered the artist Sidney Herbert Sime (1867–1945), whose "weird decorative grotesquerie" (*Selected Letters* II, 219) he admired, through Sime's illustrations to Lord Dunsany's *The Book of Wonder* (1912). Sime also did the frontispiece for Arthur Machen's novel *The Hill of Dreams* (1907).

Anthony Angarola (1893–1929) was an American book illustrator. Lovecraft may have seen his illustrations to Ben Hecht's pseudo-weird novel *The Kingdom of Evil* (1924).

ring-shaped bonfire; in the centre of which, revealed by
occasional rifts in the curtain of flame, stood a great gran-
ite monolith some eight feet in height; on top of which,
incongruous with its diminutiveness, rested the noxious
carven statuette. From a wide circle of ten scaffolds set
up at regular intervals with the flame-girt monolith as a
centre hung, head downward, the oddly marred bodies of
the helpless squatters who had disappeared. It was inside
this circle that the ring of worshippers jumped and roared,
the general direction of the mass motion being from left
to right in endless Bacchanal[32] between the ring of bodies
and the ring of fire.

It may have been only imagination and it may have been
only echoes which induced one of the men, an excitable
Spaniard, to fancy he heard antiphonal responses to the
ritual from some far and unillumined spot deeper within
the wood of ancient legendry and horror. This man, Joseph
D. Galvez, I later met and questioned; and he proved dis-
tractingly imaginative. He indeed went so far as to hint
of the faint beating of great wings,[33] and of a glimpse of
shining eyes and a mountainous white bulk beyond the
remotest trees—but I suppose he had been hearing too
much native superstition.

Actually, the horrified pause of the men was of compar-
atively brief duration. Duty came first; and although there
must have been nearly a hundred mongrel celebrants in
the throng, the police relied on their firearms and plunged
determinedly into the nauseous rout. For five minutes the
resultant din and chaos were beyond description. Wild
blows were struck, shots were fired, and escapes were
made; but in the end Legrasse was able to count some

[32] *Bacchanal*: A Roman religious festival in honor of Bacchus, the god of wine.
It later degenerated into an occasion for drunken and licentious behavior and
was banned by law.

[33] *faint beating of great wings*: An echo of "the beating of black wings" in "Supernatural Horror in Literature" (*Dagon*, 369). Lovecraft was working on this
long essay at this period.

forty-seven sullen prisoners, whom he forced to dress in haste and fall into line between two rows of policemen. Five of the worshippers lay dead, and two severely wounded ones were carried away on improvised stretchers by their fellow-prisoners. The image on the monolith, of course, was carefully removed and carried back by Legrasse.

Examined at headquarters after a trip of intense strain and weariness, the prisoners all proved to be men of a very low, mixed-blooded, and mentally aberrant type. Most were seamen, and a sprinkling of negroes and mulattoes, largely West Indians or Brava Portuguese from the Cape Verde Islands,[34] gave a colouring of voodooism to the heterogeneous cult. But before many questions were asked, it became manifest that something far deeper and older than negro fetishism was involved. Degraded and ignorant as they were, the creatures held with surprising consistency to the central idea of their loathsome faith.

They worshipped, so they said, the Great Old Ones[35] who lived ages before there were any men, and who came to the young world out of the sky. Those Old Ones were gone now, inside the earth and under the sea; but their dead bodies had told their secrets in dreams to the first men, who formed a cult which had never died. This was that cult, and the prisoners said it had always existed and always would exist, hidden in distant wastes and dark places all over the world until the time when the great priest Cthulhu, from his dark house in the mighty city of R'lyeh under the waters, should rise and bring the earth

---

[34] *Cape Verde Islands*: A group of volcanic islands in the Atlantic off the west coast of Africa settled by the Portuguese, who introduced African slaves there. Brava is the name of one of these islands. By Lovecraft's day many persons of Brava Portuguese descent were living in Rhode Island. A Brava Portuguese, Tony Gomes, figures in the plot of *The Case of Charles Dexter Ward*.

[35] *Great Old Ones*: Throughout his fiction Lovecraft called his various cosmic entities "Old Ones," "Great Old Ones," and "Elder Ones," with little consistency. See notes 88 and 90 to *At the Mountains of Madness* (*Annotated Lovecraft*, 220).

again beneath his sway. Some day he would call, when the stars were ready, and the secret cult would always be waiting to liberate him.

Meanwhile no more must be told. There was a secret which even torture could not extract. Mankind was not absolutely alone among the conscious things of earth, for shapes came out of the dark to visit the faithful few. But these were not the Great Old Ones. No man had ever seen the Old Ones. The carven idol was great Cthulhu, but none might say whether or not the others were precisely like him. No one could read the old writing now, but things were told by word of mouth. The chanted ritual was not the secret—that was never spoken aloud, only whispered. The chant meant only this: "In his house at R'lyeh dead Cthulhu waits dreaming."

Only two of the prisoners were found sane enough to be hanged, and the rest were committed to various institutions. All denied a part in the ritual murders, and averred that the killing had been done by Black Winged Ones which had come to them from their immemorial meeting-place in the haunted wood. But of those mysterious allies no coherent account could ever be gained. What the police did extract, came mainly from an immensely aged mestizo[36] named Castro, who claimed to have sailed to strange ports and talked with undying leaders of the cult in the mountains of China.

Old Castro remembered bits of hideous legend that paled the speculations of theosophists and made man and the world seem recent and transient indeed. There had been aeons when other Things ruled on the earth, and They had had great cities. Remains of Them, he said the deathless Chinamen had told him, were still to be found as Cyclopean stones on islands in the Pacific. They all died vast epochs of time before men came, but there were

---

[36] *an immensely aged mestizo*: A mestizo is a person of mixed European and American Indian blood.

arts which could revive Them when the stars had come round again to the right positions in the cycle of eternity. They had, indeed, come themselves from the stars, and brought Their images with Them.

These Great Old Ones, Castro continued, were not composed altogether of flesh and blood. They had shape—for did not this star-fashioned image prove it?—but that shape was not made of matter. When the stars were right,[37] They could plunge from world to world through the sky; but when the stars were wrong, they could not live. But although They no longer lived, They would never really die. They all lay in stone houses in Their great city of R'lyeh, preserved by the spells of mighty Cthulhu for a glorious resurrection when the stars and the earth might once more be ready for Them. But at that time some force from outside must serve to liberate Their bodies. The spells that preserved Them intact likewise prevented Them from making an initial move, and They could only lie awake in the dark and think whilst uncounted millions of years rolled by. They knew all that was occurring in the universe, but Their mode of speech was transmitted thought. Even now They talked in Their tombs. When, after infinities of chaos, the first men came, the Great Old Ones spoke to the sensitive among them by moulding their dreams; for only thus could Their language reach the fleshly minds of mammals.

Then, whispered Castro, those first men formed the cult around small idols which the Great Ones shewed them; idols brought in dim aeras from dark stars. That cult would never die till the stars came right again, and the secret priests would take great Cthulhu from His tomb to revive His subjects and resume His rule of earth. The time would be easy to know, for then mankind would have become as the Great Old Ones; free and wild and beyond

---

[37] *When the stars were right*: Lovecraft had no belief in astrology, but here it serves to explain, metaphorically at any rate, Cthulhu's interstellar migration.

good and evil, with laws and morals thrown aside and all men shouting and killing and revelling in joy. Then the liberated Old Ones would teach them new ways to shout and kill and revel and enjoy themselves, and all the earth would flame with a holocaust of ecstasy and freedom. Meanwhile the cult, by appropriate rites, must keep alive the memory of those ancient ways and shadow forth the prophecy of their return.

In the elder time chosen men had talked with the entombed Old Ones in dreams, but then something had happened. The great stone city R'lyeh, with its monoliths and sepulchres, had sunk beneath the waves; and the deep waters, full of the one primal mystery through which not even thought can pass, had cut off the spectral intercourse. But memory never died, and high-priests said that the city would rise again when the stars were right. Then came out of the earth the black spirits of earth, mouldy and shadowy, and full of dim rumours picked up in caverns beneath forgotten sea-bottoms. But of them old Castro dared not speak much. He cut himself off hurriedly, and no amount of persuasion or subtlety could elicit more in this direction. The *size* of the Old Ones, too, he curiously declined to mention. Of the cult, he said that he thought the centre lay amid the pathless deserts of Arabia, where Irem, the City of Pillars,[38] dreams hidden and untouched. It was not allied to the European witch-cult, and was virtually unknown beyond its members. No book had ever really hinted of it, though the deathless Chinamen said that there were double meanings in the *Necronomicon* of the mad Arab Abdul Alhazred which the initiated might read as they chose, especially the much-discussed couplet:

"That is not dead which can eternal lie,

---

[38] *Irem, the City of Pillars*: An ancient Arabian city, first mentioned in Lovecraft's tale "The Nameless City" (1921).

And with strange aeons even death may die.''[39]

Legrasse, deeply impressed and not a little bewildered, had inquired in vain concerning the historic affiliations of the cult. Castro, apparently, had told the truth when he said that it was wholly secret. The authorities at Tulane University could shed no light upon either cult or image, and now the detective had come to the highest authorities in the country and met with no more than the Greenland tale of Professor Webb.

The feverish interest aroused at the meeting by Legrasse's tale, corroborated as it was by the statuette, is echoed in the subsequent correspondence of those who attended; although scant mention occurs in the formal publications of the society. Caution is the first care of those accustomed to face occasional charlatanry and imposture. Legrasse for some time lent the image to Professor Webb, but at the latter's death it was returned to him and remains in his possession, where I viewed it not long ago. It is truly a terrible thing, and unmistakably akin to the dream-sculpture of young Wilcox.

That my uncle was excited by the tale of the sculptor I did not wonder, for what thoughts must arise upon hearing, after a knowledge of what Legrasse had learned of the cult, of a sensitive young man who had *dreamed* not only the figure and exact hieroglyphics of the swamp-found image and the Greenland devil tablet, but had come *in his dreams* upon at least three of the precise words of the formula uttered alike by Esquimau diabolists and mongrel Louisianans? Professor Angell's instant start on an investigation of the utmost thoroughness was eminently natural; though privately I suspected young Wilcox of having heard of the cult in some indirect way, and of having invented a series of dreams to heighten and continue the mystery

---

[39] *That is not dead . . . even death may die*: Abdul Alhazred's famous couplet, first quoted in "The Nameless City."

at my uncle's expense. The dream-narratives and cuttings collected by the professor were, of course, strong corroboration; but the rationalism of my mind and the extravagance of the whole subject led me to adopt what I thought the most sensible conclusions. So, after thoroughly studying the manuscript again and correlating the theosophical and anthropological notes with the cult narrative of Legrasse, I made a trip to Providence to see the sculptor and give him the rebuke I thought proper for so boldly imposing upon a learned and aged man.

Wilcox still lived alone in the Fleur-de-Lys Building in Thomas Street, a hideous Victorian imitation of seventeenth-century Breton architecture which flaunts its stuccoed front amidst the lovely colonial houses on the ancient hill, and under the very shadow of the finest Georgian steeple in America.[40] I found him at work in his rooms, and at once conceded from the specimens scattered about that his genius is indeed profound and authentic. He will, I believe, some time be heard from as one of the great decadents; for he has crystallised in clay and will one day mirror in marble those nightmares and phantasies which Arthur Machen[41] evokes in prose, and Clark Ashton Smith[42] makes visible in verse and in painting.

Dark, frail, and somewhat unkempt in aspect, he turned languidly at my knock and asked me my business without rising. When I told him who I was, he displayed some interest; for my uncle had excited his curiosity in probing

---

[40] *finest Georgian steeple in America*: The First Baptist Church, which Lovecraft called "that supreme landmark of Providence, finish'd in 1775." He and his friend James F. Morton explored the interior in late 1923: "This is my maternal ancestral church, but I had not been in the main auditorium since 1895, or in the building at all since 1907, when I gave an illustrated astronomical lecture to the Boys' Club. We found this fane as pleasing within as without, the panelling and the carving above the doors being especially notable as specimens of Georgian workmanship. We ascended into the organ loft, and I endeavour'd to play 'Yes, We Have no Bananas,' but was balk'd by lack of power, since the machine is not a self-starter." (*Selected Letters* I, 277)

[41] *Arthur Machen*: See note 1 to "The Horror at Red Hook."

his strange dreams, yet had never explained the reason for the study. I did not enlarge his knowledge in this regard, but sought with some subtlety to draw him out. In a short time I became convinced of his absolute sincerity, for he spoke of the dreams in a manner none could mistake. They and their subconscious residuum had influenced his art profoundly, and he shewed me a morbid statue whose contours almost made me shake with the potency of its black suggestion. He could not recall having seen the original of this thing except in his own dream bas-relief, but the outlines had formed themselves insensibly under his hands. It was, no doubt, the giant shape he had raved of in delirium. That he really knew nothing of the hidden cult, save from what my uncle's relentless catechism had let fall, he soon made clear; and again I strove to think of some way in which he could possibly have received the weird impressions.

He talked of his dreams in a strangely poetic fashion; making me see with terrible vividness the damp Cyclopean city of slimy green stone—whose *geometry*, he oddly said, was *all wrong*—and hear with frightened expectancy the ceaseless, half-mental calling from underground: *"Cthulhu fhtagn"*, *"Cthulhu fhtagn"*. These words had formed part of that dread ritual which told of dead Cthulhu's dream-vigil in his stone vault at R'lyeh, and I felt deeply moved despite my rational beliefs. Wilcox, I was sure, had heard of the cult in some casual way, and had

---

[42] *Clark Ashton Smith*: In "Supernatural Horror in Literature" Lovecraft states: "Of younger Americans, none strikes the note of cosmic terror so well as the California poet, artist, and fictionist Clark Ashton Smith, whose bizarre writings, drawings, paintings, and stories are the delight of a sensitive few." Lovecraft and Clark Ashton Smith (1893–1961) corresponded regularly from 1922 on, but never met in person. Together with Robert E. Howard, they were regarded as the three great contributors to *Weird Tales* in the late 1920s and early 1930s. Lovecraft further says in "Supernatural Horror in Literature": "In sheer daemoniac strangeness and fertility of conception, Mr. Smith is perhaps unexcelled by any other writer dead or living." (*Dagon*, 412) Despite Lovecraft's enthusiasm, today Smith remains the province of a sensitive few. See note 82 to *At the Mountains of Madness* (*Annotated Lovecraft*, 215).

soon forgotten it amidst the mass of his equally weird reading and imagining. Later, by virtue of its sheer impressiveness, it had found subconscious expression in dreams, in the bas-relief, and in the terrible statue I now beheld; so that his imposture upon my uncle had been a very innocent one. The youth was of a type, at once slightly affected and slightly ill-mannered, which I could never like; but I was willing enough now to admit both his genius and his honesty. I took leave of him amicably, and wish him all the success his talent promises.

The matter of the cult still remained to fascinate me, and at times I had visions of personal fame from researches into its origin and connexions. I visited New Orleans, talked with Legrasse and others of that old-time raiding-party, saw the frightful image, and even questioned such of the mongrel prisoners as still survived. Old Castro, unfortunately, had been dead for some years. What I now heard so graphically at first-hand, though it was really no more than a detailed confirmation of what my uncle had written, excited me afresh; for I felt sure that I was on the track of a very real, very secret, and very ancient religion whose discovery would make me an anthropologist of note. My attitude was still one of absolute materialism,[43] *as I wish it still were,* and I discounted with almost inexplicable perversity the coincidence of the dream notes and odd cuttings collected by Professor Angell.

One thing I began to suspect, and which I now fear I *know,* is that my uncle's death was far from natural. He fell on a narrow hill street leading up from an ancient waterfront swarming with foreign mongrels, after a careless push from a negro sailor. I did not forget the mixed

---

[43] *absolute materialism:* A belief, post-Darwin and pre-Einstein, that claims strict mechanical laws determine the universe and rules out the existence of the soul and hence life after death. In 1924 Lovecraft declared in a letter: "I am a sceptic and analyst by nature, and early settled into my present attitude of cynical materialism." (*Selected Letters* I, 299) See note 5 to "Herbert West—Reanimator."

blood and marine pursuits of the cult-members in Louisiana, and would not be surprised to learn of secret methods and poison needles as ruthless and as anciently known as the cryptic rites and beliefs. Legrasse and his men, it is true, have been let alone; but in Norway a certain seaman who saw things is dead. Might not the deeper inquiries of my uncle after encountering the sculptor's data have come to sinister ears? I think Professor Angell died because he knew too much, or because he was likely to learn too much. Whether I shall go as he did remains to be seen, for I have learned much now.

III. *The Madness from the Sea.*

If heaven ever wishes to grant me a boon, it will be a total effacing of the results of a mere chance which fixed my eye on a certain stray piece of shelf-paper. It was nothing on which I would naturally have stumbled in the course of my daily round, for it was an old number of an Australian journal, the *Sydney Bulletin*[44] for April 18, 1925. It had escaped even the cutting bureau which had at the time of its issuance been avidly collecting material for my uncle's research.

I had largely given over my inquiries into what Professor Angell called the "Cthulhu Cult", and was visiting a learned friend in Paterson, New Jersey; the curator of a local museum and a mineralogist of note.[45] Examining one day the reserve specimens roughly set on the storage shelves in a rear room of the museum, my eye was caught by an odd picture in one of the old papers spread beneath

[44] *Sydney Bulletin*: An actual newspaper, founded in 1880.

[45] *a learned friend . . . a mineralogist of note*: A reference to James F. Morton (1870–1941), a friend of Lovecraft's who was the curator of the Paterson (New Jersey) Museum from 1925 to his death. A fellow amateur journalist and member of the New York Kalem Club, Morton introduced Lovecraft to the work of Algernon Blackwood in 1920.

the stones. It was the *Sydney Bulletin* I have mentioned, for my friend has wide affiliations in all conceivable foreign parts; and the picture was a half-tone cut of a hideous stone image almost identical with that which Legrasse had found in the swamp.

Eagerly clearing the sheet of its precious contents, I scanned the item in detail; and was disappointed to find it of only moderate length. What it suggested, however, was of portentous significance to my flagging quest; and I carefully tore it out for immediate action. It read as follows:

MYSTERY DERELICT FOUND AT SEA
Vigilant Arrives With Helpless Armed New Zealand Yacht in Tow.
One Survivor and Dead Man Found Aboard. Tale of
Desperate Battle and Deaths at Sea.
Rescued Seaman Refuses
Particulars of Strange Experience.
Odd Idol Found in His Possession. Inquiry
to Follow.

The Morrison Co.'s freighter *Vigilant,* bound from Valparaiso, arrived this morning at its wharf in Darling Harbour, having in tow the battled and disabled but heavily armed steam yacht *Alert* of Dunedin, N. Z., which was sighted April 12th in S. Latitude 34° 21', W. Longitude 152° 17' with one living and one dead man aboard.

The *Vigilant* left Valparaiso March 25th, and on April 2nd was driven considerably south of her course by exceptionally heavy storms and monster waves. On April 12th the derelict was sighted; and though apparently deserted, was found upon boarding to contain one survivor in a half-delirious condition and one man who had evidently been dead for more than a week. The living man was clutching a horrible stone idol of unknown origin, about a foot in height, regarding whose nature authorities at Sydney Uni-

versity, the Royal Society, and the Museum in College Street[46] all
profess complete bafflement, and which the survivor says he found
in the cabin of the yacht, in a small carved shrine of common
pattern.

This man, after recovering his senses, told an exceedingly
strange story of piracy and slaughter. He is Gustaf Johansen, a
Norwegian of some intelligence, and had been second mate of the
two-masted schooner *Emma* of Auckland, which sailed for Callao
February 20th with a complement of eleven men. The *Emma,* he
says, was delayed and thrown widely south of her course by the
great storm of March 1st, and on March 22nd, in S. Latitude 49°
51', W. Longitude 128° 34', encountered the *Alert,* manned by a
queer and evil-looking crew of Kanakas[47] and half-castes. Being
ordered peremptorily to turn back, Capt. Collins refused; whereupon the strange crew began to fire savagely and without warning
upon the schooner with a peculiarly heavy battery of brass cannon
forming part of the yacht's equipment. The *Emma*'s men shewed
fight, says the survivor, and though the schooner began to sink
from shots beneath the waterline they managed to heave alongside
their enemy and board her, grappling with the savage crew on the
yacht's deck, and being forced to kill them all, the number being
slightly superior, because of their particularly abhorrent and desperate though rather clumsy mode of fighting.

Three of the *Emma*'s men, including Capt. Collins and First
Mate Green, were killed; and the remaining eight under Second
Mate Johansen proceeded to navigate the captured yacht, going
ahead in their original direction to see if any reason for their
ordering back had existed. The next day, it appears, they raised
and landed on a small island, although none is known to exist in
that part of the ocean; and six of the men somehow died ashore,
though Johansen is queerly reticent about this part of his story,

[46] *Museum in College Street*: The Australian Museum, founded as the Natural
History Museum in 1827, has a major collection devoted to Australian and
Pacific anthropology.

[47] *Kanakas*: Natives of the South Sea islands, especially those employed in
Queensland, Australia, as laborers on the sugar plantations.

and speaks only of their falling into a rock chasm. Later, it seems, he and one companion boarded the yacht and tried to manage her, but were beaten about by the storm of April 2nd. From that time till his rescue on the 12th the man remembers little, and he does not even recall when William Briden, his companion, died. Briden's death reveals no apparent cause, and was probably due to excitement or exposure. Cable advices from Dunedin report that the *Alert* was well known there as an island trader, and bore an evil reputation along the waterfront. It was owned by a curious group of half-castes whose frequent meetings and night trips to the woods attracted no little curiosity; and it had set sail in great haste just after the storm and earth tremors of March 1st. Our Auckland correspondent gives the *Emma* and her crew an excellent reputation, and Johansen is described as a sober and worthy man. The admiralty will institute an inquiry on the whole matter beginning tomorrow, at which every effort will be made to induce Johansen to speak more freely than he has done hitherto.

This was all, together with the picture of the hellish image; but what a train of ideas it started in my mind! Here were new treasuries of data on the Cthulhu Cult, and evidence that it had strange interests at sea as well as on land. What motive prompted the hybrid crew to order back the *Emma* as they sailed about with their hideous idol? What was the unknown island on which six of the *Emma*'s crew had died, and about which the mate Johansen was so secretive? What had the vice-admiralty's investigation brought out, and what was known of the noxious cult in Dunedin? And most marvellous of all, what deep and more than natural linkage of dates was this which gave a malign and now undeniable significance to the various turns of events so carefully noted by my uncle?

March 1st—our February 28th according to the International Date Line—the earthquake and storm had come. From Dunedin the *Alert* and her noisome crew had darted eagerly forth as if imperiously summoned, and on the

other side of the earth poets and artists had begun to
dream of a strange, dank Cyclopean city whilst a young
sculptor had moulded in his sleep the form of the dreaded
Cthulhu. March 23d the crew of the *Emma* landed on an
unknown island and left six men dead; and on that date
the dreams of sensitive men assumed a heightened vividness and darkened with dread of a giant monster's malign pursuit, whilst an architect had gone mad and a
sculptor had lapsed suddenly into delirium! And what of
this storm of April 2nd—the date on which all dreams of
the dank city ceased, and Wilcox emerged unharmed from
the bondage of strange fever? What of all this—and of
those hints of old Castro about the sunken, star-born Old
Ones and their coming reign; their faithful cult and *their
mastery of dreams?* Was I tottering on the brink of cosmic
horrors beyond man's power to bear? If so, they must be
horrors of the mind alone, for in some way the second of
April had put a stop to whatever monstrous menace had
begun its siege of mankind's soul.

That evening, after a day of hurried cabling and arranging, I bade my host adieu and took a train for San Francisco. In less than a month I was in Dunedin; where,
however, I found that little was known of the strange cult-
members who had lingered in the old sea-taverns. Waterfront scum was far too common for special mention;
though there was vague talk about one inland trip these
mongrels had made, during which faint drumming and red
flame were noted on the distant hills. In Auckland I
learned that Johansen had returned *with yellow hair
turned white* after a perfunctory and inconclusive questioning at Sydney, and had thereafter sold his cottage in
West Street and sailed with his wife to his old home in
Oslo. Of his stirring experience he would tell his friends
no more than he had told the admiralty officials, and all
they could do was to give me his Oslo address.

After that I went to Sydney and talked profitlessly with
seamen and members of the vice-admiralty court. I saw

the *Alert,* now sold and in commercial use, at Circular
Quay in Sydney Cove, but gained nothing from its non-
committal bulk. The crouching image with its cuttlefish[48]
head, dragon body, scaly wings, and hieroglyphed pedestal,
was preserved in the Museum at Hyde Park;[49] and I studied
it long and well, finding it a thing of balefully exquisite
workmanship, and with the same utter mystery, terrible
antiquity, and unearthly strangeness of material which I
had noted in Legrasse's smaller specimen. Geologists, the
curator told me, had found it a monstrous puzzle; for they
vowed that the world held no rock like it. Then I thought
with a shudder of what old Castro had told Legrasse about
the primal Great Ones: "They had come from the stars,
and had brought Their images with Them."

Shaken with such a mental revolution as I had never
before known, I now resolved to visit Mate Johansen in
Oslo. Sailing for London, I rembarked at once for the Norwegian capital; and one autumn day landed at the trim
wharves in the shadow of the Egeberg.[50] Johansen's address, I discovered, lay in the Old Town of King Harold
Haardrada, which kept alive the name of Oslo during all
the centuries that the greater city masqueraded as "Christiana."[51] I made the brief trip by taxicab, and knocked with
palpitant heart at the door of a neat and ancient building
with plastered front. A sad-faced woman in black answered my summons, and I was stung with disappointment when she told me in halting English that Gustaf
Johansen was no more.

He had not survived his return, said his wife, for the

---

[48] *cuttlefish*: A cephalopod mollusk having 10 tentacles or arms, 8 of which have
suction cups and 2 that are longer and can shoot out for grasping prey.

[49] *Museum at Hyde Park*: Not identical to the Australian Museum, but another
museum located in the Hyde Park neighborhood of Sydney.

[50] *Egeberg*: A mountain overlooking Oslo.

[51] *King Haardrada . . . "Christiana"*: King Harald Haardrada founded Oslo circa
1050. In more recent centuries the Norwegian capital was called Christiana or
Kristiana and only reverted to Oslo in 1925, thus shortly before Thurston's visit.

doings at sea in 1925 had broken him. He had told her no more than he had told the public, but had left a long manuscript—of "technical matters" as he said—written in English, evidently in order to safeguard her from the peril of casual perusal. During a walk through a narrow lane near the Gothenburg dock, a bundle of papers falling from an attic window had knocked him down. Two Lascar sailors[52] at once helped him to his feet, but before the ambulance could reach him he was dead. Physicians found no adequate cause for the end, and laid it to heart trouble and a weakened constitution.

I now felt gnawing at my vitals that dark terror which will never leave me till I, too, am at rest; "accidentally" or otherwise. Persuading the widow that my connexion with her husband's "technical matters" was sufficient to entitle me to his manuscript, I bore the document away and began to read it on the London boat. It was a simple, rambling thing—a naive sailor's effort at a post-facto diary—and strove to recall day by day that last awful voyage. I cannot attempt to transcribe it verbatim in all its cloudiness and redundance, but I will tell its gist enough to shew why the sound of the water against the vessel's sides became so unendurable to me that I stopped my ears with cotton.[53]

Johansen, thank God, did not know quite all, even though he saw the city and the Thing, but I shall never sleep calmly again when I think of the horrors that lurk ceaselessly behind life in time and in space, and of those unhallowed blasphemies from elder stars which dream beneath the sea, known and favoured by a nightmare cult ready and eager to loose them on the world whenever an-

---

[52] *Lascar sailors:* Lascars were Hindus from India.

[53] *sound of the water . . . stopped my ears with cotton:* Like other Lovecraft protagonists, Thurston develops a phobia over something commonplace—here running water. Like Odysseus resisting the call of the Sirens, he must stop his ears. See note 60 below for another classical allusion.

other earthquake shall heave their monstrous stone city
again to the sun and air.

Johansen's voyage had begun just as he told it to the
vice-admiralty. The *Emma,* in ballast, had cleared Auckland on February 20th, and had felt the full force of that
earthquake-born tempest which must have heaved up
from the sea-bottom the horrors that filled men's dreams.
Once more under control, the ship was making good progress when held up by the *Alert* on March 22nd, and I could
feel the mate's regret as he wrote of her bombardment and
sinking. Of the swarthy cult-fiends on the *Alert* he speaks
with significant horror. There was some peculiarly abominable quality about them which made their destruction
seem almost a duty, and Johansen shews ingenuous wonder at the charge of ruthlessness brought against his party
during the proceedings of the court of inquiry. Then,
driven ahead by curiosity in their captured yacht under
Johansen's command, the men sight a great stone pillar
sticking out of the sea, and in S. Latitude 47° 9', W. Longitude 126° 43' come upon a coast-line of mingled mud,
ooze, and weedy Cyclopean masonry which can be nothing less than the tangible substance of earth's supreme
terror—the nightmare corpse-city of R'lyeh, that was built
in measureless aeons beyond history by the vast, loathsome shapes that seeped down from the dark stars. There
lay great Cthulhu and his hordes, hidden in green slimy
vaults and sending out at last, after cycles incalculable,
the thoughts that spread fear to the dreams of the sensitive
and called imperiously to the faithful to come on a pil-
grimage of liberation and restoration. All this Johansen did
not suspect, but God knows he soon saw enough!

I suppose that only a single mountain-top,[54] the hideous
monolith-crowned citadel whereon great Cthulhu was
buried, actually emerged from the waters. When I think

---

[54] *a single mountain-top*: Another example of the "tip of the iceberg" motif in
Lovecraft. See note 36 to "The Shunned House" for the analogous "titan elbow."

of the *extent* of all that may be brooding down there I almost wish to kill myself forthwith. Johansen and his men were awed by the cosmic majesty of this dripping Babylon of elder daemons, and must have guessed without guidance that it was nothing of this or of any sane planet. Awe at the unbelievable size of the greenish stone blocks, at the dizzying height of the great carven monolith, and at the stupefying identity of the colossal statues and bas-reliefs with the queer image found in the shrine on the *Alert,* is poignantly visible in every line of the mate's frightened description.

Without knowing what futurism is like, Johansen achieved something very close to it when he spoke of the city; for instead of describing any definite structure or building, he dwells only on broad impressions of vast angles and stone surfaces—surfaces too great to belong to any thing right or proper for this earth, and impious with horrible images and hieroglyphs. I mention his talk about *angles* because it suggests something Wilcox had told me of his awful dreams. He has said that the *geometry* of the dream-place he saw was abnormal, non-Euclidean,[55] and loathsomely redolent of spheres and dimensions apart from ours. Now an unlettered seaman felt the same thing whilst gazing at the terrible reality.

Johansen and his men landed at a sloping mud-bank on this monstrous Acropolis,[56] and clambered slipperily up over titan oozy blocks which could have been no mortal staircase. The very sun of heaven seemed distorted when viewed through the polarising miasma welling out from

---

[55] *non-Euclidean:* A system of geometry that doesn't accept Euclid's Fifth or parallel postulate. Two types of non-Euclidean geometry emerged in the nineteenth century: Lobachevskian (hyperbolic) and Riemannian (elliptic). For the school year 1906–07 Lovecraft received a 92 in plane geometry, but he voluntarily retook algebra to raise his grade from 75 to 85. "Mathematics I detest, and only a supreme effort of will gained for me the highest marks in Algebra and Geometry at school," he wrote in 1915 (*Selected Letters* I, 9).

[56] *Acropolis:* The upper fortified part of a Greek city. The most famous Acropolis is in Athens.

this sea-soaked perversion, and twisted menace and suspense lurked leeringly in those crazily elusive angles of carven rock where a second glance shewed concavity after the first shewed convexity.

Something very like fright had come over all the explorers before anything more definite than rock and ooze and weed was seen. Each would have fled had he not feared the scorn of the others, and it was only half-heartedly that they searched—vainly, as it proved—for some portable souvenir to bear away.

It was Rodriguez the Portuguese who climbed up the foot of the monolith and shouted of what he had found. The rest followed him, and looked curiously at the immense carved door[57] with the now familiar squid-dragon bas-relief. It was, Johansen said, like a great barn-door; and they all felt that it was a door because of the ornate lintel, threshold, and jambs around it, though they could not decide whether it lay flat like a trap-door or slantwise like an outside cellar-door. As Wilcox would have said, the geometry of the place was all wrong. One could not be sure that the sea and the ground were horizontal, hence the relative position of everything else seemed phantasmally variable.

Briden pushed at the stone in several places without result. Then Donovan felt over it delicately around the edge, pressing each point separately as he went. He climbed interminably along the grotesque stone moulding—that is, one would call it climbing if the thing was not after all horizontal—and the men wondered how any door in the universe could be so vast. Then, very softly and slowly, the acre-great panel began to give inward at

[57] *immense carved door*: In "The Moon Pool," a novelette by A. Merritt (1884–1943) set on or near the island of Ponape near the Carolines, there is mention of a "moon-door" which, when tilted, leads to a lower region of wonder and horror. Lovecraft considered "The Moon Pool" Merrit's best work. Like the altar stone in "The Rats in the Walls," the door the sailors encounter is balanced.

the top; and they saw that it was balanced. Donovan slid or somehow propelled himself down or along the jamb and rejoined his fellows, and everyone watched the queer recession of the monstrously carven portal. In this phantasy of prismatic distortion it moved anomalously in a diagonal way, so that all the rules of matter and perspective seemed upset.

The aperture was black with a darkness almost material. That tenebrousness was indeed a *positive quality*; for it obscured such parts of the inner walls as ought to have been revealed, and actually burst forth like smoke from its aeon-long imprisonment, visibly darkening the sun as it slunk away into the shrunken and gibbous[58] sky on flapping membraneous wings. The odour arising from the newly opened depths was intolerable, and at length the quick-eared Hawkins thought he heard a nasty, slopping sound down there. Everyone listened, and everyone was listening still when It lumbered slobberingly into sight and gropingly squeezed Its gelatinous green immensity through the black doorway into the tainted outside air of that poison city of madness.

Poor Johansen's handwriting almost gave out when he wrote of this. Of the six men who never reached the ship, he thinks two perished of pure fright in that accursed instant. The Thing cannot be described—there is no language for such abysms of shrieking and immemorial lunacy, such eldritch contradictions of all matter, force, and cosmic order. A mountain walked or stumbled. God! What wonder that across the earth a great architect went mad, and poor Wilcox raved with fever in that telepathic instant? The Thing of the idols, the green, sticky spawn of the stars, had awaked to claim his own. The stars were right again, and what an age-old cult had failed to do by design, a band of innocent sailors had done by accident.

---

[58] *gibbous:* Swollen or having a hump—an adjective Lovecraft usually applies to a phase of the moon.

After vigintillions of years[59] great Cthulhu was loose again, and ravening for delight.

Three men were swept up by the flabby claws before anybody turned. God rest them, if there be any rest in the universe. They were Donovan, Guerrera, and Ångstrom. Parker slipped as the other three were plunging frenziedly over endless vistas of green-crusted rock to the boat, and Johansen swears he was swallowed up by an angle of masonry which shouldn't have been there; an angle which was acute, but behaved as if it were obtuse. So only Briden and Johansen reached the boat, and pulled desperately for the *Alert* as the mountainous monstrosity flopped down the slimy stones and hesitated floundering at the edge of the water.

Steam had not been suffered to go down entirely, despite the departure of all hands for the shore; and it was the work of only a few moments of feverish rushing up and down between wheel and engines to get the *Alert* under way. Slowly, amidst the distorted horrors of that indescribable scene, she began to churn the lethal waters; whilst on the masonry of that charnel shore that was not of earth the titan Thing from the stars slavered and gibbered like Polypheme cursing the fleeing ship of Odysseus.[60] Then, bolder than the storied Cyclops, great Cthulhu slid greasily into the water and began to pursue with vast wave-raising strokes of cosmic potency. Briden looked back and went mad, laughing shrilly as he kept on laughing at intervals till death found him one night in the cabin whilst Johansen was wandering deliriously.

But Johansen had not given out yet. Knowing that the

---

[59] *vigintillions of years*: A vigintillion is 10 to the power of 63 in American numerical notation, in British notation 10 to the 120. In either case, a time span far vaster than the estimated age of the universe. See note 116 to "The Dunwich Horror" (*Annotated Lovecraft*, 158).

[60] *Polypheme cursing the fleeing ship of Odysseus*: Polypheme is the name of the Cyclops who pursues Odysseus in Homer's *Odyssey*. There is a similar scene in Lovecraft's early tale "Dagon" (1917).

Thing could surely overtake the *Alert* until steam was fully up, he resolved on a desperate chance; and, setting the engine for full speed, ran lightning-like on deck and reversed the wheel. There was a mighty eddying and foaming in the noisome brine, and as the steam mounted higher and higher the brave Norwegian drove his vessel head on against the pursuing jelly which rose above the unclean froth like the stern of a daemon galleon. The awful squid-head with writhing feelers came nearly up to the bowsprit of the sturdy yacht, but Johansen drove on relentlessly. There was a bursting as of an exploding bladder, a slushy nastiness as of a cloven sunfish, a stench as of a thousand opened graves, and a sound that the chronicler would not put on paper. For an instant the ship was befouled by an acrid and blinding green cloud, and then there was only a venomous seething astern; where—God in heaven!—the scattered plasticity of that nameless skyspawn was nebulously *recombining* in its hateful original form, whilst its distance widened every second as the *Alert* gained impetus from its mounting steam.

That was all. After that Johansen only brooded over the idol in the cabin and attended to a few matters of food for himself and the laughing maniac by his side. He did not try to navigate after the first bold flight, for the reaction had taken something out of his soul. Then came the storm of April 2nd, and a gathering of the clouds about his consciousness. There is a sense of spectral whirling through liquid gulfs of infinity, of dizzying rides through reeling universes on a comet's tail, and of hysterical plunges from the pit to the moon and from the moon back again to the pit, all livened by a cachinnating chorus of the distorted, hilarious elder gods and the green, bat-winged mocking imps of Tartarus.[61]

Out of that dream came rescue—the *Vigilant,* the viceadmiralty court, the streets of Dunedin, and the long voy-

---

[61] *Tartarus*: A region in the Greek underworld.

age back home to the old house by the Egeberg. He could not tell—they would think him mad. He would write of what he knew before death came, but his wife must not guess. Death would be a boon if only it could blot out the memories.

That was the document I read, and now I have placed it in the tin box beside the bas-relief and the papers of Professor Angell. With it shall go this record of mine— this test of my own sanity, wherein is pieced together that which I hope may never be pieced together again. I have looked upon all that the universe has to hold of horror, and even the skies of spring and the flowers of summer must ever afterward be poison to me. But I do not think my life will be long. As my uncle went, as poor Johansen went, so I shall go. I know too much, and the cult still lives.

Cthulhu still lives, too, I suppose, again in that chasm of stone which has shielded him since the sun was young. His accursed city is sunken once more, for the *Vigilant* sailed over the spot after the April storm; but his ministers on earth still bellow and prance and slay around idol-capped monoliths in lonely places. He must have been trapped by the sinking whilst within his black abyss, or the world would by now be screaming with fright and frenzy. Who knows the end? What has risen may sink, and what has sunk may rise. Loathsomeness waits and dreams in the deep, and decay spreads over the tottering cities of men. A time will come—but I must not and cannot think! Let me pray that, if I do not survive this manuscript, my executors may put caution before audacity and see that it meets no other eye.

Pickman's Model

You needn't think I'm crazy, Eliot[1]—plenty of others have queerer prejudices than this. Why don't you laugh at Oliver's grandfather, who won't ride in a motor? If I don't like that damned subway, it's my own business; and we got here more quickly anyhow in the taxi. We'd have had to walk up the hill from Park Street[2] if we'd taken the car.

I know I'm more nervous than I was when you saw me

"Pickman's Model" was apparently written in early September 1926. It first appeared in the October 1927 issue of *Weird Tales*.

[1] *Eliot*: *Eliot* here is undoubtedly a surname; hence this character is likely a member of the eminent Boston family that includes Harvard president Charles William Eliot (1834–1926) and, by way of St. Louis, the poet T. S. Eliot (1888–1965).

[2] *Park Street*: Park Street is a stop on the Boston subway. The hill referred to has to be Beacon Hill. See note 33 below.

last year, but you don't need to hold a clinic over it. There's plenty of reason, God knows, and I fancy I'm lucky to be sane at all. Why the third degree? You didn't use to be so inquisitive.

Well, if you must hear it, I don't know why you shouldn't. Maybe you ought to, anyhow, for you kept writing me like a grieved parent when you heard I'd begun to cut the Art Club[3] and keep away from Pickman. Now that he's disappeared I go around to the club once in a while, but my nerves aren't what they were.

No, I don't know what's become of Pickman, and I don't like to guess. You might have surmised I had some inside information when I dropped him—and that's why I don't want to think where he's gone. Let the police find what they can—it won't be much, judging from the fact that they don't know yet of the old North End[4] place he hired under the name of Peters. I'm not sure that I could find it again myself—not that I'd ever try, even in broad daylight! Yes, I do know, or am afraid I know, why he maintained it. I'm coming to that. And I think you'll understand before I'm through why I don't tell the police. They would ask me to guide them, but I couldn't go back there even if I knew the way. There was something

[3] *Art Club*: Organized in 1854 and incorporated in 1871, the Boston Art Club had a clubhouse and gallery on the corner of Dartmouth and Newbury Streets in the Back Bay. By the 1920s it had become largely a social club and was in decline. It closed its doors in 1950.

[4] *North End*: The oldest part of the city of Boston, originally connected to the mainland by a narrow strip of land. A couple of years after writing "Pickman's Model," Lovecraft tried to show the story's locale to fellow writer Donald Wandrei. In a 1934 letter he reported the unexpected result: " 'Pickman's Model' describes the Boston North End as it was until a few years ago, though many of these old tangled alleys have now been swept away by civic change—the ancient houses demolished, and warehouses erected on their site. I remember when the precise location of the artist's house in the story was hit by the razing process. It was in 1927, and Donald Wandrei . . . was visiting the East for the first time. He wanted to see the site of the story, and I was very glad to take him to it—thinking its sinister quaintness would even surpass his expectations. Imagine my dismay, then, at finding nothing but a blank open space where the tottering old houses and zigzag alley-windings had been!" (*Selected Letters* IV, 385–86)

there—and now I can't use the subway or (and you may as well have your laugh at this, too) go down into cellars any more.[5]

I should think you'd have known I didn't drop Pickman for the same silly reasons that fussy old women like Dr. Reid or Joe Minot or Bosworth did. Morbid art doesn't shock me, and when a man has the genius Pickman had I feel it an honour to know him, no matter what direction his work takes. Boston never had a greater painter than Richard Upton Pickman.[6] I said it at first and I say it still, and I never swerved an inch, either, when he shewed that "Ghoul Feeding". That, you remember, was when Minot cut him.

You know, it takes profound art and profound insight into Nature to turn out stuff like Pickman's. Any magazine-cover hack can splash paint around wildly and call it a nightmare or a Witches' Sabbath or a portrait of the devil, but only a great painter can make such a thing really scare or ring true. That's because only a real artist knows the actual anatomy of the terrible or the physiology of fear—the exact sort of lines and proportions that connect up with latent instincts or hereditary memories of fright, and the proper colour contrasts and lighting effects to stir the dormant sense of strangeness. I don't have to tell you

[5] *I can't use the subway . . . or go down in cellars any more*: Like Thomas Malone in "The Horror at Red Hook" and the narrator of "Cool Air," the narrator of "Pickman's Model" has developed a phobia as a result of a supernatural encounter.

[6] *Richard Upton Pickman*: Pickman is an old Salem name. Nathaniel Pickman (c. 1615–85), a native of Bristol, England, settled there in 1639. A John Upton purchased land in Salem in 1658. As his letters reveal, Lovecraft knew one of John Upton's descendants, Winslow Upton (1853–1914): "From 1906 to 1918 I contributed monthly articles on astronomical phenomena to one of the lesser Providence dailies. One thing that helped me greatly was the free access which I had to the Ladd Observatory of Brown University—an unusual privilege for a kid, but made possible because Prof. Upton—head of the college astronomical department and director of the observatory—was a friend of the family." (*Selected Letters* IV, 398) The Nathaniel Derby Pickman Foundation funds the Miskatonic University expedition to the Antarctic in *At the Mountains of Madness*. See note 17 to that novel (*Annotated Lovecraft*, 185).

why a Fuseli[7] really brings a shiver while a cheap ghost-story frontispiece merely makes us laugh. There's something those fellows catch—beyond life—that they're able to make us catch for a second. Doré had it. Sime has it. Angarola of Chicago has it.[8] And Pickman had it as no man ever had it before or—I hope to heaven—ever will again.

Don't ask me what it is they see. You know, in ordinary art, there's all the difference in the world between the vital, breathing things drawn from Nature or models and the artificial truck that commercial small fry reel off in a bare studio by rule. Well, I should say that the really weird artist has a kind of vision which makes models, or summons up what amounts to actual scenes from the spectral world he lives in. Anyhow, he manages to turn out results that differ from the pretender's mince-pie dreams in just about the same way that the life painter's results differ from the concoctions of a correspondence-school cartoonist. If I had ever seen what Pickman saw—but no! Here, let's have a drink before we get any deeper. Gad, I wouldn't be alive if I'd ever seen what that man—if he was a man—saw!

You recall that Pickman's forte was faces. I don't believe anybody since Goya[9] could put so much of sheer hell into a set of features or a twist of expression. And before Goya you have to go back to the mediaeval chaps who did the

---

[7] *Fuseli*: Henry Fuseli (Heinrich Füssli, 1741–1825), Swiss-born painter who spent most of his life in England. His painting "The Nightmare" (1782) is one of the icons of weird art. See note 66 to "The Colour Out of Space" (*Annotated Lovecraft*, 95).

[8] *Doré . . . Sime . . . Angarola of Chicago*: Gustave Doré (1832–83), the French illustrator and painter, excelled in weird or fantastic scenes. See note 9 to "The Horror at Red Hook."
  Sidney H. Sime (1867–1941) was an artist of the weird and fantastic who illustrated many books by Lord Dunsany, while Anthony Angarola (1893–1929) was an American book illustrator. See note 31 to "The Call of Cthulhu."

[9] *Goya*: Francisco Goya y Lucientes (1746–1828), Spanish painter and graphic artist, noted for such macabre murals as "Saturn Devouring His Children," "Witches' Sabbath," and "The Three Fates." See note 8 to "The Hound."

gargoyles and chimaeras on Notre Dame and Mont Saint-Michel.[10] They believed all sorts of things—and maybe they saw all sorts of things, too, for the Middle Ages had some curious phases. I remember your asking Pickman yourself once, the year before you went away, wherever in thunder he got such ideas and visions. Wasn't that a nasty laugh he gave you? It was partly because of that laugh that Reid dropped him. Reid, you know, had just taken up comparative pathology, and was full of pompous "inside stuff" about the biological or evolutionary significance of this or that mental or physical symptom. He said Pickman repelled him more and more every day, and almost frightened him toward the last—that the fellow's features and expression were slowly developing in a way he didn't like; in a way that wasn't human. He had a lot of talk about diet, and said Pickman must be abnormal and eccentric to the last degree. I suppose you told Reid, if you and he had any correspondence over it, that he'd let Pickman's paintings get on his nerves or harrow up his imagination. I know I told him that myself—then.

But keep in mind that I didn't drop Pickman for anything like this. On the contrary, my admiration for him kept growing; for that "Ghoul Feeding" was a tremendous achievement. As you know, the club wouldn't exhibit it, and the Museum of Fine Arts[11] wouldn't accept it as a gift; and I can add that nobody would buy it, so Pickman had it right in his house till he went. Now his father has it in Salem—you know Pickman comes of old Salem stock, and had a witch ancestor hanged in 1692.[12]

I got into the habit of calling on Pickman quite often,

---

[10] *gargoyles and chimaeras on Notre Dame and Mont Saint-Michel*: Gargoyles are grotesque humans or animals carved in stone that serve as rain spouts on cathedrals such as Notre Dame (Paris) and Mont Saint-Michel. A chimaera is a fabulous monster, often with a lion's head, goat's body, and serpent's tail. See note 1 to "The Dunwich Horror" (*Annotated Lovecraft*, 103).

[11] *Museum of Fine Arts*: One of Boston's great cultural landmarks, founded in 1870.

especially after I began making notes for a monograph on weird art. Probably it was his work which put the idea into my head, and anyhow, I found him a mine of data and suggestions when I came to develop it. He shewed me all the paintings and drawings he had about; including some pen-and-ink sketches that would, I verily believe, have got him kicked out of the club if many of the members had seen them. Before long I was pretty nearly a devotee, and would listen for hours like a schoolboy to art theories and philosophic speculations wild enough to qualify him for the Danvers asylum.[13] My hero-worship, coupled with the fact that people generally were commencing to have less and less to do with him, made him get very confidential with me; and one evening he hinted that if I were fairly close-mouthed and none too squeamish, he might shew me something rather unusual—something a bit stronger than anything he had in the house.

"You know," he said, "there are things that won't do for Newbury Street[14]—things that are out of place here, and that can't be conceived here, anyhow. It's my business to catch the overtones of the soul, and you won't find those in a parvenu set of artificial streets on made land. Back Bay isn't Boston[15]—it isn't anything yet, because it's had no time to pick up memories and attract local spirits. If there are any ghosts here, they're the tame ghosts of a salt marsh and a shallow cove; and I want human ghosts—

---

[12] *a witch ancestor hanged in 1692*: The Salem witch trials occurred in Salem Village (now Danvers), Massachusetts, in 1692. See note 12 to "The Colour Out of Space" (*Annotated Lovecraft*, 64).

[13] *Danvers asylum*: Danvers State Hospital was a hospital for the insane. It opened in 1878 and closed in 1992.

[14] *Newbury Street*: Then as now a fashionable shopping street, with many art galleries.

[15] *Back Bay isn't Boston*: The Back Bay area of Boston was created in the nineteenth century by draining and filling in swamp land bordering the Charles River.

Copp's Hill cemetery (photo by Will Murray).

the ghosts of beings highly organised enough to have looked on hell and known the meaning of what they saw.

"The place for an artist to live is the North End. If any aesthete were sincere, he'd put up with the slums for the sake of the massed traditions. God, man! Don't you realise that places like that weren't merely *made*, but actually *grew?* Generation after generation lived and felt and died there, and in days when people weren't afraid to live and feel and die. Don't you know there was a mill on Copp's Hill[16] in 1632, and that half the present streets were laid out by 1650? I can shew you houses that have stood two centuries and a half and more; houses that have witnessed what would make a modern house crumble into powder. What do moderns know of life and the forces behind it? You call the Salem witchcraft a delusion, but I'll wage my four-times-great-grandmother could have told you things.

---

[16] *Copp's Hill*: Copp's Hill became the site of a cemetery, which still exists today.

They hanged her on Gallows Hill,[17] with Cotton Mather looking sanctimoniously on. Mather, damn him, was afraid somebody might succeed in kicking free of this accursed cage of monotony—I wish someone had laid a spell on him or sucked his blood in the night!

"I can shew you a house he lived in, and I can shew you another one he was afraid to enter in spite of all his fine bold talk. He knew things he didn't dare put into that stupid *Magnalia* or that puerile *Wonders of the Invisible World*.[18] Look here, do you know the whole North End once had a set of tunnels that kept certain people in touch with each other's houses, and the burying-ground, and the sea? Let them prosecute and persecute above ground— things went on every day that they couldn't reach, and voices laughed at night that they couldn't place!

"Why, man, out of ten surviving houses built before 1700 and not moved since I'll wage that in eight I can shew you something queer in the cellar. There's hardly a month that you don't read of workmen finding bricked-up arches and wells leading nowhere in this or that old place as it comes down—you should see one near Henchman Street from the elevated[19] last year. There were witches and what their spells summoned; pirates and what they brought in from the sea; smugglers; privateers—and I tell you, people knew how to live, and how to enlarge the bounds of life, in the old times! This wasn't the only world a bold and wise man could know—faugh! And to think of today in contrast, with such pale-pink brains that even a club of supposed artists gets shudders and convul-

---

[17] *Gallows Hill*: A place of public execution.

[18] *that stupid Magnalia or that puerile Wonders of the Invisible World*: The two works for which Cotton Mather (1663–1728) is best known today: *Magnalia Christi Americana* (1702), his ecclesiastical history of New England (see note 14 to "The Picture in the House"); and *Wonders of the Invisible World* (1693), an account of satanic possession in New England. Despite a certain smugness, Mather was a benevolent man, deeply interested in science and education.

[19] *the elevated*: The elevated subway, built between 1896 and 1901.

sions if a picture goes beyond the feelings of a Beacon Street[20] tea-table!

"The only saving grace of the present is that it's too damned stupid to question the past very closely. What do maps and records and guide-books really tell of the North End? Bah! At a guess I'll guarantee to lead you to thirty or forty alleys and networks of alleys north of Prince Street that aren't suspected by ten living beings outside of the foreigners that swarm them. And what do those Dagoes[21] know of their meaning? No, Thurber,[22] these ancient places are dreaming gorgeously and overflowing with wonder and terror and escapes from the commonplace, and yet there's not a living soul to understand or profit by them. Or rather, there's only one living soul—for I haven't been digging around in the past for nothing!

"See here, you're interested in this sort of thing. What if I told you that I've got another studio up there, where I can catch the night-spirit of antique horror and paint things that I couldn't even think of in Newbury Street? Naturally I don't tell those cursed old maids at the club— with Reid, damn him, whispering even as it is that I'm a sort of monster bound down the toboggan of reverse evolution. Yes, Thurber, I decided long ago that one must paint terror as well as beauty from life, so I did some exploring in places where I had reason to know terror lives.

"I've got a place that I don't believe three living Nordic men besides myself have ever seen. It isn't so very far from the elevated as distance goes, but it's centuries away

---

[20] *Beacon Street*: One of Boston's major thoroughfares. Its upper end, running along Beacon Hill, includes many fine houses, both private residences and clubs. Thurber appears to be relating his tale to Eliot at one such club.

[21] *Dagoes*: Pejorative term for persons of Spanish, Portuguese, or Italian descent. *Dago* derives from the Spanish name *Diego* meaning *James*.

[22] *Thurber*: Not surprisingly the narrator would seem to belong to an old New England family, which produced the *New Yorker* humorist, James Thurber (1894–1961). Perhaps Lovecraft had in mind the botanist and horticulturist George Thurber (1821–90), born in Providence, Rhode Island.

as the soul goes. I took it because of the queer old brick well in the cellar—one of the sort I told you about. The shack's almost tumbling down, so that nobody else would live there, and I'd hate to tell you how little I pay for it. The windows are boarded up, but I like that all the better, since I don't want daylight for what I do. I paint in the cellar, where the inspiration is thickest, but I've other rooms furnished on the ground floor. A Sicilian owns it, and I've hired it under the name of Peters.

"Now if you're game, I'll take you there tonight. I think you'd enjoy the pictures, for as I said, I've let myself go a bit there. It's no vast tour—I sometimes do it on foot, for I don't want to attract attention with a taxi in such a place. We can take the shuttle at the South Station[23] for Battery Street, and after that the walk isn't much."

Well, Eliot, there wasn't much for me to do after that harangue but to keep myself from running instead of walking for the first vacant cab we could sight. We changed to the elevated at the South Station, and at about twelve o'clock had climbed down the steps at Battery Street and struck along the old waterfront past Constitution Wharf.[24] I didn't keep track of the cross streets, and can't tell you yet which it was we turned up, but I know it wasn't Greenough Lane.

When we did turn, it was to climb through the deserted length of the oldest and dirtiest alley I ever saw in my life, with crumbling-looking gables, broken small-paned windows, and archaic chimneys that stood out half-disintegrated against the moonlit sky. I don't believe there were three houses in sight that hadn't been standing in Cotton Mather's time—certainly I glimpsed at least two with an overhang, and once I thought I saw a peaked roof-

[23] *South Station*: The railroad station at which Lovecraft arrived when traveling to Boston from Providence by train.

[24] *Constitution Wharf*: Part of the North End waterfront. The frigate U.S.S. *Constitution* is docked in nearby Charlestown.

Paul Revere's house in the North End (photo by Leigh Grossman).

line of the almost forgotten pre-gambrel type[25] though antiquarians tell us there are none left in Boston.

From that alley, which had a dim light, we turned to the left into an equally silent and still narrower alley with no light at all; and in a minute made what I think was an obtuse-angled bend toward the right in the dark. Not long after this Pickman produced a flashlight and revealed an antediluvian ten-panelled door that looked damnably worn-eaten. Unlocking it, he ushered me into a barren hallway with what was once splendid dark-oak panelling—simple, of course, but thrillingly suggestive of the times of Andros and Phipps[26] and the Witchcraft. Then he

---

[25] *pre-gambrel type*: Few seventeenth-century houses survived in Boston into the twentieth century. The notable exception is the Paul Revere house, which still stands today. Gambrel roofs, with their more efficient use of space, started to supplant peaked roofs by the late seventeenth century in New England. See note 54 to "The Colour Out of Space" (*Annotated Lovecraft*, 85).

took me through a door on the left, lighted an oil lamp, and told me to make myself at home.

Now, Eliot, I'm what the man in the street would call fairly "hard-boiled", but I'll confess that what I saw on the walls of that room gave me a bad turn. They were his pictures, you know—the ones he wouldn't paint or even shew in Newbury Street—and he was right when he said he had "let himself go". Here—have another drink—I need one anyhow!

There's no use in my trying to tell you what they were like, because the awful, the blasphemous horror, and the unbelievable loathsomeness and moral foetor[27] came from simple touches quite beyond the power of words to classify. There was none of the exotic technique you see in Sidney Sime, none of the trans-Saturnian landscapes and lunar fungi that Clark Ashton Smith[28] uses to freeze the blood. The backgrounds were mostly old churchyards, deep woods, cliffs by the sea, brick tunnels, ancient panelled rooms, or simple vaults of masonry. Copp's Hill Burying Ground, which could not be many blocks away from this very house, was a favourite scene.

The madness and monstrosity lay in the figures in the foreground—for Pickman's morbid art was preëminently one of daemoniac portraiture. These figures were seldom

---

[26] *Andros and Phipps*: Sir Edmund Andros (1637–1714), also mentioned in "The Shunned House" (see note 24 to that story), was governor of New England from 1686 to 1689. His suppression of charters and colonial assemblies did not endear him to the colonists. A popular revolt in Boston, following the news that James II had been overthrown in 1688, led to his being shipped back to England as a prisoner. Sir William Phipps (1651–95), born in what is today Maine and an opponent of Andros, became the first royal governor of Massachusetts in 1692. During the witchcraft scare he appointed the commission to try the accused. When his own wife was accused of witchcraft, he ordered an end to the trials.

[27] *foetor*: Archaic or British spelling for *fetor*, an offensive smell or stench. Lovecraft also applies this word to the invisible monster in "The Dunwich Horror."

[28] *Clark Ashton Smith*: Smith was the one living fantasist and friend that Lovecraft admired enough to cite repeatedly in his fiction. See note 42 to "The Call of Cthulhu" and note 82 to *At the Mountains of Madness* (*Annotated Lovecraft*, 215).

completely human, but often approached humanity in varying degree. Most of the bodies, while roughly bipedal, had a forward slumping, and a vaguely canine cast. The texture of the majority was a kind of unpleasant rubberiness. Ugh! I can see them now! Their occupations—well, don't ask me to be too precise. They were usually feeding—I won't say on what. They were sometimes shewn in groups in cemeteries or underground passages, and often appeared to be in battle over their prey—or rather, their treasure-trove. And what damnable expressiveness Pickman sometimes gave the sightless faces of this charnel booty! Occasionally the things were shewn leaping through open windows at night, or squatting on the chests of sleepers, worrying at their throats. One canvas shewed a ring of them baying about a hanged witch on Gallows Hill, whose dead face held a close kinship to theirs.

But don't get the idea that it was all this hideous business of theme and setting which struck me faint. I'm not a three-year-old kid, and I'd seen much like this before. It was the *faces*, Eliot, those accursed *faces*, that leered and slavered out of the canvas with the very breath of life! By God, I verily believe they *were* alive! That nauseous wizard had waked the fires of hell in pigment, and his brush had been a nightmare-spawning wand. Give me that decanter, Eliot!

There was one thing called "The Lesson"—heaven pity me, that I ever saw it! Listen—can you fancy a squatting circle of nameless dog-like things in a churchyard teaching a small child how to feed like themselves? The price of a changeling, I suppose—you know the old myth about how the weird people leave their spawn in cradles in exchange for the human babes they steal. Pickman was shewing what happens to those stolen babes—how they grow up—and then I began to see a hideous relationship in the faces of the human and non-human figures. He was, in all his gradations of morbidity between the frankly non-human and the degradedly human, establishing a sardonic linkage and evolution. The dog-things were developed from mortals!

And no sooner had I wondered what he made of their own young as left with mankind in the form of change-lings, than my eye caught a picture embodying that very thought. It was that of an ancient Puritan interior—a heavily beamed room with lattice widows, a settle,[29] and clumsy seventeenth-century furniture, with the family sitting about while the father read from the Scriptures. Every face but one shewed nobility and reverence, but that one reflected the mockery of the pit. It was that of a young man in years, and no doubt belonged to a supposed son of that pious father, but in essence it was the kin of the unclean things. It was their changeling—and in a spirit of supreme irony Pickman had given the features a very perceptible resemblance to his own.

By this time Pickman had lighted a lamp in an adjoining room and was politely holding open the door for me; asking me if I would care to see his "modern studies". I hadn't been able to give him much of my opinions—I was too speechless with fright and loathing—but I think he fully understood and felt highly complimented. And now I want to assure you again, Eliot, that I'm no mollycoddle[30] to scream at anything which shews a bit of departure from the usual. I'm middle-aged and decently sophisticated, and I guess you saw enough of me in France[31] to know I'm not easily knocked out. Remember, too, that I'd just about recovered my wind and gotten used to those frightful pictures which turned colonial New England into a kind of annex of hell. Well, in spite of all this, that next room forced a real scream out of me, and I had to clutch at the

---

[29] *lattice windows, a settle*: Small-paned windows, typically divided by diagonal lattices made of lead. A settle is a bench with a high back and arms.

[30] *mollycoddle*: A weak, often effeminate man.

[31] *France*: Like other characters in Lovecraft, Thurber is a veteran of World War I who fought on the Western front.

doorway to keep from keeling over. The other chamber had shewn a pack of ghouls and witches overrunning the world of our forefathers, but this one brought the horror right into our own daily life!

Gad, how that man could paint! There was a study called "Subway Accident", in which a flock of the vile things were clambering up from some unknown catacomb through a crack in the floor of the Boylston Street[32] subway and attacking a crowd of people on the platform. Another shewed a dance on Copp's Hill among the tombs with the background of today. Then there were any number of cellar views, with monsters creeping in through holes and rifts in the masonry and grinning as they squatted behind barrels or furnaces and waited for their first victim to descend the stairs.

One disgusting canvas seemed to depict a vast cross-section of Beacon Hill,[33] with ant-like armies of the mephitic[34] monsters squeezing themselves through burrows that honeycombed the ground. Dances in the modern cemeteries were freely pictured, and another conception somehow shocked me more than all the rest—a scene in an unknown vault, where scores of the beasts crowded about one who held a well-known Boston guide-book and was evidently reading aloud. All were pointing to a certain passage, and every face seemed so distorted with epileptic and reverberant laughter that I almost thought I heard the fiendish echoes. The title of the picture was "Holmes, Lowell, and Longfellow Lie Buried in Mount Auburn".[35]

As I gradually steadied myself and got readjusted to this second room of deviltry and morbidity, I began to analyse some of the points in my sickening loathing. In the first place, I said to myself, these things repelled because of

---

[32] *Boylston Street subway*: A subway stop that serves the Back Bay.

[33] *Beacon Hill*: One of Boston's oldest and most beautiful residential neighborhoods.

[34] *mephitic*: Noxiously smelly, especially from the earth.

Oliver Wendell Holmes's Grave, Mount Auburn cemetery (photo by Leigh Grossman).

the utter inhumanity and callous cruelty they shewed in Pickman. The fellow must be a relentless enemy of all mankind to take such glee in the torture of brain and flesh and the degradation of the mortal tenement. In the second place, they terrified because of their very greatness. Their art was the art that convinced—when we saw the pictures we saw the daemons themselves and were afraid of them. And the queer part was, that Pickman got none of his

---

[35] "*Holmes, Lowell, and Longfellow Lie Buried in Mount Auburn*": A reference to Oliver Wendell Holmes (1809–94), the author and physician; James Russell Lowell (1819–91), the poet; and Henry Wadsworth Longfellow (1807–82), perhaps the most popular American poet of his day. Mount Auburn is a cemetery in Cambridge, Massachusetts, the birthplace of both Holmes and Lowell. Lovecraft met Dr. Holmes as a small child in 1893, when the celebrated author visited the boarding house in Auburndale, Massachusetts, where the Lovecrafts were residing that summer "and on one occasion (unremembered by the passenger) is said to have ridden the future *Weird Tales* disciple on his venerable knee." (*Selected Letters* I, 296) Disturbing the graves of the great is a major theme in *The Case of Charles Dexter Ward*.

James Russell Lowell's Grave, Mount Auburn cemetery (photo by Leigh Grossman).

Longfellow's Grave, Mount Auburn cemetery (photo by Leigh Grossman).

power from the use of selectiveness or bizarrerie. Nothing was blurred, distorted, or conventionalised; outlines were sharp and life-like, and details were almost painfully defined. And the faces!

It was not any mere artist's interpretation that he saw; it was pandemonium itself, crystal clear in stark objectivity. That was it, by heaven! The man was not a fantaisiste or romanticist at all—he did not even try to give us the churning, prismatic ephemera of dreams, but coldly and sardonically reflected some stable, mechanistic, and well-established horror-world which he saw fully, brilliantly, squarely, and unfalteringly. God knows what that world can have been, or where he ever glimpsed the blasphemous shapes that loped and trotted and crawled through it; but whatever the baffling source of his images, one thing was plain. Pickman was in every sense—in conception and in execution—a thorough, painstaking, and almost scientific *realist*.

My host was now leading the way down cellar to his actual studio, and I braced myself for some hellish effects among the unfinished canvases. As we reached the bottom of the damp stairs he turned his flashlight to a corner of the large open space at hand, revealing the circular brick curb of what was evidently a great well in the earthen floor. We walked nearer, and I saw that it must be five feet across, with walls a good foot thick and some six inches above the ground level—solid work of the seventeenth century, or I was much mistaken. That, Pickman said, was the kind of thing he had been talking about—an aperture of the network of tunnels that used to undermine the hill. I noticed idly that it did not seem to be bricked up, and that a heavy disc of wood formed the apparent cover. Thinking of the things this well must have been connected with if Pickman's wild hints had not been mere rhetoric, I shivered slightly; then turned to follow him up a step and through a narrow door into a room of fair size, provided with a wooden floor and furnished as a studio. An acetylene gas[36] outfit gave the light necessary for work.

The unfinished pictures on easels or propped against the walls were as ghastly as the finished ones upstairs, and shewed the painstaking methods of the artist. Scenes were blocked out with extreme care, and pencilled guide lines told of the minute exactitude which Pickman used in getting the right perspective and proportions. The man was great—I say it even now, knowing as much as I do. A large camera on a table excited my notice, and Pickman told me that he used it in taking scenes for backgrounds, so that he might paint them from photographs in the studio instead of carting his outfit around the town for this or that view. He thought a photograph quite as good as an actual scene or model for sustained work, and declared he employed them regularly.

There was something very disturbing about the nauseous sketches and half-finished monstrosities that leered around from every side of the room, and when Pickman suddenly unveiled a huge canvas on the side away from the light I could not for my life keep back a loud scream— the second I had emitted that night. It echoed and echoed through the dim vaultings of that ancient and nitrous cellar,[37] and I had to choke back a flood of reaction that threatened to burst out as hysterical laughter. Merciful Creator! Eliot, but I don't know how much was real and how much was feverish fancy. It doesn't seem to me that earth can hold a dream like that!

It was a colossal and nameless blasphemy with glaring red eyes, and it held in bony claws a thing that had been a man, gnawing at the head as a child nibbles at a stick of candy. Its position was a kind of crouch, and as one looked one felt that at any moment it might drop its pres-

---

[36] *acetylene gas*: A colorless gas that burns with a bright flame.

[37] *nitrous cellar*: In "The Shunned House" the cellar is also nitrous. See note 8 to that story.

ent prey and seek a juicier morsel. But damn it all, it
wasn't even the fiendish subject that made it such an immortal fountain-head of all panic—not that, nor the dog
face with its pointed ears, bloodshot eyes, flat nose, and
drooling lips. It wasn't the scaly claws nor the mould-
caked body nor the half-hooved feet—none of these,
though any one of them might well have driven an excitable man to madness.

It was the technique, Eliot—the cursed, the impious,
the unnatural technique! As I am a living being, I never
elsewhere saw the actual breath of life so fused into a
canvas. The monster was there—it glared and gnawed and
gnawed and glared—and I knew that only a suspension of
Nature's laws could ever let a man paint a thing like that
without a model—without some glimpse of the nether
world which no mortal unsold to the Fiend has ever had.

Pinned with a thumb-tack to a vacant part of the canvas
was a piece of paper now badly curled up—probably, I
thought, a photograph from which Pickman meant to
paint a background as hideous as the nightmare it was to
enhance. I reached out to uncurl and look at it, when suddenly I saw Pickman start as if shot. He had been listening
with peculiar intensity ever since my shocked scream had
waked unaccustomed echoes in the dark cellar, and now
he seemed struck with a fright which, though not compa-
rable to my own, had in it more of the physical than of
the spiritual. He drew a revolver and motioned me to silence, then stepped out into the main cellar an closed the
door behind him.

I think I was paralysed for an instant. Imitating Pickman's listening, I fancied I heard a faint scurrying sound
somewhere, and a series of squeals or bleats in a direction
I couldn't determine. I thought of huge rats and shuddered.
Then there came a subdued sort of clatter which somehow
set me all in gooseflesh—a furtive, groping kind of clatter,
though I can't attempt to convey what I mean in words.

It was like a heavy wood falling on stone or brick—wood on brick—what did that make me think of?

It came again, and louder. There was a vibration as if the wood had fallen farther than it had fallen before. After that followed a sharp grating noise, a shouted gibberish from Pickman, and the deafening discharge of all six chambers of a revolver,[38] fired spectacularly as a lion-tamer might fire in the air for effect. A muffled squeal or squawk, and a thud. Then more wood and brick grating, a pause, and the opening of the door—at which I'll confess I started violently. Pickman reappeared with his smoking weapon, cursing the bloated rats that infested the ancient well.

"The deuce knows what they eat, Thurber," he grinned, "for those archaic tunnels touched graveyard and witch-den and seacoast. But whatever it is, they must have run short, for they were devilish anxious to get out. Your yelling stirred them up, I fancy. Better be cautious in these old places—our rodent friends are the one drawback, though I sometimes think they're a positive asset by way of atmosphere and colour."

Well, Eliot, that was the end of the night's adventure. Pickman had promised to shew me the place, and heaven knows he had done it. He led me out of that tangle of alleys in another direction, it seems, for when we sighted a lamp post we were in a half-familiar street with monotonous rows of mingled tenement blocks and old houses. Charter Street, it turned out to be, but I was too flustered to notice just where we hit it. We were too late for the elevated, and walked back downtown through Hanover Street. I remember that walk. We switched from Tremont

---

[38] *deafening discharge of all six chambers of a revolver*: "The Thing on the Doorstep" (1933) opens similarly: "It is true that I have sent six bullets through the head of my best friend . . ." The third section of "Herbert West—Reanimator," "Six Shots by Moonlight," begins: "It is uncommon to fire all six shots of a revolver with great suddenness when one would probably be sufficient . . ."

up Beacon, and Pickman left me at the corner of Joy,[39] where I turned off. I never spoke to him again.

Why did I drop him? Don't be impatient. Wait till I ring for coffee. We've had enough of the other stuff, but I for one need something. No—it wasn't the paintings I saw in that place; though I'll swear they were enough to get him ostracised in nine-tenths of the homes and clubs of Boston, and I guess you won't wonder now why I have to steer clear of subways and cellars. It was—something I found in my coat the next morning. You know, the curled-up paper tacked to that frightful canvas in the cellar; the thing I thought was a photograph of some scene he meant to use as a background for that monster. The last scare had come while I was reaching to uncurl it, and it seems I had vacantly crumpled it into my pocket. But here's the coffee—take it black, Eliot, if you're wise.

Yes, that paper was the reason I dropped Pickman; Richard Upton Pickman, the greatest artist I have ever known—and the foulest being that ever leaped the bounds of life into the pits of myth and madness. Eliot—old Reid was right. He wasn't strictly human. Either he was born in strange shadow, or he'd found a way to unlock the forbidden gate. It's all the same now, for he's gone—back into the fabulous darkness he loved to haunt.[40] Here, let's have the chandelier going.

Don't ask me to explain or even conjecture about what I burned. Don't ask me, either, what lay behind that mole-like scrambling Pickman was so keen to pass off as rats. There are secrets, you know, which might have come down from old Salem times, and Cotton Mather tells even stranger things. You know how damned life-like Pick-

---

[39] *the corner of Joy*: A street on Beacon Hill.

[40] *back into the fabulous darkness he loved to haunt*: Pickman later turns up as a character in *The Dream-Quest of Unknown Kadath* (1926–27), a denizen of Lovecraft's dream world. In his "History of the *Necronomicon*" (1927), Lovecraft informs us that Carter made this transition in 1926.

man's paintings were—how we all wondered where he got those faces.

Well—that paper wasn't a photograph of any background, after all. What it shewed was simply the monstrous being he was painting on that awful canvas. It was the model he was using—and its background was merely the wall of the cellar studio in minute detail. But by God, Eliot, *it was a photograph from life.*[41]

---

[41] *it was a photograph from life*: In his classic essay, "A Literary Copernicus" (1949), Fritz Leiber observes: "So closely related to his use of confirmation as to be only another aspect of it, is Lovecraft's employment of the terminal climax—that is, the story in which the high point and the final sentence coincide. Who can forget the supreme chill of: 'But by God, Eliot, *it was a photograph from life*' . . ." (*Lovecraft Remembered*, 461).

The Thing on the Doorstep

I.

It is true that I have sent six bullets through the head of my best friend, and yet I hope to shew by this statement that I am not his murderer.[1] At first I shall be called a madman—madder than the man I shot in his cell at the

---

"The Thing on the Doorstep" was written August 21–24, 1933, but still smarting over the rejection of *At the Mountains of Madness* in 1931, Lovecraft did not submit it to *Weird Tales* until the summer of 1936, along with "The Haunter of the Dark." Farnsworth Wright immediately snapped up both stories. "The Thing on the Doorstep" appeared in the January 1937 issue of the magazine.

[1] *I am not his murderer*: Not the first time a Lovecraft character has fired a gun in this fashion. See note 38 to "Pickman's Model." In a letter describing the detective agency he organized with other boys in Providence, Lovecraft says that he owned a revolver: "mine was the real thing" (*Selected Letters* III, 290).

Arkham Sanitarium. Later some of my readers will weigh
each statement, correlate it with the known facts, and ask
themselves how I could have believed otherwise than as I
did after facing the evidence of that horror—that thing on
the doorstep.

Until then I also saw nothing but madness in the wild
tales I have acted on. Even now I ask myself whether I
was misled—or whether I am not mad after all. I do not
know—but others have strange things to tell of Edward
and Asenath Derby,[2] and even the stolid police are at their
wits' end to account for that last terrible visit. They have
tried weakly to concoct a theory of a ghastly jest or warning by discharged servants, yet they know in their hearts
that the truth is something infinitely more terrible and
incredible.

So I say that I have not murdered Edward Derby. Rather
have I avenged him, and in so doing purged the earth of a
horror whose survival might have loosed untold terrors on
all mankind. There are black zones of shadow close to our
daily paths, and now and then some evil soul breaks a
passage through. When that happens, the man who knows
must strike before reckoning the consequences.

I have known Edward Pickman Derby all his life. Eight
years my junior, he was so precocious that we had much
in common from the time he was eight and I sixteen. He
was the most phenomenal child scholar I have ever
known, and at seven was writing verse of a sombre, fantastic, almost morbid cast which astonished the tutors surrounding him. Perhaps his private education and coddled
seclusion had something to do with his premature flow-
ering. An only child, he had organic weaknesses which

---

[2] *Edward Pickman Derby*: The Derbys were among the most prominent citizens
in colonial Salem. Richard Derby (1712–83), a leading New England ship-owner
and merchant, built Salem's Derby Wharf. In *The Dream-Quest of Unknown
Kadath*, Randolph Carter travels "with three helpful ghouls bearing the slate
gravestone of Col. Nehemiah Derby, obiit 1719, from the Charter Street Burying
Ground in Salem." (*At the Mountains of Madness*, 340) See note 6 to "Pickman's
Model" regarding the Pickman family.

An eighteenth-century house in Salem (photo by Amy West).

startled his doting parents and caused them to keep him closely chained to their side. He was never allowed out without his nurse, and seldom had a chance to play unconstrainedly with other children. All this doubtless fostered a strange, secretive inner life in the boy, with imagination as his one avenue of freedom.[3]

At any rate, his juvenile learning was prodigious and bizarre; and his facile writings such as to captivate me despite my greater age. About that time I had leanings toward art of a somewhat grotesque cast, and I found in this younger child a rare kindred spirit. What lay behind our joint love of shadows and marvels was, no doubt, the ancient, mouldering, and subtly fearsome town in which we lived—witch-cursed, legend-haunted Arkham, whose huddled, sagging gambrel roofs and crumbling Georgian balustrades brood out the centuries beside the darkly muttering Miskatonic.

As time went by I turned to architecture and gave up my design of illustrating a book of Edward's daemoniac poems, yet our comradeship suffered no lessening. Young Derby's odd genius developed remarkably, and in his eighteenth year his collected nightmare-lyrics made a real sensation when issued under the title *Azathoth and Other Horrors.*[4] He was a close correspondent of the notorious Bauderlarian poet Justin Geoffrey,[5] who wrote *The People of the Monolith* and died screaming in a madhouse in 1926 after a visit to a sinister, ill-regarded village in Hungary.

In self-reliance and practical affairs, however, Derby was greatly retarded because of his coddled existence. His health had improved, but his habits of childish dependence were fostered by overcareful parents; so that he never travelled alone, made independent decisions, or assumed responsibilities. It was early seen that he would not be equal to a struggle in the business or professional

---

[3] *imagination as his one avenue of freedom*: Edward Derby's childhood development has some resemblance to Lovecraft's own. In an autobiographical letter of 1915, he admitted: "As a child I was very peculiar and sensitive, always preferring the society of grown persons to that of other children. . . . Amongst my few playmates I was very unpopular, since I would insist on playing out events in history, or acting according to consistent plots. Thus repelled by humans, I sought refuge and companionship in books . . ." (*Selected Letters* I, 6–7).

[4] *Azathoth and Other Horrors*: Clark Ashton Smith created a sensation at age nineteen when he published *The Star-Treader and Other Poems* (1912). In *The Dream-Quest of Unknown Kadath* (1926–27), Lovecraft describes "the boundless daemon Azathoth" as "that last amorphous blight of nethermost confusion which blasphemes and bubbles at the centre of all infinity" (*At the Mountains of Madness*, 308). Lovecraft had first conceived of the entity in "Azathoth" (1922), a prose fragment.

[5] *Justin Geoffrey . . . The People of the Monolith*: A tip of the hat to Robert E. Howard's tale "The Black Stone," which appeared in the November 1931 *Weird Tales*.

arena, but the family fortune was so ample that this formed no tragedy. As he grew to years of manhood he retained a deceptive aspect of boyishness. Blond and blue-eyed, he had the fresh complexion of a child; and his attempts to raise a moustache were decernible only with difficulty.[6] His voice was soft and light, and his pampered, unexercised life gave him a juvenile chubbiness rather than the paunchiness of premature middle age. He was of good height, and his handsome face would have made him a notable gallant had not his shyness held him to seculsion and bookishness.

Derby's parents took him abroad every summer, and he was quick to seize on the surface aspects of European thought and expression. His Poe-like talents turned more and more toward the decadent, and other artistic sensitivenesses and yearnings were half-aroused in him. We had great discussions in those days. I had been through Harvard, had studied in a Boston architect's office, had married, and had finally returned to Arkham to practice my profession—settling in the family homestead in Saltonstall St.[7] since my father had moved to Florida for his health. Edward used to call almost every evening, till I came to regard him as one of the household. He had a characteristic way of ringing the doorbell or sounding the knocker that grew to be a veritable code signal, so that after dinner I always listened for the familiar three brisk strokes followed by two more after a pause. Less frequently I would

[6] *his attempts to raise a moustache were discernible only with difficulty*: Soon after meeting Frank Belknap Long, in New York City in the spring of 1922, Lovecraft wrote in a letter: "Long . . . is an exquisite boy of twenty who hardly looks fifteen. He is dark and slight, with a bushy wealth of almost black hair and a delicate, beautiful face still a stranger to the gillette. I think he likes the tiny collection of lip-hairs—about six on one side and five on the other—which may with assiduous care some day help to enhance his genuine resemblance to his chief idol—Edgar Allan Poe." (*Selected Letters* I, 180) Lovecraft's letters of the 1930s reflect his concern about Long's immaturity. As a grown man Long was still living with his parents.

[7] *Saltonstall St.*: Sir Richard Saltonstall (1586–1658), of a prominent Yorkshire family, was one of the early settlers of Massachusetts.

visit at his house and note with envy the obscure volumes in his constantly growing library.

Derby went through Miskatonic University in Arkham, since his parents would not let him board away from them. He entered at sixteen and completed his course in three years, majoring in English and French literature and receiving high marks in everything but mathematics and the sciences. He mingled very little with the other students, though looking enviously at the "daring" or "Bohemian" set—whose superficially "smart" language and meaninglessly ironic pose he aped, and whose dubious conduct he wished he dared adopt.

What he did do was to become an almost fanatical devotee of subterranean magical lore, for which Miskatonic's library was and is famous. Always a dweller on the surface of phantasy and strangeness, he now delved deep into the actual runes and riddles left by a fabulous past for the guidance or puzzlement of posterity. He read things like the frightful *Book of Eibon*, the *Unaussprechlichen Kulten* of von Junzt, and the forbidden *Necronomicon*[8] of the mad Arab Adbul Alhazred, though he did not tell his parents he had seen them. Edward was twenty when my son and only child was born, and seemed pleased when I named the newcomer Edward Derby Upton,[9] after him.

By the time he was twenty-five Edward Derby was a prodigiously learned man and a fairly well-known poet and

---

[8] *Book of Eibon . . . Unaussprechlichen Kulten . . . Necronomicon*: By the 1930s Lovecraft was mentioning the *Necronomicon*, along with an ever-expanding number of mythical tomes devised by fellow writers, in virtually every one of his stories, including revisions published under the names of clients. When fans wrote and asked if these books were real, he told them the truth. In a 1936 letter, for example, he stated: "Now about the 'terrible and forbidden books'— I am forced to say that most of them are purely imaginary. There never was any Abdul Alhazred or *Necronomicon*, for I invented these names myself. . . . the *Book of Eibon* is an invention of Clark Ashton Smith's. The late Robert E. Howard is responsible for Friedrich von Junzt and his *Unaussprechlichen Kulten*." (*Selected Letters* V, 285–86) See note 24 to "The Haunter of the Dark."

[9] *Edward Derby Upton*: Upton is another old Salem name. See note 6 to "Pickman's Model."

fantaisiste, though his lack of contacts and responsibilities had slowed down his literary growth by making his products derivative and overbookish. I was perhaps his closest friend—finding him an inexhaustible mine of vital theoretical topics, while he relied on me for advice in whatever matters he did not wish to refer to his parents. He remained single—more through shyness, inertia, and parental protectiveness than through inclination—and moved in society only to the slightest and most perfunctory extent. When the war came both health and ingrained timidity kept him at home. I went to Plattsburg[10] for a commission, but never got overseas.

So the years wore on. Edward's mother died when he was thirty-four, and for months he was incapacitated by some odd psychological malady. His father took him to Europe, however, and he managed to pull out of his trouble without visible effects. Afterward he seemed to feel a sort of grotesque exhilaration, as if of partial escape from some unseen bondage.[11] He began to mingle in the more "advanced" college set despite his middle age, and was present at some extremely wild doings—on one occasion paying heavy blackmail (which he borrowed of me) to keep his presence at a certain affair from his father's notice. Some of the whispered rumours about the wild Miskatonic set were extremely singular. There was even talk of black magic and of happenings utterly beyond credibility.

---

[10] *Plattsburg*: Plattsburg, New York, was a major training center for American troops in World War I.

[11] *escape from some unseen bondage*: Lovecraft's own mother, Sarah Susan Phillips Lovecraft (1857–1921), died when he was thirty. A couple of months after her death, Lovecraft wrote Frank Belknap Long: "A major bereavement has the effect of increasing one's listlessness and killing one's ambition. I cannot concentrate on any definite work, and have written nothing for aeons." (*Selected Letters* I, 141) His hitherto secluded life, however, soon opened up, with trips to amateur conventions in Boston, visits to friends in Cleveland and New York, and romance followed by marriage to fellow amateur Sonia Greene. During this period Lovecraft must have felt something similar to the exhilaration he ascribes to Edward Derby.

II.

Edward was thirty-eight when he met Asenath Waite.[12] She was, I judge, about twenty-three at the time; and was taking a special course in mediaevel metaphysics at Miskatonic. The daughter of a friend of mine had met her before—in the Hall School at Kingsport[13]—and had been inclined to shun her because of her odd reputation. She was dark, smallish, and very good-looking except for over-proturberant eyes; but something in her expression alienated extremely sensitive people. It was, however, largely her origin and conversation which caused average folk to avoid her. She was one of the Innsmouth Waites, and dark legends have clustered for generations about crumbling, half-deserted Innsmouth[14] and its people. There are tales of horrible bargains about the year 1850, and of a strange element "not quite human" in the ancient families of the run-down fishing port—tales such as only old-time Yankees can devise and repeat with proper awesomeness.

Asenath's case was aggravated by the fact that she was Ephraim Waite's daughter—the child of his old age by an unknown wife who always went veiled. Ephraim lived in a half-decayed mansion in Washington Street, Innsmouth, and those who had seen the place (Arkham folk avoid going to Innsmouth whenever they can) declared that the attic windows were always boarded, and that strange

---

[12] *Asenath Waite*: In the Bible Asenath is the name of Joseph's Egyptian wife (Genesis 41: 45), who is the mother of Ephraim. The name seems to have meant in ancient Egyptian "she belongs to her father." In the tale Asenath is literally "possessed" by her father.

[13] *Kingsport*: A fictional coastal town that Lovecraft equated with Marblehead, Massachusetts, in his tale "The Festival" (1923).

[14] *crumbling, half-deserted Innsmouth*: Among the most famous of Lovecraft's fictional New England towns, the setting for "The Shadow Over Innsmouth" (1931).

sounds sometimes floated from within as evening drew on. The old man was known to have been a prodigious magical student in his day, and legend averred that he could raise or quell storms at sea according to his whim. I had seen him one or twice in my youth as he came to Arkham to consult forbidden tomes at the college library, and had hated his wolfish, saturnine face with its tangle of iron-grey beard. He had died insane—under rather queer circumstances—just before his daughter (by his will made a nominal ward of the principal) entered the Hall School, but she had been his morbidly avid pupil and looked fiendishly like him at times.

The friend whose daughter had gone to school with Asenath Waite repeated many curious things when the news of Edward's acquaintance with her began to spread about. Asenath, it seemed, had posed as a kind of magician at school; and had really seemed able to accomplish some highly baffling marvels. She professed to be able to raise thunderstorms, though her seeming success was generally laid to some uncanny knack at prediction. All animals markedly disliked her, and she could make any dog howl by certain motions of her right hand. There were times when she displayed snatches of knowledge and language very singular—and very shocking—for a young girl; when she would frighten her schoolmates with leers and winks of an inexplicable kind, and would seem to extract an obscene and zestful irony from her present situation.

Most unusual, though, were the well-attested cases of her influence over other persons. She was, beyond question, a genuine hypnotist. By gazing perculiarly at a fellow-student she would often give the latter a distinct feeling of *exchanged personality*—as if the subject were placed momentarily in the magician's body and able to stare half across the room at her real body, whose eyes blazed and protruded with an alien expression. Asenath often made wild claims about the nature of consciousness and about its independence of the physical frame—or at least from the life-processes of the physical frame. Her crowning rage, however, was that she was not a man;[15] since she believed a male brain had certain unique and far-reaching cosmic powers. Given a man's brain, she declared, she could not only equal but surpass her father in mastery of unknown forces.

Edward met Asenath at a gathering of "intelligentsia" held in one of the students' rooms, and could talk of nothing else when he came to see me the next day. He had found her full of the interests and erudition which engrossed him most, and was in addition wildly taken with her appearance. I had never seen the young woman, and recalled casual references only faintly, but I knew who she was. It seemed rather regrettable that Derby should become so upheaved about her; but I said nothing to discourage him, since infatuation thrives on opposition. He was not, he said, mentioning her to his father.

In the next few weeks I heard of very little but Asenath from young Derby. Others now remarked Edward's autumnal gallantry, though they agreed that he did not look even nearly his actual age, or seem at all inappropriate as an escort for his bizarre divinity. He was only a trifle paunchy despite his indolence and self-indulgence, and his face was absolutely without lines. Asenath, on the other hand, had the premature crow's feet which come from the exercise of an intense will.

About this time Edward brought the girl to call on me, and I at once saw that his interest was by no means one-sided. She eyed him continually with an almost predatory air,[16] and I perceived that their intimacy was beyond un-

[15] *Her crowning rage, however, was that she was not a man*: A statement sure to provoke feminist critics if any bothered to read Lovecraft. Having little or no interest in sex, Lovecraft leaves unexplored the whole issue of gender-switching implicit in the mind-exchange premise.

[16] *She eyed him continually with an almost predatory air*: With her strong will and designs on Derby, Asenath calls to mind Lovecraft's wife Sonia, who by all accounts (including her own) took the initiative in their relationship. See her memoir "Lovecraft as I Knew Him" (*Lovecraft Remembered*, 252–63).

tangling. Soon afterward I had a visit from old Mr. Derby, whom I had always admired and respected. He had heard the tales of his son's new friendship, and had wormed the whole truth out of "the boy". Edward meant to marry Asenath, and had even been looking at houses in the suburbs. Knowing my usually great influence with his son, the father wondered if I could help to break the ill-advised affair off; but I regretfully expressed my doubts. This time it was not a question of Edward's weak will but of the woman's strong will. The perennial child had transferred his dependence from the parental image to a new and stronger image, and nothing could be done about it.

The wedding was performed a month later—by a justice of the peace, according to the bride's request. Mr. Derby, at my advice, offered no opposition; and he, my wife, my son, and I attended the brief ceremony—the other guests being wild young people from the college. Asenath had bought the old Crowninshield[17] place in the country at the end of High Street, and they proposed to settle there after a short trip to Innsmouth, whence three servants and some books and household goods were to be brought. It was probably not so much consideration for Edward and his father as a personal wish to be near the college, its library, and its crowd of "sophisticates", that made Asenath settle in Arkham instead of returning permanently home.

When Edward called on me after the honeymoon I thought he looked slightly changed. Asenath had made him get rid of the undeveloped moustache, but there was more than that. He looked soberer and more thoughtful, his habitual pout of childish rebelliousness being exchanged for a look almost of genuine sadness. I was puzzled to decide whether I liked or disliked the change. Certainly, he seemed for the moment more normally adult

---

[17] *Crowninshield*: Another old Salem name. In the eighteenth century the Crowninshields displaced the Derbys as the leading merchant family of Salem.

than ever before. Perhaps the marriage was a good thing—
might not the *change* of dependence form a start toward
actual *neutralisation*, leading ultimately to responsible independence? He came alone, for Asenath was very busy.
She had brought a vast store or books and apparatus from
Innsmouth (Derby shuddered as he spoke the name), and
was finishing the restoration of the Crowninshield house
and grounds.

Her home in—that town—was a rather disquieting
place, but certain objects in it had taught him some surprising things. He was prgressing fast in esoteric lore now
that he had Asenath's guidance. Some of the experiments
she proposed were very daring and radical—he did not feel
at liberty to describe them—but he had confidence in her
powers and intentions. The three ser\vents were very
queer—an incredibly aged couple who had been with old
Ephraim and referred occasionally to him and to Asenath's
dead mother in a cryptic way, and a swarthy young wench
who had marked anomalies of feature and seemed to
exude a perpetual odour of fish.

III.

For the next two years I saw less and less of Derby. A
fortnight would sometimes slip by without the familiar
three-and-two strokes at the front door; and when he did
call—or when, as happened with increasing infrequency, I
called on him—he was very little disposed to converse on
vital topics. He had become secretive about those occult
studies which he used to describe and discuss so minutely,
and preferred not to talk of his wife. She had aged tremen-
dously since her marriage, till now—oddly enough—she
seemed the elder of the two. Her face held the most con-
centratedly determined expression I had ever seen, and her
whole aspect seemed to gain a vague, unplaceable repulsiveness. My wife and son noticed it as much as I, and

we all ceased gradually to call on her—for which, Edward
admitted in one of his boyishly tactless moments, she was
unmitigatedly grateful. Occasionally the Derbys would go
on long trips—ostensibly to Europe, though Edward sometimes hinted at obscurer destinations.

It was after the first year that people began talking about
the change in Edward Derby. It was very casual talke, for
the change was purely psychological; but it brought up
some interesting points. Now and then, it seemed, Edward
was observed to wear an expression and to do things
wholly incompatible with his usual flabby nature. For example—although in the old days he could not drive a car,
he was now seen occasionally to dash into or out of the
old Crowninshield driveway with Asenath's powerful
Packard,[18] handling it like a master, and meeting traffic
entanglements with skill and determination utterly alien
to his accustomed nature. In such cases he seemed always
to be just back from some trip or just starting on one—
what sort of trip, no one could guess, although he mostly
favoured the old Innsmouth road.

Oddly, the metamorphosis did not seem altogether
pleasing. People said he looked too much like his wife,
or like old Ephraim Waite himself, in these moments—or
perhaps these moments seemed unnatural because they
were so rare. Sometimes, hours after starting out in this
way, he would return listlessly sprawled on the rear seat
of his car while an obviously hired chauffeur or mechanic
drove. Also, his preponderant aspect on the streets during
his decreasing round of social contacts (including, I may
say, his calls on me) was the old-time indecisive one—its
irresponsible childishness even more marked than in the
past. While Asenath's face aged, Edward's—aside from
those exceptional occasions—actually relaxed into a kind

---

[18] *Packard*: The most consistently respected American car manufacturer from
the early 1900s to until after World War II. Lovecraft never learned to drive or
owned a car, but on a number of occasions friends took him on motor trips to
parts of the New England countryside not otherwise easily accessible.

of exaggerated immaturity, save when a trace of the new sadness or understanding would flash across it. It was really very puzzling. Meanwhile the Derbys almost dropped out of the gay college circle—not through their own disgust, we heard, but because something about their present studies shocked even the most callous of the other decadents.

It was in the third year of the marriage that Edward began to hint openly to me of a certain fear and dissatisfaction. He would let fall remarks about things 'going too far', and would talk darkly about the need of 'saving his identity'. At first I ignored such refereneces, but in time I began to question him guardedly, remembering what my friend's daughter had said about Asenath's hypnotic influence over the other girls at school—the cases where students had thought they were in her body looking across the room at themselves. This questioning seemed to make him at once alarmed and grateful, and once he mumbled something about having a serious talk with me later.

About this time old Mr. Derby died, for which I was afterward very thankful. Edward was badly upset, though by no means disorganised. He had seen astonishingly little of his parent since his marriage, for Asenath had concentrated in herself all his vital sense of family linkage. Some called him callous in his loss—especially since those jaunty and confident moods in the car began to increase. He now wished to move back into the old Derby mansion, but Asenath insisted on staying in the Crowninshield house, to which she had become well adjusted.

Not long afterward my wife heard a curious thing from a friend—one of the few who had not dropped the Derbys. She had been out to the end of High St. to call on the couple, and had seen a car shoot briskly out of the drive with Edward's oddly confident and almost sneering face above the wheel. Ringing the bell, she had been told by the repulsive wench that Asenath was also out; but had chanced to look up at the house in leaving. There, at one of Edward's library windows, she had glimpsed a hastily withdrawn face—a face whose expression of pain, defeat, and wistful hopelessness was poignant beyond description. It was—incredibly enough in view of its usual domineering cast—Asenath's; yet the caller had vowed that in that instant the sad, muddled eyes of poor Edward were gazing out from it.

Edward's calls now grew a trifle more frequent, and his hints occasionally became concrete. What he said was not to be believed, even in centuried and legend-haunted Arkham; but he threw out his dark lore with a sincerity and convincingness which made one fear for his sanity. He talked about terrible meetings in lonely places, of Cyclopean[19] ruins in the heart of the Maine woods beneath which vast staircases lead down to abysses of nighted secrets, of complex angles that lead through invisible walls to other regions of space and time, and of hideous exchanges of personality that permitted explorations in remote and forbidden places, on other worlds, and in different space-time continua.[20]

He would now and then back up certain crazy hints by exhibiting objects which utterly nonplussed me—elusively coloured and bafflingly textured objects like nothing ever heard of on earth,[21] whose insane curves and surfaces answered no conceivable purpose and followed no conceivable geometry. These things, he said, came 'from outside'; and his wife know how to get them. Sometimes—but always in frightened and ambiguous whispers—he would suggest things about old Ephraim Waite, whom he had

[19] *Cyclopean ruins*: One of Lovecraft's favorite adjectives. See note 10 to "The Call of Cthulhu."

[20] *different space-time continua*: This concept of personality exchange on a cosmic scale anticipates the action in "The Shadow Out of Time" (1934–35).

[21] *objects like nothing ever heard of on earth*: Likewise in "The Dreams in the Witch House" Walter Gilman acquires an object "from outside," "the exotic spiky figure" resembling one of the barrel-shaped Old Ones (*At the Mountains of Madness*, 279).

seen occasionally at the college library in the old days. These adumbrations were never specific, but seemed to revolve around some especially horrible doubt as to whether the old wizard were really dead—in a spiritual as well as corporeal sense.

At times Derby would halt abruptly in his revelations, and I wondered whether Asenath could possibly have divined his speech at a distance and cut him off through some unknown sort of telepathic mesmerism[22]—some power of the kind she had displayed at school. Certainly, she suspected that he told me things, for as the weeks passed she tried to stop his visits with words and glances of a most inexplicable potency. Only with difficulty could he get to see me, for although he would pretend to be going somewhere else, some invisible force would generally clog his motions or make him forget his destination for the time being. His visits usually came when Asenath was away—'away in her own body', as he once oddly put it. She always found out later—the servants watched his goings and comings—but evidently she thought it inexpedient to do anything drastic.

IV.

Derby had been married more than three years on that August day when I got the telegram from Maine. I had not seen him for two months, but had heard he was away "on business". Asenath was supposed to be with him, though watchful gossips declared there was someone upstairs in the house behind the doubly curtained windows. They had watched the purchases made by the servants.

[22] *mesmerism*: Another word for hypnotism, named after the Austrian physician Friedrich Anton Mesmer (1734–1815), who developed a system of treatment based on "animal magnetism."

And now the town marshal of Chesuncook[23] had wired of the draggled madman who stumbled out of the woods with delirious ravings and screamed to me for protection. It was Edward—and he had been just able to recall his own name and my name and address.

Chesuncook is close to the wildest, deepest, and least explored forest belt in Maine, and it took a whole day of feverish jolting through fantastic and forbidding scenery to get there in a car. I found Derby in a cell at the town farm, vacillating between frenzy and apathy. He knew me at once, and began pouring out a meaningless, half-incoherent torrent of words in my direction.

"Dan—for God's sake! The pit of the shoggoths![24] Down the six thousand steps . . . the abomination of abominations . . . I never would let her take me, and then I found myself there. . . . Iä! Shub-Niggurath![25] . . . The shape rose up from the altar, and there were 500 that howled . . . The Hooded Thing bleated 'Kamog! Kamog!'— that was old Ephraim's secret name in the coven. . . . I was there, where she promised she wouldn't take me. . . . A minute before I was locked in the library, and then I was there where she had gone with my body—in the place of utter blasphemy, the unholy pit where the black realm begins and the watcher guards the gate. . . . I saw a shoggoth—it changed shape. . . . I can't stand it. . . . I won't stand it. . . . I'll kill her if she ever sends me there again. . . . I'll kill that entity . . . her, him, it . . . I'll kill it! I'll kill it with my own hands!"

---

[23] *Chesuncook*: A real town in Maine, though unbeknownst to Lovecraft inaccessible by road at the time he wrote the story. See Will Murray's article "The Chesuncook Witch-Cult," *Crypt of Cthulhu* no. 12 (Eastertide 1983): 13–16.

[24] *shoggoths*: The "multicellular protoplasmic masses capable of moulding their tissues into all sorts of temporary organs under hypnotic influence" that figure in *At the Mountains of Madness*. See note 165 to that novel (*Annotated Lovecraft*, 272).

[25] *Iä! Shub-Niggurath!*: Shub-Niggurath ranks as a sort of fertility goddess in the Lovecraft pantheon. See note 68 to "The Dunwich Horror" (*Annotated Lovecraft*, 134).

It took me an hour to quiet him, but he subsided at last. The next day I got him decent clothes in the village, and set out with him for Arkham. His fury of hysteria was spent, and he was inclined to be silent; though he began muttering darkly to himself when the car passed through Augusta—as if the sight of a city aroused unpleasant memories. It was clear that he did not wish to go home; and considering the fantastic delusions he seemed to have about his wife—delusions undoubtedly springing from some actual hypnotic ordeal to which he had been subjected—I thought it would be better if he did not. I would, I resolved, put him up myself for a time; no matter what unpleasantness it would make with Asenath. Later I would help him get a divorce, for most assuredly there were mental factors which made this marriage suicidal for him. When we struck open country again Derby's muttering faded away, and I let him nod and drowse on the seat beside me as I drove.

During our sunset dash through Portland the muttering commenced again, more distinctly than before, and as I listened I caught a stream of utterly insane drivel about Asenath. The extent to which she had preyed on Edward's nerves was plain, for he had woven a whole set of hallucinations around her. His present predicament, he mumbled furtively, was only one of a long series. She was getting hold of him, and he knew that some day she would never let go. Even now she probably let him go only when she had to, because she couldn't hold on long at a time. She constantly took his body and went to nameless places for nameless rites, leaving him in her body and locking him upstairs—but sometimes she couldn't hold on, and he would find himself suddenly in his own body again in some far-off, horrible, and perhaps unknown place. Sometimes she'd get hold of him again and sometimes she couldn't. Often he was left stranded somewhere as I had found him . . . time and again he had to find his way home from frightful distances, getting somebody to drive the car after he found it.

The worst thing was that she was holding on to him longer and longer at a time. She wanted to be a man—to be fully human—that was why she got hold of him. She had sensed the mixture of fine-wrought brain and weak will in him. Some day she would crowd him out and disappear with his body—disappear to become a great magician like her father and leave him marooned in that female shell that wasn't even quite human. Yes, he knew about the Innsmouth blood now. There had been traffick with things from the sea—it was horrible. . . . And old Ephraim—he had known the secret, and when he grew old did a hideous thing to keep alive . . . he wanted to live forever . . . Asenath would succeed—one successful demonstration had taken place already.

As Derby muttered on I turned to look at him closely, verifying the impression of change which an earlier scrutiny had given me. Paradoxically, he seemed in better shape than usual—harder, more normally developed, and without the trace of sickly flabbiness caused by his indolent habits. It was as if he had been really active and properly exercised for the first time in his coddled life, and I judged that Asenath's force must have pushed him into unwonted channels of motion and alertness. But just now his mind was in a pitiable state; for he was mumbling wild extravagances about his wife, about black magic, about old Ephraim, and about some revelation which would convince even me. He repeated names which I recognised from bygone browsings in forbidden volumes, and at times made me shudder with a certain thread of mythological consistency—of convincing coherence—which ran through his maundering. Again and again he would pause, as if to gather courage for some final and terrible disclosure.

"Dan, Dan, don't you remember him—the wild eyes and the unkempt beard that never turned white? He glared at me once, and I never forgot it. Now *she* glares that way.

And I know why! He found it in the *Necronomicon*—the formula. I don't dare tell you the page yet, but when I do you can read and understand. Then you will know what has engulfed me. On, on, on, on—body to body to body— he means never to die. The life-glow—he knows how to break the link . . . it can flicker on a while even when the body is dead. I'll give you hints, and maybe you'll guess. Listen, Dan—do you know why my wife always takes such pains with that silly backhand writing? Have you ever seen a manuscript of old Ephraim's? Do you want to know why I shivered when I saw some hasty notes Asenath had jotted down?

"Asenath . . . *is there such a person?* Why did they half think there was poison in old Ephraim's stomach? Why do the Gilmans[26] whisper about the way he shrieked—like a frightened child—when he went mad and Asenath locked him up in the padded attic room where—the other—had been? *Was it old Ephraim's soul that was locked in? Who locked in whom?* Why had he been looking for months for someone with a fine mind and a weak will? Why did he curse that his daughter wasn't a son? Tell me, Daniel Upton—*what devilish exchange was perpetuated in the house of horror where that blasphemous monster had his trusting, weak-willed, half-human child at his mercy?* Didn't he make it permanent—as she'll do in the end with me? Tell me why that thing that calls itself Asenath writes differently when off guard, *so that you can't tell its script from* . . ."[27]

---

[26] *the Gilmans*: An Edward Gilman came from Norfolk, England, to Massachusetts in 1638. One of his descendants, Arthur Gilman (1773–1836), was a prosperous Newburyport merchant. Walter Gilman, a native of Haverhill, Massachusetts, is the hero of Lovecraft's tale "The Dreams in the Witch House" (1932). In "The Shadow Over Innsmouth," the unnamed narrator describes the Gilmans as one of the four "gently bred families of the town" and stays overnight at the Gilman House.

[27] *you can't tell its script from. . . .*": In Lovecraft's fiction one's handwriting remains immutable, no matter whether one's consciousness is transferred into the body of another human being or even into an alien creature, as happens in "The Shadow Out of Time." See note 38 below.

Then the thing happened. Derby's voice was rising to a thin treble scream as he raved, when suddenly it was shut off with an almost mechanical click. I thought of those other occasions at my home when his confidences had abruptly ceased—when I had half fancied that some obscure telepathic wave of Asenath's mental force was intervening to keep him silent. This, though, was something altogether different—and, I felt, infinitely more horrible. The face beside me was twisted almost unrecognisably for a moment, while through the whole body there passed a shivering motion—as if all the bones, organs, muscles, nerves, and glands were readjusting themselves to a radically different posture, set of stresses, and general personality.

Just where the supreme horror lay, I could not for my life tell; yet there swept over me such a swamping wave of sickness and repulsion—such a freezing, petrifying sense of utter alienage and abnormality—that my grasp of the wheel grew feeble and uncertain. The figure beside me seemed less like a lifelong friend than like some monstrous intrusion from outer space—some damnable, utterly accursed focus of unknown and malign cosmic forces.

I had faltered only a moment, but before another moment was over my companion had seized the wheel and forced me to change places with him. The dusk was now very thick, and the lights of Portland far behind, so I could not see much of his face. The blaze of his eyes, though, was phenomenal; and I knew that he must now be in that queerly energised state—so unlike his usual self—which so many people had noticed. It seemed odd and incredible that listless Edward Derby—he who could never assert himself, and who had never learned to drive—should be ordering me about and taking the wheel of my own car, yet that was precisely what had happened. He did not speak for some time, and in my inexplicable horror I was glad he did not.

In the lights of Biddeford and Saco I saw his firmly set mouth, and shivered at the blaze of his eyes. The people were right—he did look damnably like his wife and like old Ephraim when in these moods. I did not wonder that the moods were disliked—there was something unnatural and diabolic in them, and I felt the sinister element all the more because of the wild ravings I had been hearing. This man, for all my lifelong knowledge of Edward Pickman Derby, was a stranger—an intrusion of some sort from the black abyss.

He did not speak until we were on a dark stretch of road, and when he did his voice seemed utterly unfamiliar. It was deeper, firmer, and more decisive than I had ever known it to be; while its accent and pronunciation were altogether changed—though vaguely, remotely, and rather disturbingly recalling something I could not quite place. There was, I thought, a trace of very profound and very genuine irony in the timbre—not the flashy, meaninglessly jaunty pseudo-irony of the callow "sophisticate", which Derby had habitually affected, but something grim, basic, pervasive, and potentially evil. I marvelled at the self-possession so soon following the spell of panic-struck muttering.

"I hope you'll forget my attack back there, Upton," he was saying. "You know what my nerves are, and I guess you can excuse such things. I'm enormously grateful, of course, for this lift home.

"And you must forget, too, any crazy things I may have been saying about my wife—and about things in general. That's what come from overstudy in a field like mine. My philosophy is full of bizarre concepts, and when the mind gets worn out it cooks up all sorts of imaginary concrete applications. I shall take a rest from now on—you probably won't see me for some time, and you needn't blame Asenath for it.

"This trip was a bit queer, but it's really very simple. There are certain Indian relics in the north woods—standing stones,[28] and all that—which mean a good deal in folk-lore, and Asenath and I are following that stuff up. It was a hard search, so I seem to have gone off my head. I must send somebody for the car when I get home. A month's relaxation will put me back on my feet."

I do not recall just what my own part of the conversation was, for the baffling alienage of my seatmate filled my consciousness. With every moment my feeling of elusive cosmic horror increased, till at length I was in a virtual delirium of longing for the end of the drive. Derby did not offer to relinquish the wheel, and I was glad of the speed with which Portsmouth and Newburyport flashed by.

At the junction where the main highway runs inland and avoids Innsmouth I was half afraid my driver would take the bleak shore road that goes through that damnable place. He did not, however, but darted rapidly past Rowley and Ipswich toward our destination. We reached Arkham before midnight, and found the lights still on at the old Crowinshield house. Derby left the car with a hasty repetition of his thanks, and I drove home alone with a curious feeling of relief. It had been a terrible drive—all the more terrible because I could not quite tell why—and I did not regret Derby's forecast of a long absence from my company.

V.

The next two months were full of rumours. People spoke of seeing Derby more and more in his new energised state, and Asenath was scarcely ever in to her few callers. I had only one visit from Edward, when he called briefly in Asenath's car—duly reclaimed from wherever he had left it in Maine—to get some books he had lent me. He

---

[28] *standing stones*: Megalithic stones crown the hilltops of Dunwich. See note 7 to "The Dunwich Horror" (*Annotated Lovecraft*, 106).

was in his new state, and paused only long enough for some evasively polite remarks. It was plain that he had nothing to discuss with me when in this condition—and I noticed that he did not even trouble to give the old three-and-two signal when ringing the doorbell. As on that evening in the car, I felt a faint, infinitely deep horror which I could not explain; so that his swift departure was a prodigious relief.

In mid-September Derby was away for a week, and some of the decadent college set talked knowingly of the matter—hinting at a meeting with a notorious cult-leader, lately expelled from England, who had established headquarters in New York. For my part I could not get that strange ride from Maine out of my head. The transformation I had witnessed had affected me profoundly, and I caught myself again and again trying to account for the thing—and for the extreme horror it had inspired in me.

But the oddest rumours were those about the sobbing in the old Crowinshield house. The voice seemed to be a woman's, and some of the younger people thought it sounded like Asenath's. It was heard only at rare intervals, and would sometimes be choked off as if by force. There was talk of an investigation, but this was dispelled one day when Asenath appeared in the streets and chatted in a sprightly way with a large number of acquaintances—apologising for her recent absences and speaking incidentally about the nervous breakdown and hysteria of a guest from Boston. The guest was never seen, but Asenath's appearance left nothing to be said. And then someone complicated matters by whispering that the sobs had once or twice been in a man's voice.

One evening in mid-October I heard the familiar three-and-two ring at the front door. Answering it myself, I found Edward on the steps, and saw in a moment that his personality was the old one which I had not encountered since the day of his ravings on that terrible ride from Chesuncook. His face was twitching with a mixture of odd emotions in which fear and triumph seemed to share dominion, and he looked furtively over his shoulder as I closed the door behind him.

Following me clumsily to the study, he asked for some whiskey[29] to steady his nerves. I forbore to question him, but waited till he felt like beginning whatever he wanted to say. At length he ventured some information in a choking voice.

"Asenath has gone, Dan. We had a long talk last night while the servants were out, and I made her promise to stop preying on me. Of course I had certain—certain occult defences I never told you about. She had to give in, but got frightfully angry. Just packed up and started for New York—walked right out to catch the 8:20 in to Boston. I suppose people will talk, but I can't help that. You needn't mention that there was any trouble—just say she's gone on a long research trip.

"She's probably going to stay with one of her horrible groups of devotees. I hope she'll go west and get a divorce—anyhow, I've made her promise to keep away and let me alone. It was horrible, Dan—she was stealing my body—crowding me out—making a prisoner of me. I laid low and pretended to let her do it, but I had to be on the watch. I could plan if I was careful, for she can't read my mind literally, or in detail. All she could read of my planning was a sort of general mood of rebellion—and she always thought I was helpless. Never thought I could get the best of her . . . but I had a spell or two that worked."

Derby looked over his shoulder and took some more whiskey.

"I paid off those damned servants this morning when

---

[29] *whiskey*: The time frame of "The Thing on the Doorstep" is vague, but it would appear the climax to the story comes in the early 1930s, not long before the repeal of Prohibition. Nonetheless it would not be unusual for a respectable household to have liquor on hand. Note that in "Pickman's Model" Thurber is able to obtain what is apparently liquor during his meeting with Eliot in Boston circa 1926. Also see note 119, on bootleg whiskey, in "The Dunwich Horror" (*Annotated Lovecraft*, 159).

they got back. They were ugly about it, and asked questions, but they went. They're her kind—Innsmouth people—and were hand and glove with her. I hope they'll let me alone—I didn't like the way they laughed when they walked away. I must get as many of Dad's old servants again as I can. I'll move back home now.

"I suppose you think I'm crazy, Dan—but Arkham history ought to hint at things that back up what I've told you—and what I'm going to tell you. You've seen one of the changes, too—in your car after I told you about Asenath that day coming home from Maine. That was when she got me—drove me out of my body. The last thing of the ride I remember was when I was all worked up trying to tell you *what that she-devil is.* Then she got me, and in a flash I was back at the house—in the library where those damned servants had me locked up—and in that cursed fiend's body . . . that isn't even human. . . . You know, it was she you must have ridden home with . . . that preying wolf in my body. . . . You ought to have known the difference!"

I shuddered as Derby paused. Surely, I *had* known the difference—yet could I accept an explanation as insane as this? But my distracted caller was growing even wilder.

"I had to save myself—I had to, Dan! She'd have got me for good at Hallowmass[30]—they hold a Sabbat[31] up there beyond Chesuncook, and the sacrifice would have clinched things. She'd have got me for good . . . she'd have been I, and I'd have been she . . . forever . . . too late. . . . My body'd have been hers for good. . . . She'd have been a man, and fully human, just as she wanted to be. . . . I suppose she'd have put me out of the way—killed her own ex-body with me in it, damn her, *just as she did before—* just as she, he, or it did before. . . .''

---

[30] *Hallowmass*: The Feast of All Saints, preceded by All Hallow's Eve or Halloween. See note 40 to "The Dunwich Horror" (*Annotated Lovecraft*, 118).

[31] *Sabbat*: Traditionally a gathering of witches and the devil.

Edward's face was now atrociously distorted, and he bent it uncomfortably close to mins as his voice fell to a whisper.

"You mush know what I hinted in the car—*that she isn't Asenath at all, but really old Ephraim himself.* I suspected it a year and a half ago, but I know it now. Her handwriting shews it when she's off guard—sometimes she jots down a note in writing that's just like her father's manuscripts, stroke for stroke—and sometimes she says things that nobody but an old man like Ephraim could say. He changed forms with her when he felt death coming—she was the only one he could find with the right kind of brain and a weak enough will—he got her body permanently, just as she almost got mine, and then poisoned the old body he'd put her into. Haven't you seen old Ephraim's soul glaring out of that she-devil's eyes dozens of times . . . and out of mine when she had control of my body?"

The whisperer was panting, and paused for breath. I said nothing, and when he resumed his voice was nearer normal. This, I reflected, was a case for the asylum, but I would not be the one to send him there. Perhaps time and freedom from Asenath would do its work. I could see that he would never wish to dabble in morbid occultism again.

"I'll tell you more later—I must have a long rest now. I'll tell you something of the forbidden horrors she led me into—something of the age-old horrors that even now are festering in out-of-the-way corners with a few monstrous priests to keep them alive. Some people know things about the universe that nobody ought to know, and can do things that nobody ought to be able to do. I've been in it up to my neck, but that's the end. Today I'd burn that damned *Necronomicon* and all the rest if I were librarian at Miskatonic.

"But she can't get me now. I must get out of that accursed house as soon as I can, and settle down at home. You'll help me, I know, if I need help. Those devilish ser-

vants, you know . . . and if people should get too inquisitive about Asenath. You see, I can't give them her
address. . . . Then there are certain groups of searchers—
certain cults, you know—that might misunderstand our
breaking up . . . some of them have damnably curious
ideas and methods. I know you'll stand by me if anything
happens—even if I have to tell you a lot that will shock
you. . . .''

I had Edward stay and sleep in one of the guest-cham-
bers that night, and in the morning he seemed calmer.
We discussed certain possible arrangements for his moving
back into the Derby mansion, and I hoped he would lose
no time in making the change. He did not call the next
evening, but I saw him frequently during the ensuing
weeks. We talked as little as possible about strange and
unpleasant things, but discussed the renovation of the old
Derby house, and the travels which Edward promised to
take with my son and me the following summer.

Of Asenath we said almost nothing, for I saw that the
subject was a peculiarly disturbing one. Gossip, of course,
was rife; but that was no novelty in connexion with the
strange ménage at the old Crowninshield house. One thing
I did not like was what Derby's banker let fall in an over-
expansive mood at the Miskatonic Club—about the
cheques Edward was sending regularly to a Moses and Abigail Sargent and a Eunice Babson[32] in Innsmouth. That
looked as if those evil-faced servants were extorting some
kind of tribute from him—yet he had not mentioned the
matter to me.

I wished that the summer—and my son's Harvard vaca-

---

[32] *Moses and Abigail Sargent and a Eunice Babson*: More typical New England
names. A William Sargent emigrated from England to Charlestown, Massachusetts, in 1638. One of his descendants was the painter John Singer Sargent
(1856–1925). Roger Ward Babson (1875–1967), a native of Gloucester, Massachusetts, was an economist and business educator who founded the Babson Institute
of Business Administration in Wellesley, Massachusetts, in 1919. By assigning
these names to servants, Lovecraft would seem to be acknowledging that not
every descendant of such old families is a member of the social elite.

tion—would come, so that we could get Edward to Europe.
He was not, I soon saw, mending as rapidly as I had hoped
he would; for there was something a bit hysterical in his
occasional exhilaration, while the moods of fright and depression were altogether too frequent. The old Derby
house was ready by December, yet Edward constantly put
off moving. Though he hated and seemed to fear the
Crowninshield place, he was at the same time queerly en-
slaved by it. He could not seem to begin dismantling
things, and invented every kind of excuse to postpone action. When I pointed this out to him he appeared unaccountably frightened. His father's old butler—who was
there with other reacquired family servants—told me one
day that Edward's occasional prowlings about the house,
and especially down cellar, looked odd and unwholesome
to him. I wondered if Asenath had been writing disturbing
letters, but the butler said there was no mail which could
have come from her.

VI.

It was about Christmas that Derby broke down one evening while calling on me. I was steering the conversation
toward next summer's travels when he suddenly shrieked
and leaped up from his chair with a look of shocking,
uncontrollable fright—a cosmic panic and loathing such
as only the nether gulfs of nightmare could bring to any
sane mind.

"My brain! My brain! God, Dan—it's tugging—from be-
yond—knocking—clawing—that she-devil—even now—
Ephraim—Kamog! Kamog!—The pit of the shoggoths—Iä!
Shub-Niggurath! The Goat with a Thousand Young! . . .

"The flame—the flame . . . beyond body, beyond life . . .
in the earth . . . oh, God! . . ."

I pulled him back to his chair and poured some wine
down his throat as his frenzy sank to a dull apathy. He

did not resist, but kept his lips moving as if talking to himself. Presently I realised that he was trying to talk to me, and bent my ear to his mouth to catch the feeble words.

" . . . again, again . . . she's trying . . . I might have known . . . nothing can stop that force; not distance, nor magic, nor death . . . it comes and comes, mostly in the night . . . I can't leave . . . it's horrible . . . oh, God, Dan, *if you only knew as I do just how horrible it is. . . .*"

When he had slumped down into a stupor I propped him with pillows and let normal sleep overtake him. I did not call a doctor, for I knew what would be said of his sanity, and wished to give nature a chance if I possibly could. He waked at midnight, and I put him to bed upstairs, but he was gone by morning. He had let himself quietly out of the house—and his butler, when called on the wire, said he was at home pacing restlessly about the library.

Edward went to pieces rapidly after that. He did not call again, but I went daily to see him. He would always be sitting in his library, staring at nothing and having an air of abnormal *listening*. Sometimes he talked rationally, but always on trivial topics. Any mention of his trouble, of future plans, or of Asenath would send him into a frenzy. His butler said he had frightful seizures at night, during which he might eventually do himself harm.

I had a long talk with his doctor, banker, and lawyer, and finally took the physician with two specialist colleagues to visit him. The spasms that resulted from the first questions were violent and pitiable—and that evening a closed car took his poor struggling body to the Arkham Sanitarium. I was made his guardian and called on him twice weekly—almost weeping to hear his wild shrieks, awesome whispers, and dreadful, droning repetitions of such phrases as "I had to do it—I had to do it . . . it'll get me . . . it'll get me . . . down there . . . down there in the dark. . . . Mother, mother! Dan! Save me . . . save me . . ."

How much hope of recovery there was, no one could

say; but I tried my best to be optimistic. Edward must
have a home if he emerged, so I transferred his servants
to the Derby mansion, which would surely be his sane
choice. What to do about the Crowninshield place with
its complex arrangements and collections of utterly inexplicable objects I could not decide, so left it momentarily
untouched—telling the Derby household to go over and
dust the chief rooms once a week, and ordering the furnace man to have a fire on those days.

The final nightmare came before Candlemas[33]—her-
alded, in cruel irony, by a false gleam of hope. One morning late in January the sanitarium telephoned to report
that Edward's reason had suddenly come back. His continuous memory, they said, was badly impaired; but sanity
itself was certain. Of course he must remain some time
for observation, but there could be little doubt of the out-
come. All going well, he would surely be free in a week.

I hastened over in a flood of delight, but stood bewildered when a nurse took me to Edward's room. The patient rose to greet me,[34] extending his hand with a polite
smile; but I saw in an instant that he bore the strangely
energised personality which had seemed so foreign to his
own nature—the competent personality I had found so
vaguely horrible, and which Edward himself had once
vowed was the intruding soul of his wife. There was the same
blazing vision—so like Asenath's and old Ephraim's—and the
same firm mouth; and when he spoke I could sense the
same grim, pervasive irony in his voice—the deep irony
so redolent of potential evil. This was the person who had
driven my car through the night five months before—the
person I had not seen since that brief call when he had

---

[33] *Candlemas*: February 2, the Christian festival that commemorates the purifi-
cation of the Virgin and the presentation of Christ in the temple. See note 32
to "The Dunwich Horror" (*Annotated Lovecraft*, 115).

[34] *The patient rose to greet me*: A situation parallel to one at the end of *The
Case of Charles Dexter Ward*, where an imposter against his will is held under
psychiatric observation at a hospital and is soon to receive retribution.

forgotten the old-time doorbell signal and stirred such nebulous fears in me—and now he filled me with the same
dim feeling of blasphemous alienage and ineffable cosmic
hideousness.

He spoke affably of arrangements for release—and there
was nothing for me to do but assent, despite some remarkable gaps in his recent memories. Yet I felt that something
was terribly, inexplicably wrong and abnormal. There
were horrors in this thing that I could not reach. This was
a sane person—but was it indeed the Edward Derby I had
known? If not, who or what was it—*and where was Edward?* Ought it to be free or confined . . . or ought it to
be extirpated from the face of the earth? There was a hint
of the abysmally sardonic in everything the creature said—
the Asenath-like eyes lent a special and baffling mockery
to certain words about the 'early liberty earned by an *especially close confinement'*. I must have behaved very awk-
wardly, and was glad to beat a retreat.

All that day and the next I racked my brain over the
problem. What had happened? What sort of mind looked
out through those alien eyes in Edward's face? I could
think of nothing but this dimly terrible enigma, and gave
up all efforts to perform my usual work. The second morning the hospital called up to say that the recovered patient
was unchanged, and by evening I was close to a nervous
collapse—a state I admit, though others will vow it coloured my subsequent vision. I have nothing to say on this
point except that no madness of mine could account for
all the evidence.

VII.

It was in the night—after that second evening—that
stark, utter horror burst over me and weighted my spirit
with a black, clutching panic from which it can never
shake free. It began with a telephone call just before mid-

night. I was the only one up, and sleepily took down the receiver in the library. No one seemed to be on the wire, and I was about to hang up and go to bed when my ear caught a very faint suspicion of sound at the other end. Was someone trying under great difficulties to talk? As I listened I thought I heard a sort of half-liquid bubbling noise— "*glub . . . glub . . . glub*"—which had an odd suggestion of inarticulate, unintelligible word and syllable divisions. I called, "Who is it?" But the only answer was "*glub-glub . . . glub-glub.*" I could only assume that the noise was mechanical; but fancying that it might be a case of a broken instrument able to receive but not to send, I added, "I can't hear you. Better hang up and try Information." Immediately I heard the receiver go on the hook at the other end.

This, I say, was just before midnight. When that call was traced afterward it was found to come from the old Crowninshield house, though it was fully half a week from the housemaid's day to be there. I shall only hint what was found at that house—the upheaval in a remote cellar storeroom, the tracks, the dirt, the hastily rifled wardrobe, the baffling marks on the telephone, the clumsily used stationery, and the detestable stench lingering over everything. The police, poor fools, have their smug little theories, and are still searching for those sinister discharged servants—who have dropped out of sight amidst the present furore. They speak of a ghoulish revenge for things that were done, and say I was included because I was Edward's best friend and adviser.

Idiots!—do they fancy those brutish clowns could have forged that handwriting? Do they fancy they could have brought what later came? Are they blind to the changes in that body that was Edward's? As for me, *I now believe all that Edward Derby ever told me.* There are horrors beyond life's edge that we do not suspect, and once in a while man's evil prying calls them just within our range. Ephraim—Asenath—that devil called them in, and they engulfed Edward as they are engulfing me.

Can I be sure that I am safe? Those powers survive the life of the physical form. The next day—in the afternoon, when I pulled out of my prostration and was able to walk and talk coherently—I went to the madhouse and shot him dead for Edward's and the world's sake, but can I be sure till he is cremated? They are keeping the body for some silly autopsies by different doctors—but I say he must be cremated. *He must be cremated—he who was not Edward Derby when I shot him.* I shall go mad if he is not, for I may be the next. But my will is not weak—and I shall not let it be undermined by the terrors I know are seething around it. One life—Ephraim, Asenath, and Edward—who now? I *will not* be driven out of my body . . . I *will not* change souls with that bullet-ridden lich[35] in the madhouse!

But let me try to tell coherently of that final horror. I will not speak of what the police persistently ignored—the tales of that dwarfed, grotestque, malodorous thing met by at least three wayfarers in High St. just before two o'clock, and the nature of the single footprints in certain places. I will say only that just about two the doorbell and knocker waked me—doorbell and knocker both, plied alternately and uncertainly in a kind of weak desperation, *and each trying to keep to Edward's old signal of three-and-two strokes.*

Roused from sound sleep, my mind leaped into a turmoil. Derby at the door—and remembering the old code! That new personality had not remembered it . . . was Edward suddenly back in his rightful state? Why was he here in such evident stress and haste? Had he been released ahead of time, or had he escaped? Perhaps, I thought as I flung on a robe and bounded downstairs, his return to his own self had brought raving and violence, revoking his discharge and driving him to a desperate dash for freedom. Whatever had happened, he was good old Edward again, and I would help him!

---

[35] *lich*: Archaic word for corpse.

When I opened the door into the elm-arched blackness a gust of insufferably foetid[36] wind almost flung me prostrate. I choked in nausea, and for a second scarcely saw the dwarfed, humped figure on the steps. The summons had been Edward's, but who was this foul, stunted parody? Where had Edward had time to go? His ring had sounded only a second before the door opened.

The caller had on one of Edward's overcoats—its bottom almost touching the ground, and its sleeves rolled back yet still covering the hands. On the head was a slouch hat pulled low, while a black silk muffler concealed the face. As I stepped unsteadily forward, the figure made a semi-liquid sound like that I had heard over the telephone—*"glub . . . glub . . ."* —and thrust at me a large, closely written paper impaled on the end of a long pencil. Still reeling from the morbid and unaccountable foetor, I seized this paper and tried to read it in the light from the doorway.

Beyond question, it was in Edward's script. But why had he written when he was close enough to ring—and why was the script so awkward, coarse, and shaky? I could make out nothing in the dim half light, so edged back into the hall, the dwarf figure clumping mechanically after but pausing on the inner door's threshold. The odour of this singular messenger was really appalling, and I hoped (not in vain, thank God!) that my wife would not wake and confront it.[37]

Then, as I read the paper, I felt my knees give under me and my vision go black. I was lying on the floor when I

---

[36] *foetid*: The adjectival form of *foetor* or *fetor*, meaning stench. A common word in Lovecraft.

[37] *I hoped . . . that my wife would not wake and confront it*: In Lovecraft a husband's natural instinct is to protect his wife from horror. In "The Dunwich Horror" Dr. Armitage warns his wife off when her eyes wander toward the notes he's been taking on Wilbur Whateley's diary, while in *The Case of Charles Dexter Ward* Theodore Howland Ward carries his wife downstairs, after she's fainted, to spare her hearing more of the strange noises coming from behind the door of their son's laboratory. With the ambiguous exception of Asenath, women are definitely the weaker sex in Lovecraft's fiction.

came to, that accursed sheet still clutched in my fear-rigid hand. This is what it said.

"Dan—go to the sanitarium and kill it. Exterminate it. It isn't Edward Derby any more. She got me—it's Asenath—*and she has been dead three months and a half.* I lied when I said she had gone away. I killed her. I had to. It was sudden, but we were alone and I was in my right body. I saw a candlestick and smashed her head in. She would have got me for good at Hallowmass.

"I buried her in the farther cellar storeroom under some old boxes and cleaned up all the traces. The servants suspected next morning, but they have such secrets that they dare not tell the police. I sent them off, but God knows what they—and others of the cult—will do.

"I thought for a while I was all right, and then I felt the tugging at my brain. I knew what it was—I ought to have remembered. A soul like hers—or Ephraim's—is half detached, and keeps right on after death as long as the body lasts. She was getting me—making me change bodies with her—*seizing my body and putting me in that corpse of hers buried in the cellar.*

"I knew what was coming—that's why I snapped and had to go to the asylum. Then it came—I found myself choked in the dark—in Asenath's rotting carcass down there in the cellar under the boxes where I put it. And I knew she must be in my body at the sanitarium--*permanently,* for it was after Hallowmass, and the sacrifice would work even without her being there—sane, and ready for release as a menace to the world. I was desperate, *and in spite of everything I clawed my way out.*

"I'm too far gone to talk—I couldn't manage to telephone—but I can still write.[38] I'll get fixed up somehow and bring you this last word and warning. *Kill that fiend* if you value the peace and comfort of the world. *See that it is cremated.* If you don't, it will live on and on, body to body forever, and I can't tell you

---

[38] *but I can still write*: Like a number of Lovecraft's characters, starting with the narrator of "Dagon" (1917), Derby can write an explanatory or warning letter in the most dire circumstances. See note 17 to "Cool Air."

what it will do. Keep clear of black magic, Dan, it's the devil's business. Goodbye—you've been a great friend. Tell the police whatever they'll believe—and I'm damnably sorry to drag all this on you. I'll be at peace before long—this thing won't hold together much more. Hope you can read this. *And kill that thing—kill it.*

Yours—Ed."

It was only afterward that I read the last half of this paper, for I had fainted at the end of the third paragraph. I fainted again when I saw and smelled what cluttered up the threshold where the warm air had struck it. The messenger would not move or have consciousness any more.

The butler, tougher-fibred than I, did not faint at what met him in the hall in the morning. Instead, he telephoned the police. When they came I had been taken upstairs to bed, but the—other mass—lay where it had collapsed in the night. The men put handkerchiefs to their noses.

What they finally found inside Edward's oddly assorted clothes was mostly liquescent horror. There were bones, too—and a crushed-in skull. Some dental work positively identified the skull as Asenath's.[39]

---

[39] *the skull as Asenath's*: This procedure for identifying a body is a minor detail in "The Horror at Red Hook." See note 53 to that story.

The Haunter of the Dark

(Dedicated to Robert Bloch)[1]

I have seen the dark universe yawning
Where the black planets roll without aim—

"The Haunter of the Dark" was written in November 1935. It was first published in the December 1936 issue of *Weird Tales*.

   In a letter dated February 20, 1937, Lovecraft answered at length the criticism
of a fan who'd apparently found it hard to believe that the tale's protagonist,
Robert Blake, behaved so passively. Part of Lovecraft's defense reads: "It is hardly
correct to attribute Blake's inability to act to 'a Hamlet-like nature'; since the
cause was a *specific hypnosis from outside*. Left to himself, Blake was not necessarily of an indecisive temperament." (*Selected Letters* V, 414) By this date
Lovecraft was seriously ill with stomach cancer and would be dead in less than
a month. That he should bother to take such pains in the circumstances suggests
the degree to which he took his work seriously.

Where they roll in their horror unheeded,
Without knowledge or lustre or name.

—Nemesis.[2]

Cautious investigators will hesitate to challenge the common belief that Robert Blake was killed by lightning, or by some profound nervous shock derived from an electrical discharge. It is true that the window he faced was unbroken, but Nature has shewn herself capable of many freakish performances. The expression on his face may easily have arisen from some obscure muscular source unrelated to anything he saw, while the entries in his diary are clearly the result of a fantastic imagination aroused by certain local superstitions and by certain old matters he had uncovered. As for the anomalous conditions at the deserted church on Federal Hill[3]—the shrewd analyst is not slow in attributing them to some charlatanry, conscious or unconscious, with at least some of which Blake was secretly connected.

For after all, the victim was a writer and painter wholly devoted to the field of myth, dream, terror, and superstition, and avid in his quest for scenes and effects of a bi-

---

[1] *Robert Bloch*: In the spring of 1935 Robert Bloch (1917–94), then a promising young writer of weird fiction, got Lovecraft's bemused permission to kill him off in a story called "The Shambler from the Stars." When it was published in *Weird Tales* (Sept. 1935), a reader wrote in and suggested that Lovecraft return the compliment in a tale dedicated to Bloch. Heartened by the recent acceptance of both *At the Mountains of Madness* and "The Shadow Out of Time" by *Astounding*, Lovecraft promptly did so. Bloch later wrote a sequel to "The Haunter of the Dark," "The Shadow from the Steeple," which was also published in *Weird Tales* (Sept. 1950).

[2] *Nemesis*: Lovecraft chose a stanza from one of his own poems as an epigraph, perhaps a sign, rare in his last years, of self-confidence. Soon after composing "Nemesis" (1917), Lovecraft described its genesis in a letter: "It was written in the sinister small hours of the black morning after Hallowe'en, which may account for the colouring & atmosphere! It presents the conception, tenable to the orthodox mind, that nightmares are the punishment meted out to the soul for sins committed in previous incarnations—perhaps millions of years ago!" (*Selected Letters* I, 51–52) He added that the meter was a cross between Poe's "Ulalume" and Swinburne's "Hertha."

zarre, spectral sort. His earlier stay in the city—a visit to a strange old man as deeply given to occult and forbidden lore as he—had ended amidst death and flame, and it must have been some morbid instinct which drew him back from his home in Milwaukee. He may have known of the old stories despite his statements to the contrary in the diary, and his death may have nipped in the bud some stupendous hoax destined to have a literary reflection.

Among those, however, who have examined and correlated all this evidence, there remain several who cling to less rational and commonplace theories. They are inclined to take much of Blake's diary at its face value, and point significantly to certain facts such as the undoubted genuineness of the old church record, the verified existence of the disliked and unorthodox Starry Wisdom sect prior to 1877, the recorded disappearance of an inquisitive reporter named Edwin M. Lillibridge in 1893, and—above all—the look of monstrous, transfiguring fear on the face of the young writer when he died. It was one of these believers who, moved to fanatical extremes, threw into the bay the curiously angled stone and its strangely adorned metal box found in the old church steeple—the black windowless steeple, and not the tower where Blake's diary said those things actually were. Though widely censured both officially and unofficially, this man—a reputable physician with a taste for odd folklore—averred that he had rid the earth of something too dangerous to rest upon it.

Between these two schools of opinion the reader must

---

[3] *Federal Hill*: Lovecraft first toured Federal Hill in November 1923, guided by his friend and revision client, Clifford M. Eddy (1896–1971). In a letter written shortly afterwards, Lovecraft said: "Italians are the most numerous foreigners in Providence, and they have a separate place of habitation in which they spend all their lives, with shops, restaurants, and theatres of their own, seldom going 'down city' (as they phrase it) from their isolated elevation. Federal Hill was sparsely settled in the Colonial period, a church and a few houses being shewn in Avery's 1777 view. It was later a stronghold of the Irish, till after 1870 the Italians drove them down the northern slope and took the crest for themselves, finally occupying the whole, almost to the foot on all sides. . . . the legions of Caesar victorious over the Celts." (*Selected Letters* I, 271)

judge for himself. The papers have given the tangible details from a sceptical angle, leaving for others the drawing
of the picture as Robert Blake saw it—or thought he saw
it—or pretended to see it. Now, studying the diary closely,
dispassionately, and at leisure, let us summarise the dark
chain of events from the expressed point of view of their
chief actor.

Young Blake returned to Providence in the winter of
1934–5, taking the upper floor of a venerable dwelling in
a grassy court off College Street—on the crest of the great
eastward hill near the Brown University campus and behind the marble John Hay Library. It was a cosy and fasci-
nating place, in a little garden oasis of village-like
antiquity where huge, friendly cats sunned themselves
atop a convenient shed. The square Georgian house had a
monitor roof, classic doorway with fan carving, small-
paned windows, and all the other earmarks of early
nineteenth-century workmanship. Inside were six-panelled
doors, wide floor-boards, a curving colonial staircase,
white Adam-period mantels, and a rear set of rooms three
steps below the general level.[4]

---

[4] *Young Blake . . . three steps below the general level.*: This paragraph describes
Lovecraft's own residence at 66 College Street, where he and his younger aunt,
Annie Emeline Phillips Gamwell (1866–1941), moved in the spring of 1933. His
letters of the period reflect his delight at finally living in a house of near colonial
vintage. He was especially pleased with his study: "Turning to look around the
room, I can honestly say that I'm damn satisfied. While only three of my pieces
of furniture are really *18th century*, there's a goodly amount of *early 19th century* material to harmonise in all essentials with the room. . . . the present room
certainly holds a strong amount of the atmosphere of 1795 or 1800. Only 9 feet
high, with Adam-period woodwork and mantel, appropriate paper, and no violent
clashes in decoration, it certainly has a Georgian grace possessed by no other
place I have ever inhabited." (*Selected Letters* IV, 189) Robert Adam (1728–92)
and his brother James Adam (1730–94) were Scottish architects and designers,
particulary known for their decorative interior work. In the 1950s the house
was moved to 65 Prospect Street to make way for Brown University's List Art
Building.
  The John Hay Library, part of Brown University, contains a number of special
collections. It was named for John Milton Hay (1838–1905), the poet, historian,
journalist, and diplomat, who served as one of Abraham Lincoln's private secre-
taries. Lovecraft's papers, presented to Brown University after his death by his
literary executor Robert Barlow (1918–1951), are housed at the John Hay Library.

Blake's study, a large southwest chamber, overlooked the front garden on one side, while its west windows—before one of which he had his desk—faced off from the brow of the hill and commanded a splendid view of the lower town's outspread roofs and of the mystical sunsets that flamed behind them.[5] On the far horizon were the open countryside's purple slopes. Against there, some two miles away, rose the spectral hump of Federal Hill, bristling with huddled roofs and steeples whose remote outlines wavered mysteriously, taking fantastic forms as the smoke of the city swirled up and enmeshed them. Blake had a curious sense that he was looking upon some unknown, ethereal world which might or might not vanish in dream if ever he tried to seek it out and enter it in person.

Having sent home for most of his books, Blake bought some antique furniture suitable to his quarters and settled down to write and paint—living alone, and attending to the simple housework himself. His studio was in a north attic room, where the panes of the monitor roof furnished admirable lighting. During that first winter he produced five of his best-known short stories—"The Burrower Beneath", "The Stairs in the Crypt", "Shaggai", "In the Vale of Pnath",[6] and "The Feaster from the Stars"—and painted seven canvases; studies of nameless, unhuman monsters, and profoundly alien, non-terrestrial landscapes.

At sunset he would often sit at his desk and gaze dreamily off at the outspread west—the dark towers of Memorial

---

[5] *mystical sunsets that flamed behind them*: Lovecraft was fond of sunsets and their image, typically linked with a sense of adventurous expectancy, crops up frequently in his poetry and prose. In May 1933 he wrote of his new abode: "My quarters—a large study and a small bedroom—are on the south side, with my working table under a west window affording a splendid view of some of the lower town's outspread roofs and of the mystical sunsets that flame behind them." (*Selected Letters* IV, 187)

[6] *Vale of Pnath*: A region in Lovecraft's dream world first mentioned in *The Dream-Quest of Unknown Kadath* (1926–27).

View of downtown Providence, looking west (approximate view that H. P. Lovecraft/Robert Blake would have had looking out his west window at 66 College street) (photo by Mollie L. Burleson).

Hall[7] just below, the Georgian court-house belfry, the lofty pinnacles of the downtown section, and that shimmering, spire-crowned mound in the distance whose unknown streets and labyrinthine gables so potently provoked his fancy. From his few local acquaintances he learned that the far-off slope was a vast Italian quarter, though most of the houses were remnants of older Yankee and Irish days. Now and then he would train his field-glasses on that spectral, unreachable world beyond the curling smoke; picking out individual roofs and chimneys and steeples, and speculating upon the bizarre and curious

[7] *Memorial Hall . . . Georgian court-house belfry*: Memorial Hall is the main building on the campus of the Rhode Island School of Design on Benefit Street. Elihu Whipple, the narrator's uncle in "The Shunned House," lives on North Court Street "beside the ancient brick court and colony house."

mysteries they might house. Even with optical aid Federal Hill seemed somehow alien, half fabulous, and linked to the unreal, intangible marvels of Blake's own tales and pictures. The feeling would persist long after the hill had faded into the violet, lamp-starred twilight, and the court-house floodlights and the red Industrial Trust beacon[8] had blazed up to make the night grotesque.

Of all the distant objects on Federal Hill, a certain huge, dark church[9] most fascinated Blake. It stood out with espe-cial distinctness at certain hours of the day, and at sunset the great tower and tapering steeple loomed blackly against the flaming sky. It seemed to rest on especially high ground; for the grimy facade, and the obliquely seen north side with sloping roof and the tops of great pointed windows, rose boldly above the tangle of surrounding ridgepoles and chimney-pots. Peculiarly grim and austere, it appeared to be built of stone, stained and weathered with the smoke and storms of a century and more. The style, so far as the glass could shew, was that earliest ex-perimental form of Gothic revival[10] which preceded the stately Upjohn period and held over some of the outlines and proportions of the Georgian age. Perhaps it was reared around 1810 or 1815.

---

[8] *Industrial Trust beacon*: The Industrial Trust Building, at 55 Exchange Place, was built 1926–28. At twenty-six stories it was the tallest building in Providence at the time.

[9] *a certain huge, dark church*: In a 1935 letter Lovecraft described it as "a less ancient & less sinister object in real life than in the story. It actually dates from the 1870's, & has no spectral associations—being St. John's Catholic (Irish, though the district has since become Italian) church. Federal Hill (the Italian quarter) as seen 2 miles away from my window is really quite a mysterious & picturesque sight—with the dark bulk & spire of St. John's rising against the remote horizon above the huddled roofs." (*Selected Letters* V, 220) In 1992 St. John's was demolished.

[10] *Gothic revival . . . stately Upjohn period*: The Gothic revival in church archi-tecture began in England in the early nineteenth century, in reaction to the Classical style that was dominant in the eighteenth century, and reached the United States in the 1830s. Prominent among American adherents of the Gothic revival was the English-born architect Richard Upjohn (1802–78), designer of New York City's Trinity Church (completed 1846).

St. John's Catholic Church, Atwell's Avenue, Providence (basis for the "Starry Wisdom Church"). Now destroyed (photo by Jason C. Eckhardt).

As months passed, Blake watched the far-off, forbidding structure with an oddly mounting interest. Since the vast windows were never lighted, he knew that it must be vacant. The longer he watched, the more his imagination worked, till at length he began to fancy curious things. He believed that a vague, singular aura of desolation hovered over the place, so that even the pigeons and swallows shunned its smoky eaves. Around other towers and belfries his glass would reveal great flocks of birds, but here they never rested. At least, that is what he thought and set down in his diary. He pointed the place out to several friends, but none of them had even been on Federal Hill or possessed the faintest notion of what the church was or had been.

In the spring a deep restlessness gripped Blake. He had begun his long-planned novel—based on a supposed survival of the witch-cult in Maine[11]—but was strangely unable to make progress with it. More and more he would sit at his westward window and gaze at the distant hill and the black, frowning steeple shunned by the birds. When the delicate leaves came out on the garden boughs the world was filled with a new beauty, but Blake's restlessness was merely increased. It was then that he first thought of crossing the city and climbing bodily up that fabulous slope into the smoke-wreathed world of dream.

Late in April, just before the aeon-shadowed Walpurgis time,[12] Blake make his first trip into the unknown. Plodding through the endless downtown streets and the bleak, decayed squares beyond, he came finally upon the ascending avenue of century-worn steps, sagging Doric porches,[13] and blear-paned cupolas which he felt must lead

---

[11] *witch-cult in Maine*: A nod to Robert Bloch's lengthy short story "Satan's Servants," written in February 1935, about a witch-cult in Maine. Lovecraft provided extensive suggestions for the revision of the tale, which was published in *Something About Cats* (1949), one of the early Arkham House collections of Lovecraft miscellany.

[12] *Walpurgis time*: Walpurgisnacht is the traditional German witches' sabbath held on the eve of one of Saint Walburga's feast days, May 1. See note 44 to "The Horror at Red Hook." In a 1934 letter Lovecraft explained how the name of a Christian saint became attached to a pagan festival: "May 1st is the day sacred to St. Walburga or Walpurgis, an English nun of the 8th century who helped to introduce Christianity into Germany. Among the Germans the old weird memories & still-surviving Sabbat-rites of May-Eve became very easily fused with the worship of the saint—especially since certain miracles were associated with her . . . or rather, with her tomb. Hence—with typical cosmic irony—one of the two most anti-Christian festivals in Europe became known by the name of a Christian saint!" (*Selected Letters* IV, 345)

[13] *Doric porches*: The simplest of the three Classical orders, the others being Ionic and Corinthian. A Doric porch would have columns topped by plain round capitals.

up to the long-known, unreachable world beyond the mists. There were dingy blue-and-white street signs which meant nothing to him, and presently he noted the strange, dark faces of the drifting crowds, and the foreign signs over curious shops in brown, decade-weathered buildings. Nowhere could he find any of the objects he had seen from afar; so that once more he half fancied that the Federal Hill of that distant view was a dream-world never to be trod by living human feet.

Now and then a battered church facade or crumbling spire came in sight, but never the blackened pile that he sought. When he asked a shopkeeper about a great stone church the man smiled and shook his head, though he spoke English freely. As Blake climbed higher, the region seemed stranger and stranger, with bewildering mazes of brooding brown alleys leading eternally off to the south. He crossed two or three broad avenues, and once thought he glimpsed a familiar tower. Again he asked a merchant about the massive church of stone, and this time he could have sworn that the plea of ignorance was feigned. The dark man's face had a look of fear which he tried to hide, and Blake saw him make a curious sign with his right hand.

Then suddenly a black spire stood out against the cloudy sky on his left, above the tiers of brown roofs lining the tangled southerly alleys. Blake knew at once what it was, and plunged toward it through the squalid, unpaved lanes that climbed from the avenue. Twice he lost his way, but he somehow dared not ask any of the patriarchs or housewives who sat on their doorsteps, or any of the children who shouted and played in the mud of the shadowy lanes.

At last he saw the tower plain against the southwest, and a huge stone bulk rose darkly at the end of an alley. Presently he stood in a windswept open square, quaintly cobblestoned, with a high bank wall on the farther side. This was the end of his quest; for upon the wide, iron-railed, weed-grown plateau which the wall supported—a separate, lesser world raised fully six feet above the surrounding streets—there stood a grim, titan bulk whose identity, despite Blake's new perspective, was beyond dispute.

The vacant church was in a state of great decrepitude. Some of the high stone buttresses had fallen, and several delicate finials[14] lay half lost among the brown, neglected weeds and grasses. The sooty Gothic windows were largely unbroken, though many of the stone mullions[15] were missing. Blake wondered how the obscurely painted panes could have survived so well, in view of the known habits of small boys the world over. The massive doors were intact and tightly closed. Around the top of the bank wall, fully enclosing the grounds, was a rusty iron fence whose gate—at the head of a flight of steps from the square—was visibly padlocked. The path from the gate to the building was completely overgrown. Desolation and decay hung like a pall above the place, and in the birdless eaves and black, ivyless walls Blake felt a touch of the dimly sinister beyond his power to define.

There were very few people in the square, but Blake saw a policeman at the northerly end and approached him with questions about the church. He was a great wholesome Irishman, and it seemed odd that he would do little more than make the sign of the cross and mutter that people never spoke of that building. When Blake pressed him he said very hurriedly that the Italian priests warned everybody against it, vowing that a monstrous evil had once dwelt there and left its mark. He himself had heard dark whispers of it from his father, who recalled certain sounds and rumours from his boyhood.

There had been a bad sect there in the ould[16] days—an

---

[14] *finials*: In architecture a finial is an ornament finishing off the apex of a roof.

[15] *mullions*: A mullion is a vertical piece within a window.

[16] *ould*: This is not a typo but rather a way of suggesting the policeman's Irish accent.

outlaw sect that called up awful things from some unknown gulf of night. It had taken a good priest to exorcise
what had come, though there did be those who said that
merely the light could do it. If Father O'Malley were alive
there would be many the thing he could tell. But now
there was nothing to do but let it alone. It hurt nobody
now, and those that owned it were dead or far away. They
had run away like rats after the threatening talk in '77,
when people began to mind the way folks vanished now
and then in the neighbourhood. Some day the city would
step in and take the property for lack of heirs, but little
good would come of anybody's touching it. Better it be
left alone for the years to topple, lest things be stirred that
ought to rest forever in their black abyss.

After the policeman had gone Blake stood staring at the
sullen steepled pile. It excited him to find that the structure seemed as sinister to others as to him, and he wondered what grain of truth might lie behind the old tales
the bluecoat had repeated. Probably they were mere legends evoked by the evil look of the place, but even so,
they were like a strange coming to life of one of his
own stories.

The afternoon sun came out from behind dispersing
clouds, but seemed unable to light up the stained, sooty
walls of the old temple that towered on its high plateau.
It was odd that the green of spring had not touched the
brown, withered growths in the raised, iron-fenced yard.
Blake found himself edging nearer the raised area and examining the bank wall and rusted fence for possible avenues of ingress. There was a terrible lure about the
blackened fane[17] which was not to be resisted. The fence
had no opening near the steps, but around on the north
side were some missing bars. He could go up the steps
and walk around on the narrow coping[18] outside the fence

---

[17] *blackened fane*: *Fane* is a poetic word for temple or, as here, church.

[18] *narrow coping*: The top, usually sloping, course of masonry in a wall.

till he came to the gap. If the people feared the place so wildly, he would encounter no interference.

He was on the embankment and almost inside the fence before anyone noticed him. Then, looking down, he saw the few people in the square edging away and making the same sign with their right hands that the shopkeeper in the avenue had made. Several windows were slammed down, and a fat woman darted into the street and pulled some small children inside a rickety, unpainted house. The gap in the fence was very easy to pass through, and before long Blake found himself wading amidst the rotting, tangled growths of the deserted yard. Here and there the worn stump of a headstone told him that there had once been burials in this field; but that, he saw, must have been very long ago. The sheer bulk of the church was oppressive now that he was close to it, but he conquered his mood and approached to try the three great doors in the facade. All were securely locked, so he began a circuit of the Cyclopean[19] building in quest of some minor and more penetrable opening. Even then he could not be sure that he wished to enter that haunt of desertion and shadow, yet the pull of its strangeness dragged him on automatically.

A yawning and unprotected cellar window in the rear furnished the needed aperture. Peering in, Blake saw a subterrene gulf of cobwebs and dust faintly litten by the western sun's filtered rays. Debris, old barrels, and ruined boxes and furniture of numerous sorts met his eye, though over everything lay a shroud of dust which softened all sharp outlines. The rusted remains of a hot-air furnace shewed that the building had been used and kept in shape as late as mid-Victorian times.

Acting almost without conscious initiative, Blake crawled through the window and let himself down to the dust-carpeted and debris-strown concrete floor. The

---

[19] *Cyclopean*: A word Lovecraft loved to use. See note 10 to "The Call of Cthulhu."

vaulted cellar was a vast one, without partitions; and in a corner far to the right, amid dense shadows, he saw a black archway evidently leading upstairs. He felt a peculiar sense of oppression at being actually within the great spectral building, but kept it in check as he cautiously scouted about—finding a still-intact barrel amid the dust, and rolling it over to the open window to provide for his exit. Then, bracing himself, he crossed the wide, cobweb-festooned space toward the arch. Half choked with the omnipresent dust, and covered with ghostly gossamer fibres, he reached and began to climb the worn stone steps which rose into the darkness. He had no light, but groped carefully with his hands. After a sharp turn he felt a closed door ahead, and a little fumbling revealed its ancient latch. It opened inward, and beyond it he saw a dimly illumined corridor lined with worm-eaten panelling.

Once on the ground floor, Blake began exploring in a rapid fashion. All the inner doors were unlocked, so that he freely passed from room to room. The colossal nave was an almost eldritch[20] place with its drifts and mountains of dust over box pews, altar, hourglass pulpit, and sounding-board,[21] and its titanic ropes of cobweb stretching among the pointed arches of the gallery and entwining the clustered Gothic columns. Over all this hushed desolation played a hideous leaden light as the declining afternoon sun sent its rays through the strange, half-blackened panes of the great apsidal[22] windows.

The paintings on those windows were so obscured by soot that Blake could scarcely decipher what they had represented, but from the little he could make out he did not

---

[20] *eldritch*: Weird or unnatural. See note 53 to "The Colour Out of Space (*Annotated Lovecraft*, 84).

[21] *sounding-board*: A board or screen placed over or behind the pulpit of a church in such a manner as to reflect the speaker's voice towards the audience.

[22] *apsidal*: Adjectival form of *apse*, an arched or domed semi-circular or polygonal recess within a church.

like them. The designs were largely conventional, and his knowledge of obscure symbolism told him much concerning some of the ancient patterns. The few saints depicted bore expressions distinctly open to criticism, while one of the windows seemed to shew merely a dark space with spirals of curious luminosity scattered about in it. Turning away from the windows, Blake noticed that the cob-webbed cross above the altar was not of the ordinary kind, but resembled the primordial ankh or crux ansata[23] of shadowy Egypt.

In a rear vestry room beside the apse Blake found a rotting desk and ceiling-high shelves of mildewed, disintegrating books. Here for the first time he received a positive shock of objective horror, for the titles of those books told him much. They were the black, forbidden things which most sane people have never even heard of, or have heard of only in furtive, timorous whispers; the banned and dreaded repositories of equivocal secrets and immemorial formulae which have trickled down the stream of time from the days of man's youth, and the dim, fabulous days before man was. He had himself read many of them—a Latin version of the abhorred *Necronomicon*,[24] the sinister *Liber Ivonis*, the infamous *Cultes des Goules* of Comte d'Erlette, the *Unaussprechlichen Kulten* of von Junzt, and old Ludvig Prinn's hellish *De Vermis Mysteriis*. But there were others he had known merely by reputation or not at all—the Pnakotic Manuscripts, the *Book of Dzyan*, and a crumbling volume in wholly unidentifiable characters yet

---

[23] *ankh or crux ansata*: A key-like cross that was a symbol of enduring life and generative energy in ancient Egypt.

[24] *Necronomicon . . . Book of Dzyan*: In addition to his own *Necronomicon* and Pnakotic Manuscripts, the latter first mentioned in "Polaris" (1918), Lovecraft invokes the various forbidden tomes invented by his friends and fellow writers. Clark Ashton Smith was responsible for the *Liber Ivonis* or *Book of Eibon*; August Derleth for the *Cultes des Goules* of Comte d'Erlette; Robert E. Howard for Friedrich von Junzt and his *Unaussprechlichen Kulten*; Robert Bloch for *De Vermis Mysteriis*. The *Book of Dzyan* is a purportedly ancient work fabricated by theosophists. See note 8 to "The Thing on the Doorstep."

with certain symbols and diagrams shudderingly recognisable to the occult student. Clearly, the lingering local rumours had not lied. This place had once been the seat of an evil older than mankind and wider than the known universe.

In the ruined desk was a small leather-bound record-book filled with entries in some odd cryptographic medium.[25] The manuscript writing consisted of the common traditional symbols used today in astronomy and anciently in alchemy, astrology, and other dubious arts—the devices of the sun, moon, planets, aspects, and zodiacal signs—here massed in solid pages of text, with divisions and paragraphings suggesting that each symbol answered to some alphabetical letter.

In the hope of later solving the cryptogram, Blake bore off this volume in his coat pocket. Many of the great tomes on the shelves fascinated him unutterably, and he felt tempted to borrow them at some later time. He wondered how they could have remained undisturbed so long. Was he the first to conquer the clutching, pervasive fear which had for nearly sixty years protected this deserted place from visitors?

Having now thoroughly explored the ground floor, Blake ploughed again through the dust of the spectral nave to the front vestibule, where he had seen a door and staircase presumably leading up to the blackened tower and steeple—objects so long familiar to him at a distance. The ascent was a choking experience, for dust lay thick, while the spiders had done their worst in this constricted place. The staircase was a spiral with high, narrow wooden treads, and now and then Blake passed a clouded window looking dizzily out over the city. Though he had seen no ropes below, he expected to find a bell or peal of bells in the tower whose narrow, louver-boarded lancet windows[26] his field-glass had studied so often. Here he was doomed

---

[25] *cryptographic medium*: A cryptogram is a text written in a cipher or code.

to disappointment; for when he attained the top of the stairs he found the tower chamber vacant of chimes, and clearly devoted to vastly different purposes.

The room, about fifteen feet square, was faintly lighted by four lancet windows, one on each side, which were glazed within their screening of decayed louver-boards. These had been further fitted with tight, opaque screens, but the latter were now largely rotted away. In the centre of the dust-laden floor rose a curiously angled stone pillar some four feet in height and two in average diameter, covered on each side with bizarre, crudely incised, and wholly unrecognisable hieroglyphs. On this pillar rested a metal box of peculiarly asymmetrical form; its hinged lid thrown back, and its interior holding what looked beneath the decade-deep dust to be an egg-shaped or irregularly spherical object some four inches through. Around the pillar in a rough circle were seven high-backed Gothic chairs still largely intact, while behind them, ranging along the dark-panelled walls, were seven colossal images of crumbling, black-painted plaster, resembling more than anything else the cryptic carven megaliths of mysterious Easter Island.[27] In one corner of the cobwebbed chamber a ladder was built into the wall, leading up to the closed trap-door of the windowless steeple above.

As Blake grew accustomed to the feeble light he noticed odd bas-reliefs on the strange open box of yellowish metal. Approaching, he tried to clear the dust away with his hands and handkerchief, and saw that the figurings were of a monstrous and utterly alien kind; depicting entities which, though seemingly alive, resembled no known life-form ever evolved on this planet. The four-inch seeming

---

[26] *louver-boarded lancet windows*: Louvers are sloping boards that overlap each other so as to admit air but exclude rain. A lancet window is a high narrow window terminating in an arch shaped like the blade of a lancet.

[27] *mysterious Easter Island*: A reference to the mysterious stone heads carved out of volcanic rock on Easter Island, a small island in the South Pacific. See note 3 to "The Picture in the House."

sphere turned out to be a nearly black, red-striated poly-
hedron with many irregular flat surfaces; either a very remarkable crystal of some sort, or an artificial object of
carved and highly polished mineral matter. It did not
touch the bottom of the box, but was held suspended by
means of a metal band around its centre, with seven
queerly designed supports extending horizontally to angles
of the box's inner wall near the top. This stone, once exposed, exerted upon Blake an almost alarming fascination.
He could scarcely tear his eyes from it, and as he looked
at its glistening surfaces he almost fancied it was transparent, with half-formed worlds of wonder within. Into his
mind floated pictures of alien orbs with great stone
towers, and other orbs with titan mountains and no mark
of life, and still remoter spaces where only a stirring in
vague blacknesses told of the presence of consciousness
and will.

When he did look away, it was to notice a somewhat
singular mound of dust in the far corner near the ladder
to the steeple. Just why it took his attention he could not
tell, but something in its contours carried a message to
his unconscious mind. Ploughing toward it, and brushing
aside the hanging cobwebs as he went, he began to discern
something grim about it. Hand and handkerchief soon revealed the truth, and Blake gasped with a baffling mixture
of emotions. It was a human skeleton, and it must have
been there for a very long time. The clothing was in
shreds, but some buttons and fragments of cloth bespoke
a man's grey suit. There were other bits of evidence—
shoes, metal clasps, huge buttons for round cuffs, a
stickpin of bygone pattern, a reporter's badge with the
name of the old *Providence Telegram*,[28] and a crumbling
leather pocketbook. Blake examined the latter with care,

---

[28] *Providence Telegram*: The *Providence Telegram*, or properly the [Providence]
Evening Telegram, was founded in 1880. In 1906 it became the *Evening Tribune
and Telegram*, at which time it published Lovecraft's astronomy columns
(1906–08).

finding within it several bills of antiquated issue, a cellu-
loid advertising calendar for 1893, some cards with the
name "Edwin M. Lillibridge", and a paper covered with
pencilled memoranda.

This paper held much of a puzzling nature, and Blake
read it carefully at the dim westward window. Its disjointed text included such phrases as the following:

"Prof. Enoch Bowen home from Egypt May 1844—buys
old Free-Will Church in July—his archaeological
work & studies in occult well known."
"Dr. Drowne of 4th Baptist warns against Starry Wisdom in sermon Dec. 29, 1844."
"Congregation 97 by end of '45."
"1846—3 disappearances—first mention of Shining
Trapezohedron"[29]
"7 disappearances 1848—stories of blood sacrifice
begin."
"Investigation 1853 comes to nothing—stories of
sounds."
"Fr. O'Malley tells of devil-worship with box found in
great Egyptian ruins—says they call up something
that can't exist in light. Flees a little light, and ban-
ished by strong light. Then has to be summoned
again. Probably got this from deathbed confession
of Francis X. Feeney, who had joined Starry Wisdom
in '49. These people say the Shining Trapezohedron
shews them heaven & other worlds, & that the
Haunter of the Dark tells them secrets in some
way."
"Story of Orrin B. Eddy[30] 1857. They call it up by gazing

---

[29] *Shining Trapezohedron*: In geometry a trapezohedron is a solid figure whose
faces are trapeziums or trapezoids, that is, irregular quadrilaterals.

[30] *Orrin B. Eddy*: Eddy, an old New England name, is most famously that of the
founder of Christian Science, Mary Baker Eddy (1821–1910). One of Lovecraft's
few Providence friends bore this surname. See note 3 above.

at the crystal, & have a secret language of their
own."

"200 or more in cong. 1863, exclusive of men at front."

"Irish boys mob church in 1869 after Patrick Regan's
disappearance."

"Veiled article in J. March 14, '72, but people don't talk
about it."

"6 disappearances 1876—secret committee calls on
Mayor Doyle."[31]

"Action promised Feb. 1877—church closes in April."

"Gang—Federal Hill Boys—threaten Dr. —— and ves-
trymen in May."

"181 persons leave city before end of '77—mention
no names."

"Ghost stories begin around 1880—try to ascertain
truth of report that no human being has entered
church since 1877."

"Ask Lanigan for photograph of place taken 1851." . . .

Restoring the paper to the pocketbook and placing the
latter in his coat, Blake turned to look down at the skeleton in the dust. The implications of the notes were clear,
and there could be no doubt but that this man had come
to the deserted edifice forty-two years before in quest of a
newspaper sensation which no one else had been bold
enough to attempt. Perhaps no one else had known of his
plan—who could tell? But he had never returned to his
paper. Had some bravely suppressed fear risen to overcome
him and bring on sudden heart-failure? Blake stooped over
the gleaming bones and noted their peculiar state. Some
of them were badly scattered, and a few seemed oddly
dissolved at the ends. Others were strangely yellowed,
with vague suggestions of charring. This charring extended
to some of the fragments of clothing. The skull was in a

---

[31] *Mayor Doyle*: Thomas Arthur Doyle was mayor of Providence for sixteen
years.

very peculiar state—stained yellow, and with a charred aperture in the top as if some powerful acid had eaten through the solid bone. What had happened to the skeleton during its four decades of silent entombment here Blake could not imagine.

Before he realised it, he was looking at the stone again, and letting its curious influence call up a nebulous pageantry in his mind. He saw processions of robed, hooded figures whose outlines were not human, and looked on endless leagues of desert lined with carved, sky-reaching monoliths. He saw towers and walls in nighted depths under the sea, and vortices of space where wisps of black mist floated before thin shimmerings of cold purple haze. And beyond all else he glimpsed an infinite gulf of darkness, where solid and semi-solid forms were known only by their windy stirrings, and cloudy patterns of force seemed to superimpose order on chaos and hold forth a key to all the paradoxes and arcana of the worlds we know.

Then all at once the spell was broken by an access of gnawing, indeterminate panic fear. Blake choked and turned away from the stone, conscious of some formless alien presence close to him and watching him with horrible intentness. He felt entangled with something—something which was not in the stone, but which had looked through it at him—something which would ceaselessly follow him with a cognition that was not physical sight. Plainly, the place was getting on his nerves—as well it might in view of his gruesome find. The light was waning, too, and since he had no illuminant with him he knew he would have to be leaving soon.

It was then, in the gathering twilight, that he thought he saw a faint trace of luminosity in the crazily angled stone. He had tried to look away from it, but some obscure compulsion drew his eyes back. Was there a subtle phosphorescence of radio-activity about the thing? What was it that the dead man's notes had said concerning a *Shining*

Trapezohedron! What, anyway, was this abandoned lair of cosmic evil? What had been done here, and what might still be lurking in the bird-shunned shadows? It seemed now as if an elusive touch of foetor[32] had arisen somewhere close by, though its source was not apparent. Blake seized the cover of the long-open box and snapped it down. It moved easily on its alien hinges, and closed completely over the unmistakably glowing stone.

At the sharp click of that closing a soft stirring sound seemed to come from the steeple's eternal blackness overhead, beyond the trap-door. Rats, without question—the only living things to reveal their presence in this accursed pile since he had entered it. And yet that stirring in the steeple frightened him horribly, so that he plunged almost wildly down the spiral stairs, across the ghoulish nave, into the vaulted basement, out amidst the gathering dusk of the deserted square, and down through the teeming, fear-haunted alleys and avenues of Federal Hill toward the sane central streets and the home-like brick sidewalks of the college district.

During the days which followed, Blake told no one of his expedition. Instead, he read much in certain books, examined long years of newspaper files downtown, and worked feverishly at the cryptogram in that leather volume from the cobwebbed vestry room. The cipher, he soon saw, was no simple one; and after a long period of endeavour he felt sure that its language could not be English, Latin, Greek, French, Spanish, Italian, or German. Evidently he would have to draw upon the deepest wells of his strange erudition.

Every evening the old impulse to gaze westward returned, and he saw the black steeple as of yore amongst the bristling roofs of a distant and half-fabulous world. But now it held a fresh note of terror for him. He knew the heritage of evil lore it masked, and with the knowledge

---

[32] *foetor*: Archaic or British spelling of *fetor*, an offensive smell or stench.

his vision ran riot in queer new ways. The birds of spring were returning, and as he watched their sunset flights he fancied they avoided the gaunt, lone spire as never before. When a flock of them approached it, he thought, they would wheel and scatter in panic confusion[33]—and he could guess at the wild twitterings which filed to reach him across the intervening miles.

It was in June that Blake's diary told of his victory over the cryptogram. The text was, he found, in the dark Aklo language[34] used by certain cults of evil antiquity, and known to him in a halting way through previous researches. The diary is strangely reticent about what Blake deciphered, but he was patently awed and disconcerted by his results. There are references to a Haunter of the Dark awaked by gazing into the Shining Trapezohedron, and insane conjectures about the black gulfs of chaos from which it was called. The being is spoken of as holding all knowledge, and demanding monstrous sacrifices. Some of Blake's entries shew fear lest the thing, which he seemed to regard as summoned, stalk abroad; though he adds that the street-lights form a bulwark which cannot be crossed.

Of the Shining Trapezohedron he speaks often, calling it a window on all time and space, and tracing its history from the days it was fashioned on dark Yuggoth,[35] before ever the Old Ones[36] brought it to earth. It was treasured and placed in its curious box by the crinoid things of Ant-

---

[33] *wheel and scatter in panic confusion*: The whippoorwills in "The Dunwich Horror" behave similarly when they go after the soul of Wilbur Whateley: "above the murmurs of the gathering crowd there came the sound of a panic-struck whirring and fluttering. Against the moon vast clouds of feathery watchers rose and raced from sight, frantic at that which they had sought for prey." (*Annotated Lovecraft*, 141)

[34] *Aklo language*: A term found in Arthur Machen's "The White People." See note 108 to "The Dunwich Horror" (*Annotated Lovecraft*, 155).

[35] *Yuggoth*: The planet we humans know as Pluto, home of the crab-like Winged Ones or Mi-Go, as revealed in "The Whisperer in Darkness" (1930).

[36] *Old Ones*: A seeming reference to the Great Old Ones in "The Call of Cthulhu." See note 35 to that story and note 37 below.

arctica,[37] salvaged from their ruins by the serpent-men of
Valusia,[38] and peered at aeons later in Lemuria[39] by the
first human beings. It crossed strange lands and stranger
seas, and sank with Atlantis before a Minoan fisher
meshed it in his net and sold it to swarthy merchants from
nighted Khem.[40] The Pharaoh Nephren-Ka[41] built around it
a temple with a windowless crypt, and did that which
caused his name to be stricken from all monuments and
records. Then it slept in the ruins of that evil fane which
the priests and the new Pharaoh destroyed, till the delver's
spade once more brought it forth to curse mankind.

Early in July the newspapers oddly supplement Blake's
entries, though in so brief and casual a way that only the
diary has called general attention to their contribution. It
appears that a new fear has been growing on Federal Hill
since a stranger had entered the dreaded church. The Italians whispered of unaccustomed stirrings and bumpings
and scrapings in the dark windowless steeple, and called
on their priests to banish an entity which haunted their
dreams. Something, they said, was constantly watching at
a door to see if it were dark enough to venture forth. Press
items mentioned the long-standing local superstitions, but
failed to shed much light on the earlier background of the

[37] *the crinoid things of Antarctica*: Otherwise known as the star-headed Old
Ones in *At the Mountains of Madness*. Aware that he had been imprecise in
his terminology in the past, Lovecraft here is careful to distinguish the Great
Old Ones of "The Call of Cthulhu" from these creatures. See note 36 above.

[38] *serpent-men of Valusia*: An invention of Robert E. Howard in "The Shadow
Kingdom," published in *Weird Tales* (Aug. 1929). The serpent-men are described
as having ruled Valusia before human beings drove them out.

[39] *Lemuria*: A mythical continent supposedly sunken in the Indian Ocean. See
note 12 to "The Call of Cthulhu" and note 130 to *At the Mountains of Madness*
(*Annotated Lovecraft*, 250).

[40] *Atlantis . . . Minoan . . . Khem*: For Lovecraft's views on Atlantis, see note
129 to *At the Mountains of Madness* (*Annotated Lovecraft*, 250). *Minoan*, from
King Minos, is a descriptive of the ancient Cretan civilization (3000–1500 B.C.).
See note 158 to *At the Mountains of Madness* (*Annotated Lovecraft*, 267). *Khem*
means "black" in Egyptian and was the native name for Egypt.

[41] *Nephren-Ka*: A fictional king of ancient Egypt.

horror. It was obvious that the young reporters of today are no antiquarians. In writing of these things in his diary, Blake expresses a curious kind of remorse, and talks of the duty of burying the Shining Trapezohedron and of banishing what he had evoked by letting daylight into the hideous spire. At the same time, however, he displays the dangerous extent of his fascination, an admits a morbid longing—pervading even his dreams—to visit the accursed tower and gaze again into the cosmic secrets of the glowing stone.

Then something in the *Journal*[42] on the morning of July 17 threw the diarist into a veritable fever of horror. It was only a variant of the other half-humorous items about the Federal Hill restlessness, but to Blake it was somehow very terrible indeed. In the night a thunderstorm had put the city's lighting-system out of commission for a full hour, and in that black interval the Italians had nearly gone mad with fright. Those living near the dreaded church had sworn that the thing in the steeple had taken advantage of the street-lamps' absence and gone down into the body of the church, flopping and bumping around in a viscous, altogether dreadful way. Toward the last it had bumped up to the tower, where there were sounds of the shattering of glass. It could go wherever the darkness reached, but light would always send it fleeing.

When the current blazed on again there had been a shocking commotion in the tower, for even the feeble light trickling through the grime-blackened, louver-boarded windows was too much for the thing. It had bumped and slithered up into its tenebrous steeple just in time—for a long dose of light would have sent it back into the abyss whence the crazy stranger had called it. During the dark hour praying crowds had clustered round the church in the rain with lighted candles and lamps somehow shielded with folded paper and umbrellas—a guard of

---

[42] *Journal*: The *Providence Journal* was founded in 1828.

light to save the city from the nightmare that stalks in darkness. Once, those nearest the church declared, the outer door had rattled hideously.

But even this was not the worst. That evening in the *Bulletin*[43] Blake read of what the reporters had found. Aroused at last to the whimsical news value of the scare, a pair of them had defied the frantic crowds of Italians and crawled into the church through the cellar window after trying the doors in vain. They found the dust of the vestibule and of the spectral nave ploughed up in a singular way, with pits of rotted cushions and satin pew-linings scattered curiously around. There was a bad odour everywhere, and here and there were bits of yellow stain and patches of what looked like charring. Opening the door to the tower, and pausing a moment at the suspicion of a scraping sound above, they found the narrow spiral stairs wiped roughly clean.

In the tower itself a similarly half-swept condition existed. They spoke of the heptagonal[44] stone pillar, the over-turned Gothic chairs, and the bizarre plaster images; though strangely enough the metal box and the old mutilated skeleton were not mentioned. What disturbed Blake the most—except for the hints of stains and charring and bad odours—was the final detail that explained the crashing glass. Every one of the tower's lancet windows was broken, and two of them had been darkened in a crude and hurried way by the stuffing of satin pew-linings and cushion-horsehair[45] into the spaces between the slanting exterior louver-boards. More satin fragments and bunches of horsehair lay scattered around the newly swept floor, as if someone had been interrupted in the act of restoring

[43] *Bulletin*: The *Evening Bulletin* was founded in 1863. In 1976 it merged with the *Providence Journal* to become the *Providence Journal-Bulletin*.

[44] *heptagonal*: Seven-sided, from the Greek *hepta* meaning seven.

[45] *cushion-horsehair*: Victorian furniture was often stuffed with the hair from a horse's mane or tail.

the tower to the absolute blackness of its tightly curtained days.

Yellowish stains and charred patches were found on the ladder to the windowless spire, but when a reporter climbed up, opened the horizontally sliding trap-door, and shot a feeble flashlight beam into the black and strangely foetid space, he saw nothing but darkness, and an heterogeneous litter of shapeless fragments near the aperture. The verdict, of course, was charlatanry. Somebody had played a joke on the superstitious hill-dwellers, or else some fanatic had striven to bolster up their fears for their own supposed good. Or perhaps some of the younger and more sophisticated dwellers had staged an elaborate hoax on the outside world. There was an amusing aftermath when the police sent an officer to verify the reports. Three men in succession found ways of evading the assignment, and the fourth went very reluctantly and returned very soon without adding to the account given by the reporters.

From this point onward Blake's diary shews a mounting tide of insidious horror and nervous apprehension. He upbraids himself for not doing something, and speculates wildly on the consequences of another electrical breakdown. It has been verified that on three occasions—during thunderstorms—he telephoned the electric light company in a frantic vein and asked that desperate precautions against a lapse of power be taken. Now and then his entries shew concern over the failure of the reporters to find the metal box and stone, and the strangely marred old skeleton, when they explored the shadowy tower room. He assumed that these things had been removed—whither, and by whom or what, he could only guess. But his worst fears concerned himself, and the kind of unholy rapport he felt to exist between his mind and that lurking horror in the distant steeple—that monstrous thing of night which his rashness had called out of the ultimate black spaces. He seemed to feel a constant tugging at his will, and callers of that period remember how he would sit abstractedly at his desk and stare out of the west window at that far-off, spire-bristling mound beyond the swirling smoke of the city. His entries dwell monotonously on certain terrible dreams, and of a strengthening of the unholy rapport in his sleep. There is mention of a night when he awaked to find himself fully dressed, outdoors, and headed automatically down College Hill toward the west. Again and again he dwells on the fact that the thing in the steeple knows where to find him.

The week following July 30 is recalled as the time of Blake's partial breakdown. He did not dress, and ordered all his food by telephone. Visitors remarked the cords he kept near his bed, and he said that sleep-walking had forced him to bind his ankles every night with knots which would probably hold or else waken him with the labour of untying.

In his diary he told of the hideous experience which had brought the collapse. After retiring on the night of the 30th he had suddenly found himself groping about in an almost black space. All he could see were short, faint, horizontal streaks of bluish light, but he could smell an overpowering foetor and hear a curious jumble of soft, furtive sounds above him. Whenever he moved he stumbled over something, and at each noise there would come a sort of answering sound from above—a vague stirring, mixed with the cautious sliding of wood on wood.

Once his groping hands encountered a pillar of stone with a vacant top, whilst later he found himself clutching the rungs of a ladder built into the wall, and fumbling his uncertain way upward toward some region of intenser stench where a hot, searing blast beat down against him. Before his eyes a kaleidoscopic range of phantasmal images played, all of them dissolving at intervals into the picture of a vast, unplumbed abyss of night wherein whirled suns and worlds of an even profounder blackness. He thought of the ancient legends of Ultimate Chaos, at whose centre sprawls the blind idiot god Azathoth, Lord of All Things, encircled by his flopping horde of mindless and amorphous dancers, and lulled by the thin monotonous piping of a daemoniac flute held in nameless paws.[46]

Then a sharp report from the outer world broke through his stupor and roused him to the unutterable horror of his position. What it was, he never knew—perhaps it was some belated peal from the fireworks heard all summer on Federal Hill as the dwellers hail their various patron saints, or the saints of their native villages in Italy. In any event he shrieked aloud, dropped frantically from the ladder, and stumbled blindly across the obstructed floor of the almost lightless chamber that encompassed him.

He knew instantly where he was, and plunged recklessly down the narrow spiral staircase, tripping and bruising himself at every turn. There was a nightmare flight through a vast cobwebbed nave whose ghostly arches reached up to realms of leering shadow, a sightless scramble through a littered basement, a climb to regions of air and street-lights outside, and a mad racing down a spectral hill of gibbering[47] gables, across a grim, silent city of tall black towers, and up the steep eastward precipice to his own ancient door.

On regaining consciousness in the morning he found himself lying on his study floor fully dressed. Dirt and cobwebs covered him, and every inch of his body seemed sore and bruised. When he faced the mirror he saw that his hair was badly scorched, while a trace of strange, evil odour seemed to cling to his upper outer clothing. It was then that his nerves broke down. Thereafter, lounging exhaustedly about in a dressing-gown, he did little but stare from his west window, shiver at the threat of thunder, and make wild entries in his diary.

---

[46] *Ultimate Chaos . . . nameless paws*: Lovecraft describes the entity Azathoth in similar terms in *The Dream-Quest of Unknown Kadath* (1926–27). See note 4 to "The Thing on the Doorstep."

[47] *gibbering*: To gibber is to speak fast and inarticulately.

The great storm[48] broke just before midnight on August
8th. Lightning struck repeatedly in all parts of the city,
and two remarkable fireballs were reported. The rain was
torrential, while a constant fusillade of thunder brought
sleeplessness to thousands. Blake was utterly frantic in his
fear for the lighting system, and tried to telephone the
company around 1 a.m., though by that time service had
been temporarily cut off in the interest of safety. He recorded everything in his diary—the large, nervous, and
often undecipherable hieroglyphs telling their own story
of growing frenzy and despair, and of entries scrawled
blindly in the dark.

He had to keep the house dark in order to see out the
window, and it appears that most of his time was spent
at his desk, peering anxiously through the rain across the
glistening miles of downtown roofs at the constellation of
distant lights marking Federal Hill. Now and then he
would fumblingly make an entry in his diary, so that detached phrases such as "The lights must not go"; "It
knows where I am"; "I must destroy it"; and "It is calling
to me, but perhaps it means no injury this time"; are
found scattered down two of the pages.

Then the lights went out all over the city. It happened
at 2:12 a.m., according to power-house records, but Blake's
diary gives no indication of the time. The entry is merely,
"Lights out—God help me." On Federal Hill there were
watchers as anxious as he, and rain-soaked knots of men
paraded the square and alleys around the evil church with
umbrella-shaded candles, electric flashlights, oil lanterns,
crucifixes, and obscure charms of the many sorts common
in southern Italy. They blessed each flash of lightning, and
made cryptic signs of fear with their right hands when

---

[48] *great storm*: Lovecraft was on an extended visit to his friend Robert Barlow
in Florida at the time. That fall in a letter, however, he said that St. John's
Catholic Church "lost its steeple in a storm last summer while I was away"
(HPL to Duane W. Rimel, 12 November 1935; ms, John Hay Library), which
suggests that lightning did strike the church.

a turn in the storm caused the flashes to lessen and finally to cease altogether. A rising wind blew out most of the candles, so that the scene grew threateningly dark. Someone roused Father Merluzzo of Sprito Santo Church, and he hastened to the dismal square to pronounce whatever helpful syllables he could. Of the restless and curious sounds in the blackened tower, there could be no doubt whatever.

For what happened at 2:35 we have the testimony of the priest, a young, intelligent, and well-educated person; of Patrolman William J. Monahan of the Central Station, an officer of the highest reliability who had paused at that part of his beat to inspect the crowd; and of most of the seventy-eight men who had gathered around the church's high bank wall—especially those in the square where the eastward facade was visible. Of course there was nothing which can be proved as being outside the order of Nature. The possible causes of such an event are many. No one can speak with certainty of the obscure chemical processes arising in a vast, ancient, ill-aired, and long-deserted building of heterogeneous contents. Mephitic[49] vapours— spontaneous combustion—pressure of gases born of long decay—any one of numberless phenomena might be responsible. And then, of course, the factor of conscious charlatanry can by no means be excluded. The thing was really quite simple in itself, and covered less than three minutes of actual time. Father Merluzzo, always a precise man, looked at his watch repeatedly.

It started with a definite swelling of the dull fumbling sounds inside the black tower. There had for some time been a vague exhalation of strange, evil odours from the church, and this had now become emphatic and offensive. Then at last there was a sound of splintering wood, and a large, heavy object crashed down in the yard beneath the

---

[49] *Mephitic*: Noxiously smelly, especially from the earth. An adjective also applied to the monsters in "Pickman's Model."

frowning easterly facade. The tower was invisible now that the candles would not burn, but as the object neared the ground the people knew that it was the smoke-grimed louver-boarding of the tower's east window.

Immediately afterward an utterly unbearable foetor welled forth from the unseen heights, choking and sickening the trembling watchers, and almost prostrating those in the square. At the same time the air trembled with a vibration as of flapping wings, and a sudden east-blowing wind more violent than any previous blast snatched off the hats and wrenched the dripping umbrellas of the crowd. Nothing definite could be seen in the candleless night, though some upward-looking spectators thought they glimpsed a great spreading blur of denser blackness against the inky sky—something like a formless cloud of smoke that shot with meteor-like speed toward the east.

That was all. The watchers were half numbed with fright, awe, and discomfort, and scarcely knew what to do, or whether to do anything at all. Not knowing what had happened, they did not relax their vigil; and a moment later they sent up a prayer as a sharp flash of belated lightning, followed by an earsplitting crash of sound, rent the flooded heavens. Half an hour later the rain stopped, and in fifteen minutes more the street-lights sprang on again, sending the weary, bedraggled watchers relievedly back to their homes.

The next day's papers gave these matters minor mention in connexion with the general storm reports. It seems that the great lightning flash and deafening explosion which followed the Federal Hill occurrence were even more tremendous farther east, where a burst of the singular foetor was likewise noticed. The phenomenon was most marked over College Hill, where the crash awaked all the sleeping inhabitants and led to a bewildered round of speculations. Of those who were already awake only a few saw the anomalous blaze of light near the top of the hill, or noticed the inexplicable upward rush of air which almost stripped the leaves from the tees and blasted the plants in the gardens. It was agreed that the lone, sudden lightning-bolt must have struck somewhere in this neighbourhood, though no trace of its striking could afterward be found. A youth in the Tau Omega[50] fraternity house thought he saw a grotesque and hideous mass of smoke in the air just as the preliminary flash burst, but his observation has not been verified. All of the few observers, however, agree as to the violent gust from the west and the flood of intolerable stench which preceded the belated stroke; whilst evidence concerning the momentary burned odour after the stroke is equally general.

These points were discussed very carefully because of their probable connexion with the death of Robert Blake. Students in the Psi Delta[51] house, whose upper rear windows looked into Blake's study, noticed the blurred white face at the westward window on the morning of the 9th, and wondered what was wrong with the expression. When they saw the same face in the same position that evening, they felt worried, and watched for the lights to come up in his apartment. Later they rang the bell of the darkened flat, and finally had a policeman force the door.

The rigid body sat bolt upright at the desk by the window, and when the intruders saw the glassy, bulging eyes, and the marks of stark, convulsive fright on the twisted features, they turned away in sickened dismay. Shortly

---

[50] *Tau Omega*: Then as now College Street was lined with fraternity houses. In a 1933 letter Lovecraft states: "The main Brown campus with its great clock tower can be seen from our easterly windows, and a goodly quota of our neighbours are fraternity-houses." (*Selected Letters* IV, 216)

[51] *Psi Delta*: That first fall after his move to 66 College Street, the cat-loving Lovecraft discovered a feline fraternity outside his window: "One thing I like about this place is the refined and sedate club of felidae on the roof of a shed across the garden, in plain sight of my study windows. There are seldom fewer than one or two old Toms at the 'clubhouse', and occasionally as many as five or six or seven. . . . In view of the prevalence of fraternity-houses in this neighbourhood, I am calling this pleasing sodality the Kappa Alpha Tau." (*Selected Letters* IV, 274)

afterward the coroner's physician made an examination, and despite the unbroken window reported electrical shock, or nervous tension induced by electrical discharge, as the cause of death. The hideous expression he ignored altogether, deeming it a not improbable result of the profound shock as experienced by a person of such abnormal imagination and unbalanced emotions. He deduced these latter qualities from books, paintings, and manuscripts found in the apartment, and from the blindly scrawled entries in the diary on the desk. Blake had prolonged his frenzied jottings to the last, and the broken-pointed pencil was found clutched in his spasmodically contracted right hand.

The entries after the failure of the lights were highly disjointed, and legible only in part. From them certain investigators have drawn conclusions differing greatly from the materialistic official verdict, but such speculations have little chance for belief among the conservative. The case of these imaginative theorists has not been helped by the action of superstitious Dr. Dexter, who threw the curious box and angled stone—an object certainly self-luminous as seen in the black windowless steeple where it was found—into the deepest channel of Narragansett Bay. Excessive imagination and neurotic unbalance on Blake's part, aggravated by knowledge of the evil bygone cult whose startling traces he had uncovered, form the dominant interpretation given those final frenzied jottings. These are the entries—or all that can be made of them.

"Lights still out—must be five minutes now. Everything depends on lightning. Yaddith[52] grant it will keep up! . . . Some influence seems beating

[52] *Yaddith*: A planet first mentioned in "Through the Gates of the Silver Key" (1933), a collaboration with E. Hoffmann Price (1898–1989), a fellow *Weird Tales* writer. Yaddith does not appear to be a part of our solar system, the way for example Yuggoth is another name for Pluto. It could in fact exist in another galaxy. See note 53 below.

through it . . . Rain and thunder and wind deafen. . . . The thing is taking hold of my mind. . . .

"Trouble with memory. I see things I never knew before. Other worlds and other galaxies[53] *. . . Dark . . . The lightning seems dark and the darkness seems light. . . .*

"It cannot be the real hill and church that I see in the pitch-darkness. Must be retinal impression left by flashes. Heaven grant the Italians are out with their candles if the lightning stops!

"What am I afraid of? Is it not an avatar of Nyarlathotep,[54] *who in antique and shadowy Khem even took the form of man? I remember Yuggoth, and more distant Shaggai, and the ultimate void of the black planets. . . .*

"The long, winging flight through the void cannot cross the universe of light . . . re-created by the thoughts caught in the Shining Trapezohedron . . . send it through the horrible abysses of radiance.

"My name is Blake—Robert Harrison Blake of 620 East Knapp Street, Milwaukee, Wisconsin.[55] *. . . I am on this planet. . . .*

"Azathoth have mercy!—the lightning no longer flashes—horrible—I can see everything with a monstrous sense that is not sight—light is dark and dark is light . . . those people on the hill . . . guard . . . candles and charms . . . their priests. . . .

"Sense of distance gone—far is near and near is far. No light—no glass—see that steeple—that

---

[53] *galaxies*: Edwin Hubble (1889–1953), the American astronomer, demonstrated the existence of galaxies beyond the Milky Way in 1925. Lovecraft first refers to galaxies in "Through the Gates of the Silver Key."

[54] *Nyarlathotep*: An early member of the Lovecraft pantheon, first appearing in the prose-poem "Nyarlathotep" (1920). See note 51 to "The Rats in the Walls" (*Annotated Lovecraft*, 53).

[55] *Milwaukee, Wisconsin*: Robert Bloch's address at the time Lovecraft wrote "The Haunter of the Dark."

tower—window—can hear—Roderick Usher[56]—am mad or going mad—the thing is stirring and fumbling in the tower—I am it and it is I—I want to get out . . . must get out and unify the forces. . . . It knows where I am. . . .

"I am Robert Blake, but I see the tower in the dark. There is a monstrous odour . . . senses transfigured boarding at that tower window cracking and giving way. . . . Iä . . . ngai . . . ygg. . . .

"I see it—coming here—hell-wind—titan blur—black wings—Yog-Sothoth[57] save me—the three-lobed burning eye. . . ."

---

[56] *Roderick Usher*: The central character of Poe's "The Fall of the House of Usher." Usher was preternaturally sensitive to distant sounds, such as the stirrings of the corpse of his sister Madeline in the family crypt.

[57] *Yog-Sothoth*: A cosmic entity first mentioned in *The Case of Charles Dexter Ward* that figures prominently only in "The Dunwich Horror." See note 42 to "The Dunwich Horror" (*Annotated Lovecraft*, 120).